Tales of Asculum

Servant Queen

By V. J. O. Gardner

Tales of Asculum
Servant Queen
V 1.5
By V.J.O. Gardner

V&E Enterprises
142 W 300 S
Springville, UT 84663

Table of Contents

A price paid in suffering, pain and blood. One life given that another is spared. Out of death a new life begins

Chapter 1 – The End of a Life

The water tasted like blood but it cooled Marriah's sore tongue. There was a pounding on the door as she put down her cup. Father opened the door revealing a young man. He had straight black hair and thin eyebrows. His pointed face and brown skin reminded her of the small rodents that tried to nest in their house and eat their food. It was the same young man who killed her mother and split her tongue yesterday.

"It is you!" the young man exclaimed. "I've seen a painting of you."

"Impossible," Father countered. "Where would a fifteen year old boy have seen a painting of me?"

"Sixteen! Where do you think I would have seen it?" he responded angrily. "My father was treating a kitchen worker when I saw it. I also saw your brother pass by on his way to that little cemetery off the garden. I listened as he confessed everything to whoever is buried there."

Father's dark skin turned ashen.

"I have all your cattle and if you want any back you will pay me twenty gold coins for each one," the young man growled.

"I don't have that much money," Father protested.

"To get your cattle back you will work for me. It's my turn to be master and you will be my servant."

Father fell to his knees and buried his face in his hands.

"That's right Langward, you and your daughter are mine now. You will call me Master Larkin from now on. You will build me a house to live in. It will be at least three times the size of this house. If you displease me I'll tell you brother exactly where you are!"

"Yes, Master Larkin," Father sobbed before he slowly got to his feet.

"Get your tools," Master Larkin ordered. "I'll show you where you will build it."

"Stay here Marriah," Father said and left with him.

Although it was eight tortuous years ago, that day's events had not faded in her memory. He was an evil beast that took great joy in their misery.

1

Servant Queen

Marriah pinned back her curly hair that was the same dark brown her mother's had been. Father's hair now had grey strands among the black curly hair that went with his darker skin. She straightened her quilt on the mattress pad before climbing down the ladder. Father was already milking the cows and would soon be finished. She quickly swept the floor in the main room which was just large enough for the table and four chairs along with the trunk in the corner. The fireplace was at the end of the room next to the door to Father's small bed room. For the last couple of weeks Master Larkin had tried to touch her breasts. Yesterday when she pulled away from him his evil grin had faded to a beastly scowl as he reached for his whip. Her back was still sore from being whipped. Since there had been no time to repair her ripped dress she put on her tattered cape before leaving the house.

Marriah knew she couldn't put off fixing his breakfast any longer as much as she wished she could. She hurried down the road through the forest to Master Larkin's house that was at the edge of the village. She was grateful to find the main room empty when she arrived. Marriah got the empty bucket and went to the well near the center of the village. The people were heading out to the fields and paid little attention to her as she drew the water. Back at the beast's house she hung a pot of water in the fireplace to heat. As she stirred in the porridge the beast grabbed her by the arm.

He turned her around roughly to face him, "You will not refuse me anymore. I will touch your breasts whenever I please."

"As her father I will not allow that!" Father's voice said from the door.

"You are now my wife." Master Larkin declared with that same evil grin and began dragging her toward the bedroom.

Marriah was knocked to the floor as Father leapt on the beast.

"Run!" Father yelled at her as she scrambled to her feet. "It is time!"

"You'll pay for that!"

Marriah headed toward the door but looked back to see Master Larkin hit Father as he swore.

"Run, Ka Messi, run to the castle!" Father screamed.

Marriah ran out the door and down the road. She knew she could not stop. With her split tongue she was not able to form words to gain help from the villagers. They would stop her and return her to the last place she wanted to be. She ran south through the trees

2

around the village and the fields to the eastern forest. She did not know how far it was to the castle, only that she had to get there before Master Larkin caught her. Father had made her promise that when he told her it was time she was to never turn back or wait for him.

She found a stream and paused. Her breath was ragged and her legs trembled. She drank some of the water before crossing the stream. Before her mother died there were stories about the Lords of Dracona being evil men born in the black mountain at the center of the forest. They stole cattle and drove everyone from the forest. Some who dared enter the forest were found dead at the edge of the fields. Everything she had heard from the villagers about the Lords of Dracona terrified her, but Father never feared them. In spite of her fears she kept going straight to the heart of the forest toward the castle. She didn't know what they would do to her, but the thought of being the beast's wife made her fall to her knees and throw up.

Marriah screamed silently in her head knowing Father was fighting their evil master for her freedom. She forced her legs under her and ran as fast as she could make them move. Before long it began to rain. It slowed her down, but she kept moving until it was too dark to see. She trembled with exhaustion as she fell to her knees. She knew she must keep moving forward. She tried to force her legs under her as her vision blurred and she passed out.

Marriah woke to darkness and no rain. She slipped and fell several times before she was able to stand. The trees were barely visible as she began walking again. She didn't know if she was even going the right direction, but had to keep going. She stumbled and fell. The ground was hard packed. As she got up she noticed the ground under her right hand was hard, but there was mud squishing up between the fingers of her left hand. She felt farther to her left and found the hard packed ground again. She felt an urge to go right along the trail. She began to run in spite of the branches that seemed to be grasping at her clothing as if to capture her.

She was losing her strength as the dawn finally revealed her surroundings to her. The trail was very narrow, but clear between the trees. She slowed to a trot as she wondered if she should stay on the trail or get off it before the beast found her. She felt an urge to follow the trail. She began running again knowing she could not stop before she reached the castle. The trail made it easier for her to run. There were berry bushes along the trail so she grabbed some as she ran by. Even mixed with the mud from her hands the berries renewed her strength.

Marriah's ripped skirt tripped her and she fell to the hard ground. Ignoring the pain of her scraped hands she tore the bottom of the skirt off and was going to throw it away, but something stopped her. She got to her feet and tied it around her waist like a sash before continuing on the path. She heard crashing in the forest and that drove her to run faster. When the trail forked the word 'left' came to her mind as clearly as if it had been spoken by someone with a deep voice. She took the left fork without hesitating and saw the trail was lined with berry bushes. She snatched and ate as many as she could without slowing down. They quenched her thirst and enabled her to keep running.

The day wore on as she wondered if she would ever reach the castle. As the sun began to set the rain began again causing her to slip and fall. She curled up into a ball and sobbed. She couldn't go on.

'Get up.'

The words were spoken in the same deep voice that had told her to take the left fork in the trail.

'Quickly!'

She trembled as she got to her feet.

'Get off the trail. Go to the right.'

She obeyed knowing the voice had led her to the berries. She didn't know if it was leading her to the castle or away from it, but it was her only hope.

'Hide under that tree's branches.'

She dove through the thick branches that touched the ground as they scratched at her face and hands. There was a clear space around the trunk cushioned with the needle like dead leaves.

'Lie very still and silent.'

A nearby crashing in the forest was punctuated by Master Larkin's voice cursing. Marriah's heart froze in her chest as she held her breath. She heard her name among the foul oaths as the sound of hoof beats and breaking sticks came closer.

"Where are you, Marriah? You are mine, you foul little animal! I'll take you back to where females know their place! You'll bear me a son," the beast stormed as he passed near the very tree where she hid.

As a wave of nausea came over Marriah she clenched her hands into fists and fought her churning stomach. She would die before she carried any child of his! He killed her mother and probably her father. She wept tears of anger and sorrow as she tried to remain still.

'Wait and I will tell you when it is safe,' the voice said. 'Help will be waiting at the castle.'

The words gave her strength and hope. As she lay there her limbs felt heavy and numb. She couldn't keep her eyes open any longer.

'Wake up!' the voice demanded. 'It is time to go!'

She got to her knees and crawled out from under the branches. It was so dark she could barely make out the trees. There were small patches of stars among the black clouds.

'To your left. Get back on the trail and follow it right.'

She soon found the trail and ran as fast as she dared. The rain had stopped but the ground was slippery and her dress was heavy with the wet mud. The moon came out to light her way . . . and Master Larkin's!

It was nearing dawn when the rain began again as she reached where the forest gave way to fields. The thunder made her jump, but she could hear the beast not far behind her. As she ran, she found a path that led her straight through the fields to the homes around the castle. She followed the voice as it told her where to turn among the houses and found her way to the castle courtyard just as Master Larkin caught her by the arm. She heard a low growl as a door burst open.

Lightning flashed as a tall man with broad shoulders came out of the door. He was wearing pants and holding a sword. She struggled against the beast's grip and managed to break free. She ran toward the open door only to stumble and fall at the man's feet.

"What's going on here?" the man demanded as lightning flashed again.

"It's none of your concern!" Master Larkin proclaimed as he dismounted his horse. "I'm just passing through with my servant. I'll take what's rightfully mine and be gone."

Marriah gasped as a white light surrounded the man. She scrambled to her knees as he stepped past her. His blond hair and white skin seemed to glow.

"As Regis of Dracona, I will decide what is and is not my concern," the man proclaimed. "This is definitely my concern."

"Her father owed me," Master Larkin argued. "She's mine in payment of his debt. She won't even speak at all. She's hardly more than a stupid animal."

"She is no animal to be traded. She will not be forced to go with you." Regis replied to Marriah's relief.

Her master dropped the reins as he declared, "You're not my king and I don't have to obey you. She's mine and there is no one to say any different."

Master Larkin lunged at Regis who caught him as the sword clattered to the cobble stones. Marriah scrambled away from the two as they wrestled. Soon Regis was on top of the beast and had his arms twisted behind his back. She untied the strip of cloth from her waist and held it out to Regis as he looked up. Quickly he bound the beast's hands behind his back.

"Can you put one knee here on his neck?" Regis asked as he pointed. "I need the key so I can lock him up."

Marriah nodded and put one knee on the beast's neck.

"Get off me you filthy little animal!" Master Larkin growled as the man stood and walked away. "Untie me! I am your master and you will obey me!"

He began to squirm and Marriah feared he would get loose so she pressed her knee a little harder on the beast's neck. It didn't make sense to her that her light weight was enough to hold him to the ground. He began to swear at her and kick his feet. She looked up as she heard a horrible screeching sound near the gate. The light around Regis revealed an open door. He returned and retrieved his sword before nodding to Marriah. She removed her knee from Larkin's neck. He began to struggle to his knees until he felt the point of the sword on his back. Regis moved the sword then grabbed Larkin by the arm and pulled him to his feet before dragging him over to the open door. Larkin struggled as he was shoved into the dark doorway.

"If you don't cooperate I'll leave your hands tied behind your back," Regis said as a man surrounded by a blue light came through the gate.

The door screeched as Regis pushed it closed and locked it. He then spoke to the man who bowed before walking toward Larkin's horse. Regis returned to her and dropped to one knee in front of her. She was too exhausted to even try to stand.

His eyes were blue as he met hers and said, "Let's get in out of the rain."

She didn't know what he would do to her, but he said she wasn't an animal. Lightning flashed and was followed immediately by a loud crack of thunder. She was more afraid of the lightning than she was of him. She nodded quickly.

He helped her up with gentle hands, put her arm around his shoulders and supported her while they entered the castle. Once safely inside, he eased her down to the floor.

"What happened to her?" a woman asked as she knelt beside Marriah.

She put her hand over her mouth as Marriah looked at her.

"I don't know, Sonje" he responded. "But right now she needs our help. Go get a pen and paper. I want a record of her injuries."

Sonje nodded and went into the doors behind her. The man with the blue light entered with a person wearing a hooded cape. The person pushed back the hood revealing a young woman with straight hair almost as dark as Marriah's. She began to say words Marriah had never heard as the man left shutting the door behind him. Regis replied in the same strange language. Marriah was startled by a door shutting behind her. She turned to see Sonje had returned. She too spoke in the strange language.

Again fear began to rise within Marriah. Who could she trust? This was farther than she had ever been from home. She was in a strange dark place surrounded by strange people and so far just as much a prisoner has she had been in the village. She was too weak and injured to go any further. She couldn't understand what they were saying. She could not form words with her split tongue. Even Father had never been able to understand her when she tried. How would she be able to tell them what happened to her and that the beast must have killed Father? The thought brought tears to her eyes.

"It's alright," Sonje said as she knelt next to Marriah.

"You are safe. Bethesda is a healer," Regis said and Marriah nodded once.

She flinched as someone pulled her ripped dress revealing the wounds on her back.

"Who did this to you?" Bethesda asked softly as Marriah turned to see who had touched her.

She pointed toward the door. Bethesda looked at Regis.

"He's locked up at least until we find out exactly who she is and why he claimed to own her," Regis said.

7

Marriah looked up into his eyes. She still didn't know if he was one of the lords of Dracona, but he must be a leader if the other man had bowed to him. She gathered her courage as she scraped some mud from her dress and spread it on the floor. She drew the symbol from her father's cattle that looked like two mountains divided by a line between them. Regis looked down at the drawing.

"Are you Langward's daughter?" Regis asked as he met her eyes again.

She nodded.

"Where is he? Is he safe?" Regis asked.

Marriah shook her head before burying her face in her hands as she began to sob. Even if Father still lived she knew he would be gravely injured. She heard them talking in the strange language again.

'You are safe and they will care for you,' the deep voice told her.

She raised her head and looked around. Sonje was gone, but Regis and Bethesda were still there. She could not see anyone else. A flash of lightning revealed an enormous room with stairs in front of her and more across the room. She flinched at the thunder that followed. She had not seen any other people during that brief glimpse.

'You will meet me later after Bethesda has healed your wounds and you have rested,' the deep voice assured her.

"I'm going to carry you upstairs," Regis said. "You can stay in the room I lived in as a young man."

Marriah stared at him for a moment before nodding. He gently lifted her into his arms and stood up. Bethesda followed as Regis began to climb the stairs. At the top he turned and walked back toward the front of the castle before climbing more stairs. Again at the top he walked back to the front of the castle. At the top of the next set of stairs he began walking away from the stairs on what had to be the fourth floor. He carried her past large windows that showed the dark mountain and lightning cutting through the sky behind it. Rain pounded on the clear glass of the windows. She had never seen glass that clear or large.

At last Regis turned to a door that Bethesda opened for him. He waited as she lit a torch. She lit others around the room before opening another door. Marriah saw a bed that was larger than Father's along with several tables and chairs before Regis carried her into the next room. There was a basin large enough for a person to sit in and it had the head of a creature coming down from the wall as if to drink from the basin. The head was much larger than a horse, but similar in shape. It also had horns and pointed teeth.

Regis set her down on a stool. He had mud and blood on his bare skin from carrying her. She was still afraid of what would happen to her, but Regis knew Father's name. He said this was where he lived as he grew up, but still she felt like she was a prisoner. She fought against her fears and the panic she felt rising in her. They hadn't hurt her yet. Regis knelt and looked into her eyes.

"Don't be frightened. We just want to help you. Bethesda will heal your wounds. I'll run a basin of warm water for you to bathe in and find some dry clothing," he told her. "There will be some food here soon and there is a soft bed you can rest in."

That was certainly better than cruel Master Larkin had ever done.

"When you feel up to it, we need to know what happened," he said gently. "If necessary, you can tell Haskell, the dragon. He guided you to the castle and told me you needed help."

She looked at him for a long time as she tried to make sense of what had he said before finally nodding. She decided she had to trust him for now even though she was overwhelmed and wanted to hide. He stood and went over to the basin. He twisted one of the ears and water began to pour out of the mouth. Bethesda wet a cloth in the water and began to clean her wounds. Sonje came in and closed the door behind her with Regis on the other side of the door.

Bethesda spoke the strange language again as Sonje wrote on some paper she had brought. When Bethesda touched Marriah's wounds with her hands they closed. Although they spoke gently to her she was both frightened and confused. How could wounds be instantly healed? Sonje helped Bethesda remove Marriah's clothing to reveal the wounds hidden beneath. She felt uncomfortable to be naked in front of strangers but when they finished her pain was gone.

The two women helped her to her feet and into the basin full of water. She was surprised that the water was warm. It was relaxing as the two women washed her. They wrapped her in a large cloth and took her back into the bed chamber. Bethesda returned to the small room and Sonje dried Marriah's hair with another cloth while she sat on a cushioned stool eating the porridge and drinking the warm cider that was waiting for her on the table. Regis returned with a new dress. He went into the small room and closed the door behind him. Once Marriah was dressed, Sonje opened the door to the small room. Marriah dropped to her knees and bowed with her face to the floor at Regis' feet. It was how her Father said one should bow to a leader.

"Rise," he told her gently. "You need to rest now. I'll post two men at the door for your protection. They will bring you to me when you are ready to leave the room."

She nodded and sat down on the bed. She watched them leave, shutting the door behind them. Marriah lay down on the large bed. Although she was allowed to leave the room she still didn't know if she was a prisoner or not.

'No, you are not a prisoner,' the deep voice assured her. 'My name is Haskell and I will watch over you. Sleep now.'

What would happen to her now? She doubted her father survived their master's wrath. Marriah could no longer hold back the tears.

'Someone has been sent to the village to find him,' Haskell told her. 'You need to sleep and recover your strength.'

Chapter 2 – Meeting Her Guardian Dragon

Marriah awoke confused by her surroundings until she saw the bruising on her arms where there had been open wounds. She remembered that she was in Dracona's castle and the beast of a man who had enslaved her and her father for so long was locked up. She smiled as she remembered kneeling on his neck to keep him from escaping. Marriah slowly sat then stood up. When she cautiously opened the outer door two men stood in the hall near the door.

"We will take you to Regis Bryant and Regina Sonje," one of them said.

"General Edgard asked us to escort and protect you," the other added.

She nodded and followed them down a long hallway, past the stairs to a second staircase. She realized Regis was a title, not a name. The men opened the door and she looked inside to see Regis Bryant and Regina Sonje looking up from a table.

"Come in," Regis Bryant said. "Are you hungry?"

She nodded slowly. They met her near the door.

"It's time for lunch," Regina Sonje said. "Come with us."

They sat at a table that was raised up on a short platform on the far end of the large room. Marriah heard the whispers among the people as she ate hardly tasting her food. She wanted to run away from the stares. The meal seemed to last forever before they led her to a room with a large desk and a creature's head on the wall behind it. Was this fierce face what Haskell who had helped her looked like? At last she sat down.

"We know that this must be very hard for you," Regis Bryant began in a gentle tone. "We are glad that you have turned to us for help. Your father once helped mine when he was injured. His kindness gave my father hope. He had me give your father his first two cattle as a wedding gift."

It now made sense why Father had not feared the lords of Dracona.

"We need to know what has happened to you," Regina Sonje said. "We understand that you do not speak."

"The dragon, Haskell, can speak for you if you wish," Regis Bryant said. "He can relay to us both words and images as you think them in your mind."

She looked to Regis Bryant and then to Regina Sonje. She pointed at the head on the wall, then to herself.

"Would you like to meet him?" Regina Sonje asked and she nodded.

"Come with us," Regis Bryant said with a smile. "I'm sure he is anxious to see you as well."

They led her out to the great hall and to the back wall. Regis Bryant turned a strange wheel and the wall began to open in the center. They led her into a great cavern where a large creature was lying on a ledge. It had a head was taller than she was and claws the length of her forearm. There were wings folded against its body that continued into an opening in the cavern wall. Haskell was enormous, but his face was not fierce. She went up the stairs to the ledge then knelt and bowed before the dragon.

'Please get up,' his deep voice told her gently. 'I have been very worried about you, Marriah. Since dragons speak through thought, your silent cries for help woke me from a sound sleep. I knew I was the only one who could help you.'

"Will you let Haskell tell us what happened?" Regina Sonje asked as she knelt beside Marriah.

She thought for a moment about where to start.

'You should sit down, Bryant,' Haskell spoke in the minds of all three. 'Marriah says it is a long story.'

Regis Bryant and Regina Sonje sat down and Haskell lay down. Marriah sat down on his foreleg knowing no harm could come to her while she was with him.

'She says this really all started about eight years ago,' Haskell began. 'She and her parents lived on the outskirts of the village. One day when she was about ten years old, she and her mother were gathering their cattle from the forest. A young man came on a horse and began to herd their cattle away. When Marriah's mother tried to stop him, he struck her down. Then he got off his horse and grabbed Marriah. He took his knife and split her tongue.'

"Was it the same man that chased her this morning?" Regis Bryant asked as Regina Sonje put her hand on his arm.

'Yes. Her father had little besides his family and those few cows. Marriah's mother was dead when he found her and Marriah couldn't tell him what had happened,' Haskell paused for a moment while Marriah wiped tears from her eyes.

It took Marriah a few minutes to regain her composure and continue. Haskell helped her explain Master Larkin's cruel treatment of them and his intent to take her as a wife that prompted her father to finally attack him so she could escape.

"The village council will be here within a few days," Bryant said. "You are free to do as you wish. I suggest that you rest as much as possible to regain your strength. I will send for you if you are needed."

Marriah nodded and for the first time smiled. She settled back against Haskell.

'She feels safe here with me,' Haskell said and Regis Bryant nodded.

"We will meet with the council of Dracona and explain this to them," Regina Sonje said. "By the time the village council arrives we should have some idea of what needs to be done."

"Larkin will remain locked in the cell in the courtyard until his fate is decided," Regis Bryant added as they both stood. "Haskell can tell us if you need anything."

She watched as they exited the cavern leaving the door open.

'What will I do now, Haskell?' Marriah asked as tears began to run down her cheeks. 'I'm certain Father is dead. He never fought back until Master Larkin said I was his wife. He just kept screaming at me to run.'

'He sacrificed himself so you would survive,' Haskell said in his soothing deep voice. 'Your life was more important to him than his own. You must remember that and live to honor that sacrifice.'

'My life isn't worth that much,' she sobbed. 'Master told me every day that I was worthless, that I was an ugly little animal. Sometimes he would tie us up to make Father watch as he whipped me and laughed.'

'You are a beautiful young woman. You are very smart. I've been listening to your thoughts since I first heard you. You fought against your fears knowing that no matter how afraid you were you were not in the same danger that you had been in when Larkin controlled your life. Stop calling him Master. You understand that no one should be treated like that which makes you better than him.'

'Where will I live? What will I do? How can I take care of myself?' she asked as she felt even more overwhelmed with each question. 'I know that my father loved my mother even after she died. I would hear him crying in his sleep and saying her name over and over again. To be loved like that.'

She couldn't go on. Haskell softly nuzzled her with his nose.

'I know,' Haskell said softly to her as she sobbed. 'I can't give you the answers you seek, but I can tell you that if you want to stay here you will be safe and cared for. For now you need to heal both physically and emotionally. Take things as they come and deal with them one at a time. Evelina tells me that you are important to others in ways that you don't yet understand.'

'Who is Evelina?' she asked as she looked up at Haskell's large eye.

'The queen dragon, my mate,' Haskell said. 'She can see the future, but you must learn what she has seen as you are ready to accept it. For now just rest and heal.'

Marriah eventually fell asleep nestled against Haskell. When she woke she was hungry. At Haskell's urging she went toward the door. She stopped as she heard familiar men's voices. She peeked out to see men she recognized as the village council speaking to Regis Bryant and the man who had bowed before taking care of Larkin's horse.

"Where is Larkin?" Wyman, the oldest council member asked. "He galloped through the village covered in blood the other morning. We found Langward dead at his house, but can't find Langward's daughter."

"We followed Larkin to see if we could find out what happened," the blacksmith Barrnar said. "We couldn't find either of them, but ran into your messenger. After what he told us we're not certain what really happened."

"Edgard, please ask Regis Auberon and the other council members to join us for a meeting before supper. If no one minds, we will meet in the cavern," Regis Bryant said and the man bowed before leaving. "Langward's daughter arrived early this morning seeking my aid and protection. Haskell will be Marriah's voice since she is unable to speak."

The villagers glanced at each other. Marriah hurried back up the stairs to Haskell before they entered. Regina Sonje soon followed with General Edgard, two other men and a woman. Regis Bryant smiled as Marriah sat down on Haskell's forearm. He stepped up to Haskell's side.

V.J.O. Gardner

"Haskell, this is Wyman, Barnarr, Kyle, and Sebastian," Regis Bryant introduced them by pointing to each man. "Gentlemen, this is Haskell."

'I remember helping Bryant rescue you, Wyman,' Haskell said allowing Marriah to hear him as well.

"I am grateful for your help," Wyman responded as he looked up at the dragon.

"Since dragons speak through thought, Marriah's cries for help woke him. He woke me in time to stop Larkin from capturing her," Bryant explained.

"Capturing?" Sebastian asked in a surprised tone.

"The past eight years have been torture at the hands of Larkin beginning with her mother being killed by him and then him splitting her tongue to prevent her from speaking," Regis Bryant revealed grimly.

"Larkin told everyone that she and her father owed him a debt," Wyman stated breaking the shocked silence.

"Haskell, please tell them what Marriah told you," Regina Sonje requested.

Marriah watched them closely as they heard the tale. She could see the color drain from their faces. The woman and some of the men wiped at tears.

"Since this happened in the village, we felt we should first see if the village has any laws regarding these crimes," Regis Bryant prompted.

The villagers looked at one another and shook their heads. "There have been occasional fights, but nothing like this. We found Langward beaten to death at Larkin's house," Wyman admitted as Haskell revealed to Marriah what he had seen.

The image from Wyman's memory showed Father lying on a blood stained floor. The brief image also showed just how brutal the beating had been. Marriah tried hard to not react to the image as her heart broke.

"Where is Larkin?" Kyle asked.

"He is locked in a cell out in the courtyard. He is being fed and has a bed to sleep on. I want to get a decision on Larkin's fate as soon as possible," Regis Bryant replied. "As I see it we have two options. The first option is imprisonment for life shaping stone blocks in the quarry. The second is death."

The cavern fell silent again.

Regis Bryant broke the silence, "We will meet after breakfast. We all need time to decide our vote. Come have supper."

"There will be rooms prepared for you," The woman informed them as she stood up. "Will you go upstairs for night, Marriah?"

Marriah looked up at Haskell as she wondered why she would care.

'Agatha is Dracona's Minister of the Interior. Part of her job is to make certain people have somewhere to live,' Haskell explained.

'I thought she was one of the cooks,' Marriah said.

'She is,' Haskell chuckled at her.

After a moment she stood up and nodded. She stayed close to Regina Sonje as they went to the dining hall. Marriah felt more relaxed than before knowing that the village council now knew the truth of what Larkin had done. After the meal she went upstairs to the room she had been in that morning. She looked into the smaller room and found it clean. Her torn dress was missing, but the one she was wearing fit better than the old one had. A quiet knock at the door drew her attention. She opened the door cautiously.

"I brought you a key to the room," Regis Bryant said as he held it out to her. "You can lock the door so you will feel safe. I have another key, but I won't use it unless Haskell tells me you need us but can't open the door on your own."

She nodded as she took the key from him.

"I know how hard it is to be alone. I don't think I would have survived my father's death if not for Haskell," he confessed softly. "I can't give back what has been taken from you, but I promise we will help you recover and make a new life for yourself."

Marriah nodded. He turned and walked toward the end of the hallway. Marriah locked the door and put the key on the small chest of drawers beside the bed before she lay down.

Chapter 3 - Revelations and Decisions

Marriah woke after a night disturbed by dreams of the past and images of her father lying dead on Larkin's floor, but she had been aware of Haskell's presence in her dreams. She dressed and went down to the dining hall. She was a bit nervous about walking around unescorted, but people smiled and nodded to her. Haskell assured her that no one here would hurt her. Regis Bryant and Regina Sonje already sat at the head table as she sat beside them. Regina Sonje was eating meat and cheese on bread, but Regis Bryant wasn't eating. Soon the room began to fill up and porridge was brought out. It tasted good and Regina Sonje seemed to enjoy it as well. Once breakfast was over they went to the large room with chairs and tables in it between the great hall and Regis Bryant's office. The village council and the council from the castle joined them along with Bethesda.

"We are here to decide the fate of Larkin," Regis Bryant announced. "Are you ready to vote?"

Everyone's face was serious and some shifted in their seats before nodding. Marriah's heart was beginning to pound as she tried to sit still awaiting their decision.

"All in favor of life imprisonment?" Regis Bryant asked.

She held her breath as the room fell silent.

"Death?"

Their voices were grim, but without hesitation. Marriah was relieved. General Edgard stood and knelt before Regis Bryant.

"I volunteer to carry out the execution," General Edgard stated.

Regis Bryant smiled and put his hand on his shoulder.

"No, I cannot ask that of anyone," Regis Bryant responded. "I swore an oath on Fanchon's Sword. It is my duty."

Although Regina Sonje's face remained unchanged, the other's faces showed shock at his words. The man sitting next to Regina Sonje half rose before Regis Bryant spoke again.

"We will take Larkin to the village. They need to know what Larkin has done and that it will not be tolerated. We will dispatch a messenger to Merton. They need to know about the changes to the law."

17

"I will prepare the dispatch for your approval, Regis," the man sitting between Agatha and General Edgard offered.

"I will get a messenger ready to leave at once," General Edgard added.

"Can you ride a horse, Marriah?" Regis Bryant asked and she nodded. "You, Sonje and two guards will ride ahead through the forest to reach the village in just one day. The rest of us will take the road and arrive the next day."

Marriah was glad she would not be traveling with Larkin. People began to leave, but the man next to Regina Sonje approached Regis Bryant.

'That is Sonje's father, Auberon,' Haskell told Marriah. 'He was regis before Bryant.'

"A word with you, Regis," he said with a bow.

"In a moment," Bryant replied. "Bethesda, could you see if you can determine what has made Sonje nauseous this morning?"

Regis Bryant led Auberon into his office and shut the door.

Bethesda put her hand on Regina Sonje's stomach and felt around a bit as she and Regina Sonje spoke in the strange language they had used yesterday. After a while Bethesda came over to where Marriah still sat.

"Regina Sonje told me your tongue is split making it impossible for you to speak," Bethesda said and Marriah nodded. "I'd like to try to repair your tongue so you can speak again. Can I see it?"

Marriah opened her mouth. Bethesda looked inside and began to glow red as she touched Marriah's tongue with two fingers. She felt he tongue coming together along the center.

"You should find eating easier as well now," Bethesda commented as she felt Marriah's throat. "Your voice box is very tight from not being used. There, I've loosened it a little. With some practice you should be able to speak now."

Marriah felt tears begin to run down her cheeks.

"I don't know everything that has happened to you, but to suffer the injuries you have in silence is unimaginable to me," Bethesda said as she wiped at Marriah's tears. "I love being able to help others by healing their wounds. I'm so glad I've been able to help you."

She gave Marriah a quick hug before standing up. She went over to the office door and knocked.

Regis Bryant opened the door.

"I've healed Marriah's tongue," she said. "And I found Regina's problem."

"What was it?" Regis Bryant asked.

"I want to tell both of you at the same time. You should hear it as well, Regis Auberon," Bethesda answered.

Regis Bryant and Auberon followed her to where Sonje waited.

"I'm afraid you will have to get used to nights with frequent trips to the bathing chamber and morning nausea," Bethesda said. "The good news is that in about six months, you will be parents."

Regis Bryant stood staring at Regina Sonje for a moment.

"Congratulations, Son," Auberon smiled, patting him on the back.

Regis Bryant took Regina Sonje's hands in his.

"Well?" Auberon asked. "Are you happy about this?"

"Beyond words," Regis Bryant answered.

"Yes," Regina Sonje agreed.

"You can do what ever you feel like, just don't push yourself too hard," Bethesda advised. "You will be eating more and tire easily."

"You should find an assistant," Regis Bryant suggested as he put his arm around Regina Sonje.

Marriah knew she had no family left. She didn't want to return to live in the village alone. She didn't know what being an assistant meant, but it had to be better than being Larkin's slave. Here she had been treated with kindness. The people here treated her as a person, not an animal. She knelt before Regina Sonje and bowed her head.

"Please, I want to be your assistant," she stammered, struggling to form the words with her newly healed tongue.

"Marriah," Regina Sonje said gently and she looked up. "You do understand that you owe us no debt. You are free to do as you wish. If this is truly what you want to do, I accept your offer."

Marriah hesitated before she took the hand Regis Bryant offered her and stood up.

"I have no reason to live in the village anymore," Marriah spoke slowly. "There are too many bad memories there."

"Then welcome to your new home," Regis Bryant approved and she felt a surge of joy that they would let her stay. "I've got to write a letter to my mother before we tell Larkin his fate. You don't have to be there if you don't want to."

"I'll watch, but I don't want him to see me," she replied as Regina Sonje patted her shoulder.

"You can watch from the second floor balcony," Regina Sonje suggested as Regis Bryant returned to his office. "We'll find you some more dresses and when we return from the village we'll have the tailor make some for you."

"I have no money to pay for clothes," Marriah said softly.

"Don't worry about that," Regina Sonje assured her. "You are part of our family now. Your father was the one person from the village Bryant would have welcomed to the castle before I met him. Your father gave him hope that not everyone hated and feared him."

"Father always told me that I shouldn't fear the lords of Dracona but I should respect their desire for privacy," Marriah revealed. "When Larkin came he told me that the day would come for me to seek their help. He trusted that I would be safe here. I just don't want to be a burden to you."

"You are not a burden," Regis Bryant insisted as he walked into the room with a folded paper in his hand. "Can you give this to Edgard while we get changed?"

Marriah nodded as Haskell showed her General Edgard standing with a thin, grey haired man near the center of the great hall. She followed them out of the room and saw General Edgard where Haskell had shown her he was. She swallowed hard and began to walk toward him with the paper in hand. She recognized the older man from the meeting and Haskell told her his name was Hoyt.

"Here is the letter for Regis Bryant's mother," Marriah spoke slowly as she struggled to pronounce the words clearly.

"Could you take this to him for his approval?" Hoyt asked as General Edgard took the paper from her.

She nodded and took the paper he held out to her. She returned to the stairs and began going up them. Haskell showed her that Regis Bryant and Regina Sonje's room was at the very end of the hall. When she reached the door she cautiously knocked.

Regis Bryant answered the door dressed in black pants and a crimson shirt with a black jacket over it.

"Hoyt asked you to approve this," Marriah said as she held out the paper.

He opened it and looked at it for several minutes before setting it on a table. He opened a drawer and brought out a small bottle of ink and a pen. She had seen her father writing before, but he never taught her how to read and write. Regis Bryant made some marks at the bottom of the page then blotted it carefully with a thin paper before folding it again. He dripped some wax from a lit candle and pressed one of his rings into it leaving a mark.

"Tell Edgard we'll be down soon to deal with Larkin," Regis Bryant said as he handed her the sealed paper.

Marriah nodded and returned to where General Edgard and Hoyt were waiting.

"Regis Bryant and Regina Sonje will be down soon to deal with Larkin," Marriah informed them as she held out the paper.

"I'll get the messenger on his way and get Larkin ready," General Edgard nodded as he took the paper from her.

"I'm so glad you are able to speak now," Hoyt smiled. "I'll get the rest of the council members together."

Marriah made her way up to the second floor where she could look out over the great hall. Regina Sonje patted her shoulder as they passed. Both were wearing crowns and capes. Regis Bryant's black cape was clasped with a brass dragon whose wings went from one shoulder to the other. The smaller dragon clasp on Regina Sonje's white cape sparkled with jewels. They stopped in the center of the great hall near where the council members stood. After Regis Bryant nodded to a man waiting at the door Larkin was led in between four men.

"Do you have anything to say before learning your fate?" Regis Bryant asked.

Larkin scowled and spit in Regis Bryant's direction. The men moved to restrain Larkin, but stopped as Regis Bryant shook his head slightly.

"The abuse to Marriah at your hands was enough for a life of imprisonment and hard labor," Regina Sonje informed him sternly. "But the deaths of her parents at your hands are punishable by death."

"You will be transported to the village before being executed," Regis Bryant added. "It is important for all of Dracona to understand that the intentional killing of another person will be punished with death. We will leave as soon as a wagon to transport you in is prepared."

Before the men could stop him, Larkin lunged at Regis Bryant with a growl. Marriah gasped as Larkin suddenly shot into the air with his legs still running. He stopped and looked around him.

"What?! Who's doing this?" Larkin demanded.

"I am," Regis Bryant answered calmly. "I am able to lift things with my mind."

"Coward!" Larkin shouted in frustration. "You're no better than I am forcing everyone to do your bidding!"

"On the contrary," Regis Bryant replied calmly. "I ask only what I, myself, am willing to do. They have the freedom to refuse without fear. You will meet your death at my hand."

Larkin seemed stunned as Regis Bryant set him down. He gave no resistance as they led him back to his cell.

"Edgard, get some men working on building a cage in the bed of a wagon to transport him. Put a solid panel behind the driver's seat and a seat for Larkin. Also put a tarp over it and extend it over the driver's seat," Regis Bryant commanded and General Edgard bowed before leaving.

"We will return to the village now to prepare the people for your arrival," Wyman offered and Bryant nodded.

*****

The days were filled with preparations for the journey to the village and the execution of Larkin. Since Marriah had only ridden bareback Regina Sonje taught her to ride side saddle. Marriah heard the men building the cage on the wagon talking about what they would have done to Larkin. They all would have beaten him to death. Marriah wished they had.

'No, that would have perpetuated the violence Larkin started,' Haskell told her. 'Bryant knows that how Larkin is treated and how he dies reflects on what kind of leaders he and Sonje are. They need their people to trust them to be both fair and compassionate even when someone must die for their crimes.'

'I hadn't thought about that,' Marriah admitted.

'This gives Larkin a chance to think about what he did to you and your father,' Haskell explained. 'He is thinking a lot about his past and that he has become just like his father who beat and tortured him when he was growing up.'

Marriah never thought about what type of childhood Larkin had. To her, he had always been a beast she must obey or face the consequences. Now it was Larkin who would face the consequenses for his behavior.

Chapter 4 - Even Death Brings New Life

At last the day came that the cage on the wagon was complete. After an early breakfast Regina Sonje, Auberon, Marriah and two guards started out for the village. She learned that Regina Sonje's sister Cherie lived in the village with her husband Olvan and their two children. They reached Cherie and Olvan's house just before dark after a hard ride through the forest. Cherie dished up some soup for them to eat before they settled in to sleep. The following morning Marriah stayed inside the house, not wanting to see the familiar sights any sooner than she really had to. She swept the floor and helped with the dishes. She also thought about what Haskell had told her about Larkin's childhood.

"They're arriving," Regina Sonje said when it was nearly noon

"You don't have to watch, Marriah. You can stay here in the house," Cherie offered

"I need to see it," she replied. "I need to know beyond a doubt that he can never hurt anyone again. I want to speak with him before he is executed."

Her emotions churned inside of her as she walked with Regina Sonje to meet Regis Bryant. He was standing next to the wagon.

"I still don't understand," Larkin said as they got close enough to hear.

"Understand what?" Regis Bryant asked.

"Why you would take such an interest in her. She's nobody important."

"Everyone is somebody and important to someone, even you," Regis Bryant explained with a sigh. "Langward helped my father when he was injured. It wasn't something my father expected from any of the villagers. Even so, I would have helped Marriah regardless of who she was or where she came from. I don't understand why you did what you did."

Larkin just shrugged his shoulders and said, "Perhaps because it was my father's way of doing things."

Marriah walked closer until she could see Larkin clearly through the bars of the cage. Regis Bryant drew a dragon gripped sword from the scabbard at his side. The blade gleamed in the sunlight.

"I am the only man to safely touch this sword since my great-grandfather forged it in dragon's fire," Regis Bryant told Larkin. "When I first held it in my hand, I swore an oath to protect those in need. This will be the blade I will use today. Your death will be swift and painless."

"I'm sure that is kinder than what others may think I deserve," Larkin admitted quietly as he rubbed at his arm.

She noticed a thick scar beside one from a burn on Larkin's arm as his shirt sleeve moved up. Larkin looked up at Regis Bryant then pulled up his sleeve. There were more scars further up on his arm. He lifted his shirt revealing additional scars from cuts and burns.

"From my father," Larkin explained as he glanced at her. "He cared only for himself. I could never quite please him. He nearly killed me a couple of times. He wouldn't even teach me how to read like he did my older brother. She who bore me, my mother, cared for me."

"We learn how to treat others from our parents, but it is up to us to choose to follow their example or to make a new example for our children," Regis Bryant said.

"I will never have children that learn from my bad example," Larkin observed. "I guess it's best for everyone this way."

"You knew how it felt to be humiliated, beaten and tortured," Marriah stated. "Why did you do that to us?"

"I knew your father would never tell anyone," Larkin admitted.

"What did you hear his brother confess?" Marriah demanded. "Where did you see his portrait?"

Larkin shook his head.

"Tell me!" she commanded.

"I will take that secret to my grave. It's the one thing I promised him that first day," Larkin insisted. "I owe him that much after everything I did to both of you. He swore to me he would do anything I asked him to if I would promise to never reveal his past to anyone, including you."

'He knows I can hear his thoughts,' Haskell told her. 'He won't even think about what he saw or heard. He is confused as to why it was so important to your father.'

'I am too,' Marriah admitted as Regina Sonje led her away with one arm around her shoulders.

They went to a stand built on the edge of the village. Regis Bryant led them onto the stand as Marriah tried to control her urge to run and hide from the villagers.

"By now, most of you know what has happened," Regis Bryant began. "It has been determined that Larkin will be executed for the deaths of Marriah's mother and father. All that Larkin owns becomes hers, but it cannot be enough to repay her for the years of torture suffered at his hands."

Larkin followed with his head bowed as General Edgard and the guards escorted him to the stand.

"Do you have any last words?" Regis Bryant asked.

Larkin met Regis Bryant's gaze before turning to Marriah. Her heart froze in her chest as her nails dug into her palms.

"I now know it was wrong to treat you as my father treated she who bore . . . my mother and me," Larkin began in a tone she had never heard from him before. "I killed my own father after he beat my mother to death in front of me. Your father was right to call you his princess."

She was stunned by the confession as Larkin knelt before Regis Bryant.

"I am ready to die for my crimes," he said. "Take care of her. She deserves better than I treated her."

Marriah saw the single tear run down Larkin's cheek as he bowed his head. Regis Bryant drew his sword and held it high above his head.

"I, Regis Bryant Donley, Lord Dracona, put you, Larkin, to death for the lives taken at your hands," he said as the blade turned to flame.

The sword sliced cleanly through Larkin's neck. The smothering weight of enslavement lifted from Marriah as his body crumpled and his head rolled off the end of the stand. The body along with the head was placed in a simple wooden coffin. The crowd quieted as she stepped forward with her head held high.

"Other than a few items, I have no desire to keep any of the property belonging to me," Marriah announced. "I will be staying at the castle as our Regina's assistant. I give the property to the village."

The village council came to the stand as the crowd dispersed.

"We want to let you know that we are sorry that we did not realize what was happening," Wyman apologized.

"Larkin did not allow us much contact with anyone," Marriah replied. "He split my tongue to prevent me from speaking. It would be hard for someone to realize what he was doing unless they saw or heard it."

"We will try to be more vigilant in the future," Sebastian promised.

"Your gift of the property is appreciated, but we are not certain what to do with it," Kyle admitted.

Marriah turned to Regis Bryant.

"Do you have a school for your children?" Regis Bryant asked.

"A school?" Barnarr repeated in a confused tone.

"A place to teach your children to read and write," he explained.

The men shook their heads.

"Cherie would be able to help set the school up," Regina Sonje offered. "I'm certain we could send someone from Glynis to help."

"I can read and write," Sebastian said. "But I don't have any books simple enough for children."

"I will help find the materials you will need," Hoyt volunteered as he joined them. "I have been setting up a school at the castle."

"Is a school only for children?" Marriah asked. "I would like to learn to read and write."

"Sonje and I thought you might," Regis Bryant replied. "We've already asked Hoyt to teach you."

"Thank you, Regis," Marriah said as she fell to her knees at his feet. "You have done so much for me."

She felt a hand under her chin that gently lifted her face until she met Regis Bryant's gaze.

"For about a hundred years, my father and I stayed alone at the castle to care for the dragons. My father died about six years ago, leaving me completely alone," he told her. "I know how alone and helpless you must have felt. You do not need to feel that way anymore. We believe that every individual person is very important. We will provide you what you need to heal and make a new life for yourself."

26

"I know you will learn so much and that will make you an even better assistant to me," Regina Sonje assured her. "But right now I am hungry."

"My wife is preparing a meal," Wyman said. "It should be ready soon. Come with me."

After lunch, Regina Sonje and Regis Bryant went with Marriah to gather the few things she cared to keep. There were so many memories as she gathered the stack of paper Father had bound together for her to draw on and her mother's shawl. She took Father's cup from the shelf as well. They stopped at Olvan and Cherie's house afterward. Regina Sonje was talking to her sister about the baby she was carrying while Cherie's son and daughter played near the fireplace. A knock at the door interrupted them. Olvan opened the door. A man entered and bowed. He rubbed his eyes before looking around the room.

"King Archelaus sends an urgent message for Regis Bryant and Regina Sonje," he said and drew a scroll from a satchel at his side.

He bowed again after Regis Bryant took the scroll from him. Regina Sonje joined Regis Bryant as he unrolled the scroll. Her hand went to her mouth as she read it.

"What's wrong?" Auberon asked as he turned to look at them.

"Xylia has died. Archelaus will meet us for the burial," Regis Bryant answered.

Regina Sonje put her hand on his arm and he smiled briefly at her. Agatha, Hoyt and General Edgard entered through the open door.

"Bryant, Marriah and I must travel north before returning to Dracona," Regina Sonje told them. "Agatha, I will give you a list of things we will need you to pack and send on Haskell as soon as you can."

"What is going on, Regis?" Hoyt asked.

"A funeral for Xylia," he answered tersely. "Edgard, I want you to accompany us."

"Yes, Regis," General Edgard replied with a bow.

Cherie brought writing materials to Regina Sonje. Marriah watched preparations being made. Regis Bryant was staring at a second piece of paper with a serious look on his face. As Hoyt and Agatha left, Marriah touched Regina Sonje's arm.

"Who is Xylia?" Marriah asked. "She seems very important to you."

"She is a very dear friend who helped Bryant when he went to find the true king of Burton and brought to Dracona clues to the future of the people of Dracona," she answered. "We will miss her."

Marriah nodded. Swift preparations were made while the messenger ate and rested. Some food was packed for the journey. Rain began to fall as they mounted their horses. As they left the village, they were greeted by a pack of wolves and an eagle.

"You have heard of Xylia's death?" Regis Bryant asked.

Marriah gasped with surprise as the eagle and wolves nodded.

"You may accompany us to pay our respects," Regis Bryant said.

The eagle launched itself into the air and the wolves parted to allow their passage. Regis Bryant rode ahead with the messenger from Burton and a large black wolf. General Edgard followed behind Regina and Marriah. By nightfall, they were nearing Burton. After they ate a simple supper Marriah sat quietly watching the men pitch two tents. Regina Sonje stood silently beside a tree at the edge of the clearing. Suddenly Regis Bryant dropped the rope he had been holding and crossed to her side. Marriah's heart beat faster as he reached out towards Regina Sonje. She let her breath out slowly as he tenderly wiped away her tears. Regina Sonje seemed to collapse into his arms. Regis Bryant held her in his arms and stroked her hair.

Marriah's attention was broken by a touch at her hand. A grey wolf nuzzled her hand again and lay down beside her. A movement drew her attention back to her mistress. Marriah stood as Regis Bryant carried Regina Sonje to the tent.

"Please help me get her into the tent and into bed," he asked her quietly.

Marriah picked up the bedding and entered the tent while the messenger was staking the last rope. Quickly she spread out the bedding before holding the tent flap for Regis Bryant. She could see the tears on his face in the white light that centered on him. Gently, he laid his wife on the bedding and covered her. Marriah let the tent flap close with her on the outside.

"Thank you," Regis Bryant said as he laid his hand on her shoulder.

Her heart froze at his touch. As he sat down, the large black wolf laid down next to him. Marriah sat down also.

"Is Regina alright?" she asked him.

"Yes," he answered. "She is just very tired and mourning for Xylia."

"Was her death unexpected? Does she leave behind any family?"

"Not exactly, she was about ninety years old," he replied. "Her half sister Riva will miss her very much. Riva will need the support of her friends to adjust since she will live for another seven hundred years or more."

Marriah sat in stunned silence. The last eight years without her mother had been hard and lonely, but seven hundred years would seem like forever. Regis Bryant was looking down at the ground before him.

"How old are you?" Marriah asked.

"Two hundred seventy one," he answered as he met her gaze. "When I met your father I could tell he was different than the other villagers. He was the first person in a very long time who had not feared or hated me. I'm sorry that he is gone."

The corners of his mouth were turned down as he looked at her, but it was as though he saw past events instead of her.

"Father said that your father understood why we drove people from the forest," Bryant continued. "He once mentioned that Langward had his own past he had left behind and wanted to forget, but he would not tell me anything more."

"Father refused to speak of his past. He never spoke of where he came from or why he left his home and family. I do know that something in his past was very painful to him," Marriah acknowledged. "All I have figured out is it has something to do with his brother. May I ask why Xylia and Riva are so important to you?"

"They saved my life once," Regis Bryant responded.

"Today has been hard on all of us," she said and stood up.

"Yes and tomorrow will be a long day," he replied as he rose to his feet. "The wolves will keep watch. We need to get some sleep."

Marriah looked from one tent to the other. The other two men had gone into one tent and Regis Bryant had entered the other where Regina Sonje slept.

"Come in," Regis Bryant invited as he opened the tent flap for her. "You can sleep on the other side of Sonje."

Servant Queen

She hesitated before walking towards the tent. Trust was something that she had to learn anew. She entered the tent and sat down. He lay down and covered himself. Marriah watched in amazement as Regina Sonje rolled over and put her arm across Regis Bryant's chest. A silent tear rolled down her cheek.

Chapter 5 - New Friends and a Prediction

Marriah was awake with the first light of dawn. Quietly she left the tent. The grey wolf rose from beside the door of the tent and followed her. It was raining lightly as she entered the edge of the forest. Soon she found some dry wood under a tree with low, thick branches. She gathered it in her skirt and sheltered it with her cape. All was quiet as she returned to the camp. She found a suitable spot to make a fire. As she knelt down, the grey wolf began digging at the spot she had chosen. Soon the ground was bare. Marriah sheltered the wood with her cape until it was burning well.

She was startled as General Edgard emerged from the other tent. He looked at her before ducking back into the tent. Soon he returned with a pair of saddlebags and a skin of water. He took a pot out of the bags and filled it with water. He smiled at her as he placed a stone into the fire and set the pot on it. She watched silently as General Edgard placed another three stones in the fire before placing a shallow pot on them. He poured in some water then stirred in some course ground oats.

"This should warm us up for our journey," he said with a smile.

A stirring and a groan caught their attention. General Edgard drew two cups from the bags and measured tea into them before adding the hot water.

"Here, they will want this," General Edgard said as he handed her the cups.

His hands were large and his arms scarred. She nodded and headed for the tent. Regina Sonje looked pale and Regis Bryant's face was drawn.

"What's the matter?" Marriah asked with concern.

Regis Bryant took a sip of tea before he drew a pendant of clear stone out of his shirt. Its center glowed red. Regina Sonje drew an identical pendant from the neck of her dress.

"Malvin's Heart enables us to speak to each other as the dragons do," he said before taking another sip of tea. "Our thoughts and feelings are as one, so I feel her morning nausea."

"Oh," Marriah said in surprise. "I noticed that you two seemed to think alike. I had no idea it went that far. General Edgard is making breakfast. Are you going to want anything?"

"Soon," Regina Sonje answered. "But not just yet."

"Is there anything I can get for you?"

"No," Regis Bryant replied. "Go have your breakfast."

Marriah left the tent and returned to the fire. General Edgard handed her a bowl of porridge.

"Regis and Regina are not yet ready to eat," Marriah said as he reached for another bowl.

General Edgard nodded as he picked up his own bowl and began to eat. The messenger from Burton was also eating. Marriah watched them closely while she ate. The grey wolf lay between her and them as if it knew she did not quite trust them. After she had finished, General Edgard cleaned Marriah's bowl and placed it back in the saddlebags.

A noise drew her attention to the tent as the royal pair emerged from it and approached the fire. They looked like they felt better. General Edgard handed them each a bowl of porridge. Soon they had eaten and Marriah put out the fire while the men packed the tents. Marriah stayed close to Regina Sonje as they continued their journey. The rain turned to snow before the end of the second day. Marriah pulled her cape close around her, grateful for its warmth. Around noon on the third day, Marriah heard the loud flapping of wings that announced Haskell's arrival. A bend in the road revealed a small village. Haskell circled once before landing in a snow covered field. Regina Sonje said something about finding Archelaus as she continued to the village with General Edgard. There were three people mounted on Haskell's shoulders. There was a young woman with red hair, an older woman with blonde hair and a young man with light brown hair.

'It is good to see you, Marriah,' Haskell's words brought a smile to her face. 'How are you doing?'

'A little better,' she responded silently as she dismounted and approached him. 'It is good to see you again too.'

"Mother!" Regis Bryant exclaimed as he helped the older woman from the dragon's back. "I didn't expect you to come."

"You didn't think you could keep me away after the letter you sent with that dispatch," she replied with a laugh. "You'll make a great father."

"I want you to meet Marriah," Regis Bryant said as Marriah peeked hesitantly from behind Haskell's head.

'It's alright,' Haskell reassured her. 'They won't hurt you.'

"Marriah, this is my mother, Lady Miranda. Brenndah and Raphello are Merton's healers," Regis Bryant said as each nodded in turn.

Brenndah looked at her intently then looked at Regis Bryant and touched her face. She then pointed to Raphello and herself before pointing to Marriah.

"Is there anything we can help with?" Raphello asked. "Perhaps Brenndah knows how to clear the bruises from Marriah's face."

Brenndah nodded.

"Yes, please," Marriah said in answer to Regis Bryant's questioning look. "I don't like to be stared at."

Brenndah smiled and began to glow a fiery red glow as she stepped forward. Her hands felt surprisingly warm as she gently stroked Marriah's face. Brenndah smiled and stroked Marriah's arms and hands one at a time. Marriah gasped to see her bruising and scars disappear leaving her skin smooth and unblemished. She fell to her knees at Brenndah's feet. Her eyes were blurred with tears as a hand lifted her face. Brenndah smiled and shook her head as she pulled Marriah to her feet.

"Thank you," she whispered as Brenndah hugged her.

"Sonje is waiting for us. She and Edgard found Riva and Archelaus," Regis Bryant said.

*****

Archelaus was relieved to see Sonje and General Edgard approaching.

"Riva, they're here," Archelaus said and Riva turned from talking to the woman who was letting them stay in her home. "I'm so glad to see you here."

"We wouldn't miss this for anything," Sonje replied as she hugged Riva, then him. "Bryant will be along shortly with my new assistant, Marriah. We just found out I'm with child. Her father was killed so she decided to become my assistant rather than return to the village."

Sonje began to tell them the full story with General Edgard occasionally adding some details. Archelaus' heart ached to think of a girl growing up being enslaved and beaten. He knew how awful that was from his own experience. Soon Bryant showed up with Lady Miranda followed by a man and woman he recognized as healers.

"I'm grateful you sent us that message," Bryant said.

Servant Queen

"We're so glad you could come," Archelaus welcomed as he bowed.

"We wouldn't think of missing this," Bryant replied, bowing low in return. "Xylia will be sorely missed."

Archelaus noticed a young woman standing behind Sonje as Riva made a comment. The woman had dark brown hair and skin that was darker than the tanned skin of the farmers. His heart skipped a beat as she glanced up then quickly looked back at the ground. She was far more beautiful than any princess he had met since taking the throne of Burton. As he approached her she backed away a step then swallowed.

"Sonje told us of you," he said, taking her hand and kissing it. "I'm glad you were able to come. Please call me Archelaus."

"I am pleased to meet you," Marriah answered with a curtsey as she finally looked up at him.

"Sonje told us of your ordeal," Archelaus said as he looked into her dark eyes. "I'm sorry to hear that your parents are both dead. Is there anything I can do for you?"

"Regina Sonje and Regis Bryant have taken care of my needs. I am Regina Sonje's assistant now," Marriah replied.

*****

A woman came out of the house and announced that lunch was ready. Marriah followed the others inside where a generous meal was laid out on the table. She was ushered to a seat and served before she had a chance to protest. Archelaus had blonde hair that was lighter than Regis Bryant's and sky blue eyes. His hand had been very gentle and his lips touching her hand sent her heart pounding. She had never seen a man kiss a woman's hand before. She noticed he kept glancing towards her and would smile at her.

After the meal they all went to the village cemetery. Marriah listened as the others shared their memories of Xylia. She was amazed to learn that Archelaus was the king of Burton and what part Xylia had played in putting him on the throne. After the coffin had been lowered into the grave, Marriah felt something touch her hand. She looked down to find the grey wolf at her side. She followed as the wolf led her to the edge of the forest. It stopped at a large stone shaped roughly like a lying wolf. The grey wolf looked back to the grave and then at Marriah. As she turned, she saw King Archelaus headed towards her.

"What have you found?" he asked.

"The wolf found it, King Archelaus," she said as she curtsied low. "For the grave, I think."

"Just call me Archelaus," he said as she rose. "I think we should show the others."

Marriah followed him back to the grave where the others were still talking.

"Marriah and that grey wolf found a stone for a foot marker," King Archelaus announced. "It almost looks like a wolf lying down."

Marriah was surprised as Riva hugged her.

"Xylia would want that," Riva wept. "Thank you."

Marriah led them to where the stone lay. She watched in amazement as Regina Sonje put her hands on the stone and the features of the wolf became clear on it. A small wagon was found and the stone was placed at the foot of the new grave.

As they returned to the house where they had eaten lunch, one of the women from the village approached them. She bowed low before Regis Bryant.

"I have something that must belong to you, a box with a dragon on it," the woman said. "It looks just like the one on your cape."

*****

Archelaus was curious. Bryant's eyebrows were almost touching as he glanced at Archelaus.

"Where is this box?" Bryant asked. "Take me to it."

"I'll come with you." Archelaus offered and Bryant nodded.

They followed the woman to a house near the field where Haskell was curled up asleep. Once inside, she opened a trunk and drew out a box made of a strange metal. It was about the size of a large book and indeed had a dragon with outstretched wings on its surface that matched the clasp on Bryant's cape.

"It was found in Xylia's house after she and her sister left," the woman explained as she drew something else out of the chest. "My mother found it and this bundle of cloth behind the bed when the house was cleaned out. Something prompted her to keep them."

"Thank you for remembering them," Bryant said as he held the box. "I think this could be very important. Is there anything I can give you in return?"

"I always knew it did not belong here. It is enough to know that I found its rightful owner," the woman said, then paused. "Could I touch your dragon? We have never seen a dragon before."

The woman held out the bundle of cloth.

"Of course," Bryant replied as Archelaus took the bundle from her. "Come with me."

The woman and Archelaus followed him out to the field where Haskell was watching them approach. The dragon put his head down. Some villagers paused to watch as the woman hesitantly put her hand on Haskell's nose.

"It's smoother than I thought it would be," she commented as she stroked the dragon's nose. "He is beautiful in the sunlight."

Archelaus could feel Haskell's smug enjoyment of her compliment.

"Yes, he is beautiful," Bryant replied. "He is a dear friend to me."

"Thank you for letting me touch him," the woman said. "I'd best get back to my chores."

Bryant seemed lost in thought as they made their way across the village to where the others were waiting. Bryant sat quietly by the fire examining the box while supper was being prepared. Archelaus put the bundle of cloth on Bryant's saddlebags. He watched Marriah help prepare the meal and set the table. She moved with grace but avoided touching anyone. She went over to Bryant and hesitated before she touched his arm.

"It is time to eat, Regis," Marriah informed him.

"Thank you," he replied as he stood up.

Archelaus went over to the table. After the meal was finished, the table and chairs were pushed into the corner and bedding was laid out on the floor.

*****

Marriah stayed near Regina Sonje as everyone settled in for night. Soon almost everyone was asleep. Marriah watched as Riva moved closer to the fire and sat watching the flames dance. She saw a tear roll down Riva's cheek. Marriah knew what Riva was going through. Carefully, she stepped around the sleeping forms to join Riva near the fire. She put her arm around Riva's shoulders.

"I can't believe that she is really gone," Riva whispered. "And yet, I don't look much older than I did the day we left this village."

"She is not completely gone as long as your heart remembers," Marriah replied softly.

"I feel so empty inside," Riva quavered. "I feel so alone. Where should I go? What will I do?"

"You have these people for friends. You are not alone. They will help you."

"I know. It will just take a while to get used to Xylia being gone."

"You have a long life ahead of you."

"Xylia said she had been a burden on me for too long," Riva sobbed as her tears began anew. "But I never thought she was a burden."

"She must have been a wonderful person. She would want you to get on with your life."

"You're right," Riva conceded. "I should sleep, but I'm afraid to."

Marriah shifted and leaned back against a chest.

"Come, lay your head in my lap," Marriah offered. "I'll keep watch over you while you sleep."

Riva lay down and put her head in Marriah's lap. Marriah stroked her hair softly as she remembered her mother doing when she was little. Riva's breathing became slower and more regular as the fire slowly died.

*****

Archelaus was one of the first to awaken in the morning. He sat up and looked around. In the fireplace, the embers cast a red glow and softly lit the surrounding area. As he rose he saw someone leaning against a chest near the fireplace. When he moved closer, he could see that it was Marriah. He smiled as he saw Riva's head cradled in Marriah's lap. Sonje quietly got up and stoked the fire before putting some water on to heat. Archelaus gently touched Marriah's shoulder and her eyes fluttered open. She lifted her head. Archelaus leaned closer to Marriah and Riva as Bryant sat up.

"Thank you, Marriah," Archelaus whispered in her ear.

"She needs to not be alone," Marriah responded.

Bryant joined them as Riva began to stir.

"How do you feel this morning?" Bryant asked as Riva sat up.

"A little better thanks to Marriah," Riva replied as she turned to look at Marriah. "After breakfast I want to do something for you in return."

"You don't need to," Marriah protested. "I know what you are going through. I know what it is like to go through it alone."

"Still, I want to do this for you," Riva replied. "I have a good feeling about this."

37

Archelaus was intrigued.

*****

Marriah helped to fold up the bedding and set the table for breakfast. As she listened to the cheerful conversation at breakfast, Marriah wondered what it was Riva wanted to do for her. Soon breakfast was cleared and Riva turned two chairs to face each other. She had Marriah sit in one and then sat down to face her. Riva smiled at Marriah as she took her hands and the others gathered around. Even King Archelaus seemed interested in what was going to happen. Riva closed her eyes and the room fell silent.

"Out of darkness and into the light, from unknown to renowned. Love will come from one who has suffered as you have."

Marriah gasped as Riva released her hands. She looked to find King Archelaus staring at her with his mouth open, but Regina Sonje was smiling. The rest of the day was a blur as Riva's words repeated in her head. As she rode beside her mistress, she wondered what it meant.

'Wait and see,' Haskell told her with a chuckle. 'Riva's gift is to see the future.'

That evening, Marriah sat by the fire as she stroked the grey wolf. She sat watching the flames, thinking about how her life had changed in the last few days. She had left behind a life of torture and begun a new life. Regis and Regina's friends had not treated her as a servant, but as an equal. Even the king of Burton had insisted that she call him by name, not title.

"You've had a long day," General Edgard's words broke into her thoughts. "You should get some sleep."

"There is so much to think about," Marriah replied. "So much has changed."

"I can guarantee that life will never go back to the way it was," General Edgard said with a smile. "I am glad to see that Brenndah has cleared the bruises and scars from your face and hands. You are a very beautiful young woman."

"Why doesn't Brenndah speak?"

"Regis Bryant told me that when the town was burned, Brenndah saw her parents die in the flames and she hasn't spoken since," he replied. "She could heal her own scars, but is not ready to."

"She could heal your scars," Marriah said.

"My scars are from teaching others to use a sword. I earned them and they are a part of me," he responded as he pointed to a scar on his cheek. "This one here I got while defending my brother Lucjen."

Marriah noticed his left eye twitch before he quickly rubbed the corner with his fingertips. He ran his hand through his short hair as he looked at the ground in front of him.

"You must love your brother very much," Marriah commented and he looked back up at her.

"He left Glynis about one hundred years ago. I haven't seen or heard from him since. I'm not even certain if he still lives," General Edgard said. "Go to bed. It is still a long ride to Dracona."

Marriah slipped quietly into the tent where Regis and Regina already slept. Soon she too was asleep.

The night brought more snow. The horses went slower through the deepening snow. They reached the village outside of Dracona's forest just after dark on the third day. Marriah was glad for Regis Bryant and Regina Sonje's white light and General Edgard's blue light to light their way in the dark. She realized how tired she was when they dismounted at Cherie and Olvan's house. She sat down gratefully in front of the fire.

Marriah woke with a start in the morning. She found herself lying in front of the fire place with a blanket and pillow. She had no memory of anything after sitting down in front of the fire. She sat up as she smelled something cooking. Soon everyone was crowded around the table and eating. Marriah listened to the conversation as she ate. When she finished, she began to help clear the table.

"Thank you, Marriah," Cherie said as she brought the last of the dishes to the washtub. "I am so excited to get the school set up for the village children. I'm glad that you are Sonje's assistant because I know that you will take good care of my sister."

"You are older than she is," Marriah observed. "Yet she is Regina."

"Yes, I am older by about a hundred years," Cherie replied. "But when I fell in love with Olvan, I knew that the people of Glynis would never accept him as their leader."

"I've seen how happy you are. I have always wished to be like you."

"Someday you will be as happy as I am," Cherie replied and gave her a hug. "I am glad that Sonje became Regina instead of me. I would not trade my life for anything in the world."

Soon the goodbyes were said and they headed back to Dracona. The snow on the ground got shallower as they traveled toward the town and castle. By the time they stopped for nightfall, the ground was clear of snow. In the morning, a skiff of snow covered everything. They ate quickly and continued on to the castle. Marriah was tired and numb by the time Agatha and Hoyt met them at the door of the castle.

"Come in and warm up," Agatha said. "I'll have food sent up to your rooms."

Chapter 6 - An Invitation and Memories of the Past

Archelaus returned to Burton still thinking about Riva's prediction. Winter wore on while his days were filled with his duties as king. More kingdoms sent princesses to him, but he found himself comparing them to the shy young woman who had been through so much yet still cared for Riva as she grieved. Spring was approaching when Charles reminded him that the Spring Festival had to be planned.

"Your birthday falls during the Spring Festival, My King," Charles said as they were nearly finished with the plans. "There should be a party for you on your birthday."

"I don't want a party," he replied. "I'm used to my birthday being just another day."

"Certainly there is something special you'd like to do on your birthday," Charles said. "Maybe a dance."

"Fine, we'll have a dance," Archelaus replied then had an idea. "I think I'll invite Bryant and Sonje to come."

Later in his quarters he wrote an invitation to Bryant and Sonje before staring at a blank sheet of paper trying to figure out how to make certain Marriah would be coming with them. He started the letter several times only to crumple up the paper and throw it into the fireplace. He finally went to bed, but couldn't sleep as he thought about Marriah.

*****

Life had settled into a routine for Marriah. During the last four months her days started with lessons in the library with Hoyt for an hour or two before beginning her duties with Regina Sonje. She was excited to be learning to read and write. She was even learning the language of Glynis. Hoyt seemed both surprised and pleased at how quickly she learned.

She was surprised when Regis Bryant mentioned that he was meeting with the village council and asked her for details on how to recognize if someone was being abused like she and her father had been. General Edgard had been teaching Marriah self defense and how to use a sword. For this she was grateful. Her

41

nightmares of Larkin were slowly fading as she felt less helpless, but she missed her father.

She was talking with Haskell in the great cavern when Regina Sonje looked in and said, "I thought I'd find you here."

"Yes, Regina?" Marriah answered.

"A messenger has come from Burton," Sonje said as she climbed the stairs to the ledge. "He brought an invitation to the Spring Festival and this."

Marriah was puzzled as she took the envelope from Regina Sonje. The envelope had Marriah's name on the front and a wax seal on the back. A crown and scepter were imprinted into the wax. Marriah opened it with trembling hands. Slowly she read the letter.

'Dear Marriah,' it began. 'Since our meeting, I have thought of you often. I am looking forward to seeing you again at the Spring Festival. I hope you will give me the chance to get to know you better. Sincerely, Archelaus.'

Marriah sat down in surprise.

"What is it?" Regina Sonje asked with concern.

"The king of Burton is looking forward to seeing me at the Spring Festival," Marriah answered in disbelief. "He says he wants to get to know me better."

"That's great."

"But, why me?" Marriah asked. "I am just a servant."

"That doesn't matter. In order to hide from Gustave, Archelaus was disguised as a mute, hunchbacked kitchen boy. For years, he labored hard until he had the opportunity to regain Burton's throne," Sonje explained. "As king, he is a servant to all of Burton. And you are so much more than a servant."

Marriah looked at her in surprise.

"You are my friend," Sonje explained. "And you have shown us all that we must work hard to give every individual person the best life possible."

"Me?" Marriah asked incredulously.

Sonje glanced at Haskell.

'Before you arrived seeking help, Bryant did not know such cruelty existed,' Haskell told her. 'You taught him a very important lesson, that as regis, it is his duty to protect the people of Dracona, not only from invasion, but from themselves.'

"That is why Bryant is working so hard on the book of laws," Sonje added. "To prevent others from suffering as you have.

It shouldn't matter where you came from or what you do. Everyone deserves to be treated as equals."

'It is late,' Haskell said. 'You are both looking tired.'

"Good night," Marriah said as she rose. "Thank you."

*****

Sonje and Haskell watched her leave.

'There is still much pain and distrust in her,' Haskell told Sonje. 'It will take a lot for her to lose that.'

'She has changed so much since she first came here,' Sonje thought back. 'She is turning from a frightened child into a confident young woman. Yet she still seems so sad at times.'

'Like Brenndah, part of her died with her parents,' Haskell replied. 'She may never quite feel whole again.'

*****

That night, Marriah slept fitfully, her dreams were disjointed memories of the handsome young man who was king of Burton, and of Larkin. She rose early. She bathed and dressed quickly, not wanting to linger long enough to recall her dreams. She hurried down to the library and found some paper. She then went down to the kitchen, grateful to find it still empty. She opened the door of the oven and drew out a few pieces of charred wood. Quietly she shut the door and went out into the garden. She quickly went around to the courtyard and up the stairs behind the armory. She walked along the courtyard wall to the castle wall and sat down. There she began to draw a picture of Larkin beating her father. She drew her mother lying murdered in the meadow and her father crying over her body. Then she drew Regis Bryant carrying Regina Sonje to the tent. The expression on his face revealed the deep love that he held for her in his heart. Finally she drew the face that she could not forget; the face of kind and handsome King Archelaus.

She sat staring at the face of the man who insisted she not use his title. He had treated her not as a servant, but as an equal. Her heart ached wondering if someone could love her as Regis Bryant loved Regina Sonje. She dared not believe it possible that anyone could actually love her.

As she wiped away the tear that rolled unbidden down her cheek she heard footsteps on the stairs. She looked up to see Regis Bryant go straight from the stairs to the corner of the wall and stand motionless watching the people in the bustling streets below him. She stood up and carefully approached him. He suddenly sighed and sat down looking at the stones beneath his feet. The papers rustled as a breeze caressed her cheek. Regis Bryant looked up to find her standing before him.

"What is the matter, Regis?" she asked with concern.

"I have just learned more about why the people of Glynis live so much longer than the other people of this world," Regis Bryant began. "We are not even from this world. There is a large ship in the ocean near Merton. It is called the Temple of Origin and brought us here."

"Does that mean that you will leave?" Marriah asked, frightened to have the only people she had learned to trust abandon her.

"Not right away," he answered quickly. "There is much more to learn and prepare before we could even consider leaving. We have a responsibility to you and the village. We would have to make certain your futures were secure."

Marriah nodded.

"I think it would be more than a year before we could even consider it," Regis Bryant said as he stood up. "Have you eaten yet?"

"No," she admitted. "I hope that Hoyt and Regina Sonje aren't upset with me."

"No, they were just worried about how you were doing. They weren't the only ones who asked where you were and if you were alright," he answered to her surprise.

"When things trouble me, I draw. It helps me sort things out in my mind. Sometimes I draw the horrible things and then burn them."

"I write in my journal for the same reasons," Regis Bryant said with a smile. "You could throw the ones you want to burn in the volcano."

"Yes, please," Marriah responded as she decided to trust him with what had been troubling her. "I do have one I would like to show you."

Marriah shuffled through the stack of drawings before handing him the one of him carrying his wife to the tent when they had traveled to Xylia's funeral.

"It was then that I saw how deeply you care for Regina Sonje," Marriah whispered as her heart ached. "How much you love her."

Regis Bryant looked up as a tear rolled down her cheek.

44

"Last night I lay awake wondering if ever anyone would care for me that way," she confessed as her voice cracked. "If ever anyone could love me."

*****

Bryant wiped the tear from her cheek.

"I can't tell the future like Riva can, but I can tell you that you are worthy of that love," Bryant assured her. "Let's go to the volcano. Do you mind if Sonje joins us?"

"Please," Marriah replied. "I would like for her to come."

They found Sonje waiting at the rear of the great hall. She hugged Marriah as Bryant opened the doors. They walked to the volcano. Haskell was waiting there for them along with the queen dragon, Evelina.

"You can keep that drawing if you would like," Marriah said. "I want to keep this one."

Bryant smiled as he took the drawing from her.

"It's Archelaus," Sonje exclaimed.

Marriah nodded as she released the rest of the drawings into the volcano.

"After lunch we will go down to the tailor's shop," Sonje said as she put her arm across Marriah's shoulders. "You need a new dress."

Bryant smiled as Haskell chuckled softly.

'Marriah will protest when she finds out what Sonje has planned,' Haskell told Bryant.

'Not that it will do her any good,' Bryant replied silently. 'When Sonje gets through with her, Marriah will look like a princess.'

*****

At lunch, Marriah was surprised by the number of people who came up and asked where she had been. She hadn't realized that anyone would have cared. At the tailor's shop, she patiently stood as the tailors, Darryl and Aurora, measured her.

"What color would you like?" Darryl asked.

"I don't care," Marriah replied in surprise.

"What is your favorite color?" Regina Sonje asked.

"I've never thought about it," Marriah admitted. "I remember the pink roses Mother had growing by the house."

Marriah felt suddenly sad. The roses had died right after her mother had.

45

Aurora brought some fabric out of the back room. There were several shades of pinks and greens.

"It's alright to miss your mother," Regina Sonje reassured her. "She would be very proud of you now and she would want you to find happiness."

Aurora had arranged the fabric in pairs of pink and green. Marriah chose a pink that closely matched the roses she remembered. Next Regina Sonje took her to the cobbler's shop.

"Some new shoes too?" Marriah asked. "I don't need new shoes."

"Yes, you do," Regina Sonje said with a laugh. "You can't dance properly in those boots."

"I don't know how to dance," she protested.

"We have a week to teach you then."

Marriah sighed as the cobbler traced and measured her feet.

"Your shoes will be ready before the week is up," the cobbler said with a bow.

"Thank you," Marriah replied, surprised at his courtesy.

Regina Sonje led her back to the castle and to the music room. Regis Bryant and Aloysia were waiting for them.

"First watch, then it will be your turn," Regis Bryant said.

He bowed then offered his hand to Regina Sonje. She placed her hand in his and curtsied. Aloysia began to play as they walked to the center of the room. Marriah watched as they began to dance. She could see that Regina Sonje's steps followed Regis Bryant's. Soon it was her turn. She swallowed hard before placing her hand in Regis Bryant's outstretched hand. Nervously she placed her left hand on his arm as she felt his hand on the back of her waist.

"Just relax and let me guide you," Regis Bryant said as her eyes met his.

She nodded, not trusting her voice. His hands were firm, but gentle as they stepped in time to the music. At first her feet kept hitting his, but after a while she realized that she was doing better.

"You have a good sense of rhythm," he told her as the music ended.

"That was great," Regina Sonje added. "By the time we leave for Burton, you will be ready to dance."

"Thank you," Marriah said as she followed them out of the room.

The following days were filled with preparations for going to the Spring Festival in Burton. Hoyt had organized a group of young men and women who were also learning to dance. Marriah found that she enjoyed dancing and was no longer afraid of being hit every time someone touched her. Haskell told her he was very proud of her for that. When she returned to the tailor's shop for her dress, she was amazed as she stood in front of the polished shield. The bodice was a bright green with pink gathered around the top leaving the shoulders bare. The skirt was pink and full. They had made her several other dresses as well. The cobblers shop was their next stop. Her new shoes were also pink. They had a short heel on them and fit comfortably. She could hardly wait to leave for Burton.

*****

The morning finally arrived when they left for Burton. Marriah was nervous but excited. She had not been to a fair or festival since her mother died. It was warmer than when they had traveled to Xylia's funeral. General Edgard and Bethesda were waiting in the courtyard along with four men in guard uniforms. In addition to the large carriage, a wagon waited to take their trunks, bedding and tents. General Edgard and Regis Bryant helped the women into the carriage before mounting their horses. Marriah was glad when they stopped for the night. Regina Sonje seemed very tired. Marriah helped get food prepared and made sure Regina Sonje's bed was ready before eating. When she finally lay down beside Bethesda, she fell asleep immediately.

The next morning she awoke to the smell of breakfast cooking. As she exited the tent, she was surprised to find the grey wolf waiting for her. She patted it on the head before joining the others for breakfast. Soon they were packed and on their way. During their journey, Marriah saw wolves running in the trees keeping pace with them. Evening was approaching when Burton came into sight. The streets were bustling with people and carts. Near the center of the city the sight of a man beating a boy in front of a shop made Marriah's heart freeze.

As the man grabbed the boy and drug him into the shop Marriah leapt from the carriage and shouted, "Stop!"

When she got into the shop the man was beating the boy again.

"Don't hit him!" she exclaimed.

"Who are you to say what I can or cannot do?" the man growled angrily. "This clumsy lout keeps dropping things!"

As the man raised his arm again, a soldier stepped between him and Marriah.

"You will do as she says," the soldier ordered.

Marriah looked at the boy and saw his tight, tattered clothes and shoes.

"He would not be so clumsy with proper fitting shoes and clothes," she said. "Beating him will not make him less clumsy."

The man turned red and opened his mouth as if to speak, then closed it again.

"See to it that the boy is properly dressed," a familiar voice commanded.

Marriah turned in surprise. King Archelaus stood in the doorway.

"If the boy is ever beaten again, you will face the consequences," the king declared as the man knelt with head bowed. "Check on this situation tomorrow."

Marriah curtsied to King Archelaus as he approached. He bowed to her as he took her hand and kissed it.

"You must be tired from your journey," he said with a smile as his eyes met hers. "Your room is ready and waiting with a warm bath and dinner."

"Thank you, King Archelaus," Marriah replied as he placed her hand on his arm and led her back to the street.

"Please call me Archelaus," he insisted as he led her to a fine carriage next to the one from Dracona.

Marriah was speechless as King Archelaus helped her into the carriage then sat next to her. She glanced at Regina Sonje and found her smiling back.

"Bryant says that you have inspired him to make new laws against that type of abuse," King Archelaus said as the carriage began to move. "I too am working on some new laws and would like your advice."

"My advice?" Marriah asked, stunned.

"I suffered beatings and abuse as a kitchen boy, but nothing like you survived," King Archelaus confessed as he took her hand in his. "I need your help to make certain no one in Burton could ever suffer as you did."

"I will help you in any way I can," Marriah replied as she met his gaze.

*****

He smiled at her answer. He was grateful that she had come. Bryant's reply had not been clear on if she would come or not. He knew that Marriah had a hard time trusting new people and new

48

situations. He was pleased with her look of wonderment as they entered the castle. He led her upstairs to her room. He was happy with the surprise she showed as the door was opened. He had picked the room personally.

"This is where I will be staying?" Marriah asked as two women came into the room and curtsied.

"Yes," he replied. "These two women will serve you while you stay in Burton."

"Regina Sonje will . . ," Marriah protested.

"Will have servants caring for her every need as well," he interrupted her before she could finish. "You are here to relax and enjoy the festival. Dinner will be in one hour. I will see you then."

The hour seemed to last forever as Archelaus waited for it to be time for dinner. Marriah was even more beautiful than he had remembered. He had so wanted to kiss more than her hand.

"You look like you have a lot on your mind," Aunt Althea said as she put a hand on his shoulder.

"Yes, Aunt," Archelaus replied. "Marriah came. She is so wonderful."

"I heard about what happened on the way to the castle," she said.

"I can't tell you how happy that made me," he admitted as he watched Marriah enter the dining room. "I think she is the one."

Soon Bryant and Sonje arrived and they sat down to eat. Marriah was seated on Archelaus' right and Bryant to his left. He noticed how tired Sonje looked. The meal was simple, but filling. Once in bed, Archelaus had trouble getting to sleep. The events of the day kept running through his mind. When Charles woke him, it was as if he had barely gotten to sleep.

"Is something troubling you, My King?" Charles asked with concern as he laid out clothing for Archelaus.

"You heard about what happened yesterday?"

"Involving the young woman from Dracona?"

"Yes," Archelaus said as he began to dress. "Her name is Marriah."

"The same one who was at Xylia's funeral?"

Archelaus nodded as he picked up his jacket.

"It is time for some changes in Burton," Archelaus said as he buttoned his jacket. "That is some of why I invited Bryant, Sonje and Marriah. I needed some advice on some new laws forbidding the type of abuse that Marriah and that boy suffered."

"I suspect there is another reason you wanted Marriah to come," Charles asserted as he handed Archelaus his crown. "I saw the extra envelope sent with the messenger."

Archelaus smiled as he placed the crown on his head.

"Just working on a promise I made at my coronation."

Charles smiled and nodded.

The others were waiting in the dining room when Archelaus arrived. Marriah looked beautiful in a pink dress with white trim. Breakfast was eaten quickly.

"After I declare the official beginning of the festival, we can do whatever you would like," Archelaus said as he stood up. "Come with me please."

He caught Bryant's smile as Marriah placed her hand on the arm he offered to her. Bryant's understanding would make things easier later, if all went well. He led them to the same balcony that his coronation was held on. He smiled at Marriah's gasp of surprise at the number of people crowded among the tents and booths in the plaza. Archelaus raised his hand and the crowd fell silent.

"Burton has come through winter and spring is finally here with promises of new growth and change," Archelaus began with a smile. "I would like to welcome any visitors to our city. I extend a special welcome to Regis Bryant and Regina Sonje of Dracona, and the others here from Dracona including Lady Marriah."

He felt her hand tighten on his arm as she bobbed down in a shallow curtsey.

"Let the Spring Festival begin!"

A cheer rose from the crowd. Archelaus turned to see Bryant wink at him before leaving the balcony. He hoped that meant Bryant knew that he was interested in more than a friendship with Marriah.

"Would you like to see the booths first?" Archelaus asked as he turned to face Marriah.

"I would like to check on that boy first," she replied.

"Of course," he agreed with a smile. "Aunt Althea and Charles will make sure the others have escorts and we can meet back here for lunch."

Just then a soldier approached and bowed.

"Report," Archelaus ordered.

"We found the boy's condition improved," the soldier responded.

"We wish to confirm your findings."

50

"As you wish, My King. I can ready a carriage," he replied.

"Horseback will be fine," Marriah said and the soldier bowed before hurrying off.

Archelaus led Marriah down stairs and through halls until they reached the stables. The soldier was waiting with three horses. Archelaus smiled at Marriah's surprised look as he clasped his hands to help her mount.

"But, you are king," Marriah protested. "I am just a servant. You should not be helping me mount."

"One thing I learned from Bryant is, as King of Burton, I am a servant to all the people of Burton," Archelaus replied. "Here in Burton, you are my honored guest and I am at your service."

*****

The soldier smiled and nodded to Marriah as King Archelaus bowed low before her. King Archelaus again offered his clasped hands to her. She placed her foot in his hands and mounted without further protest. She remembered what Regina Sonje had told her. Perhaps she was right, he was not concerned that she was a servant. He had introduced her to the people of Burton as Lady Marriah.

They followed the soldier to the same shop Marriah had been in the day before. The man and the boy both bowed low to King Archelaus and her as they entered the shop.

"He hasn't dropped anything all morning," the man confessed with his head bowed. "You were right."

"Beating someone creates more problems than it solves," Marriah said. "Sometimes it teaches children that it is alright to abuse others and it will be passed down to their children."

"It will not happen again," the man vowed.

"Thank you for helping me," the boy said.

"You're welcome," she replied.

"It is time to see the festival," King Archelaus said as he led her back out to the street.

Marriah allowed him to help her mount and soon they were back at the main plaza. The soldier took their horses after they had dismounted. King Archelaus put her hand on his arm and they spent the rest of the morning looking at all the goods for sale.

In one tent there were books, paper, pens and ink for sale. A small book bound in white leather caught Marriah's eye. She opened it to find all the pages blank. She closed it and put it back where she had found it. Next to it was a board with a stack of paper fastened to it.

"Does M'Lady like to draw?" the man in the tent asked her.

"Yes," Marriah answered.

"There are some paints and inks over there," he told her.

*****

Archelaus watched as she looked over the paint and felt the brushes. He had noticed her interest in the white journal. Her hand had lingered on it as she looked at the drawing board.

"Are you enjoying the Festival, My King?" the man asked him.

"Yes," he responded as he glanced to see if Marriah's back was turned. "How much for the journal and your finest pen and ink set?"

"Two gold coins, My King."

Archelaus nodded and placed two coins in the man's hand. Marriah turned to the man with a questioning look.

"Would you consider a trade for the board?" she asked.

"What have you got to trade?" the man asked, glancing at Archelaus.

Marriah drew a small pouch from the purse hanging from her wrist. She loosened the strings and drew out a chain with a heart-shaped stone the color of blood on it.

"A gem from the mountain of Dracona," she answered.

The man lifted the stone and took a closer look at it.

"The board, five brushes, and a complete paint set," the man said. "My wife told me to bring her something. This will please her."

"How do I use the paints?"

"Mix a little of the powder with a drop or two of oil on the stone tray. Clean the brushes with lamp oil or they will go hard," the man responded as he gathered the items together.

Archelaus smiled at Marriah's surprise as he handed her the journal he had purchased for her. Her eyes widened as the man set the beautiful pen and ink set down with the other items.

"For me?" she asked.

"A gift," Archelaus answered.

"Thank you!" Marriah said and kissed him on the cheek.

She then blushed bright red and began to open her mouth.

"I'm glad you like them," he said with a smile before she could speak.

52

His heart was racing as he gathered up the items and they left the tent.

"It's time to get back to the castle for lunch," he said as he noticed the position of the sun.

"I am getting hungry," she admitted.

They met up with Bryant and Sonje as they entered the castle gate. Marriah began talking to Sonje, leaving Archelaus free to talk to Bryant.

"I need to meet with you," Archelaus said. "In private."

"I think right after lunch would be a good time," Bryant responded.

Archelaus dropped Marriah's things off at her room before going to the dining hall. Charles was waiting there.

"Enjoying the Festival?" Charles asked him.

"Very much," he replied. "I found out that Marriah likes to draw. I bought her a journal with a pen and ink set."

"Did she like it?"

"She kissed me on the cheek," he smiled.

Before Charles could respond, the door opened and the others came in. Archelaus hardly tasted the food he was eating. The women were talking about what they saw at the booths. Bryant was listening and making comments to General Edgard. He wondered how Bryant would react to his question. He was originally going to wait a few days, but Marriah's kiss had given him courage to approach the matter sooner. He was glad when the meal was over. The women went to their rooms for a rest before the afternoon's activities. General Edgard and Charles went off to the armory. Archelaus led Bryant to the office off of the throne room. Bryant sat down, but Archelaus was too nervous to sit.

"I need to ask something of you," he began.

"You know you can ask me anything," Bryant replied.

"Since Marriah's parents are both dead, then you and Sonje are the closest thing she has to a family."

"I suppose so."

"I would like your permission to ask her to marry me," Archelaus blurted out as his heart began to race.

Bryant laughed, "I was wondering how long it would take you to get the courage to ask."

"Has it been that obvious?" Archelaus asked as he sat down, his knees weak with relief.

"I could see your interest in her at Xylia's funeral," Bryant affirmed. "Then when you leapt out of your carriage and ran into that shop, it was obvious."

"What do you think she will say when I ask her?"

"Do it in private so she won't feel pressured by the crowd. And wait for the right moment."

"How do I know when?"

"I think she will let you know."

Archelaus' heart leapt. Without actually saying it, Bryant had given him the answer he was hoping for. He felt better.

"I bought her a journal today and she kissed me on the cheek," he confessed.

"She told Sonje all about it and about you helping her mount the horse," Bryant commented.

Archelaus felt the blood rushing to his cheeks. Bryant laughed.

"It's just hard for her to understand how a king could have an interest in a servant," Bryant explained. "She once confided in me that she didn't know if she was deserving of true love."

"I've never thought of her as a servant, but you have given me a lot to think about," he admitted. "Thank you, my friend."

"Now I need to ask something of you," Bryant said as his face grew serious. "As you know, the people of Glynis are much longer lived than anyone else."

"Yes," Archelaus replied remembering what he had learned on an earlier visit to Dracona for Bryant and Sonje's wedding and coronation.

"I have learned that the people of Glynis must someday return home," Bryant revealed.

"But the volcanos."

"We are not originally from the north," Bryant interrupted him. "We are not even originally from this world."

Archelaus sat in stunned silence.

"I was shocked too," Bryant admitted. "I don't know exactly when or how, but we will eventually need to leave here."

Archelaus still did not know what to say.

"I need to ask you if you and Burton could help me with something very important," Bryant continued after a few minutes. "We can work out the details later, and you can turn me down if you want to."

"You know I would do anything to help you, Bryant," Archelaus replied. "What is it you need?"

"When the people of Glynis leave, the villagers will need protection and guidance," Bryant pointed out. "They have their own council but need watching over."

"I would be happy to," Archelaus replied.

"Thank you," Bryant smiled. "That makes me feel a lot better. By the way, do you have a ring?"

"A ring?" Archelaus repeated in confusion.

"For Marriah," Bryant explained. "Sonje says she would be happy to make one if you don't."

"No, I don't," Archelaus confessed. "I would appreciate it if she could make one. I'll get her whatever she needs."

Chapter 7 - No One Else's Opinion Matters

Marriah could not believe the gift that King Archelaus had given her. She had been thinking of writing about what had happened to her and her family. Haskell told her that writing about it might help and that Regis Bryant wrote in his journal almost every day. The ink bottle stood on a stone base with a groove for the pen to lie in. A gold filigree basket kept the ink bottle in place. The pen had matching filigree inlaid on it. It was unlike any pen she had seen while at Dracona. She wondered why King Archelaus should have such an interest in her that he would give her such an obviously expensive gift. She knew little about him other than he had been a scullery boy before becoming king. Maybe it was time to learn more about him and his past.

She left her room and started towards the dining room. A man who was walking towards her stopped and bowed low to her.

"My name is Charles," the man said. "May I be of assistance, Lady Marriah?"

"I was looking for King Archelaus," she replied.

"Right this way," Charles responded and led her down the hall.

They passed the dining room and went down some stairs. Charles opened a pair of double doors into a large hall with a raised platform at the other end. On the platform were two thrones.

"Wait here a moment, please," Charles said as he went up the stairs.

After he went behind a curtain at the side of the platform, Marriah began to look around the room. Over the double doors hung a large painting of a man, a woman and a young boy. The man looked a lot like King Archelaus, but much older. He was wearing the same crown that King Archelaus wore and the woman wore a smaller matching crown.

"My parents and me."

She jumped at the sound of King Archelaus' voice behind her.

"I wanted it there to remind me of how my father would have ruled," King Archelaus said with a note of sadness in his voice.

"What happened to them?" Marriah asked.

"About nine years ago, my mother fell ill," King Archelaus began as he sat on the stairs. "Gustave took advantage of that and killed both my parents. Aunt Althea saved me and had some of the faithful servants hide some of the things Gustave wanted destroyed."

Marriah sat down on the steps next to him. She took his hand as a tear rolled down his cheek.

"Aunt Althea and I hid in a cave for about a year. Gustave convinced everyone that we had all become ill and died."

"Gustave lied just like Larkin did," Marriah observed softly.

"I realized that if I ever wanted to claim the throne, I needed to get back into the castle. I was about thirteen at the time."

"But Gustave would have killed you if he recognized you."

"Exactly the problem. Aunt Althea felt that if we could change my appearance enough, Gustave would be fooled. She had discovered she had the ability to heal wounds while we were in hiding. She thought that she could use the same power to disguise me."

King Archelaus stood up and climbed to the top of the stairs. He pulled a cord hanging near the thrones before returning to Marriah's side. Charles entered through the double doors and bowed.

"Ask Aunt Althea to come here," King Archelaus requested.

Charles bowed and left. King Archelaus took Marriah's hand and kissed it.

"I want you to see how I spent almost eight years," he said as he looked into her eyes. "I hope it will help you to understand me better and why I want to know you better."

Marriah nodded as his Aunt Althea entered the throne room. She curtsied to Marriah and King Archelaus. King Archelaus stood and stepped beside her before turning to face her.

"I want to show Marriah my disguise," King Archelaus said as he removed his jacket and shirt.

King Archelaus was standing with his side toward Marriah. Althea stood facing him and placed her hands on his shoulders. Marriah gasped as King Archelaus' back bent and a hump swelled up. When King Archelaus turned towards her, his face was twisted and strange.

"We decided he should be mute so his voice would not be recognized," Althea explained. "It turned out that Gustave preferred a mute servant to carry out his most sensitive tasks."

King Archelaus turned back to Althea and she changed him back to his former appearance.

"Thank you, Aunt," King Archelaus said.

"I'll see you in a half an hour," she said and left the room.

King Archelaus turned to watch her leave. Marriah stood in shock as she saw the scars that crossed his back. She reached out and felt the uneven skin.

"You were whipped!" she exclaimed.

"A price I paid to work so close to Gustave," King Archelaus replied. "The cook beat me when he was in a bad mood."

"Why didn't you have your Aunt Althea repair these when you became king?"

"To remind myself that the people of Burton could suffer from such abuse," King Archelaus said as he turned to face her.

Marriah saw a crown and scepter in red on his chest. She reached out and found it to be smooth and flat.

"My birthmark," King Archelaus explained.

Marriah met his gaze as he took her hand in his and raised it to his lips. He kissed the palm of her hand. She trembled at the sensation.

"You understand how it feels to live in fear and danger. You want to protect others from that. That is why I invited you here. I have thought of you every day and every night since we first met," King Archelaus confessed.

"I have thought often of you," Marriah admitted. "I remember that at Xylia's funeral, you seemed more interested in my welfare than in yourself and your title."

King Archelaus smiled and took her other hand in his.

"Your welfare and happiness are more important," he insisted. "If there is anything, anything at all that you want or need, just tell me and I will take care of it."

"What do you want from me in return?"

"Only your company," he replied and kissed both of her hands. "We had better be going to meet the others at the stables. They will be there soon."

"Can you show me where you stayed when you were in disguise?"

"Yes."

King Archelaus released her hands and put his shirt back on. She handed him the jacket. He smiled as he put it on. He led her from the throne room and to the bustling kitchen. He led her to a corner near the great oven.

"Here is where I slept. One of my jobs was to keep the fire burning."

"No bed or blanket?"

"Only an old flour sack that was full of holes."

"What did you do with the cook when you became king?"

Just then a man came into the kitchen. His eyes widened at the sight of King Archelaus and he dropped to his belly on the floor.

"He doesn't beat the kitchen workers anymore," King Archelaus grinned. "Rise, Cook. This is Lady Marriah. She is to be treated with the same respect that I am due."

"As you wish, Kind and Generous King," the cook responded. "If there is anything you want, just ask."

"I will," Marriah said as the man bowed low to her.

King Archelaus led her outside and across the courtyard.

"I told him he could continue to be the castle cook only if he stopped beating people when he was angry," King Archelaus told her. "He just about died of shame when he realized what he had done was to the rightful king. The other kitchen workers told me later that he slept in that corner for a whole month."

"You didn't have to punish him, he punished himself," Marriah commented in amazement.

"Yes, but I need to decide what punishment should have been warranted," he said. "I need your help with that."

Marriah nodded. Regis Bryant had asked for the same thing. They walked through the stables in silence. She patted the noses of the curious horses as they walked by. At the end of the stables were two horses that were a color Marriah had never seen before. They were a golden yellow with white manes.

"I received these as a gift from a king northeast of here after I withdrew Burton's soldiers and sent a messenger announcing Gustave's dethronement," King Archelaus explained, seeing her questioning look.

She stroked their golden necks and laughed as they sniffed her hair.

*****

"There you are."

Archelaus turned to see Bryant approach.

"The others are in the courtyard," Bryant said. "Are you two ready?"

"Yes, Regis," Marriah replied with a curtsey.

Archelaus and Marriah followed Bryant back out to the courtyard. Sonje, Aunt Althea, and Bethesda were already in the carriage. General Edgard had mounted his horse as well. Sonje smiled at Archelaus as he helped Marriah into the carriage. He mounted his horse and led the way to the field where the afternoon's events were to take place. Bryant rode beside him.

"How did things go?" Bryant asked.

"Quite well," Archelaus smiled. "She wanted to learn more about my past."

"Althea mentioned you showed Marriah your disguise."

"Yes," Archelaus acknowledged. "Marriah felt the scars on my back, and then my birthmark. She has the gentlest touch."

"She is telling Sonje all about it and how you kissed the palm of her hand. You are definitely getting through to her."

As they watched the races and other events, Archelaus was acutely aware of Marriah sitting next to him. She was obviously enjoying herself. Often she would touch his arm and point out something. Occasionally her hand would linger on his arm. This filled him with hope. He knew she had changed and learned a lot since she first sought help escaping Larkin. But would she be ready to accept his proposal?

As they left the stand, Marriah took his offered arm. When he turned from helping her into the carriage, he found Bryant smiling at him.

"I have never seen her so happy," Bryant revealed as he prepared to mount.

They returned to the castle as the sun began to set. As Archelaus helped Marriah from the carriage, she met his gaze and smiled at him. A large meal was waiting for them in the dining room. After eating, Bryant and Sonje excused themselves.

"I'm too excited to sleep yet," Marriah admitted. "Could we walk in the castle garden?"

"Anything you want."

He kissed her hand before placing it on his arm and leading her out to the garden. Lanterns had been lit and the moon was coming out. As they passed the well, Marriah stopped.

"This is where it happened," she said.

"Yes."

She walked over to the stone marker near the well.

"On this site greed and cruelty were defeated, but we must be ever vigilant against their return," she read out loud.

"There's more on the other side," Archelaus told her.

She went to the other side of the stone and read, "A man is not elevated by standing on the backs of others, but by reaching down to help those less fortunate than himself."

"Some people wanted a large statue. I felt this was much more appropriate."

"I like it."

Archelaus' heart skipped a beat as she put her hand in his and they continued their walk. They soon came to a bench near the fountain. She led him to the bench and sat down. He sat down beside her.

"What do you want to do tomorrow?" he asked her.

"I would like to see the rest of the city," Marriah answered. "And the cave that you lived in."

"Then that is what we will do," he happily agreed. "Sometime, I would like to see where you lived and grew up."

Marriah turned to face him. Her eyes met his as if searching for something.

"You really do," she whispered.

"Yes," Archelaus said and kissed her hand. "I care very deeply for you and want to know everything about you."

"Then I must show you something that might help," Marriah said. "It is in my room."

Archelaus went with her to her room. She lit the lamps and candles around the room.

"This room is bigger than the house I grew up in," she said as she drew a paper from the trunk of clothes. "I drew this the morning after receiving your invitation."

Archelaus took the paper and was stunned to see his own face staring back at him.

"The day I escaped from Larkin, he told me I was his wife," Marriah revealed with a tremor in her voice. "I knew that I could never be the wife of a man I could never love."

"Without love, there is no point in marriage," Archelaus agreed as he put the drawing on the table.

"For a long time, I believed I would never find it in my heart to love any man. Regis Bryant and Regina Sonje taught me that life could be worthwhile and that there was love in this world."

Archelaus could see the tear begin to roll down her face. He drew out his handkerchief and stepped closer to her. She did not flinch as he gently wiped the tear from her cheek. She took the handkerchief from him and wiped her nose.

"I have often wondered if I could ever find love," she revealed as her voice cracked. "Or if I deserved to be loved."

Her admission made his heart ache. Archelaus drew her gently to him as tears began to stream down her face.

"Of course you deserve to be loved," he promised gently. "I love you."

"Then it is alright for me to love you even though you are king of Burton?" Marriah whispered.

"It is alright with me," Archelaus assured her as his heart began to beat faster. "And no one else's opinion matters."

She buried her face against his shoulder and began to sob. He held her close and stroked her hair softly. After a while she seemed to be calming down.

"I know you have had a hard life, and it will take time for you to learn to trust again," he said softly. "I want you to know that you can trust me."

"I don't want to be alone tonight," Marriah quavered. "Stay with me."

"I will. Come, sit down."

He led her to a lounge. The back on one end was high enough for him to lean his head against if he fell asleep. Marriah sat beside him.

"Do you have nightmares?" she asked.

"Yes," Archelaus answered truthfully. "Less often now, but I still wake up screaming sometimes."

"I do too," Marriah admitted. "The next day, I draw what I saw in the nightmare and then burn the drawing to make the images go away."

"I talk to Aunt Althea about my nightmares."

"I feel dizzy."

"Lay down. I'll hold you while you sleep."

Marriah put her feet up on the lounge and lay down across his lap. He cradled her head in his arm and drew her closer. He brushed a curly wisp of her hair from her face before kissing her on the forehead. After a while, her eyes were closed and she relaxed.

*****

Charles was worried. He knew that King Archelaus was not in his room and it was getting late. A guard had seen the king and Lady Marriah come in from the garden, but now he couldn't be found. There was one last place to look, Lady Marriah's room. Charles was relieved when he saw Lady Althea coming down the hall.

"Have you seen Archelaus?" she asked.

"No, but he was last seen with Lady Marriah," Charles said with a bow. "Would you come with me to her room?"

"Yes."

Charles tapped softly at the door. There was no response. Lady Althea turned the knob and quietly opened the door. As the door opened, Charles could see King Archelaus put his finger to his lips. Lady Marriah was asleep in his arms. The king motioned them in. Charles leaned over so the king could whisper to him.

"She asked that I stay with her tonight."

Charles nodded. He got a quilt from the bed and covered Lady Marriah. Lady Althea brought another and tucked it around her nephew. Silently he and Lady Althea left the room.

"He loves her," Lady Althea said.

"Yes," Charles replied. "Perhaps soon Burton will have a queen."

"She is kind and noble of spirit."

"Just as he promised at his coronation."

Chapter 8 - An Announcement

Marriah awoke slowly. She had been dreaming of Mother and Father. Gradually, she became aware that there were arms holding her. She opened her eyes and realized that the King of Burton had kept his promise. King Archelaus had stayed with her all night, holding her in his arms.

Slowly, she sat up, surprised to find she had been covered by a quilt. King Archelaus' eyes began to open. He smiled as he met her gaze. Tenderly he brushed the hair from her face as she wondered about what it would feel like if he kissed her lips.

"How do you feel?" he asked.

"Much better."

"I'm glad. I was worried about you."

"Someone will be looking for you," Marriah said, realizing that someone would have checked his room by now.

"No, Charles and Aunt Althea found us last night," he answered with a smile.

Marriah felt herself blush.

"It's nothing to be embarrassed about. I have told them of your suffering at Larkin's hand and both of them have spent some very rough nights with me."

"We had better get ready for breakfast," Marriah pointed out as she stood up.

"Do you have a riding habit?"

"Yes."

"Good, I'll see you in an hour," King Archelaus said as he stepped closer.

He lifted her chin gently and leaned closer. His lips met hers tenderly. He smiled at her and left the room. She stood for a few minutes with her heart pounding, surprised at his kiss. He saw her as worthy of his love. For the first time she saw him not as a king, but as a man, a man she could love as her husband.

She found her riding habit before going into the bathing chamber where the two servants were preparing her bath. She was still uncomfortable with having servants and someone helping her bathe. Just after she was dressed there was a knock at the door. Marriah opened the door to find Lady Althea standing there.

"Are you feeling better?" Lady Althea asked.

"Yes, thank you."

"I wanted to talk to you," Lady Althea said. "I wanted you to know that I appreciate what you have done for Archelaus."

Marriah was shocked. She hadn't done anything for King Archelaus.

"He has been happier with you at his side than I have seen him since before Gustave killed his parents," Lady Althea confided with a smile.

"Last night King Archelaus told me that he loves me," Marriah confessed quietely.

"I guessed that after seeing him holding you last night while you slept. I'm glad that he has found someone as wonderful as you are to fall in love with. You seem quite fond of him as well."

"Yes," Marriah admitted as Lady Althea hugged her.

"Other kingdoms have sent princesses to meet him, but none of them were quite what he was looking for."

Marriah had to sit down. Lady Althea sat next to her and put an arm across her shoulders.

"He never showed any of them his disguise. They were all disgusted by the fact he was a scullery boy at all. Two of them even drove the servants to tears with their spitefulness."

"That's terrible," Marriah agreed.

"Charles says that the servants enjoy serving you. That is part of why Archelaus is so happy," Lady Althea said. "Let's go to breakfast."

Marriah walked with Lady Althea down to the dining hall where the others were waiting for them. Regina Sonje handed a box to King Archelaus. He looked into the box before hugging Regina Sonje.

"Come and eat," King Archelaus said before kissing Marriah's hand.

When he sat down, he placed the box on the table on the other side of him. Marriah was curious. The box was wooden and flat like a book, but a little larger. No mention of it was made during the conversation at breakfast.

When they arrived at the stables, the two golden horses were saddled. King Archelaus slipped the box into the saddlebags of his mount before helping Marriah to mount the other. Soon they were making their way through the city streets. King Archelaus pointed out various shops and landmarks. They rode past very large houses and past tiny houses. He pointed out the repairs some of the houses needed to be fit to live in.

She was glad when they headed back towards the castle. She was beginning to get hungry. Marriah was surprised when they passed by the castle. They left the city and went through a field before stopping.

"We will eat here," King Archelaus announced before dismounting.

He placed his hands on her waist and lifted her from the saddle before taking the saddlebags from his horse. As he smiled at her, she smiled back. When he touched her, his hands were strong, yet gentle like Father's. He took her hand and led her up a small hill. Marriah gasped as she saw the view on the other side of the hill. She was looking over the edge of a tall, steep hill. There were some fields towards the city and then forest as far as she could see to the north.

"This is beautiful," Marriah sighed as she turned to look at King Archelaus.

"I thought you would like it," he smiled. "Are you hungry?"

"Yes."

She sat down as King Archelaus took some items out of the saddlebags and divided up the food. They ate in silence, enjoying the view. When they were finished, he gathered everything up and put it back into the saddlebags. He then moved closer to her and took her hand in his.

"What do you think of my kingdom?"

"It is very different from the village I grew up in and from Dracona," she replied. "But I like it a lot."

"It makes me happy to hear that."

"People have been so nice to me here."

"It is because you are kind to them," King Archelaus suggested and kissed her hand. "You will always be welcome here in Burton."

Marriah turned to face him. He was looking at her and smiling like he had that morning.

"I have something to ask you," King Archelaus admitted. "You can take as much time as you want before you answer."

Marriah remembered what Lady Althea had told her. King Archelaus was a kind and caring man. He knew what she had been through and didn't think any less of her. In fact, he respected her for it. Finally she nodded. She felt his hands begin to tremble as he took her other hand before taking a deep breath.

He met her gaze and said, "Marriah, will you marry me and become my queen?"

"Yes," she replied without hesitation as her heart began to pound.

Archelaus rose to his knees and pulled her up on her knees before him. He released her hands and she put her arms around his neck. He leaned closer until his lips met hers. She could feel the emotion in his kiss and was glad for his arms around her because she suddenly felt a bit dizzy. When their lips parted, she laid her head on his shoulder and heard his heart beating as quickly as hers was.

"I have something for you," he said.

Marriah sighed as he released her. He drew the wooden box from the saddlebags and handed it to her. Her hands were trembling as she opened the box. Inside was a gold ring with a purple stone and two diamonds. There was also a circlet of gold with a large purple stone on it. Archelaus took the ring and separated it into two rings. He placed the one with the purple stone on the third finger of her left hand. Then he took the circlet and placed it on her head.

"At my coronation, I promised the people of Burton that I would find a woman who was kind and noble of spirit, and pure of heart to be their queen," Archelaus said with a smile. "And that we would be their representatives and servants. You have proven that you meet all of those qualifications."

"From the moment I met you, I was impressed by your kindness and sincerity," Marriah admitted in a shaky voice. "You respected me and made me feel important. That is what made me fall in love with you."

"When Sonje told me of your ordeal, I was very saddened, but your beauty startled me. When I returned to Burton, Riva's prediction for you kept repeating in my head. That is why I invited you to the Spring Festival."

"She said I would find love with someone who had suffered as I had," she recalled.

"When I saw you defending that boy, you stole my heart. When you came looking for me yesterday, I was asking Bryant for his permission to marry you."

"Then Regina Sonje knows as well."

"She made the rings and circlet," Archelaus replied. "I know that you must have obligations to take care of in Dracona before making Burton your home."

"Yes, I need to make certain that Regina Sonje finds a new assistant."

"One of the women who has been serving you and one of the castle guards have volunteered to accompany you to Dracona. They recently got married."

"They volunteered?" she asked, not quite sure she had heard him right.

"Yes. Janina was so impressed with you that when she realized you would be leaving, she insisted that she and her husband be allowed to go with you," Archelaus affirmed. "I thought it was a great idea. It will make me feel better knowing Gavynn will be there to protect you."

Marriah nodded. She would have to get used to the idea of someone serving her in Dracona. Haskell would be certain to tease her about it.

"Would you like to see the cave now?" Archelaus' voice broke into her thoughts.

"Yes," Marriah replied. "Then I think I need some time to rest."

"That's a good idea," he agreed. "Tonight is a dance that will last until late. I wouldn't want you to be too tired to dance."

They put the saddle bags back on Archelaus' horse before mounting up. They rode along the edge of the hill until they reached the city. They rode through the streets to where the castle wall met the edge of the hill. There was a small group of trees and bushes growing nearby. Archelaus led her behind the trees revealing a path going down the face of the hill. At the end of the trail there was a wide ledge in the face of a rocky cliff. A few trees grew along the face of the cliff, but Marriah could see no cave entrance. Archelaus dismounted and tied their horses to a tree before lifting her from her horse. He drew a short torch from the saddlebags and lit it. Marriah followed him between two trees and into an opening behind the trees.

"Aunt Althea continued to live here until Bryant and Riva came to Burton. Without them, I would probably still be a scullery boy."

"Regis Bryant saved both our lives in many ways," Marriah commented as they reached a bend in the cave tunnel.

Just around the bend was a large chamber. Torches were still wedged in crevices along the walls. Archelaus lit the torches and wedged the small torch in a crevice near the entrance. There was a rough table and a couple of chairs left behind.

"It must have been awful to live here," Marriah commented. "It's cold in here."

"Like you, we had little choice," Archelaus said as he took off his jacket and put it around her shoulders. "Gustave would have killed us. If not for a member of the castle staff sneaking food to a dropoff point, we would have starved."

*****

The memory was still painful for him. Marriah reached out her hand and stroked his cheek.

"I'm glad that not everyone agreed with Gustave's plans," she said softly. "It has taken me quite a while to realize that most people are kind and honest. When I escaped from Larkin, I knew that if I stayed he would have eventually killed me. When I reached the castle courtyard and Regis Bryant came running out of the castle with a sword, I thought he would kill me until he put himself between me and Larkin."

Archelaus saw the tears beginning to form in her eyes. He put his arm around her and led her to a ledge in the side of the chamber to sit down.

"Bryant is the kind of king I hope to be," Archelaus admitted. "He treats everybody as though they were more important than him. Because of that, people trust him and are completely loyal to him."

"He is kind and patient with others," Marriah agreed. "He has taught me a lot about trust."

"We had better get back to the castle before too much longer," he said realizing he had best get the box now since he was already here. "But there is one thing I need to do before we leave."

Marriah nodded. Archelaus stepped up onto the ledge and walked along it as it rose along the wall. Across the chamber, he entered a small opening near the top of the cave. After a few moments, he found the box hidden behind some rocks under some firewood. He brought the box and placed it gently on the ledge beside Marriah. He put out all of the torches except the small one.

"Would you carry the torch?" he asked as Marriah stood up.

"Yes," she replied and took it from him.

He looked around one last time before following Marriah out of the chamber. When they reached the entrance, Marriah put out the torch. Archelaus set the box down and put on the jacket Marriah handed to him.

"I will lead my horse," he told her, seeing her curious look. "It is too valuable to risk dropping it from horseback."

Marriah nodded and untied the horses as he picked up the box. She handed him the reins of his mount. The climb seemed longer than he remembered. After they had walked along the castle wall for a while, two soldiers came out of a side street.

"There you are, My King," one said as they bowed. "Lady Althea was getting worried about you."

"Deliver this box to Charles," Archelaus ordered. "He will know what to do with it."

The men bowed and took the box. He helped Marriah to mount before mounting his horse. He urged his mount to a trot and they were soon at the castle door. Aunt Althea was there waiting for them.

"I was so worried," she greeted them as he lifted Marriah from her horse. "You should have taken a couple of guards with you."

"We needed some privacy," he replied as he hugged her.

"You've been there," Aunt Althea guessed. "I can smell it on you. Did you bring it with you?"

"It will be delivered to Charles," he acknowledged with a smile. "We will need it soon."

Aunt Althea hugged him again and then hugged Marriah.

"You two should get some rest and get ready for tonight then."

Marriah gave him a puzzled look as he took her hand. He gave her hand a quick squeeze before placing it on his arm. At the door of her room, he kissed her hand before leaving. In his room, two servants were drawing a bath for him. Soon he was clean and ready to lie down. There was a knock at the door.

"Come," he responded.

Charles entered and bowed.

"Marriah and I will have an announcement to make this evening," Archelaus said.

"I gathered that from the contents of that box the soldiers bought," Charles responded. "Have you set a date yet?"

"No, but she will need a month or two in Dracona to settle things there," he admitted. "I need rest before the dance."

"I'll come wake you in two hours," Charles replied as he bowed.

Archelaus lay down on the bed. It seemed to be only a few moments before Charles awakened him. He was glad for Charles' help choosing his clothes. He was feeling excited, but nervous. As he stood in front of the polished shield, he looked a lot calmer than he felt. The deep purple suit with gold trim reminded him of the crown that would complete the outfit.

"Very regal," Charles complimented after placing the crown on Archelaus' head. "The colors suit you."

Archelaus took one last look before going to the dining room. Aunt Althea was waiting there with Bethesda and General Edgard. They bowed as he approached. He listened to their conversation without joining in. When the door finally opened, it startled him. Bryant entered followed by Sonje who stepped aside to reveal Marriah behind her. Her beauty took his breath away. His heart quickened at the sight of her shoulders that were left bare by the pink and green gown. She smiled at him and curtsied. He crossed to her and bowed. He took her hand in his and kissed it before turning to face the others.

"We would like you to be the first to know that I have asked Marriah to marry me, and she has accepted," Archelaus announced.

Everyone congratulated them as the servants brought the food. The women talked about wedding plans.

"I will be in need of some advice," Archelaus told Bryant.

"Not to worry," Bryant assured him. "I will help you. I'm sure that Charles has some idea of how to get everything ready."

"Thank you. I know Marriah will need a couple of months to take care of things at Dracona."

"It will take a couple of months for the women to straighten out the details as well," Bryant laughed.

"I don't know if I can wait four months," Archelaus fretted.

"Two and a half months," Marriah proposed.

"I think I can handle waiting that long."

"Good, then the date is settled," Marriah answered with a smile.

"If everyone is done eating it is almost time to begin the dance," Charles announced as he approached the table.

Archelaus glanced at Bryant who nodded. He felt a touch on his right hand. He turned to meet Marriah's gaze. He stood and took her hand in his.

"Once it is announced, there is no turning back," he told her knowing she must be as nervous as he felt.

"I'm ready," she replied to his unspoken question.

Her trembling betrayed the nervousness hidden by her calm reply. Archelaus squeezed her hand before placing it on his arm. They went to the balcony over the plaza as the sun was beginning to set. Archelaus swallowed as he viewed the throng of people in the plaza. He felt Marriah's grip tighten as he raised his hand.

"Good people of Burton," he began as the crowd quieted. "The Spring Festival is to celebrate the end of a long winter and the beginning of a new and prosperous season. Today I have another reason to celebrate. At my coronation, I promised to find a woman who was kind and noble of spirit and pure of heart to become your queen. I have found that woman."

Archelaus paused to let the crowd quiet down again. The feel of Bryant's hand on his shoulder reassured him.

"That woman is Lady Marriah of Dracona. She has agreed to become my wife and your queen."

He felt Marriah jump as a cheer went up from the crowd. He took her hand in his and raised it high for the crowd to see. It was several minutes before the people quieted down again.

"Let the dance begin!" Archelaus commanded with a smile.

Music began to play as they left the balcony. Archelaus could feel Marriah trembling again. He put his arm around her and pulled her closer as they entered the throne room.

"Are you alright?" he asked softly as they waited for the others to enter the room.

Marriah nodded. Her face was pale as she turned towards him.

"Come sit for a moment," he suggested as he led her to a chair along the wall.

Bethesda came over with a concerned look on her face.

"I didn't expect such a response," Marriah admitted softly.

"News travels fast in Burton," Archelaus said. "I'm certain everyone has heard about the boy you helped. They have probably also heard of how kind you are to the servants."

"Out of darkness and into light. From unknown to renowned," Marriah quoted.

72

"I couldn't tell you outright," a voice said from the door.

"Riva," Archelaus exclaimed as he turned to see her standing in the doorway.

"You had to discover it for yourselves," Riva finished.

"We've been wondering where you have been," Sonje said as she hugged Riva.

"I couldn't miss the hatching," Riva replied. "And I have a prediction for you as well, but it can wait until later."

Archelaus turned back to find Marriah looking more relaxed. She smiled back at him and stood up. Soon they were all down in the castle garden. Lanterns lit the gardens with a soft light that reflected off of Marriah's dark brown hair.

*****

"You look so beautiful," Archelaus told her as they danced.

"I have never thought of myself as beautiful," Marriah admitted. "My mother was very beautiful."

"You are more beautiful every time I see you," he insisted and kissed her forehead. "I see the couple who will go to Dracona with you. Would you like to meet Gavynn and Janina?"

"Yes."

Archelaus led her to where he had seen the couple dancing. They stopped dancing as they saw Archelaus and Marriah approach them.

"This is Janina," Archelaus introduced as the woman curtsied. "And this is Gavynn."

"We are at your service, M'Lady," the man said as he bowed low.

"Thank you," Marriah replied and stepped forward. "I hope you will enjoy Dracona."

"I'm certain we will, M'Lady," Janina responded with a smile.

When she turned back to Archelaus he looked concerned. He took her hand and led her back to a quiet corner of the castle garden.

"You have a heart-shaped birthmark on your shoulder," he told her. "Two men came through Burton last year looking for a man with a heart-shaped birthmark on his shoulder."

"My father had such a birthmark on his right shoulder," Marriah acknowleged. "What did they want?"

"They wouldn't say," he replied. "I'm glad Gavynn will be going to Dracona with you, just in case."

"General Edgard has been teaching me to handle a sword and the art of self defense."

"That makes me feel a lot better," Archelaus said as he drew her close. "I wouldn't want anything to happen to you."

Gently he kissed her lips before releasing her. Slowly they returned to the others. She really enjoyed dancing with Archelaus. Marriah noticed that Janina and Gavynn stayed nearby the rest of the evening. It was very late when Archelaus escorted her to her room. She was asleep almost as soon as she lay down.

Chapter 9 - Hatching and Vision of the Future

'Wake up!' a voice demanded. 'You must come now!'

Marriah sat up, confused. She could see no one in the room.

'Haskell will come to get you,' the voice informed her. 'Be ready.'

Marriah quickly dressed and peeked into the hall. No one was in sight. She shut the door and checked the bathing chamber, but no one was there either. She jumped as she heard a soft tap at the door. She opened it to find Regina Sonje at the door.

"What is going on?" Marriah asked as Regina Sonje entered the room.

"Evelina is dying."

"The queen dragon?"

"Yes. The new queen will hatch soon. Evelina has sent Haskell to take you and me back to Dracona."

"Why me?"

"It is queen's business she said," Regina Sonje replied. "To a dragon, a wedding and coronation mean nothing. Archelaus has chosen you as queen of Burton, and so you are."

Marriah grabbed her cape and followed Regina Sonje out to the hall.

"I should tell Archelaus," Marriah insisted.

"Bryant is waking him. They will meet us at the stables."

When they reached the stables where the horses were being saddled the sun had not yet risen. The cook came running out in his bare feet with bread and cheese for them.

"Thank you," Marriah said as he handed her the food.

He bowed low before leaving. Regis Bryant and Archelaus came out as the cook reappeared with more food.

"Bryant explained it to me," Archelaus said as he took her hand. "I'll see to it that everything gets packed. I'll be there in three days. I hope I arrive in time to see the hatching."

"I'll be waiting for you," Marriah promised. "I'll miss you."

Archelaus kissed her before helping her to mount. Two soldiers mounted and rode with them to a field outside of town.

Marriah dismounted and reassured her horse as Haskell approached. The soldier looked a bit unnerved as he took the reins from her.

"He won't hurt you," Marriah assured him. "He is my friend."

She patted Haskell's cheek before helping Regina Sonje to mount. She could feel his sadness as she mounted behind Regina Sonje. She held on tight as he launched into the air. The ride was very cold. Marriah was stiff from the cold when they landed in the courtyard. She placed a hand on Haskell's cheek before entering the castle. Everyone bowed low as they passed. Lady Miranda was waiting for them at the doors to the caverns. Marriah was glad for the warmth as they approached the volcano.

'Come closer,' a voice said.

A soft glow lit a large dragon lying next to the volcano. Marriah knew the voice that had awakened her was Evelina's.

'My time is coming to an end. I have given all my knowledge to the new queen. Her name is Tasia. She will hatch tomorrow. The others will hatch a few days later.'

"We will care for these dragons as if they were our own children," Regina Sonje promised.

'A time will come for dragons and their people to leave this place,' Evelina said as Regina Sonje led Marriah closer. 'You will care for those who remain here. I see a great nation that you will lead.'

Marriah glanced at Regina Sonje who smiled.

'In the queen's chamber you will find a large smooth sphere of stone. Sonje will mount it for you. It is my gift to you.'

"Thank you," Marriah said and bowed.

Haskell entered the chamber and nuzzled Evelina tenderly. Marriah followed Regina Sonje out of the caverns, leaving Lady Miranda with the dragons. Hoyt was waiting for them in the great hall. He bowed low as they approached.

*****

"Welcome home," Hoyt greeted them. "Breakfast is ready."

"Good," Sonje said. "We have some announcements to make."

She knew that some of the people might be shocked by what she had to say, but Marriah's circlet had already gotten a few stares. The dining hall was noisy with conversation as they entered. Sonje stood for a moment at the head table with Marriah at her side. She raised her hands and soon the hall fell silent.

"You have probably heard that our queen dragon, Evelina, is dying. The new queen, Tasia, will hatch sometime tomorrow," Sonje said then waited for the people to quiet down again. "The rest of the dragons will hatch in a few days. Some of you will begin hearing a voice. That will be the voice of a dragon who has chosen you to care for it. Hoyt has been preparing information packets to help you know how to care for your dragons."

It was several minutes before the hall was quiet again.

"I have some other happy news," Sonje announced with a smile. "Marriah has an announcement to share with everyone."

"First, I want to thank all of you for being so kind to me since I arrived in Dracona," Marriah began. "While we were in Burton as guests of King Archelaus, he asked me to marry him."

Sonje glanced at Marriah who was smiling as the people began to whisper among themselves.

"I have accepted his proposal and will make Burton my home. I will miss all of you when I leave Dracona," Marriah beamed. "You have helped me more than I can ever thank you for."

There was much conversation as they ate breakfast. Many people came up and congratulated Marriah after they had eaten. Sonje felt tired and excused herself. The stairs felt longer than she remembered. She was glad to get to her apartment and lay down.

It was afternoon before she woke up. Marriah was sitting at the table drawing something. Miranda was watching her.

"We brought up some food for you," Miranda said as Sonje sat up. "Evelina is gone."

Sonje nodded. The news made her sad even though she had expected it. She went to the table and began to eat.

'Bryant!' she called out in her mind.

'Sonje, I was getting worried about you,' Bryant's reply had a relieved tone to it.

'Evelina is gone. Tasia will hatch tomorrow,' Sonje told him. 'The rest should hatch in a few days.'

'Good, we left Burton about two hours after you did,' Bryant said and then paused a moment. 'Archelaus is asking how Marriah is doing.'

"Archelaus wants to know how you are doing," Sonje said out loud.

Marriah held up a drawing of Haskell and Evelina.

"Alright, but a little sad," Marriah admitted. "I wish he was here."

'She wishes he was here,' Sonje told Bryant. 'She is a little sad.'

'Tell her we will be there as soon as we can,' Bryant replied. 'I expect to hear from you tomorrow.'

'Tomorrow then, My Love,' Sonje responded.

She patted Marriah's hand and stood up.

"They will be here as soon as they can," she told Marriah. "Let's go down to the queen's chamber and find your gift."

*****

Marriah stood and followed Regina Sonje and Lady Miranda out of the room. When they reached the caverns, Haskell was on the ledge in front of his den. Marriah ran up the stairs to him.

'How are you?' she asked as she stroked his cheek.

'I'll be alright,' Haskell's voice was sad. 'I see that you and Archelaus discovered the meaning of Riva's prediction.'

'Yes,' Marriah replied.

'It makes me feel better to know you are happy and your future is secure,' Haskell said. 'I know you will have a good life as Archelaus' wife and queen of Burton.'

Sonje patted Haskell's cheek before leading Marriah to the queen's chamber. Lady Miranda stayed with Haskell. Near the wall behind the smoothed out sleeping area, something reflected Regina Sonje's light on the wall and the floor. Marriah picked up the sphere of stone that was almost as large as her head. It was clear with bands of color in it.

"It's beautiful!" Marriah exclaimed.

"I'll gather some gold over the next few days and mount it for you," Regina Sonje promised as they walked back to Haskell's den. "Evelina had a very specific design in mind for it."

As they approached Haskell, they could hear crying. Lady Miranda was sobbing against Haskell's shoulder. Regina Sonje put her arms around her and stroked her hair. Marriah stroked Haskell's cheek.

*****

"When our people left Dracona, Evelina insisted I go with them," Miranda sobbed. "I feel I abandoned her."

"Merton needed your leadership," Sonje said gently. "She knew that."

"She was my responsibility."

"The survival of your people is your responsibility as well," Sonje replied. "Without them, there may not have been anyone to care for Evelina's offspring. And no one to help bring Glynis to Dracona."

They stood in silence for a while, when suddenly Sonje felt something strange.

"Oh!" Sonje said. "The baby just kicked me."

Miranda put a hand on Sonje's stomach. Sonje felt it again.

"How much longer do you have?" Miranda asked.

"About two months."

"Are you sure? You look farther along than that."

"Bethesda said I was very large, too," Sonje replied.

"I am looking forward to having a grandchild. I just wish that I could be closer," Miranda admitted.

"That will not last forever," Sonje said. "Bryant and I have some things you need to know before you return to Merton. You and Archelaus should be there too, Marriah."

Marriah came over to where Sonje and Lady Miranda stood.

"Haskell needs to rest," Marriah observed. "We should rest as well. Tomorrow will be a big day."

"Check with Agatha and have some food sent up," Sonje requested. "I don't think I will be down for supper."

Marriah nodded and left.

"She has changed a lot since Xylia's funeral," Miranda said as they left the caverns.

"She has been an enormous help to me," Sonje replied. "I will miss her when she goes."

Sonje was awakened early the next morning by Tasia's struggles to hatch. As she bathed and dressed, she encouraged Tasia to struggle harder. Agatha was busy in the kitchen when she got there.

"Tasia is hatching," Sonje told her. "I need to eat quickly."

Agatha handed her a bowl of porridge and a slice of bread.

"I'll get someone to bring in food for her," Agatha volunteered. "Have Haskell let me know when."

Sonje nodded. Soon she had finished eating. She hurried to the mechanism for the great doors to the caverns. A man opened the doors for her. She walked quickly across the warm sands to where Tasia's egg was wiggling and rocking. She could hear faint voices whispering around her.

'I want out!' Tasia's voice was defiant as her egg rocked violently and cracked more.

'Push harder!' Sonje instructed.

She could feel the tension in Tasia's muscles as the egg cracked more.

'A little more,' Sonje encouraged her.

She could feel Haskell's breath as he leaned down from the ledge for a better look. Four men brought bowls of meat and set them nearby before leaving.

'I have food for you,' Sonje told Tasia.

With a loud crack, the split in the shell widened and a clawed foot emerged followed by a golden nose.

'I want it!' Tasia demanded.

'Come out and get it,' Sonje replied. 'It is here for you.'

The egg split open, spilling out the dragon. She quickly gained her feet and began eating. She was a small replica of Evelina.

"She's beautiful," Marriah whispered as she set down two buckets and some rags.

"Yes, she is," Sonje agreed as Tasia moved to the next bowl of meat.

Once Tasia had finished eating, Sonje and Marriah began to wash her down. After she was clean and dry, they rubbed her down with oil. The black stripes on her face, legs and wings glistened against the gold. Suddenly she yawned, revealing her teeth like rows of daggers. Marriah stepped back in surprise.

*****

'Sorry,' Tasia's voice was soft in Marriah's mind. 'I didn't mean to startle you. I won't eat you.'

"You must be tired," Marriah replied.

"Come," Regina Sonje said gently. "I need to rest as well."

They led Tasia to the queen's chamber, her golden glow softly lighting the tunnels. Tasia yawned again before curling up and going to sleep.

When Regina Sonje and Marriah returned to the great cavern, some men were there taking the buckets and bowls away. Regina Sonje went up to her room for a nap. Marriah went to the library where Hoyt was waiting for her.

"You have changed," Hoyt observed with a bow.

Marriah felt herself blush.

"You are more relaxed and sure of yourself than when you left for Burton," Hoyt continued. "And you seem happier."

"In Burton, I found the one thing my life was missing," Marriah admitted with a smile. "I found love."

"We are all very happy for you," Hoyt said.

"I want to thank you for teaching me to read and write. You have taught me many things that will help me in my new duties as queen of Burton."

"You're welcome," Hoyt smiled. "It has been a pleasure."

Regina Sonje and Tasia slept most of the day. Lady Miranda spent the afternoon with Marriah. They talked of many things, but Lady Miranda seemed sad. Haskell made several trips to Merton for people who would care for a new dragon. Brenndah and Raphello were among them. Agatha had Marriah help her with room assignments that evening. They were able to put Janina and Gavynn in the room next to Marriah. She hoped they would like Dracona.

'Don't worry about that,' Haskell interrupted her thoughts. 'Tomorrow will be a big day. Get some sleep.'

Marriah was up early the next morning. She quickly bathed and dressed before going to the library. The maps of the caverns and castle had been copied and marked so she could direct everyone to where they would stay. She carefully rolled them up and tied them with a string. She picked up Agatha's lists with some extra paper, ink and a pen before heading down for breakfast. She looked around the dining hall as she ate. There were many new faces mixed with the familiar ones. Regina Sonje was talking to Lady Miranda and Auberon.

After breakfast, a table was set up near the center of the north wall of the great hall. Marriah unrolled the maps and set out the lists. Hoyt joined her and laid out a pile of envelopes.

"Could you watch these while I get the rest of them?" Hoyt asked.

"Of course," she replied.

She watched as people hurried through the great hall. She stood as Brenndah and Raphello approached the table.

"It's good to see you again," Marriah greeted them.

Brenndah reached out and touched Marriah's circlet.

"Archelaus gave it to me," Marriah said with a smile. "With this."

"Wow," Raphello said as Marriah held out her left hand. "Then the talk we've heard is true."

"I shall marry Archelaus in two and a half months," Marriah confirmed as Brenndah hugged her. "He's coming for the hatching."

Brenndah and Raphello suddenly froze.

"What's the matter?" Marriah asked.

"Rubetta is hatching," Raphello explained.

"Here," Marriah said, handing Brenndah an envelope. "Rubetta can have this den above Haskell's. Get in there and take care of Rubetta."

As Marriah added Rubetta's name to the map, Raphello and Brenndah hurried to the open doors of the caverns. Hoyt came with more envelopes and Marriah assigned more rooms and dens. Just before noon, there was a loud clatter in the courtyard. The doors burst open and Regis Bryant ran through, cape flying behind him.

*****

Bryant was breathing hard as he reached the egg that held the dragon struggling to hatch. It rocked and cracked as he touched its bumpy surface.

'Try again, Peregryn!' he thought to the dragon.

'I want out!' Peregryn answered.

The crack in the egg widened and the dragon spilled out onto the sand next to Bryant. Peregryn began eating from a nearby bowl of meat. He was almost the color of the clasp on Bryant's cape with black striping.

"He's beautiful," Sonje said as she handed Bryant a clean rag and took his cape.

"He wasn't going to wait for me," Bryant replied with a laugh. "I had to ride on ahead. The others should be here later today."

"There was some excitement this morning," Sonje revealed as he washed Peregryn. "Brenndah and Raphello's dragon, Rubetta, got hiccups and caught Raphello's sleeve on fire."

"Is he alright?" Bryant asked with concern.

"Yes," Sonje replied. "In healing his burns, Brenndah healed herself. The first word she spoke was Raphello's name."

Bryant laughed, "Somehow, I am not surprised. I'm glad she has finally realized she doesn't need to mourn any longer."

Peregryn was soon cleaned, oiled and fed. Bryant put his arm around Sonje as Peregryn settled in to sleep in his den next to Haskell's.

"Come have some lunch," Sonje insisted gently.

Bryant went with her to the dining hall. Marriah joined them. After lunch, Bryant and Sonje went to their apartment for a nap while Marriah went back to the table in the great hall.

"There are only ten eggs left," Hoyt told her as she sat down. "Forty two new dragons have hatched."

"It is so exciting to know that there will be more dragons in the caverns," Marriah replied. "Poor Haskell seemed so alone."

"Yes," Hoyt agreed. "You too seemed lonely. But you have changed since leaving for Burton."

Marriah smiled as she felt herself blush.

"I'm glad your future is secure," Hoyt continued. "You have become almost like a daughter to me."

Marriah looked at him in surprise.

"You have taught me so much," Marriah said. "You, Regis Bryant and Regina Sonje have become my family in a way."

Their conversation was interrupted by another family picking up an envelope and getting a den assignment. More people lined up before that family left for the caverns. In just over an hour there was only one envelope left.

"I wonder who," Marriah mused as the door opened and a tired looking young man stepped in.

He looked around in obvious confusion before approaching the table. He looked sweaty and dirty as though he had traveled far.

"Kaeden has called me here," the man announced. "I rode in from Merton."

Before Hoyt or Marriah could respond, the door opened and a woman entered.

"Riva!" Marriah said as she recognized her.

"You are Jonath," Riva said to the man. "Kaeden has told me you would be here."

"Kaeden's den will be here," Marriah told them as she pointed to the map. "Opposite Haskell's."

Hoyt handed the young man the envelope.

"Here are instructions for Kaeden's care," he explained.

Jonath nodded and followed Riva to the caverns. Marriah turned toward the outside door in time to see Archelaus enter. Janina and Gavynn entered behind him with two guards. Marriah met him halfway. Archelaus bowed low to her before taking both her hands in his and kissing them. Janina, Gavynn and the guards then bowed to her.

"I'm so glad you are here," Marriah told them. "Riva's dragon is the last one to hatch."

"May we watch?" Archelaus asked.

"Of course," she replied. "Come with me."

She led them through the doors at the rear of the great hall and across the sand to where Riva and Jonath were standing. The egg containing the dragon named Kaeden was rocking. A small crack in it began to run across it surface and then widened. Janina gasped as a claw pushed through the crack followed by another. The egg was still for a moment before it rocked again. A nose poked through above the claws before the shell finally opened up.

"Kaeden," Jonath said as he stepped forward. "Let us help you."

Riva pushed a bowl of meat in front of the dragon as Jonath helped him to stand. As Kaeden ate, they washed him down. He was bright violet except for the black striping. As they watched, Marriah felt a warm breeze from behind. She turned to find Haskell standing behind them.

'You haven't introduced me to your new friends yet,' Haskell told her in a jealous tone.

"Oh, Haskell," Marriah replied with a laugh. "I hadn't forgotten."

She heard his chuckle as Gavynn leapt between him and Marriah. The guards stepped in to protect Archelaus.

"Haskell," Marriah said as she placed her hand on Gavynn's shoulder. "This is Gavynn and his wife Janina, they are here from Burton to serve me until I return to marry Archelaus. Gavynn and Janina, this is my dear friend Haskell."

Gavynn's eyes were wide as he watched Marriah stroke Haskell's cheek.

'Welcome to Dracona,' Haskell told them.

Gavynn, Janina and the two guards looked puzzled.

"Dragons speak through thought," Marriah explained. "Haskell always knows what is going on around here before anyone else does."

They glanced at each other before bowing to Haskell.

"It is a pleasure to meet you," Gavynn said.

'You look tired,' Haskell replied. 'There are rooms prepared for you and your belongings have been taken up.'

"Thank you," Janina said.

"Go on," Archelaus told his guards. "I want to visit with Haskell for a while."

"But," one of the guards protested.

"No harm will come to him," Marriah assured them. "Not here, nor anywhere in Dracona."

"I will see you later," Archelaus said before kissing her lips tenderly.

"You will have the room next to Regis and Regina's apartment," she told him. "Your guards will be in the next room. My room is Regis Bryant's old room."

Marriah led them to their rooms before going to her own room. Her trunk had been delivered there. She unpacked the paints and drawing board. She would try the paints later. Next, she unpacked the journal with the pen and ink set.

She sat at the table to write. She began with her earliest memories. She felt the tears coming before they began to roll down her face. She did not realize how long she had been writing until there was a tap at her door. She glanced at the window to see the sun was approaching the tree tops.

"Come," she responded.

"Are you coming down for supper?" Archelaus asked as he stepped in. "What's the matter?"

"Nothing," Marriah replied as she wiped her eyes. "I've just been writing about my past."

"I understand," Archelaus said as he put his arms around her. "I've been talking to Haskell. He showed me what Larkin put you through. He felt I should know."

"I'm glad," Marriah sighed as she put her arms around his neck. "I've wanted to tell you about what I went through but didn't know where to begin."

"You have to be the bravest and strongest person I know. When I am ready to grieve for my parents I know you will be there to help me through it," he admitted before kissing her lips tenderly. "Are you ready for supper now?"

"Let me wash my face before we go," she replied.

They knocked at Gavynn and Janina's door to make sure they knew where to get supper.

"There must be some mistake, My Lady," Janina protested after curtsying. "These are not servant's quarters."

"There is no mistake," Marriah assured them. "There are no servant's quarters in Dracona. All of the chambers are pretty much the same except for Regis Bryant and Regina Sonje's."

"Dracona is very different from what you were used to in Burton," Archelaus explained. "You will see. Come with us to have supper."

As they ate, Marriah could see Gavynn and Janina looking around in wonderment. Regina Sonje looked happy, but tired. After supper, Regina Sonje asked Riva, Lady Miranda, Archelaus and Marriah meet in the sitting room.

"With Marriah getting married I was wondering if you would become my new assistant Riva," Regina Sonje said as they sat down.

"I have some predictions to give before I give you my answer," Riva replied. "I've been having visions pertaining to the people of Glynis along with some regarding Marriah and Archelaus."

Marriah was both curious and anxious.

"Sonje, you carry two babies that will link our distant past to our future. One to rule the skies, one to rule the oceans, and both to bind the land together. Both will be born with wings."

Regis Bryant and Regina Sonje both looked shocked. Lady Miranda covered her mouth with her hand.

"I've recently learned that our people come from a different world," Regis Bryant admitted. "We will need to return to our home world within the near future."

"Before we leave this world all of our people will have wings," Riva revealed. "Marriah, you will soon claim your birthright and learn the truth about your father's past. With Archelaus at your side, you will unite three kingdoms into one."

Marriah suddenly felt the blood drain from her face. Archelaus's hand trembled as he took her hand in his.

"That is all I have for now. Sonje, I knew you would ask me to be your assistant and I am prepared to accept," Riva admitted. "I have seen the dragons sleeping through the journey in clear eggs."

"We've all had a long day," Regis Bryant said. "Let's get some sleep. We'll need to find some nursemaids for the babies soon."

"Perhaps Aunt Ruth can suggest someone," Regina Sonje said as they left the sitting room.

Marriah felt numb as Archelaus led her to her room.

*****

As Bryant helped Sonje get ready for breakfast his mind kept returning to the fact that she was carrying two babies. Haskell chuckled at him.

"We'll work it out," Sonje told him as they walked down to breakfast. "I'm glad Riva will be my assistant. I don't know how much longer I can take those stairs. What will I do about Tasia's care?"

"Haskell and I will deal with that," Bryant promised. "I will have to care for Peregryn anyway."

"I can let you know when she needs something."

"Good. That will help a lot," he said as he saw Aunt Ruth sitting down with Hoyt.

"Aunt Ruth," Sonje said as they reached the table. "I found out that I'm carrying two babies. Can you help me find two nursemaids?"

"Of course," Aunt Ruth replied. "You will have your hands full with twins on top of being Regina."

"Thank you," Sonje said and kissed her on the cheek.

After breakfast they went to the office to take care of a few things. They were just finishing when there was a knock at the door.

"Come," Bryant responded.

"I hope we are not disturbing you," Aunt Ruth said as she entered with two young women.

"Not at all," Bryant replied.

"I've found someone to help you, Sonje," Aunt Ruth informed them. "Hannah and Lizette would be honored to be of service."

The young women curtsied.

"That is wonderful," Sonje responded. "Every day it is more difficult to do things and Marriah has things she needs to do now besides assisting me."

"You may want to start getting things set up for the arrival of the babies," Bryant suggested with a smile. "I must attend to some business in the village. I believe that Marriah and King Archelaus will be going as well."

"Thank you, Regis," Hannah said.

"Do you wish us to move into the castle?" Lizette asked.

Bryant looked at Sonje for a moment before replying.

"There are two small bedrooms in our apartment that you may stay in until other quarters are available."

"I think I want to go lie down for a bit anyway," Sonje admitted as she got to her feet. "We'll show them to you now."

Aunt Ruth excused herself as the rest of them went upstairs. When they reached the top of the fourth flight of stairs, they paused for Sonje to catch her breath. As they approached the end of the hall, Marriah opened the door to her chamber. She curtsied to Bryant and Sonje.

"We are almost ready to leave for the village, Regis," she said.

"Good," he replied. "I will be ready in about a half an hour. These are the new nursemaids, Hannah and Lizette."

"It's good to meet you," Marriah smiled then headed down the hall towards the stairs.

Bryant showed the women their rooms while Sonje lay down on the bed. They both knew that she would soon be unable to climb the stairs at all. Bryant sat on the bed next to her and took her hand.

"Don't overtire yourself while I'm gone. Hannah and Lizette can bring you anything you need. I know Riva will be a great assistant for you. The others will understand."

"I'll take it easy," Sonje promised as he kissed her hand.

When he opened his saddlebags he noticed the bundle of cloth tucked into the bottom corner of one.

"What is that?" Sonje asked.

"I got it in the village at Xylia's funeral," Bryant explained as he pulled loose the knotted string that bound it.

As the cloth unfolded he held it up and found it to be a long shirt with pants attatched. The cloth was soft and stretched easily.

"There are slits in the back for wings," Sonje whispered.

He turned it around there were indeed slits for wings. As he stared in shock his back itched right where the slits would be if he were wearing the shirt and pants.

"Riva said the twins would be born with wings," Bryant recalled softly. "I'm certain it won't be long before I grow out my own wings."

"Along with the rest of our people," Sonje added as he folded the clothes and set them on the table.

He packed his saddlebags with a change of clothes and his journal. He kissed her lips tenderly before taking his bedroll and saddlebags down to the stables. Marriah, Gavynn, and Janina were already there ready to leave. Archelaus and his two guards came out soon after Bryant. The wagon was soon loaded and they mounted up. They kept up a quick pace, stopping only briefly for lunch. They stopped at a clearing off the side of the road at dusk. There was little conversation as the tents were set up and supper cooked. A nearby howl startled them. The guards leapt up with swords drawn.

"Put away your swords," Bryant said calmly. "You will not need them."

Marriah put her hand on Gavynn's arm and nodded when his eyes met hers. The other guards looked to Archelaus, who also nodded. Their eyes widened as Bryant began to glow and walked in the direction of the howl. Bryant smiled as the black wolf stepped out of the trees, followed by the grey wolf.

"Will you keep watch tonight?" Bryant asked.

The black wolf nodded.

"Thank you, my friend," Bryant said.

The wolves followed him back to where the group stood. The grey wolf took her place beside Marriah. The black wolf sat next to Bryant.

"Get some sleep," Bryant said as he scratched behind the wolf's ears. "They will keep watch and protect us."

The guards seemed doubtful until Archelaus laughed as the grey wolf licked his hand.

"We will be safe," Archelaus assured them.

They bowed before heading to their tent.

"Sleep well," Archelaus said and kissed Marriah before following Bryant into their tent.

Chapter 10 - Return to the Village

Marriah awoke when the first light of dawn softly lit the camp. She was careful not to disturb Janina as she left the tent. The camp was still and silent as she approached the remains of last night's fire. The embers glowed a fierce red against the blackened wood and white ash. The grey wolf silently accompanied her as she gathered tinder and kindling to revive the fire. As she watched the the flames lick the wood, she sat thinking about the week's events. She had not expected Riva's prediction. She knew that her mother was from the village, but her father never spoke of his past. If her grandparents were still alive, she might be able to ask them, but they died a year before her mother had been killed. Her mother had no brothers or sisters. Considering he submitted himself to slavery to insure Larkin's silence in regards to his past she doubted Father had told her grandparents anything. What had the strangely dressed men wanted with her father?

A movement broke into her thoughts. Regis Bryant emerged from his tent. He quietly joined her at the fire. He seemed lost in thought as well. She studied him while they sat in silence. His appearance was youthful despite being over two hundred years old. His broad shoulders and chest showed the years he had worked alone to repair Dracona's town. He reminded her of her father in that respect, but his golden blonde hair, light skin and piercing blue eyes contrasted her father's dark brown eyes, skin and hair. Regis Bryant displayed the same commanding presence that her father had before her mother died. After that, he became a shadow of his former self. She still hated Larkin for that.

"Is something troubling you Regis?" Marriah asked softly and he met her gaze.

"I have wings," Regis Bryant admitted. "Soon more of our people will have wings and it will be time for us to leave. There is so much that must be done in preparation."

"I have faith that your people will trust and follow you and Regina Sonje," Marriah assured him.

"I'm just worried about how the villagers will take the news, yet I don't think it should be hidden from them."

"They trust you. If you tell them, they will believe you."

The rest of the camp began to stir. When Archelaus came out of his tent Regis Bryant walked with him to the wagon for the pot and water for porridge. Archelaus seemed slender in comparison, yet he carried the same proud bearing that set him apart from other men.

Soon they were finished with breakfast and loading the wagon. They were back on the road before the sun was fully up. When they reached the village well before noon, they were greeted with bows and puzzled looks. Marriah knew that the circlet she wore and the golden horses were in part the source of their curiosity. They dismounted near Cherie and Olvan's house. Cherie came out to meet them as a crowd of curious people began to gather.

"It's good to see you," she said as she gave Regis Bryant a quick hug. "How is Sonje?"

"Wishing it was time for the babies to come already," he laughed.

"Babies?" Cherie asked.

"Two babies," Marriah confirmed.

"It looks as though that is not the only news," Cherie surmised as she took Marriah's hand in hers to examine her ring more closely.

"There will be time later for the official announcements," Regis Bryant said. "We need to meet with the village council first. Could we meet here in your home?"

"Of course," Cherie replied. "Come in. There's some cider in the pitcher on the table. I'll go get the council members while you rest."

They tied the horses to the hitching post before going into the house. Gavynn and Janina sat on the bench in front of the house while the two guards waited with the wagon. Marriah was glad to sit down and drink the cider Cherie offered. Soon she returned with the village council. Cherie went to the back door to leave, but Regis Bryant stopped her.

"You should stay, Cherie," he insisted. "This concerns you too. I want you to hear it directly from me."

Marriah could see the puzzled look on her face as she shut the door and returned.

Marriah stood up and suggested, "You should sit down."

Cherie glanced at Regis Bryant, who nodded. The men were beginning to look puzzled as well.

"What is this news you have?" Wyman asked.

91

"You all know that Cherie and I along with all of the people from Glynis and Merton are longer lived than the people from this village," Regis Bryant began. "And that we have some unusual abilities."

"Barbara told me about Regina Sonje making the circlet you wear into a chain with a touch of her finger," Barnarr said.

"And we have seen you produce light without fire," Sebastian added.

"We recently learned why we are different," Regis Bryant replied. "Cherie, do you know where the people of Glynis came from before they found Glynis?"

"No one remembers," Cherie admitted. "Only that the clothing they wore was not really warm enough to survive long in the snows."

"You're right," Regis Bryant acknowledged. "When I met Riva and Xylia, I got some clues to our past. Sonje discovered that the mysterious island off the coast of Merton is some sort of strange ship named 'Temple of Origin' that brought our people here."

"Is that where your people came from?" Kyle asked. "They couldn't have always lived in a ship."

"At Xylia's funeral, I was given some strange clothes and a box with a dragon on its lid," Regis Bryant continued, seeming to ignore the question. "These had belonged to Riva's father. The clothes are similar to some passed to Sonje from her mother."

Marriah could see Cherie begin to tremble. She placed her hand on Cherie's shoulder and gave it a gentle squeeze.

"The box is a communicator that allows us to talk to the guardians of the Temple of Origin," he continued. "From them, Sonje and I learned that the true origin of our people is a place named Trinan far from here with tall cliffs over the ocean."

Regis Bryant paused to let them grasp what he had just told them. Marriah could see and understand their apprehension. It had taken her a while to accept it herself. She wondered how they would take the rest of the news.

"This means you will be leaving us, doesn't it?" Kyle asked.

"Not immediately, but soon," Regis Bryant answered. "There is a good reason for that. The reason we were sent here is complicated, but there was a sickness in our homeland. We were sent here while our homeland was cleansed of the cause of the sickness."

"Did the sickness come with you?" Wyman asked.

"No," Regis Bryant said as he shook his head. "But Trinan is ready to be reborn."

"Why must you leave?" Barnarr asked. "Can't you just stay?"

"We learned from the guardians that soon we will have to leave because the differences between our peoples will be even more visible," he said gently. "Once our people had wings like dragons. The strange clothing has slits in the back for the wings."

"The wings are coming back," Sebastian reasoned.

"Yes. Regina Sonje is carrying two babies that will probably have wings. Other babies have wings as well."

"I can understand why you must return to Trinan," Wyman said. "But what will happen to us?"

"As you know, King Archelaus of Burton is a very different ruler than Gustave was and we now have an alliance with Burton," Regis Bryant said. "I have asked Archelaus to look after this village and Dracona. Everything else will remain the same. This council will continue to govern the village, but Burton will offer protection and guidance when needed."

"Perhaps our announcement should be made now," Marriah offered, seeing the concern in the men's faces.

Regis Bryant nodded his approval as the men looked at her as if seeing her for the first time.

"Marriah?" Barnarr asked in a puzzled tone. "I didn't recognize you."

"A lot has happened since Larkin's execution," Marriah acknowledged with a smile. "At Dracona, I learned to read and write. I also learned that I was more than I thought I was. I now know that I am important to others, that I am worthy of friendship and love."

Marriah moved to stand next to Archelaus. He took her hand in his and kissed it.

"At my coronation, I promised the people of Burton a queen that was kind and noble," Archelaus spoke for the first time since entering the village. "I have chosen Marriah to be my wife and queen of Burton."

Marriah was pleased with the men's surprised expressions.

"Archelaus suffered at the hand of Gustave as I suffered at Larkin's hand," Marriah told them. "He has seen the suffering of the people under Gustave's rule. You can ask the woman and men outside about Archelaus' treatment of the people."

"I have no interest in conquering new territories," Archelaus assured them. "I will protect this village, but I will not force my rule over you. I am happy to help you in any way you want."

"What about taxes?" Kyle asked.

Archelaus shook his head, "I see no reason to tax this village at this point. I have repealed the taxes Gustave imposed on Burton. I am creating a system where each family pays a small percentage of their yearly income."

"We would like a chance to discuss this amongst ourselves," Wyman stated.

"Of course," Archelaus responded with a bow. "There are some things that I wished to see while I am here, if Marriah will be my guide."

"I had some places in mind," Marriah replied.

"Send your people in," Sebastian requested. "We would like to ask them some questions."

Archelaus opened the door for Marriah. Cherie followed her. Archelaus signaled to the guards.

"You are wanted inside," Marriah told Gavynn and Janina. "They need to ask you some questions."

"At least one of us should stay with you, M'Lady," one of the guards protested.

"No," Marriah insisted as Regis Bryant came out of the house. "I grew up here. We will be fine."

They bowed and entered the house. Regis Bryant and Cherie sat on the bench. Marriah took the arm Archelaus offered and led him down the street. She knew where she wanted to start. They got some strange looks from the people they passed.

"I don't think anyone recognizes me," Marriah speculated as they entered the forest. "I guess I have changed."

"Yes, you have," Archelaus agreed with a smile.

They came to a small clearing. Marriah stopped and pointed to the rough stone jutting out of the ground.

"This is where it all started," she said quietly.

She was grateful for the arm he put around her. He kissed her forehead. She led him out of the clearing and through the forest to the house where she grew up. Her hand shook as she opened the door.

"My parents slept in there," she said pointing to the open door. "And I slept up there."

"This was your stairs?" Archelaus asked as he grasped a rung of the ladder near the wall.

She watched as he climbed up to take a look. Soon he came back down.

"There's not enough room to stand up there," he commented. "You were right about how small this house is."

"You can see why I decided to stay in Dracona and give this to the village," Marriah said. "When Larkin was executed, I was given all of his property as well, but I didn't want any of it. Besides, the village didn't have a school for the children."

Archelaus nodded as he wiped a tear from her cheek.

"There is one last place I want to show you," she said after taking a moment to regain her composure.

As they left, she took one last look at the house and noticed her mother's roses were beginning to grow again. She led him down the narrow dirt road leading back to the village. They passed the large house with many children playing in front of it.

"Larkin's house?" Archelaus asked.

She nodded without taking her eyes off the road. They walked through the village to the cemetary behind the church. When she found the graves she was looking for, she was surprised to find the wooden marker for her mother's grave was replaced with a new stone marker. Next to it was a similar marker bearing her father's name. She knelt before the markers.

"Carita, beloved mother, wife of Langward," she read with a trembling voice. "Langward, beloved father, husband of Carita. Let us remember his suffering that others remain free and unafraid."

Marriah could no longer hold back her tears. She sat with her face in her hands and cried. She felt Archelaus' arm around her and was comforted by it. It took several minutes for the tears to slow. Her heart ached as she lifted her head. Archelaus handed her a handkerchief which she took gratefully. She looked at Archelaus to find that there were tears on his face as well. She wiped his tears and he kissed her forehead.

"This is the first time I have visited her grave since just after she was buried," Marriah confessed quietly.

Archelaus nodded then turned to look behind her. She listened and heard voices approaching.

"There is a man named Langward buried over here," a woman's voice said. "He did have a daughter."

"Where might we find her?" a man's voice asked.

"She went to Dracona," the woman replied.

Marriah stood up. Something in the man's way of speaking reminded her of the way that her father had spoken. Archelaus stood by her side waiting for the people to come. Marriah recognized Barbara who had always given Marriah something to eat when she brought Larkin's horse to the blacksmith. The men's skin and hair were darker than her own, as dark as her father's had been. They wore long shirts that were not tucked into their pants. The shirts had no sleeves and had bright colored designs along the edges.

"They were the ones looking for a man with a heart-shaped birthmark," Archelaus whispered.

Marriah nodded as the group neared.

"Hello, Barbara," Marriah said, glad that her voice was steady.

She studied Marriah's face for a moment before speaking again.

"Marriah!" she exclaimed. "You look wonderful. I didn't recognize you at first. Erta has something she thinks you should have."

"We'll go there next," Marriah said. "This is Archelaus from Burton. Archelaus, this is Barbara, wife of the blacksmith, Barnarr."

"Pleased to meet you," Archelaus said as he bowed slightly.

"It's good to meet you," Barbara responded as she curtsied. "What brings you to our humble village?"

"Marriah wanted me to see where she grew up before I married her," he replied.

"Who carved the markers for my parents' graves?" Marriah asked as she gestured to the stones. "I would like to thank them personally."

"You are the daughter of Langward?" one of the men asked.

"Yes," Marriah answered.

"Did he have a birthmark shaped as a heart on his shoulder?" the other asked.

"I have one in the same place he did," Marriah confirmed.

The men drew their swords and knelt at her feet with heads bowed and swords on upturned palms. Marriah had not expected this response at all. She looked to Archelaus for an explanation. As their eyes met, he looked surprised as well. Suddenly it became clear.

"Riva," she said quietly.

Archelaus nodded.

"Rise," Marriah commanded. "Why have you come looking for my father?"

"We are sent by Queen Aurita to find him," one of them replied.

"Perhaps we should go somewhere that we can sit down," Marriah suggested. "I have a feeling this could be a long story."

"You could go pick up those things from Erta. I'm sure she would let you use her house," Barbara offered. "I'll walk with you. I needed to talk to her anyway."

Marriah nodded. Barbara led the way to the modest house. Erta was in the yard hanging clothes on a line to dry. She gave Barbara a puzzled look.

"You remember Marriah," Barbara said. "And this is Archelaus."

"Pleased to meet you," Erta said with a brief curtsy.

"These gentlemen are from a kingdom west of these mountains," Barbara explained. "They were looking for Marriah's father."

"Come in and sit down," Erta welcomed them. "I have something for you, Marriah. It was under a false bottom in the chest in your house."

They followed her into the house. Erta took a cloth bundle and a book from the shelf over the fireplace and handed them to Marriah. Marriah drew in a quick breath as she realized that the book and cloth both bore the same designs as the shirts worn by the men. Archelaus pulled a chair out from the table for her to sit on. She laid the book on the table and began to untie the string on the cloth bundle. The cloth turned out to be a shirt, just as she suspected, but what was inside was completely unexpected.

"What is that?" Archelaus asked as she held it up.

"The royal armband," one of the men said reverently.

Marriah turned it in her hands to find that on each end of the silver band was the outline of a shield with a sword and arrow crossed on its face. The two ends would be one above the other when worn on the arm. From its size, she knew her father would have worn it on his upper arm. She placed it on the table and turned her attention to the book. Inside she found drawings and strange lettering. As she turned the pages, she felt Archelaus' reassuring hand on her shoulder. There were many drawings of her mother and

97

of her as a child. She closed the book knowing that she should view the rest later.

"Barbara, Erta, I need to speak to these gentlemen in private for a few minutes," she said.

"I'll be outside hanging the laundry," Erta replied.

"I'll help you with that," Barbara offered and followed Erta out, closing the door behind them.

"Tell me who you are and why you were searching for my father," Marriah demanded as she met their eyes.

"This is Fyodor and I am Garman," the taller of the two said. "We have traveled far from Brinley to many kingdoms in search of Prince Langward."

Archelaus sat down next to Marriah and took her hand in his.

"Years ago," Fyodor began, "King Brook died and his son, Prince Burkhart, became king to rule the kingdom of Brinley. The day he took the throne, King Burkhart had a fight with his brother, Prince Langward. It was a petty matter, but King Burkhart ordered his brother out of the castle. Prince Langward left with only the clothes he wore and that book, vowing to never return to Brinley."

Marriah at last knew where her father was from, but why would vow to never return?

"The next morning, King Burkhart called for his brother, but Prince Langward was nowhere to be found," Fyodor continued. "Within a few days, their mother, Queen Aurita, locked herself in her room for a week and would eat nothing but bread and water. King Burkhart waited for word of his brother, but none came. Eventually he realized that Prince Langward kept his vow."

Archelaus took her hand in his and gave it a gentle squeeze.

"Time passed and Queen Aurita kept Prince Langward's room locked and untouched. Last winter was harsh and many fell ill. King Burkhart died. Queen Aurita sent us to find Prince Langward and beg his return. She is very old and is concerned since there is no heir to the throne," Fyodor concluded.

"We beg you return with us that Brinley be yours to rule," Garman pled.

Marriah sat in silence for a moment before speaking.

"So I am now heir to the throne of Brinley," Marriah stated and the men nodded. "Riva's prediction makes more sense now."

The men looked confused and concerned.

Archelaus smiled and said, "I have asked Marriah to become my wife and queen of Burton."

"We went through Burton over a year ago and King Gustave was in power," Garman said.

"I'd been in hiding, working in the kitchens until I could take my father's throne back from Gustave," Archelaus replied. "He was an evil man with a violent temper. Most of the palace staff members bear scars from his beatings. I have scars from when he whipped me."

"How did Prince Langward die?" Fyodor asked.

"A man named Larkin enslaved Father and I," Marriah answered. "He finally attacked Larkin and was beaten to death so I could escape. I barely survived."

"Where is this man who did wrong to you, Princess?" Fyodor asked as he and Garman stood drawing their swords. "We will deal with him in swift order."

"Regis Bryant defended me as I escaped Larkin and then executed him when he was condemned to death," she responded. "Regis Bryant also defended Archelaus against the evil King Gustave, killing him."

"We must meet this man and thank him," Fyodor insisted as they sheathed their swords. "Where can we find him?"

"We will take you to him," Marriah offered.

She picked up the book, armband and shirt. Garman opened the door

"Thank you, Erta, for saving these for me," Marriah said as the women turned to look at them.

"You're welcome," Erta replied.

Chapter 11 – An Unexpected Legacy

Marriah and Archelaus led the men back to Cherie's house. Olvan was in front of the house, but Regis Bryant and Cherie were gone.

"Olvan, do you know if Regis Bryant is inside?" Marriah asked.

"No, he went out to the barn with Cherie," Olvan replied with a puzzled look on his face.

"You don't recognize me, do you?" Marriah surmised. "I am Marriah."

"You look so different than," Olvan started then hesitated, "than."

"Than at Larkin's execution," she finished for him.

"Yes," Olvan confirmed. "What is the circlet?"

Marriah smiled and said, "Perhaps I should introduce you to the man I will marry, King Archelaus of Burton."

Archelaus gave a shallow bow.

"Now I remember you from Bryant and Sonje's wedding," Olvan responded. "Who are these gentlemen?"

"Fyodor and Garman of Brinley," she replied.

"We wish to find Regis Bryant to thank him for protecting our Princess Marriah," Fyodor said.

Olvan looked at Marriah with a stunned expression.

"My father came from Brinley," Marriah explained. "I just found out."

Olvan replied. "I'll take you to the barn. He and Cherie should still be in there."

"Thank you," Garman said.

They followed Olvan to the barn. The door was shut.

"Bryant," Olvan yelled. "Marriah needs to speak to you."

Regis Bryant opened the door for them to come in.

"This is Bryant Donley, Lord of Dracona, Regis of Glynis, Merton and Dracona," Marriah announced, using his full title.

Fyodor and Garman fell to their knees as they had before Marriah. Regis Bryant gave her a puzzled look.

"Rise," he commanded the men.

The men got to their feet.

"Brinley is forever grateful to you for protecting our Princess Marriah," Fyodor said.

"Riva was right," Marriah answered Regis Bryant's questioning look. "They want me to return to Brinley with them to meet my grandmother, Queen Aurita."

"Do they know about the changes?" Regis Bryant asked.

"Not yet," Marriah replied.

Olvan looked puzzled. Regis Bryant laughed as the village council joined them. The two guards, Gavynn, and Janina were with them.

"Cherie wanted to see," he explained. "Sonje is happy for you, Marriah. She says I should show all of you."

"We have made a decision Regis," Wyman interjected.

"Show us what?" Olvan asked as Bryant began to take off his shirt.

Regis Bryant handed his shirt to Archelaus and turned his back to the group. Marriah could see the frightened looks on Fyodor and Garman's faces as Regis Bryant's wings grew from his back. They looked very much like Haskell's wings.

"Do not be afraid," Marriah told them. "He will not hurt you. The people of Glynis and Dracona are different from us, but they are our friends. Where we may live a hundred years, they may live a thousand years."

"Bryant is over two hundred and seventy years old," Archelaus explained. "He and his people can make a colored glow around them and can do amazing things with their minds."

Bryant began to glow, followed by Cherie.

"Watch this," Regis Bryant said and pointed to a stack of wood in the corner of the barn.

A stick floated off the stack and into his waiting hand. In his hands, the stick shaped itself to match the armband Marriah held. His glow faded and he leaned against a nearby stall.

"There is a price to be paid for such talents," Cherie revealed as she took the wooden band from him.

Garman nodded as she handed him the band. He and Fyodor examined it closely before Garman knelt and offered it to Marriah. She saw the mischievous smile on Regis Bryant's face as he saw her discomfort at the gesture. The villagers looked confused.

"Haskell says that in time you will get used to it," he chuckled as she took the armband. "Put it on."

"I'm certain he derives great enjoyment from all of this," she replied as Archelaus took the armband and placed it on her right arm.

"Of course," Bryant confirmed. "He says that if you don't return in ten days, he will come get you."

"Who is this Haskell?" Garman asked.

"Where is this man?" Fyodor added.

"Haskell is not a man," Marriah said. "He is a dragon and my friend."

Their faces went pale.

"We will personally escort you to Brinley and back to Dracona within ten days," Fyodor stammered. "How is it that we do not hear his words?"

"Dragons speak through thought," Regis Bryant explained.

"How is it you speak to the woman, Sonje, and she is not here?" Garman asked. "Is she a dragon also?"

Regis Bryant held up the pendant that hung against his bare chest and said, "My wife wears the other half. It allows us to speak through thought as well."

"Tell my sister we will return with you to Dracona to see the new dragons," Cherie said.

"She'll have Agatha arrange quarters for you," he replied after a moment.

"May I touch the wings, Regis?" Kyle asked.

"Of course," Regis Bryant replied and spread his wings wider.

"Regina Sonje has wings as well?" Sebastian asked as he stroked a wing with his fingertips.

"Yes," Regis Bryant confirmed. "And so will the twins that she carries. Other babies will soon be born having wings as well. You can now understand why we wanted to let you know about this as soon as we did. We did not want anyone to panic over it. We are going to have enough trouble getting our own people to accept that they too will have wings and that soon we must leave for Trinan."

"Yes," Wyman said. "You were wise to not just announce it before speaking to us."

Regis Bryant turned to face them again and the wings began to shrink. When they were gone, Archelaus handed him his shirt.

"There have been some new developments since this morning," Regis Bryant said. "Marriah can explain those. You said you had come to a decision."

"Yes," Wyman answered. "The people will be asked to accept or reject our decision, but we feel they will trust our judgement in this."

Wyman then knelt on one knee before Marriah and Archelaus. He was soon joined by the other members of the council.

"We will accept your leadership, King Archelaus and your queen," Wyman vowed. "We will recommend that the people of this village accept your rule as well."

"Rise," Archelaus told them. "We promise to never give you cause to regret your decision."

"What are the developments that Regis Bryant spoke of?" Barnarr asked, meeting Marriah's gaze.

"These are Fyodor and Garman of Brinley," she said. "They came in search of Prince Langward."

"Prince?" Wyman asked in surprise.

"Yes," she replied. "Brinley's king has died. My father was his brother. Apparently I am now heir to the throne of Brinley."

There was silence for a moment before Cherie said, "It is past lunch time. We should take a break to eat."

"Yes," Marriah agreed, suddenly realizing how hungry she was.

Olvan opened the door and they left the barn. As they walked towards Cherie and Olvan's house, Marriah saw Barbara coming towards the house as well.

"There you are," she said as she got near enough. "We have a meal ready for all of you."

"Thank you," Regis Bryant replied.

"Come this way," she said. "We set it up at Erta and Wyman's home."

Soon they were eating. Fyodor and Garman were deep in conversation, speaking rapidly in a strange language. Marriah noticed that Regis Bryant seemed a little distracted. He leaned across the corner of the table and whispered something to Archelaus who then nodded.

Janina touched her arm and said, "Gavynn and I are going with you to Brinley."

"Thank you," Marriah replied. "It will help a lot to have you with me."

Almost as soon as they were finished eating, there was a knock at the door. Erta opened the door and a young man stepped in and bowed.

"The villagers are assembled and waiting, Regis," he said.

"Thank you," Regis Bryant replied. "I guess it's time to tell them."

They all followed the young man to the small platform at the edge of the village. It was the same one where Larkin's execution took place. Regis Bryant and the village council stepped up on the platform. After a moment the crowd fell silent.

"As most of you have probably heard I have been meeting with the village council this morning," Regis Bryant began. "At the meeting, we discussed the future of this village. Over the last few weeks, Regina Sonje and I have learned some very important things about the people of Glynis that will affect you as well."

Marriah felt Archelaus' grip on her waist tighten as Regis Bryant waited for the crowd to quiet down.

"Before now, no one knew where the people of Glynis came from before they found Glynis. As you all know, there are certain differences between the people of Glynis and everyone else. In discovering our forgotten past, we have discovered another difference that will soon become more and more obvious."

Again, the crowd whispered amongst themselves, forcing Regis Bryant to pause.

"We now know that the people of Glynis originally came from a place called Trinan. It is a place of tall cliffs rising out of an ocean. The dragons also came from Trinan. At that time, the people of Glynis had wings like the dragons to glide between the cliffs. Soon, our people will have wings again and we must return to Trinan."

The crowd stood in shocked silence.

After a few minutes a man asked, "Will you have wings?"

"Actually, I do have wings," Regis Bryant replied. "Just not all the time."

"Show us," another man demanded then was echoed by others in the crowd.

"I'll show you," he responded as he began to take off his shirt. "Just remember that I am still the same person that I have always been. I will keep my obligation to provide protection and guidance for this village regardless of anything else."

Marriah held her breath as Regis Bryant turned his back to the crowd and his wings began to form. There was a collective gasp from the crowd followed by some whispering. She let out her breath slowly as he turned to face the villagers again.

"I wanted all of you to know about this from me instead of having rumors and half truths begin to spread," Regis Bryant said. "We will be waiting at least four months before we can think about leaving for Trinan. Partially because that is after Regina Sonje is due to deliver our twin babies."

Marriah smiled as the news about the babies caused more of a stir in the crowd than the wings had. It was several minutes before the crowd of villagers quieted down again. While waiting, Regis Bryant was talking to the village council.

"In order to insure the safety and prosperity of this village, I have spoken to a good friend of mine and he has agreed to take on my obligations to this village," he said as Archelaus kissed Marriah's cheek and moved to the stairs of the platform. "As you have heard, Gustave is no longer king of Burton. His death enabled the rightful heir to claim the throne."

Archelaus stepped up on the platform at Regis Bryant's gesture.

"I would like to present King Archelaus of Burton," Regis Bryant announced as Archelaus bowed low to the villagers. "We have agreed that nothing should change except that you turn to Burton for aid instead of Dracona. In a few moments we will let you make the final decision, but first I think there are a few things that Archelaus would like you to know."

The crowd was restless, but quiet as Archelaus began to speak.

"First of all, I want to sincerely apologize for Gustave's attack on this village. I have recalled all of Burton's soldiers and have no desire to conquer anyone."

Marriah could see the villagers begin to settle down again.

"Secondly, the people of Burton suffered greatly under Gustave's rule. For years I disguised myself as a mute scullery boy for fear that Gustave would kill me as he had my parents. Since becoming king, I have repealed Gustave's cruel taxes and laws."

The crowd began to whisper among themselves again.

"I understand your hesitation to believe based on my words alone," Archelaus said and silence fell. "I will show you how I suffered along with the people of Burton. What price I paid to stay in the castle so I could one day take the throne from Gustave."

Regis Bryant nodded as Archelaus removed his vest and shirt. He turned his back to let the villagers see his scars. There was a lot of talking among the crowd before they quieted down again and Archelaus turned to face them.

"Archelaus has one more thing that he wants to tell you," Regis Bryant said.

Marriah handed her father's things to Janina as Archelaus began to speak.

"At my coronation, I promised the people of Burton that I would find a queen for them," Archelaus said as he moved towards the platform's stairs. "I have found a very noble woman and she has agreed to be my wife and queen."

As Marriah went to the platform's stairs, Archelaus knelt on one knee and extended his hand. She put her hand in his and climbed the stairs to join the others on the platform. He kissed her hand before placing it on his arm.

"Marriah visited Burton during the Spring Festival and stole my heart," Archelaus confessed. "We are to be wed in two and a half months."

Marriah felt herself blush as the villagers applauded.

When the villagers began to quiet down, Regis Bryant said, "I believe that Marriah has something to tell you as well."

"Most of you knew my father, Langward, but never knew much about where he came from," she said. "That was a subject he never talked about, even to me. Today I showed Archelaus some places here that hold meaning for me. While we were at the cemetery, Barbara was helping two visitors find what they were looking for. Fyodor and Garman were sent by Queen Aurita of Brinley to find her long lost son since her other son, King Burkhart, had fallen ill and died. The man they were searching for had also died. That man was Prince Langward of Brinley, my father."

Marriah paused as the crowd began to whisper to each other. She waited until it got quiet again before continuing.

"I will travel with them to Brinley to meet my grandmother, Queen Aurita," she said. "I know that this must all come as quite a surprise to you. The decision is now yours. If you accept Regis Bryant's proposal, Archelaus and I promise that you will not regret it. If you reject his proposal, we will honor your wishes, but will be happy to help if you ask us."

Archelaus placed his hand over hers while they waited for the villagers' decision. She knew how much they had feared Burton after Gustave's attack. This would take a lot of faith for them to agree, yet she knew it was their choice to make. She met Regis Bryant's gaze.

"I'm very proud of you," he said in the language of Glynis. "So are Sonje and Haskell."

"I'm pleased with how well they took the news," she replied in the same language.

Archelaus gave them a questioning look. Marriah leaned closer and repeated it quietly to him so he could understand.

"So am I," he replied.

After a while, the crowd finally quieted down. Wyman stepped forward to address them.

"Have you come to a decision?" he asked.

A man stepped forward as the rest of the villagers stepped back to allow him through.

"We have made two decisions actually," the man responded. "Since this village has never really had a name, we have decided to name this village Langward after Princess Marriah's father."

Marriah's heart caught in her throat at hearing the honor bestowed upon her father and that they had accepted her new found title.

"The second decision was made having faith in Regis Bryant," the man continued. "We have decided to place the same faith in King Archelaus. After all that Princess Marriah has been through, if she has agreed to marry him, then we can accept his rule over us."

"Long live King Archelaus and Princess Marriah!" the villagers shouted.

Marriah was relieved as they heard the sound of Haskell's wings flapping. Marriah saw him land at the end of the street, just outside the village. The villagers parted as Haskell walked toward them. He stopped in front of the stand and bowed. She could see that he was carrying two large bags.

"Is that?" Fyodor asked with a tremor in his voice and his eyes wide.

Garman backed up a step.

"It is my dear friend, Haskell," Marriah acknowledged. "It was he who woke Regis Bryant after hearing my silent cries for help."

Fyodor nodded before he and Garman knelt before Haskell with their swords on upturned palms, heads bowed.

'You're welcome,' Haskell's voice came softly to Marriah's mind.

The two men looked up, startled by the response.

'You had better keep Marriah safe on your journey,' Haskell said with a stern tone.

Marriah laughed silently to herself.

"We will guard her with our very lives," the men replied.

Marriah could hear Haskell laughing.

"We thought you might need some things for your trip," Regis Bryant explained.

Archelaus helped Regis Bryant get the bags off Haskell's shoulders while Marriah stroked Haskell's cheek. The dragon turned his face toward her.

'I will miss you,' he told her. 'Safe journey.'

'Thank you,' she thought back to him as she rubbed his nose. 'I will miss you too.'

'Tasia says that Evelina knew it all along,' Haskell told her. 'Everyone is very excited and happy for you.'

Marriah returned to Archelaus' side as Haskell carefully turned and walked out into the fields before taking off. They turned around to face the villagers.

"We want to thank you for giving us the opportunity to serve as your rulers," Archelaus said. "I'll begin sending a messenger to you on a weekly basis so that you can send any requests or messages that you may have."

"I want to thank you for naming this village after my father," Marriah said. "It means a lot to me. My father would be very honored."

As the crowd began to disburse, the village council came over and bowed. Kyle handed Regis Bryant and Archelaus their shirts.

Suddenly, a boy and girl came at a full run shouting, "Uncle Bryant! Uncle Bryant!"

"Mayetta, Alleyn, have you been to school?" he asked with a big smile as he knelt down on one knee.

"Yes," Mayetta replied as she threw her arms around his neck and kissed his cheek.

"Where did you get the wings?" Alleyn asked as he reached out to touch one. "Can I have wings too?"

Regis Bryant laughed and said, "You might just get your own wings some day. If you do, they will grow right out of your back just like mine did."

"Does Aunt Sonje have wings too?" Mayetta asked as she cautiously ran her hand along the edge of his wing.

"Yes, but only when we want to have wings," Regis Bryant replied. "Did you know that in about two months you will have two new baby cousins?"

"I hope one's a boy!" Alleyn shouted, jumping up and down.

"I don't know," he said. "I guess we'll just have to wait and see."

"Are you going to stay with us tonight, Uncle Bryant?" Mayetta asked.

"If your Mom and Dad don't mind, I suppose I could."

"Let's go ask," Alleyn insisted as he pulled at his uncle's arm.

Marriah heard Archelaus laugh as the three went to find Cherie and Olvan.

"He certainly loves those children," he commented. "And they love him."

"Yes," she replied as she saw a familiar looking young woman and an older couple approach.

The women curtsied and the man bowed before Marriah. As she rose, Marriah could see that the young woman held something in her hand.

"I don't know if you remember me," the young woman began, not quite meeting Marriah's eyes. "It's been so long ago."

"You do somehow look familiar," Marriah said.

The woman held out her hand and opened it to reveal a little doll. Marriah took it with trembling hands. The young woman collapsed to her knees before Marriah. The doll had been her own . . . before . . . before Larkin.

"Katina?" Marriah remembered as she knelt down.

She stroked Katina's check and felt the tears that were streaming down her face.

"You left her at my house," Katina explained with a trembling voice. "I tried to return her a few days later, but he . . . he."

"Larkin," Marriah provided the name.

"He drove me off saying you were angry," she continued. "That you hated me."

"I wondered why you wouldn't look at me when I saw you after that," Marriah said gently. "But Larkin never allowed much contact with anyone."

"Can you forgive me?" Katina pled as she finally met Marriah's gaze.

"Oh, Katina," she said as she drew her into her arms. "There is nothing to forgive."

"I should have told someone," she replied. "I hid and watched. I saw what he did to you and your father."

"What is important is that it is out in the open now," Marriah told her gently. "Now every person will know that if they report such a thing, the incident will be investigated and dealt with."

Marriah patted Katina's back and held her until her sobbing subsided.

"There's something I want you to see," Marriah said gently as she pulled Katina to her feet. "Janina, bring that book over here."

As Janina came over, Archelaus said, "We know that you are not responsible for what happened. There must have been adults that saw what was going on and did nothing."

Marriah opened the book that Janina handed her. She soon found the drawing she was looking for. She held it for Katina to see.

"This is how I remember you," Marriah told her. "I remember sitting in the sun, talking while you braided my hair."

"I loved to braid your hair," Katina admitted softly. "I have talked it over with my parents, and I want to go with you, to Brinley, to Dracona, even to Burton and serve you."

Her mother and father nodded at Marriah's questioning look. When she glanced at Archelaus, he just shrugged his shoulders.

"I would be happy to let you serve me," Marriah said. "We will leave first thing in the morning."

"Where are you sleeping tonight?" Katina's mother asked. "We would be honored to have you stay with us tonight."

Regis Bryant came up and said, "You can stay with me at Olvan and Cherie's, Archelaus."

"That sounds good, but what about the others?" Archelaus replied.

"Garman and I will sleep at the front door of where Princess Marriah sleeps," Fyodor stated.

"Gavynn and I will sleep in a tent behind the house," Janina said.

"We will sleep outside Cherie and Olvan's house to keep you and Regis Bryant safe, My King," one of the guards volunteered.

"Then that's settled," Marriah said. "Let's see what Haskell brought."

Regis Bryant knelt and opened one of the sacks. He drew out a sword in a scabbard which he gave to Marriah.

"Sonje discovered that Jonath can also shape metal and stone, so she had him place some jewels in the hilt to make it more befitting a princess," he told her. "Edgard sharpened it and hardened it. It has a permanent edge that will never dull and will cut through anything."

"It's beautiful," Marriah commented as she buckled the belt around her waist.

Next he drew out a cloth that Marriah unfolded to discover was a purple dress that only had a sleeve on the left side and would leave her right shoulder completely bare. The one sleeve was open, flowing and trimmed with gold.

"Evelina gave the design to Sonje before she died and told her you would need it when you learned the truth of your father's past. Sonje gave the design to Darryl and Aurora. This goes with it," he explained as he held up another piece of folded purple cloth.

Katina unfolded it revealing a large triangle with gold trim and two long ties attached to the longest side of the triangle. Regis Bryant stood up and took the dress from Marriah and handed it to Janina. Then he took the other piece from Katina and folded it in half so the ties were even.

"Sonje said this goes over your right shoulder then the ties cross on the left side, over the ends and tie on the right side."

"So that piece could be removed to expose the heart shaped birthmark," Fyodor pointed out.

"Exactly," Regis Bryant affirmed with a smile.

While Janina and Katina folded the dress back up, he drew her drawing board and a long narrow box from the other bag. He handed the box to her. Inside she discovered several long pieces of charcoal, a pen and a small bottle of ink.

"And finally," he said as he reached in the bag again. "We thought you might want this."

He held out her white journal. She hugged him tight and kissed his cheek.

"Oh, thank you," she said. "This is all so thoughtful. I really appreciate this."

"Sonje says that the first thing you must do when you return to Dracona is come straight to our apartment and tell her everything," he said.

"And the second thing is to write it all down and send it to me," Archelaus added. "There will be a messenger waiting to take it to Burton."

"I promise," Marriah laughed. "I suppose that Haskell and Hoyt will want a full report as well."

"Yes, they do," Regis Bryant aknowledged after a moment.

Suddenly Marriah realized that the writing in her father's book was something she had seen before.

"The writing," she said and everyone looked puzzled. "Give me my father's book again."

Katina handed her the book. She opened up the book and looked again at the writing. It had wavy lines and dots intermixed with short straight lines. Suddenly it occurred to her where she had seen it.

"Can either of you read this?" Marriah asked and held the book open for Fyodor and Garman to see.

They both nodded. She shut the book.

"We must go to Larkin's house," Marriah announced.

"We can take care of these things," Janina volunteered.

"Thank you," Marriah responded. "Come with me."

She led them to Larkin's house with Regis Bryant, Fyodor, Garman, and the two guards following Marriah and Archelaus.

The woman who was sweeping the front step curtsied and asked, "Can I be of service, Regis?"

"We need to see something inside," Marriah said.

The woman glanced at Regis Bryant who nodded. Once inside, Marriah led them to the fireplace.

"Larkin took this off the front of our house," Marriah explained, pointing to the wooden plaque hanging there. "He liked it so much that later he forced my father to carve it all around the room."

The men had shocked expressions as they saw the lettering along the tops of the walls.

"The plaque says, 'Langward, Carita and Marriah.' The rest appears to be a letter to Queen Aurita," Fyodor revealed.

"My grandmother," Marriah said. "Will you read it for me?"

"We should write it down," Regis Bryant suggested.

"Yes, Princess," Fyodor agreed. "Garman can write it down."

"Regis, can you write it down while Garman writes it in their language?" she asked.

"Of course," he replied.

"You can use these," the woman offered and set out some paper and ink with two pens.

The woman left closing the door behind her. The two men sat down and Fyodor began to read.

"Dear Mother, I know you may never read this, but it must be said before I die. I write this that you may understand why I left Brinley behind. I always understood that one day, Burkhart would be king, but I too had the desire to learn the skills of leadership, defense and negotiation. I needed to have the respect of others. I know that you loved me, but next to Burkhart, I felt invisible."

"When Father died, Burkhart became king. I was not jealous. I always knew that I would not be king, but when he ordered me to my knees to honor him as if I were a stranger, I could take no more. You knew not of the times he would use his training to pin me to the ground and humiliate me. I fought back, but he outmatched me in strength and skills. Still, I blame only myself for not being more assertive. I should have demanded the training.

When I left Brinley, I made a new happy life for myself. I worked hard to provide a home for my beautiful wife, Carita. She worked by my side without complaint and provided a beautiful daughter, Marriah. She reminds me so much of you. She has been so very strong and brave in this adversity.

A man, a monster, has killed my beloved wife and enslaved Marriah and me. We have worked for years now under his cruel hand. The bruises I now bear are far worse than those I hid from you. My fears are now for Marriah. She has grown into a woman and I know the look in his eye when he is near her. I will defend her honor from this monster. Even to my death."

Archelaus put his arms around her and stroked her hair as she buried her face against his shoulder. She trembled as she sobbed out loud. She felt Archelaus' arms tighten around her. Other hands stroked her hair and patted her back until her sobbing finally subsided.

"Will you be alright, Princess?" Garman asked softly.

Marriah nodded, not trusting her voice.

"That is all there is," Fyodor said.

"He walked in from the barn when Larkin decided I should be his wife," Marriah sobbed. "He told me to run as he attacked Larkin. I never looked back."

"He must have known when he engraved this," Garman concluded. "King Burkhart never said why Prince Langward left. He never married."

"There was always as sad tone to his voice when he spoke the name," Fyodor added.

"I need some time alone," Marriah said.

"I'll get your drawing board and case for you, Marriah," Regis Bryant offered. "Where will you be?"

"The clearing," Marriah replied with a nod. "Ask Haskell."

"We will guard a perimeter so no one disturbs you," one of the guards said.

"I will stay near in case you need me," Archelaus promised as they stepped outside.

The words her father had written ran through her mind as she led them to the clearing. He had known that Larkin would kill him. She felt numb all over as they reached the clearing where Larkin had killed her mother. Regis Bryant arrived not long after they had. After handing the board and case to her, he stroked her cheek tenderly. He did not speak, but his eyes told her how much they all cared for her.

They left her in the clearing. Although she could no longer see them, she could hear them. As she sat down against a large rock, the grey wolf stepped silently out of the forest. It lay down next to her as she flipped through the drawings to a blank page. She began drawing as she thought about the past and how her life had changed since she had escaped from Larkin. She drew her mother and father before drawing her father as he was just before his death. She then drew the two individuals who had rescued her, Regis Bryant and Haskell. At last her heart had quit aching. As she looked up, she realized night was approaching. She stood up, muscles stiff from sitting so long, and walked back the way she had entered the clearing. Archelaus and Fyodor were talking quietly as she and the wolf approached them. They turned around suddenly as they heard her footsteps.

"Princess!" Fyodor gasped as he drew his sword.

"No," she said as she stepped between him and the wolf. "This wolf is my friend. Put your sword away."

He did then knelt before her with his sword on his upturned palms. The wolf gave her a questioning look as Garman and the two guards joined them at a run. Garman dropped to his knees as Fyodor had and the two guards bowed low.

"Rise," she told them. "This wolf and the rest of its pack may travel to Brinley with us. They are not to be harmed. They will keep watch over us at night."

"Yes, Princess," Garman and Fyodor answered.

"Now I must eat and rest," she said.

As she led them back to Katina's home she felt exhausted. She was grateful for the arm Archelaus put around her as they walked. When they arrived there was a most delicious smell as the door opened. She sat down at the table. A bowl of stew was set before her.

*****

Archelaus watched Marriah closely as they ate. Her eyes began to close after she had only eaten half of her stew. He knew she was asleep in her chair. He gently lifted her into his arms. Katina led him into a room where there was a single narrow bed. Katina pulled back the quilt and he laid her gently on the bed. He kissed her forehead tenderly. He left the room as Katina covered her up.

Archelaus finished eating his stew before thanking Katina's mother and leaving. He and his guards followed Bryant to Cherie and Olvan's home. He was very tired as he got into bed and fell asleep immediately.

Chapter 12 – Becoming Royalty

Archelaus found himself standing in a large room draped in white. The drapes parted across from him and Marriah entered flanked by a man and a woman. The man's hair and skin were darker than Marriah's. The woman had light skin like the villagers and brown hair. He could hear no sound as they crossed the room. Marriah had her hand on the man's arm. The woman held a strip of cloth with a light blue stone at each end in both hands, palms up, before her. When they reached Archelaus, the man kissed Marriah's cheek and placed her hand in his. The woman wrapped the cloth around their hands, binding Marriah's hand to his. The woman then placed her hand on the man's arm where Marriah's had been. Archelaus turned to face Marriah and kissed her lips tenderly. When he looked back at the man and woman, they smiled before vanishing.

Archelaus sat up and found he was still in bed. It had all seemed so real. His heart was pounding in his chest. He quickly dressed in the predawn light and went downstairs. The guards jumped to attention as he opened the door.

"My King?" one asked as he hurried past them without stopping.

They followed him to Katina's house. Garman and Fyodor were getting to their feet as he approached. He tapped quietly on the door. Marriah opened the door. Her face seemed pale as she sat down at the table. The men followed Archelaus into the house. On her drawing board was a picture of him standing with his parents in front of white drapes.

"I dreamed I was standing in a room," Archelaus said. "The drapes parted and you walked in with a man and a woman. The man kissed your cheek then put your hand in mine. The woman bound our hands with a cloth. I kissed you, they smiled and vanished."

"I had the same dream just a few minutes ago," Marriah confirmed.

"What you just described is . . . is," Garman began.

"Is a . . . a wedding ceremony in . . . in," Fyodor added.

"In Brinley?" Archelaus finished for him.

Both men nodded. He turned back to Marriah. She had turned the pages on the drawing board to one of the man and woman from his dream.

"That is who I saw in my dream," Archelaus said.

"Prince Langward," Garman said reverently.

"My parents," Marriah confirmed what Archelaus had already guessed.

He took Marriah's hand in his. He pulled her gently to her feet. Her eyes met his as he tenderly stroked her cheek. She sighed as he leaned toward her. He kissed her lips tenderly. His heart began to race as he felt her hands draw him even closer. He kissed her again, this time with more of the passion he felt for her in his heart. When their lips parted, she laid her head on his shoulder as she leaned against him.

"Even if it was a dream, I feel that your parents have given their blessings on our marriage. Still it's going to be a long two and a half months," he whispered as he stroked her hair.

"Seventy days," she responded.

"This brings up another good point," Archelaus said as he reluctantly released her from his arms. "Since we will be uniting three kingdoms, perhaps we should combine parts of their wedding ceremonies to reflect that."

"I like that idea," she said. "I still need to introduce our plans to the people of Brinley."

Archelaus nodded.

"We have a long journey ahead of us," Fyodor said. "We should leave within an hour."

"I should be leaving soon as well," Archelaus admitted reluctantly. "Safe journey, My Love."

"Take care as well," Marriah told him. "We are a part of each other now."

*****

Archelaus kissed her once more before leaving. She stood watching him leave. The guards bowed to her before following him. Katina came into the room. She looked confused.

"We need to leave within the hour," Marriah told her. "Wake the others. We need to get packed and have breakfast."

Marriah gathered her things and packed her saddlebags. The things that would not fit, she put into one of the large bags that Haskell had brought. Katina set a pot of porridge over the fire and her mother came in to set the table. Her father helped to saddle the horses. Soon they had eaten breakfast.

"The rest of your things can be sent to Dracona," Marriah told Katina as the horses were loaded and they mounted up.

Many people were out in the streets as they rode out of the village. Garman and Fyodor led the way. Katina and Janina rode on either side of Marriah. Gavynn followed behind. By nightfall they had stopped only briefly for lunch. As the men pitched the tent, Janina and Katina prepared a cold supper. Marriah fell gratefully into her bedroll after eating.

The next day, they crossed the summit of the mountains and had begun their decent down to the valley. It was beautiful country. Marriah was glad when they stopped for night. It was not quite dusk as they found a large clearing to camp in. Katina lit a fire as the men pitched the tent.

"Look," Gavynn said suddenly.

Marriah turned to see the grey wolf step into the clearing followed by another wolf. They each dropped a rabbit at her feet.

"Thank you," she said and the wolves disappeared back into the forest.

The cooking rabbits smelled delicious. Marriah was happy when they were ready to eat. As they ate, she listened to Garman and Fyodor talking to each other in the language of Brinley. She realized that both she and Archelaus would need to learn to speak the language as well as read and write it. Once they finished eating, she went to her saddlebags and got out her journal, the pen case and her father's armband. She sat down by the fire and wrote about what had happened in the village as daylight began to fade. Soon it was too dark to see to write, so she just sat holding the armband.

"You look concerned about something, Princess," Fyodor said as he knelt down next to her. "Is there anything I can do to help?"

"Just thinking that King Archelaus and I should learn your language," Marriah replied. "And I will need someone to translate for me while in Brinley."

"It is a wise idea to learn Brinley's language," he agreed. "Garman's wife also speaks your language. She can help Garman and me translate for you in Brinley."

"Thank you," she said with a smile. "That makes me feel a lot better. I was also wondering how your Queen Aurita will take her son's death."

"And your appearance in his place."

"Yes," Marriah admitted. "And how the people of Brinley will feel about joining with Burton and Dracona."

"If your grandmother accepts your claim to Brinley's throne as genuine and rightful, the people will accept her decision as law," Fyodor said. "After her official decree, they will follow you and King Archelaus without question."

"I guess that our biggest challenge will be convincing my grandmother," Marriah said with a sigh.

"Get some sleep," Fyodor told her. "It won't take long to reach the city from here."

Marriah nodded and took her things with her into the tent. Janina and Katina were already asleep on either side of her bedroll. When Marriah awoke, she was alone in the tent. Outside she heard the quiet sounds of breakfast being made. As she rolled onto her side, her hand fell upon her father's armband. Her father had left a lot behind when he left Brinley, but at least she understood why.

She sat up suddenly at the sound of strange voices outside. Although she did not understand the words, she understood the tone of voice, their presence here was being challenged. As she stood up, with the armband still in hand, Fyodor answered in the language of Brinley.

"Is there a problem?" she asked as she stepped out of the tent.

As Garman knelt Fyodor said something including the word messi to the three men and gestured to her before kneeling. The men's eyes widened at the sight of her and they too fell to their knees. One of them muttered something she did understand, the name Aurita.

"Rise," she commanded.

Fyodor repeated her order to the men who also stood back up and sheathed their swords.

"Who are these men?" Marriah asked.

"Brinley's territory is patrolled by soldiers against attack, Princess," Fyodor answered. "They are one of the patrols."

"We should send one of them ahead to announce our arrival," she suggested.

"Excellent idea," Fyodor replied.

"Perhaps if we have him just say that I bear news of Queen Aurita's son," Marriah began.

"You are wise," he said. "She should learn the rest directly from you."

"Let them eat before sending the messenger. They look hungry."

Janina added another pot of porridge to heat while Fyodor explained things to the men. They soon produced bowls and spoons from their saddlebags. Katina dished up a bowl for Marriah before serving the men. Marriah watched them as she ate. They seemed very curious about her.

"What did Fyodor tell them?" she asked Garman as he sat down near her.

"That they were in the camp of visiting royalty," Garman answered with a smile on his face. "When you came out of the tent, he told them you were a princess."

"Perfect," Marriah replied.

Once finished eating, one of the men knelt before her.

"This man will bear your message to Queen Aurita," Fyodor explained. "He has asked where he should tell Queen Aurita that you are from."

"Have him tell her that I will explain everything to her, also that I request an opportunity to clean up before presenting myself to her."

Fyodor nodded before translating for the man. The man got up and went to his horse. Marriah watched as he galloped away.

"Let's break camp," she ordered as she stood up.

Soon everything was packed. Gavynn helped Marriah to mount before getting on his own horse. The two men led them to a road and turned south.

As they rode, Marriah's mind wandered over the events in the village, but her thoughts kept returning to Archelaus' kiss. It stirred something deep within her that she could not ignore. It was going to be a long wait for their wedding day; especially with a three day journey between Dracona and Burton.

'Haskell says that Archelaus can not keep his mind off you,' a voice said, faint but clear.

'Tasia!' Marriah thought back in surprise. 'Did he arrive in Burton safely?'

'Yes,' Tasia confirmed after a brief pause. 'He is telling Charles and Aunt Althea about everything. Charles is protesting the combined wedding ceremony. Charles told him that it would be easier on him if you were married for real instead of just in a dream.'

'Archelaus should tell Charles that we wouldn't want to deprive him of the honor of coordinating such an important event,' Marriah thought back, trying not to laugh out loud.

'He just did,' Tasia said in a very pleased tone. 'Charles rolled his eyes, bowed and told Archelaus he was right.'

'I bet Haskell is enjoying this,' Marriah replied.

'Haskell is laughing so hard he had to lie down before he fell down,' Tasia said with just a hint of a giggle.

'How is Regina Sonje?' Marriah asked. 'I miss her.'

'She is doing well,' Tasia responded after a moment. 'She wants you to know how proud she is of you, and that she misses you too.'

As they came around a bend in the road, a city came into view. At the center was a large castle surrounded by a wide area of green, then a tall stone wall.

"Oh," Marriah said aloud in surprise.

"This is Brinley," Fyodor told her.

'You are Queen Marriah,' Tasia reminded her. 'Carry yourself tall and proud.'

The man sent as a messenger returned before they were halfway to the castle wall. He spoke to Fyodor who nodded. Fyodor dropped back to Marriah's side.

"It is as you requested, Princess," he told her. "It is two and a half hours until lunch is served. You are assigned to a suite to stay in. There you can recover from the journey before dining with the ministers and district governors. You have audience with Queen Aurita directly after lunch."

"Thank you," she said.

The people stopped what they were doing and watched as they rode by. Marriah did not turn her head to look at anything as they continued on their way. At the portcullis the guards stopped them. Fyodor spoke to the guards, who opened the gates before kneeling as they passed by. She could hear the people talking excitedly before the gates were closed behind them. The wide area of green was some sort of short grass. She knew from General Edgard that this was actually a very good defense, leaving an enemy nowhere to hide. There was a wide body of water that encircled the castle making it appear to be in the middle of a lake. A bridge was lowered for them to cross. Once in the courtyard, they dismounted.

Their saddlebags and belongings were removed before the horses were led away.

A young woman appeared with six men. They knelt with their faces down and palms up before saying anything. The woman spoke after standing back up. Garman took her hands and kissed them both.

"This is my wife," Garman informed them. "Her name is Aurella."

"I am so happy to meet you," Marriah said. "This is Katina, Janina and Gavynn."

"Please follow me," Aurella responded.

The men picked up their things and followed behind. They went down hallways and up stairs before Aurella opened a set of double doors. There were chairs, a settee, and several tables in the room as well as open doors along the walls.

"Servants' quarters, bed chamber, bathing chamber, balcony," Aurella said pointing out each door in turn.

Fyodor and Garman picked up their belongings and excused themselves. Janina and Katina took Marriah's things into the bedchamber while Gavynn took their belongings and went into the servants' quarters. Aurella led Marriah into the bathing chamber. It was enormous. There was a large pool of water in the center of the room. It was fed by a waterfall along one edge of the pool. There were drying sheets waiting nearby.

"Queen Aurita asked me to attend to you personally," Aurella said.

"How long has Garman been away from Brinley?" Marriah asked.

"Four months," she replied without meeting Marriah's eyes.

"You can best serve both me and your queen by being with your husband right now," Marriah told her as she lifted Aurella's chin to meet her gaze. "There is much for him to explain to you before my audience with Queen Aurita. Also she may need you late into the night."

"As you wish," she said with a smile. "Thank you."

Aurella left quickly. Marriah smiled as she shut the door and undressed. She sank gratefully into the water. Janina and Katina entered through the door to the bedchamber. She didn't argue as they washed her. Once they had dried her, they dressed her in the purple and gold dress. She sat patiently as they put her hair up.

"What has you smiling so much?" Marriah asked Katina as she placed the circlet on Marriah's head.

She blushed, "I wonder if Fyodor is married. He is so handsome."

"Go get cleaned up while you have a chance," Marriah said with a laugh.

They went to the servant's quarters as she went to the bedchamber. She took out her drawing board and a piece of charcoal. It didn't take her long to draw Fyodor. She carefully tore the page from the board and placed it on the bed before taking out her father's shirt, book and armband. She would need them for her audience with her grandmother.

As she turned to leave the bedchamber, a framed drawing of a man and a familiar looking woman caught her eye. She opened her father's book and soon found the page she was looking for. The woman in the drawing was younger than in her father's book, but it was the same woman.

"My grandmother," Marriah whispered.

Then she knew the man was her grandfather. It was definitely her father's work. She went into the sitting room without putting down the book. Across from the double doors was a large framed drawing of a man. This too she recognized. There was a tap on the door.

"Enter," she said without turning around.

"It is true!" Aurella's voice betrayed her shock.

Marriah turned to find Aurella, Garman and Fyodor on the floor before her.

"Rise," she commanded them. "Yes, it's true. I didn't believe it at first, but I now know it to be true. This portrait is of King Burkhart drawn by my father."

"Yes," Garman aknowledged. "My father hung it on Queen Aurita's order."

Just then, Katina entered followed by Janina and Gavynn.

"Please sit down," Marriah said. "I have thought about how to best break the news to Queen Aurita ever since leaving the village. I think it best that I start by showing her the shirt and armband. Next I will show her this book of his drawings. Then the hard part."

"The letter," Fyodor stated, drawing the folded piece of paper from his pouch.

"Yes," Marriah agreed with a sigh. "The letter. After that I will show her the drawings on my board and explain the changes facing Dracona and Burton."

"Will you tell her about your shared dream?" Garman asked.

"I must," she replied. "She needs to know all of it. Does she speak my language or only that of Brinley?"

"Queen Aurita does speak your language, but not fluently," Aurella replied. "Garman told me you plan to learn our language."

"Yes," she said. "Archelaus and I will both need to learn the language, but it will make it much easier to get through today knowing that not everything needs translating."

There was a knock at the door and Fyodor went to answer it at Marriah's nod. He soon returned.

"It is time to assemble for lunch," he announced.

"Katina, help me with the other sleeve," Marriah requested.

Katina followed her into the bedchamber. She gasped as she went to the bed to retrieve the sleeve.

"I thought you might like that," Marriah said.

"Oh, yes! Thank you," Katina gushed as she unfolded the sleeve.

Soon Marriah was following Aurella to the dining hall.

"You will be eating with the ministers and district governors," she informed Marriah. "Queen Aurita dines alone in the Royal Suite. I will remain to translate for you."

In the dining hall, the table was set, but they were the first to arrive.

"Queen Aurita wishes for you to be seated facing the entrance at the head of the table," Aurella told her. "The rest have their assigned seats. The four ministers will be seated nearest you and the eight district governors finish the table."

"That leaves one seat open," Marriah observed.

"It has been left open waiting for Prince Langward's return," she explained as she stopped before reaching the head of the table. "You will stand here for the introductions I will stand behind you at all times to translate."

"Thank you," Marriah said just as the doors opened again.

Aurella stepped behind her as the first man entered. He spoke before kneeling as Marriah now knew to be customary in Brinley. Aurella repeated his name and title to Marriah. He rose to face her.

124

"Princess Marriah," she said bowing only her head slightly. Aurella said, "Messi Marriah."

The man looked puzzled, but had no chance to ask anything before the next man entered.

"That is perfect," Aurella whispered before the second man stopped to kneel.

Marriah was glad when the last man had been introduced and was standing by his chair. She went to her chair and sat down. As the men sat down, servers entered and began to dish up the meal.

Eldwin, the Minister of the Interior spoke and Aurella translated, "Rumor has it that you have Prince Langward's royal armband. Is that true?"

"Yes," Marriah answered.

"Is he returning to Brinley?" one of the district governors asked.

"No," she replied.

The men all appeared very annoyed. She heard Aurella stifle a giggle.

"Perhaps a woman as beautiful as you could have persuaded our King Burkhart to marry and produce an heir to the throne," Adamok, the Prime Minister, who sat on her right, said. "Then we would not be in this awkward position of asking Prince Langward to break his vow."

"There are events that can change a man forever," Marriah countered. "Your Prince Langward will not break his vow."

"You have spoken to Prince Langward?" General Caddaric, the Minister of Defense on her left asked. "What did happen between him and King Burkhart?"

"What I know is for Queen Aurita's ears only," she replied firmly.

There were protests, but she would not waiver in her resolve. They finally gave up that line of questioning.

"Where do you come to us from?" one of the district governors finally asked.

"From the east and the north," she replied cryptically.

Aurella stifled another giggle before translating.

"We have heard rumors of giant flying dragons to the east," one of the district governors near the head of the table said.

"That is no rumor," Marriah stated. "I have seen these dragons."

"Were you afraid of being eaten?" Bretton, the Minister of Finance, asked.

Marriah tried not laugh as she replied, "Not at all. They live with people who care for them, in turn they protect those people."

"What if they invade us?" someone asked in an alarmed tone. "We would be defenseless."

"I have met with their king," she replied. "They have no interest in conquest."

Silence fell as they considered her answer. She noticed a pair of paintings flanking the entrance. One was obviously of King Burkhart. He had a very commanding gaze and a self assured posture. The other painting was of her father, Prince Langward, the one Larkin had seen. Father looked much younger and although he wore a smile, there was something there that betrayed the emotion lying beneath.

The prime minister noticed her interest and said, "Our royal painter is quite talented. Prince Langward was very talented as well."

"Yes," Marriah agreed. "I have seen some of his work."

Before anyone could ask further questions, the doors opened and Garman entered.

"Queen Aurita is ready to grant audience with Princess Marriah," he announced, first in the language of Brinley, then in Marriah's language.

Marriah rose as the men scrambled to stand. She was relieved to get away from their questioning.

"You did very well, Princess," Aurella complimented her. "I have seen those men pry secrets out of many emissaries. You left them more confused than when they entered the room."

Marriah smiled.

Chapter 13 – Meeting Her Grandmother

When they reached a pair of ornate doors, Fyodor handed her the shirt and armband that had belonged to her father. Aurella took her position in front of Marriah, between Garman and Fyodor. Katina held the drawing book and Janina the drawing board as they stood behind and to each side of her with Gavynn following them. Marriah took a deep breath as the guards opened the doors revealing an enormous room that was ornately decorated. Opposite the doors a woman sat on one of two thrones. A sword in a sheath occupied the other throne. They crossed to stop just before reaching the dais. Marriah recognized the woman from her father's book. The armband she wore was made of gold and embellished with jewels. Marriah curtsied as low as possible while the others knelt.

"Come, bring me news of my son," Queen Aurita's voice was stern, yet gentle.

"Where did you get these?" she asked as Marriah handed her the shirt and armband.

"It is a long story," Marriah replied. "I will start at the beginning. After leaving Brinley, Prince Langward settled in a small village east of the mountains."

She motioned to Katina who brought the book forward. Marriah opened the book to the first page with a picture of her mother on it.

"I have found love, and her name is Carita," Queen Aurita read before commenting, "She is beautiful."

Marriah turned the pages to one with her as a baby.

"I have never been happier. Our baby is the most beautiful thing I have ever seen. We have named her," Queen Aurita stopped reading and met Marriah's eyes for the first time. "You have his eyes and her mouth."

"Yes," Marriah said softly as she untied the ties and removed the right sleeve of her dress. "And my father's birthmark."

Marriah turned so Queen Aurita could see for herself. She felt fingers softly trace its outline.

"Granddaughter."

The word was music to Marriah's heart, but she knew she must reveal the rest. She held out her hand and Fyodor handed her the paper containing the letter.

127

"There is more you must know," she said gently as she turned to face her grandmother. "It will not be easy to hear. That is why I would not send it with a messenger. I knew it best if I were the one to tell you."

"He is never returning," Queen Aurita surmised.

"This was written for you," Marriah said handing her the paper. "It explains a lot."

She could see tears forming as Queen Aurita read the letter. Marriah took her hand as the letter fell to the floor and she felt tears running silently down her own cheeks.

"He always kept his word," Queen Aurita's voice trembled. "How could I not have known?"

"I have learned that such things can easily be overlooked. Father was too proud to show he needed help," Marriah confessed softly. "He never spoke of his past. I learned of it only four days ago when Fyodor and Garman found the village that is now named Langward in his memory."

"How did he die?" she asked softly after a moment.

Marriah began to tell her grandmother the story with the help of the drawings she had made. She told of meeting Archelaus at Xylia's funeral and how he was genuinely concerned for her and her wellbeing.

"Have you seen him since then?" her grandmother asked with obvious interest.

"Yes," Marriah answered with a smile. "Actually he is the reason that I returned to the village. We were there for two reasons really. The first being he wanted to see where I grew up."

"What was the second reason?"

"The second reason was to announce our engagement," Marriah revealed. "He gave me this ring and circlet. We are to be married in sixty eight days. Something strange happened before we left the village. Archelaus and I shared a dream involving us and our parents. Garman and Fyodor said that what happened in the dream was a wedding ceremony in Brinley."

Marriah turned to the drawing of the cloth from their dream. "Our hands were bound to each other with this."

Queen Aurita's eyes widened before she glanced at Aurella who was standing beside her and nodded. Aurella left, but soon returned with a long box. She opened the box and Queen Aurita lifted a cloth from the box and held it for Marriah to see. Marriah gasped as she saw it was the same as the one in the dream.

"I must meet this King Archelaus," Queen Aurita insisted as Marriah sat on the steps at her feet. "And Regis Bryant. I will have messengers sent for them."

"No need," Marriah replied. "I have contact with Tasia, the queen dragon."

"How soon can they get here?"

After a few moments, Marriah answered, "They will arrive tomorrow after breakfast. Haskell will bring them. I had them told that it will be a formal occasion."

"I assume that the sword you carry is not just for decoration," Queen Aurita stated.

"General Edgard has trained me well in the use of the sword and self defense," Marriah replied. "I can now beat both him and Regis Bryant in a duel."

"There is one more thing then I'll let you rest from your journey," she told Marriah. "I can see that you are indeed your grandfather's true heir. He left you a letter which I will have Fyodor deliver to you along with a scroll which he said you should also read. Tomorrow I will declare you Queen Marriah of Brinley."

"You understand that Brinley must then join Burton?" Marriah asked her.

"That is why I want to meet your Archelaus," was her reply. "His parents are both dead as well?"

"Yes."

"I thought so. You have your father's talent. May I look through these?" she indicated the book and drawing board.

"Of course," Marriah agreed

"After supper we can finalize the plans for your coronation."

Back in her chambers, Marriah stood out on her balcony. It was hard to believe that soon she would be queen of all of Brinley. She heard a step behind her and turned to see Fyodor drop to his knees.

"Rise," she said.

"May I have a word with you, Princess?" he requested, as he handed her a scroll and a sealed letter.

"What do you want?"

"I was wondering if you know if Katina is . . . has," he stammered.

"No," Marriah said. "In fact, I think you should take Katina for a tour of the city or something."

"As you command, Princess," he replied.

"No, as you wish," Marriah told him.

"But, only you or Queen Aurita can approve such a relationship between servants in the castle."

"I don't see why, as long as it doesn't interfere with your duties."

"Do you think that Katina would. . . ," he began then trailed off.

"I have seen her watching you," Marriah revealed and the man blushed. "This morning she mentioned how handsome you are."

Marriah struggled to keep a straight face as his blush spread from his cheeks to the rest of his face.

"I wouldn't know how to ask her," Fyodor admitted.

"Why don't you let me handle that," Marriah suggested. "Where would you take her? I know, I think I need some flowers for the sitting room. She can help you get them."

"The royal gardens are very beautiful this time of year," Fyodor noted as he followed her back inside.

"Katina!" Marriah called.

Katina came from the servants' quarters. Marriah saw her glance at Fyodor before curtseying low.

"This room needs flowers," Marriah declared. "Fyodor will assist you."

Fyodor bowed low to Katina, who blushed. Marriah returned to the balcony and shut the door behind her before she began to laugh.

'You have a sense of humor similar to Haskell's,' Tasia's voice accused in her mind.

She just laughed again. A soft tap on the door caught her attention.

"Come," she said once she had composed herself.

Aurella opened the door and knelt before her.

"Rise," Marriah said.

"Queen Aurita has ordered a dress be made for you for tomorrow," Aurella said. "The seamstresses are here to take measurements."

Marriah nodded and followed Aurella into the sitting room.

"Take your measurements," she ordered.

The women were quick as they measured her thoroughly writing down every measurement.

"They were commenting that you look a lot like Queen Aurita," Aurella revealed after the women had left. "You really do look much like her and your father."

"Tomorrow they'll know why," Marriah said. "I need some time to myself."

Aurella knelt and left. Marriah opened the letter. She was surprised that it was not written in Brinley's language, but in her own.

'My Dear Grandchild,' the letter began. 'I write this knowing that I will never meet you. The scroll contains the prophecy which told me of your existence. Through it I know that by the time you have read this, you will have suffered great sorrow and pain. I wanted you to know that it will be worth what you have been through. After your father, Langward, was born I knew that it would be through him that you would inherit my throne. I realize that you may not understand why I did not intervene on his behalf even though I knew what he suffered at his brother's hand. I knew that he had to leave Brinley behind before the prophecy could be fulfilled. You will be the first to read the prophecy since I wrote it down and sealed it. My father and General Kannan are the only others who have been told more than brief hint about its contents. Even your grandmother does not know the full prophecy. I have only told her that when all seems lost she must search you out. I told her that the search will be difficult, but she must not give up hope and promised her that she would live to see your face. You and I share a bond that time and death cannot break, for I know that you are my true heir just as certainly as I know that my heart-shaped birthmark can be found on your right shoulder. I know that all will prosper under your rule. I want you to know that I love both you and your father very much. With all my love, your grandfather, King Brook of Brinley.'

She sat in shock as she felt the letter slip from her hand. Her father had once told her that everything happened for a purpose and that even death brought new life. He had always taught her to treat everyone with kindness and respect. When her mother's parents had died, she asked about his parents. He had simply said that what was past, was past and not important. When he turned away, she thought she had seen a tear run down his cheek.

She was startled by a knock on the door. She composed herself and folded the letter before bidding them to enter.

Servant Queen

Garman entered and said, "Queen Aurita summons you to the study, Princess."

She followed him down to a room that was lined with shelves of books. There was a desk at one end and a window at the other. A table with six chairs sat in the middle of the room. There was another door opposite the one they had entered. Her grandmother was sitting at the table with several papers and a map.

"Garman, come read this announcement for her," Queen Aurita said as she looked up.

The announcement stated that as the daughter of Prince Langward Marriah was the rightful heir to the throne of Brinley. It also told of her engagement to Archelaus and the joining of Brinley with Burton. Marriah recommended a couple of minor changes before Garman sat down to write out copies to be taken and read around the kingdom. They discussed the coronation ceremony before going over the map.

"Princess, after you and King Archelaus are married you will rule a kingdom larger than any other," Garman observed.

"It's a little overwhelming to think about," Marriah admitted. "I'm grateful that Regis Bryant and Regina Sonje taught me many of the skills I'll need as queen."

"I'm grateful that both you and Archelaus understand the lives of the people you will rule over," Queen Aurita said. "His experience in ruling a kingdom will be valuable in reassuring the people that they are in good hands."

"It will probably be a while before we can spend much time in one place," Marriah theorized. "I'm glad that you will be here, Grandmother."

"I will not live forever, my dear granddaughter," Queen Aurita reminded her. "You will need to use the council to help you rule Brinley. They are good dedicated men who care very much for the welfare of our people."

"I have a question," Marriah said. "My father often called me Ka Messi. I figured out that messi means princess, but what does Ka mean?"

"Ka Messi means My Princess," Queen Aurita said as she wiped a tear from her cheek. "In his drawing book he often referred to you and your mother as his beautiful princesses. He loved both of you with all of his heart. It is just about supper time and I'm tired. Garman will take you down to supper."

V.J.O. Gardner

She followed Garman down to the dining hall. Aurella was waiting there for them. The ministers and district governors again questioned her about where she was from and what news she had of Prince Langward, but she gave them no more information than she had before.

As they entered Marriah's chambers, they heard laughter in the bedroom. Aurella shrugged as Marriah glanced at her. Marriah put her finger to her lips and quietly crossed the room to look into the bedchamber. Katina and Fyodor were arranging flowers in a large bowl on the table. They were talking and laughing. Marriah led Aurella out to the balcony and shut the door.

"I haven't seen Fyodor this comfortable talking to a woman or this happy in years," Aurella revealed before laughing.

"You should have seen how red his face got when I told him I had seen Katina watching him."

Aurella laughed even harder.

"I really didn't need flowers, but it was the perfect way to get them talking to each other," Marriah confessed. "You should have seen her face when I told her that he would be assisting her and he bowed to her."

They both laughed so hard that they had to sit down. It was several minutes before either of them could speak again.

"You realize that, when you are queen, you will have the power to marry them," Aurella revealed.

"In that case, I will need to have Fyodor accompany us back to Dracona so he can ask her father for her hand in marriage," Marriah replied.

"I wonder what happened," Aurella pondered. "Fyodor is usually very shy around women."

"I think we can find out," Marriah said and went to the door.

She opened the door slowly. They looked into the sitting room to see Fyodor and Katina kissing. Fyodor left and Katina just stood there watching him go. Marriah walked into the room, followed by Aurella. Katina turned around and just smiled.

"You look like you had a good time," Marriah commented as she sat down.

"The garden was so beautiful," Katina gushed as she sat down. "Fyodor knew where all of the best flowers were. There were some perfect flowers on the end of a tall branch, so I stepped up on a rock wall to bend the branch down. Suddenly I fell backwards."

"Were you hurt?" Aurella asked.

"I found myself in his strong arms, looking up into his big brown eyes. At first he looked surprised, but then his smile melted my heart. My hand went to his cheek then he leaned down and kissed me."

Katina leaned back and sighed. Marriah smiled at Aurella.

"Then he set me on my feet, but my knees were wobbly. He held me close until I could stand on my own," Katina confided. "Then we laughed and started to talk. He is so wonderful!"

"Go on to bed," Marriah told her. "Tomorrow will be a big day."

As Katina stood up there was a knock on the door.

She opened the door and said, "Oh. Hi, Garman."

Then she went into the servant's quarters and shut the door behind her. Marriah and Aurella broke out into laughter as Garman stood there looking confused.

"I just passed Fyodor in the hall. He had the same expression on his face and said exactly the same thing. What happened to them?" he asked

It took Marriah a moment before she could speak. After she and Aurella finished telling Garman they were all laughing. It was several minutes before any of them could quit laughing.

"That explains it," Garman chortled. "You know you can marry them if you want."

"Yes, but I thought I would give him the opportunity to ask her father's permission first," she confessed.

This sent Garman into another fit of laughter. After they finally quit laughing, Marriah stood up.

"I needed a good laugh," she admitted. "Today was just too tense. I'm going to bed now."

"Do you need help?"

"No," Marriah replied. "Go get some sleep."

When Marriah woke up, she could hear Janina and Katina talking in the bathing chamber. They curtsied low as she joined them. They had been talking about Fyodor.

"I'm glad that you and Fyodor are getting along so well," Marriah said as she stepped into the water. "I want him to return to Dracona with us to teach me Brinley's language."

"Oh, thank you," Katina beamed. "I was hoping he would be coming with us."

She knew how Katina felt. It was hard for her to know how long she and Archelaus would be apart before the wedding. She wondered if it was as hard for him.

Chapter 14 - Summoned to Brinley

Archelaus was up well before dawn. Marriah's message had been very brief with no explanation of what he was being summoned to Brinley for. At least he would get to see her. He put on the clothes that Charles had laid out for him. He settled his cape around his shoulders and picked up his crown. Two guards were waiting for him with horses. They arrived at the appointed place just as Haskell landed.

"Ready?" Bryant asked as he mounted.

He put his arm through his crown and said, "Ready."

Even Haskell had little to say. Archelaus suspected he knew more, but wasn't saying.

'It wouldn't be much fun if I told you everything,' Haskell taunted. 'Some things you just have to find out on your own.'

He watched the ground as they flew trying to recognize things that were less familiar from dragonback. Among the trees he glimpsed the buildings of town south of Burton. He vaguely remembered visiting an abandoned town that was overgrown with his father when he was quite young.

As they approached Brinley, Archelaus was impressed. The city was larger than Burton's city. The castle was enormous. Haskell landed in the wide green field surrounding the castle. Archelaus had noticed the large throng of people crowded just outside the wall that divided the field from the city. Gavynn and Janina were waiting with four very nervous looking guards. Archelaus settled his crown on his head after he dismounted. Bryant drew a gold ball from his pocket. As he held it in both hands, it turned into his crown.

"Welcome to Brinley," Gavynn greeted them as he bowed low.

The guards stood dumbfounded for a moment before bowing as well. Gavynn led them across a drawbridge over the moat and through a courtyard. Once inside the castle he led them into a large throne room. Twelve men stood waiting at the bottom of the dais steps. The woman sitting on one of the thrones looked older, but was the same as from Marriah's father's book. Archelaus and Bryant stopped at the bottom of the stairs and bowed low.

The woman said, "Welcome King Archelaus, Regis Bryant. I have heard much about both of you. These men are the ministers and district governors of Brinley. I am Queen Aurita. To explain why you are here, I will read a letter to these men, the letter which you have heard already."

She then read in the language of Brinley. As they listened some fell to their knees in tears. When she finished the room fell silent for a time.

Queen Aurita spoke again. Archelaus heard her say Dracona, then Larkin and Regis Bryant several times. One of the men asked something. Bryant looked up to Queen Aurita for an explanation.

"He lived next to a couple who had a son named Larkin. One morning the two were found beaten to death and the son was nowhere to be found," Queen Aurita explained.

"Tell him that I personally executed Larkin. Before he was executed Larkin admitted to killing his father after his father killed his mother," Bryant requested.

He looked at Bryant and asked something.

"May he see the sword that executed Larkin?"

"Yes," Bryant responded. "Warn him that this sword serves only one master and I am the only one to handle it safely since it was forged. He must not touch it."

Queen Aurita looked from Bryant to Archelaus with a questioning look. He nodded his confirmation of Bryant's warning. She told the man, who nodded and stepped toward Bryant.

Bryant flipped his cape back over his left shoulder, revealing Fanchon's Sword. He drew it slowly from its sheath. There were gasps from the men as he lifted it high and the blade appeared as a flame briefly. Bryant then laid the blade over his open palm. The men were obviously impressed as Bryant showed each man in turn. Once the sword was sheathed again, the man returned to his place with the others.

"Come here, King Archelaus of Burton," Queen Aurita commanded.

Archelaus climbed the steps then dropped briefly to one knee before her. She spoke in Brinley's language for a while, saying his name and Gustave several times.

"Before we adjourn to the outer wall for Marriah's coronation I have something for you," she said as Fyodor came forward holding a sheathed sword. "My husband forged it himself.

He told me to give it to his true heir thinking it would be a man not a woman. As Marriah already has a sword, this one I present to you."

He took the sword and buckled it in place before glancing down at Bryant who smiled. She spoke again and the doors opened. Marriah entered, flanked by Garman and a woman. She was even more beautiful than he remembered. She was wearing a dress that though similar in design to the purple dress that Sonje had sent, featured plates of silver and gold forming a pattern along the top and sleeve. On her right arm, she wore a silver armband. The men quickly dropped to their knees as she passed. He and Bryant dropped to one knee and bowed their heads. Marriah smiled at him as she stopped on the step beside him. Archelaus rose, took her hand and kissed it.

"Welcome to Brinley," Marriah smiled. "The carriage should be waiting for us."

"We saw a crowd of people by the outer wall," Archelaus commented as Queen Aurita stood.

He offered her his arm and helped her down the stairs.

"I met your father several times. He was a good man and king. I was saddened when I heard about his death," Queen Aurita mentioned as they walked toward the courtyard. "I met Gustave once and disliked him immediately."

"All of Burton suffered under Gustave's rule," Archelaus replied, surprised by her comment.

"I know you will take good care of Marriah and the people of Brinley. You have my permission to marry her. You remind me very much of your father."

"Thank you. For Marriah I would give up everything," Archelaus assured her.

"Yes, I can see the love you have for her," Queen Aurita smiled as he helped her into the waiting carriage.

He helped Marriah into the carriage before joining Bryant and the rest of the men waiting behind the carriage. It was a long walk to the outer wall. The men seemed frightened of Haskell as they passed by him. When they reached the outer wall a guard opened a door in a tower. Marriah helped Queen Aurita up the narrow staircase that wound around the outside of the tower and came out on the battlements.

A cheer went up from the gathered crowd as they stepped up on a wooden platform so they were visible above the battlements. Queen Aurita raised her arms and silence fell. She began speaking mentioning Langward and Marriah several times. Archelaus noticed even the guards seemed emotionally affected by what she was saying. Queen Aurita continued and mentioned Bryant who stepped forward and bowed. A cheer went up from the crowd.

Queen Aurita had to raise her hands again before continuing. Soon she mentioned Burton and his name. Archelaus stepped forward and bowed to the crowd before turning to take Marriah's hand. He brought it to his lips and kissed it as a cheer went up from the crowd.

"Give her a proper kiss," Queen Aurita dared him.

Marriah smiled at him as he stepped closer. He kissed her passionately as the crowd roared its approval. After silence finally fell again Queen Aurita spoke again as she took the jeweled gold band from her arm and held it high. Marriah removed the silver arm band from her arm and Queen Aurita replaced it with the jeweled gold band. The crowd suddenly knelt for a moment before rising.

There were shouts of 'Empri Marriah!' that echoed off the buildings. Queen Aurita led them back down to the carriage to be greeted by a large group of guards and servants that were also cheering.

"I want to meet Haskell," Queen Aurita said as Marriah settled into the carriage next to her.

Bryant seemed amused by the look of dismay on the faces of the council members as they stopped in front of Haskell. Archelaus helped Marriah from the carriage and Bryant helped Queen Aurita. Haskell put his head down and Queen Aurita reached out to touch his nose as Marriah stroked his cheek.

'The men are terrified,' Haskell chuckled.

Cautiously the men came forward and bowed to the dragon. One of the men who was wearing a uniform similar to the guards stepped forward and knelt to Haskell. When he stood Haskell gently touched the man's cheek with his nose. The man slowly lifted his hand and stroked Haskell's nose. When he returned to the other men he spoke rapidly to them.

"General Caddaric is telling them how warm Haskell is and what his scales feel like," Queen Aurita laughed. "Let's go have lunch. I haven't eaten in the dining room for years, but today is a day to celebrate."

Haskell had a very pleased look about him.

'You look very pleased yourself,' Haskell commented. 'I've never seen either of you this happy.'

'I just wish I didn't have to go back to Burton without her,' Archelaus replied.

'I promise it will be worth the wait,' Haskell chuckled.

When they reached the dining room they stood near the head of the table as each of the ministers was introduced in turn, followed by the district governors. The men waited at their places as Queen Aurita and Marriah led him and Bryant to the head of the table. Marriah took her place at the head of the table with Archelaus next to her and Queen Aurita around the corner from her. Bryant took the place around the corner from Archelaus. The men took their seats after Marriah and Queen Aurita sat down. Garman stood behind him, Fyodor behind Bryant and the woman behind Marriah. As he looked around the room, he noticed there were two paintings on either side of the entrance.

"Your father and uncle?" he asked Marriah.

"Yes," she said. "There is something about his eyes, his smile."

Archelaus studied the portrait of Prince Langward for a moment.

"Yes," he replied. "There is something, something almost sad."

"He would be very proud of you," Bryant said. "And very happy."

"It broke my heart to learn what abuse he took from his brother without telling me. I am glad to know he found the happiness he deserved even though it was so brief," Queen Aurita admitted. "I will be forever grateful that both of you have cared for Marriah after his death."

"He came to my father's aid when he was injured once. Prince Langward expected nothing in return. I met him briefly once when I gave him his first two cattle. I know he was a good and honorable man," Bryant replied. "To be able to repay his kindness by caring for his daughter means a lot to me."

As they ate, the conversation was light. Archelaus found the food to be delicious. Marriah seemed surprisingly comfortable in her new role as Queen of Brinley. She smiled at him when she saw him watching her. He noticed that the ministers and district governors had a lot of respect for their new queen.

After lunch, Marriah and Archelaus were escorted out to a waiting carriage. The ministers and district governors mounted horses and followed the carriage out of the castle. The the streets were lined with cheering people as they rode in a great circle through the city. This made Archelaus happy. He had been concerned about how the people of Brinley would feel about merging with Burton and Dracona. He was glad to get back to the castle.

Garman was waiting for them when they returned. He led them to a set of double doors on an upper floor. Inside was a short hall crossed by a longer hall. There was a large sitting room at the end of the hall where Queen Aurita and Bryant were talking. Aurella was there to translate if necessary.

"Bryant was telling me more about meeting Langward," Queen Aurita said.

"It was hard for me to see how happy he and all the villagers were when I was so alone. I was glad to see how happy Langward was with you and your mother," Bryant recalled. "I was concerned when he suddenly vanished about the time I was almost desperate enough to try to ask him for some help."

"Shortly after Larkin enslaved us Father told me that the day would come for me to seek you out Regis," Marriah commented.

"You don't need to use my title, Marriah," Bryant interjected. "You never have needed to. Sonje feels the same way."

Marriah smiled as Queen Aurita picked up two rings and a set of keys that had been on the table next to the settee.

"I have something for you," she said. "Come sit down."

Once Marriah was seated she held out one ring and the keys to Marriah.

"My signet ring and the keys to your father and uncle's rooms," she explained. "I've kept them locked and untouched since your father left and your uncle died."

Marriah put on the signet ring on the third finger of her right hand as Queen Aurita held out the other ring to him.

"My husband's signet ring," she said. "Burkhart took it off about a month after Langward left and refused to wear it except when meeting with other leaders or their emessaries. It is now yours."

"I am not the king of Brinley yet, Queen Aurita," Archelaus protested.

"Not officially, but your dream of being married to Marriah is real enough for me because your hands were bound together with the royal wedding cloth," Queen Aurita insisted as she slipped the signet ring onto the third finger of Archelaus' right hand.

"The royal what?" he stammered.

"I saw it myself," Marriah said as he looked at her in shock. "Every last detail, right down to the blue gems at each end of the cloth."

"I want you to call me Grandmother from now on," Queen Aurita added. "Bryant told me more about you. I know I couldn't have chosen a better husband for Marriah or king for Brinley."

"I've always been so very curious about my father's past," Marriah said as she looked at the keys in her open hand. "I want to see his room, but I want to see Uncle Burkhart's room first."

"Yes, My Queen," Aurella responded and led them halfway down the entrance hall and down the longer one to a set of double doors.

Marriah placed one of the keys in the key hole. She turned it slowly. The room was dark. Archelaus smiled at Aurella's gasp as Bryant lit their way.

"Garman didn't tell you?" Marriah asked.

"Only that Regis Bryant had saved you," Aurella replied. "We were a . . . a little busy."

"Actually, I knew you would be," Marriah confessed. "Why do you think that I wanted you to be with Garman? He had been gone four months. It wouldn't have been fair to keep you two apart."

Aurella turned to light a lamp near the door, but not before Archelaus saw her blush. Marriah's comment had surprised him as well. He glanced at Bryant who grinned at him. The room was surprisingly plain for the bedroom of a king. Marriah went over to the bed and began to look at the headboard. It had sections of wood inlayed with brass, gold and silver.

"I remember that the headboard of my bed had a hidden compartment where I kept my journal. It's probably still there," Archelaus remembered with a twinge of sadness.

"I wonder if there could be one in this headboard," she said as she began to feel around. "It seems thick enough."

A thin rectangle of silver popped up as her fingers passed above it. She tugged at it gently. A large panel opened up and a book fell out. Marriah handed the book to Aurella.

142

After flipping through a few pages, she began to read, "Why is Langward so stubborn? He was willing to kneel before Father. Am I not his king? He'll come back, he always has."

"It has been a week, and still no sign of Langward. This is not like him at all. Even when I beat him until he was bruised, he would act as if nothing happened. He never even told Mother."

Aurella flipped a few more pages before continuing, "It has been a month and Langward is still gone. Even the border patrol did not see him leave our territory. I dare not tell Mother why he was angry."

Aurella flipped through more pages before reading, "Mother says I should marry, but I have no interest. How can I, knowing how I have failed? Langward was a good brother and friend, but I never understood that until it was too late. He always stood up for me and even took the blame for most of the things I had done. He is never coming back, I know that now. His place still remains empty in the dining hall, his room locked and untouched."

Aurella paused and looked at Marriah.

"He finally realized that what he had done to Father was not right and that to demand an unearned show of respect from him was unreasonable," Marriah observed. "Is there more?"

Aurella flipped through more pages before looking up.

"This is the last entry," she said. "I know I will die soon. My regrets in life are many. I leave behind a kingdom with no heir to the throne, yet my greatest regret is not knowing Langward's fate. Last night my dreams were troubled. I saw Langward fighting with a man. There was a young woman who runs without looking back. Both Langward and the woman are battered, bruised and bleeding. I watch helplessly as Langward dies at this man's hand. It all seemed so real. I heard the man curse and swear as he beat Langward to death, but the only words from my brother's lips were to the woman, urging her to run. If this is truly Langward's fate, then though king, I am nothing. Langward is truly a greater man than I. He gave his life that another might live."

They sat in silence after Aurella closed the book. Archelaus took Marriah's hand in his. Marriah was the first to break the silence.

"That explains a lot," she said. "I want to take that journal with me. Fyodor will be teaching me to read and write as well as speak the language of Brinley. I want to look at Father's room now."

Aurella led them back down the hall to the door on the opposite end. The lock was stiff and the hinges squeaked as the door was opened. Aurella lit some lamps. There were many drawings and a few paintings scattered about the room. There were several books on a shelf similar to the one Marriah had brought with her. There was a space where two were missing in the middle. The drawer of the desk was open as was the closet door.

"He did leave in a hurry," Bryant commented.

Marriah let go of Archelaus' hand and went to the bed. After a moment, she found the secret panel. A journal fell out with a drawing book. Marriah opened the drawing book and gasped. Archelaus quickly went to her. She handed him the book. He could see why Langward had kept the book hidden. The drawings showed a side of Burkhart that reminded him of Gustave. He flipped through some pages. Among the drawings of Burkhart were some showing happy families in front of small houses.

"He knew where he wanted to be when he left," Archelaus said and handed the book back to Marriah.

"This looks like our home in the village," Marriah said softly. "The man looks like him. I can't see the woman's face, but she is holding a baby."

"Prince Langward found what he always wanted; a home where he had control over his own life, a wife who loved him, and a daughter," Aurella remarked.

"Beyond that, nothing much matters," Bryant agreed with a smile.

"I know I am looking forward to having children," Marriah said as she took Archelaus' hand in hers.

Archelaus could only smile and hope that she didn't notice his pulse was racing. He was definitely looking forward to starting a family with her.

"I want to take the two journals and the drawing book with me to Dracona," Marriah said. "I think for now the rooms should remain as they are."

They returned to where Queen Aurita waited.

"What are these?" she asked.

When they explained what they had discovered a tear ran down her cheek.

"I had a dream the night before you arrived," she said softly. "In it Burkhart knelt with his head in his hands sobbing uncontrollably. When I asked him what was wrong all he would say

144

was that it was his fault. I could get nothing more out of him. A mist formed behind him and turned into Langward. He knelt with a hand on Burkhart's back and whispered, 'I forgive you.' Langward then vanished leaving Burkhart still sobbing."

"I can forgive Uncle Burkhart for how he treated Father," Marriah assured her.

"It has been years since I visited Brook's grave even though I can see it from the balcony," Queen Aurita commented. "Will you go with me to visit it?"

"We both will," Archelaus volunteered and Marriah nodded.

"May I come as well?" Bryant asked and Queen Aurita nodded as she stood. "Losing those you love can leave you feeling very alone as you mourn for them. For me even five years seemed like a lifetime."

"That is what I have seen in your eyes as you spoke of your father," Queen Aurita said. "Come and we will spend a little time mourning together for those we love."

Queen Aurita took Bryant's offered arm and led them through the castle to a lower level. The stonework was older than that of the upper floors. There were two guards at a door who knelt before opening it for them. The room inside was very dusty. There were brown stains on the floor and the bedding. A drawer remained open in one of the nightstands beside the bed.

"This room has remained mostly untouched since the day I was born," Queen Aurita said softly. "A part of my father died with my mother that day. Brook's father became King Langward and spared his life so he could raise me."

Bryant patted her hand softly as Archelaus put his arm around Marriah. Queen Aurita opened a door that led to a small courtyard. There were six stones marking the graves and room for one more. Queen Aurita broke into tears. Bryant gently pulled her toward him and she collapsed sobbing against his chest. Garman quietly read the inscriptions on the stones to Marriah and Archelaus. The graves belonged to Queen Aurita's parents, King Brook's parents, King Brook, and Marriah's Uncle Burkhart. Marriah put her arms around Queen Aurita and cried with her. Archelaus softly stroked her back as tears ran down his own face. He remembered that he and Aunt Althea had lit two candles in memory of his parents. There had been a stone marker on his empty grave in Burton. That stone had been destroyed when he became king of

Burton. Bryant kept one hand on Queen Aurita's back. He wiped at his eyes before looking up at Archelaus.

When Queen Aurita finally settled down she looked at Bryant and said, "Thank you. You remind me so of Brook and his father. I'm certain you are a good ruler over your people."

"It is a hard thing to mourn those you love when you are alone. I had to bury my own father with only Haskell there to help," Bryant confessed before wiping his face with his hands.

"I think it's time I return to the royal quarters," Queen Aurita admitted. "I've had more excitement today than I've had in a very long time. I need to rest."

They walked with her back to the sitting rooms where Aurella was waiting for them. She quickly knelt

"Supper is soon," she announced after standing.

Marriah picked up the journals and drawing book before saying, "These things must be taken to my room."

"I will see to that personally," Garman volunteered.

He took the three books and left.

"I'll take my meal here," Queen Aurita ordered. "I've climbed enough stairs for one day."

Marriah kissed her cheek before they followed Aurella down to the dining hall. Garman and Fyodor arrived to help translate. The ministers and district governers all seemed to be in a good mood as they sat down to eat.

As they were eating, one man asked, "Rumor is that you will be leaving us soon for a while, My Queen. What will happen to us while you are gone?"

"My grandmother will continue her duties as queen while I am gone. That will help the transition to go smoother. King Archelaus and I will be joining three kingdoms into one so we have a lot to do," Marriah explained. "I want weekly reports sent by messenger to Dracona. I will provide a map of Brinley, Dracona, Langward and Burton. While we are gone, King Archelaus and I will be learning your language. Aurella and Garman will return to Burton with King Archelaus. Fyodor will return to Dracona with me."

"Three kingdoms?" another man asked.

"It is time for the people of Dracona and Merton to return to their original homeland," Bryant informed them. "We are leaving our kingdom to Archelaus and Marriah. It will take some time

before we are ready to leave but soon we will leave Dracona empty.
It will take longer for Merton to be emptied."

"The dragons?" one man began.

"Will leave with us," Bryant affirmed and the men looked
relieved.

"What about your wedding?" Prime Minister Adamok
asked. "Where will you hold it?"

"Will it follow our traditional ceremony?" Minister of the
Interior Eldwyn added. "I've heard that the ceremonies in other
kingdoms are very different from ours. In Okiah they cut the back of
the bride's hand near the wrist."

"We are the servants of our people and must keep their
interests a priority," Archelaus replied. "We have obligations to the
people of Burton and Langward. One of those obligations is a public
wedding ceremony that they will accept as binding."

"We have decided that we should combine aspects of the
three wedding ceremonies into one ceremony," Marriah announced.
"We should find a central location to hold the ceremony. We will
expect all of you to be in attendance."

The men looked at one another in surprise then nodded. A
central location was a good idea for the wedding. Perhaps that
abandoned town would be a good place. He would have to
investigate it and why it was empty.

When they finished eating each man bowed to Bryant and
knelt to Marriah and him before leaving.

"Thank you," Marriah said and gave Aurella a hug. "Thank
you for everything. Go and prepare for your stay in Burton. Haskell
will take you safely there."

"We are to fly?" Garman stuttered.

"Not on the dragon!" Aurella objected.

"Dress warmly," Archelaus acknowledged. "Riding on
dragon back can be cold. I need you in Burton immediately. I have a
lot to learn and only a short time to learn it."

Aurella and Garman knelt before Archelaus.

When they stood up they said, "As you command, My
King."

"You will want to pack in two sacks," Bryant suggested.

They began talking rapidly in low tones halfway to the
door. Fyodor led them back to the courtyard. They talked about the
wedding and when Dracona would be empty while they waited for
Aurella and Garman. They arrived with two large sacks with them.

"We will need to tie these together," Bryant said as he lifted the two sacks. "They need to weigh about the same."

Aurella handed Archelaus and Bryant their capes while Garman drew two capes out of one of the sacks. Aurella then shifted two books into the other sack. Bryant put on his cape before lifting the sacks again.

"That's better," Bryant commented as Archelaus put on his cape.

Aurella tied the sacks closed. Fyodor brought a small length of rope and tied the sacks together. Garman and Aurella put on their capes. Archelaus turned to face Marriah. Her smile was a little sad. He stroked her cheek with his hand.

"My heart goes with you," she said as she stepped closer.

His heart quickened at her words.

"My heart stays with you," he replied as he drew her into his arms.

He kissed her gently. She smiled at him before she kissed him back. Her kiss told him just how much she would miss him. He held her close while he caught his breath.

"Sixty seven days until we can truly become one," she whispered in his ear.

"Sixty seven days," he repeated with a sigh.

He released her reluctantly as a carriage pulled up. Archelaus put his arm around Marriah's shoulders as he sat next to her. No one spoke as they rode out to where Haskell waited. Aurella and Garman looked anxious, but Haskell looked eager to leave.

"Safe journey," Fyodor said as they got out of the carriage.

"Take care of her," Archelaus commanded.

"I will guard her with my very life," Fyodor vowed solemnly as he knelt before Archelaus.

"I'll see you again in about five or six days," Marriah told Haskell as she patted his cheek. "Then I'll tell you about everything."

By then, Bryant had the bags secured. Archelaus kissed Marriah goodbye and held her tight.

"I'll send you a letter the moment I return to Dracona," she promised.

"Take care," he replied. "I wouldn't want anything to happen to you. I love you too much to lose you."

"I love you in the same way," Marriah said. "I checked my sword. General Edgard has it razor sharp. I'll make certain that

Fyodor and Gavynn's are just as sharp before we leave. The wolves will travel with us as well."

Archelaus kissed her forehead before releasing her. He mounted Haskell, followed by Aurella and Garman. Bryant gave Marriah a quick hug before mounting behind Garman. Haskell moved away from the others before taking off. Aurella clung tightly to Archelaus and buried her face in his back. Once Haskell quit climbing and leveled out, Aurella relaxed a little.

It was well after dark when they reached Burton. Haskell had contacted Charles and told him to have a carriage waiting. Haskell landed softly near the torches marking the waiting carriage. Bryant helped Garman and Aurella dismount. Charles and several guards were waiting as Archelaus dismounted. They bowed to Archelaus and his companions.

"Welcome home, My King," Charles said. "The cook has food waiting for you."

"Thank you, Charles," he replied. "This is Aurella and Garman of Brinley. They will be staying with us at least until the wedding."

"Pleased to meet you," Charles said and bowed low.

Archelaus stifled a laugh at the surprised looks on Aurella and Garman's faces. Bryant handed the two sacks down to Garman before remounting. He waved to Archelaus before Haskell moved away and took off. The sacks were put in the carriage and they headed for the castle.

"It's not nearly as large as Brinley," Archelaus said. "But it is home."

"It's cooler than Brinley," Aurella commented as she drew her cape around her.

"If you want, we can get you some warmer clothing," he replied. "Burton is on a hilltop."

Two of the guards took their sacks and Archelaus led them to the dining hall. The cook was waiting for them. He dropped to the floor before Archelaus.

"Rise," Archelaus ordered. "This is Aurella and Garman of Brinley. They will be staying with us until the wedding."

"I am at your service," the cook replied. "How is our Lady Marriah?"

"She is doing well," he answered. "She is now Queen Marriah of Brinley."

"That is wonderful," the cook commented. "If you need anything else, please call."

"We will," Archelaus said as Charles entered.

"May I take your capes?" Charles asked after bowing.

"Yes, please," Archelaus said as he removed his cape.

"My King!" Charles exclaimed. "What went on in Brinley today? I've never seen that sword before nor that signet ring."

"It is the signet ring of the king of Brinley and the sword belonged to Marriah's grandfather, King Brook," Archelaus acknowledged. "I'll tell you everything tomorrow, but Queen Aurita of Brinley gave her blessings for me to marry Marriah. I am to call her Grandmother."

"You didn't get?" Charles asked then hesitated. "Did you?"

"Get married?" Archelaus laughed. "No."

Garman and Aurella were grinning.

"The people of Brinley also approve of the union," he added. "I'll fill in the details tomorrow."

"Yes, My King," Charles said. "You must be tired."

"Yes. You must be tired as well. I'll escort our guests to their room."

"Thank you, My King."

Charles bowed and left. Archelaus was glad to have something to eat. He led Aurella and Garman to their room. They protested about it not being servant's quarters, but relented when he insisted. He was glad to finally get into bed. His dreams were of Marriah and his trip to Brinley.

Chapter 15 - A Proposal for a New City

"Wake up, My King."

Archelaus opened his eyes to find Charles standing at his bedside.

"I hated to wake you, but it's well past dawn," Charles said as he sat up. "You looked as though your dreams were happy. You were smiling in your sleep."

"Very happy," Archelaus admitted with a smile.

"The cook said that Lady Marriah is now queen of Brinley."

"Yes," Archelaus replied as he went to the bathing chamber.

While he bathed, dressed and ate, he gave Charles details of his trip to Brinley.

"I have some questions you may be able to answer," Archelaus said as Charles handed him his crown. "Come to my study after breakfast."

"I am at your service," Charles replied and bowed low as Archelaus left the room.

After breakfast Archelaus went to his study and found Charles waiting at the door. Charles followed Archelaus into the study and waited as he looked through the maps. He knew the town didn't appear on the maps he had been using so he looked for one that seemed older than the the the rest. Charles helped him weight down the corners with stones that were worn from use then touched the map in the corner that bore a name and a date.

"This map was made by your great grandfather," Charles commented. "Why not use a newer map?"

Archelaus located Burton's hilltop city and then looked south towards Brinley. He was pleased to find the town labled Carleton on the map where he had glimpsed the buildings among the trees.

"I wanted to ask if you knew anything about this town south of Burton, but this map answers one of my questions," Archelaus admitted as he looked up at Charles.

"Most people have forgotten about that town. The people moved here to Burton," Charles said as Archelaus looked back at the map.

"Why did they move? It's ideal for a town with the small lake and a river there."

"I've heard rumors about the area being dangerous and no one goes there," Charles replied. "You might find some answers in your great grandfather's journal. May I ask why you want to know about it? Certainly there's nothing left there."

"I noticed there was something there as we flew over it on the way to Brinley. I'm interested in it because we need a central location to hold the wedding," Archelaus pointed out. "Building a town would take too long, but repairing this one might be possible. Find a soldier who just came off of patrol in that area. I'll want a report on what is actually there. I'll need a messenger ready to go to Dracona."

"At once, My King," Charles said as he bowed.

Archelaus found the journal before sitting down at his desk. He skimmed through it looking for any references to Carleton. Burton had originally been built on the hilltop for a clearer view to watch for dragons coming from the east. As the kingdom grew some people settled in Carleton. As the dragons became more active the people of Carleton abandoned the town and fled to the city of Burton. He closed the journal when Charles returned with a soldier.

"Sergeant Thaxter just returned from the area you require information on," Charles informed him. "Also there is someone here requesting an audience with you."

He nodded and Charles left.

"What information can I give you My King?" Sergeant Thaxter asked as Archelaus stood.

"Tell me about the condition of this town south of Burton," Archelaus requested as he pointed to Carleton on the map.

"Oh," Sergeant Thaxter said as he looked at the map. "It's abandoned. My father always said it was cursed or haunted."

"I know it was abandoned because people feared the dragons to the east. The dragons are not something we need to fear. What condition are the buildings in? What would be required to make it inhabitable again?" Archelaus demanded. "Have you seen the town or not?"

"I slept there all of last week," the man said. "Most of the buildings are intact but need repair. There are trees growing in the roads and some homes would need to be completely rebuilt."

"Are there any shops or public buildings like churches or meeting halls?" Archelaus persisted, excited by the possibilities.

"It appears there was once a central plaza with a church at one end and a large building at the other. The bulding had a large meeting hall and several smaller rooms including one that has an oven. There is also a natural ampetheater on the south end of the town," Sergeant Thaxter replied.

"Perfect," Archelaus grinned. "I'll want to tour it myself. Charles will inform you when I need you to be my guide."

"I am at your service, My King," Sergeant Thaxter said. "I was a bit frightened the first time I stayed there, but I soon realized my father was wrong about it. It seemed a shame for it to be abandoned."

"Thank you," Archelaus said. "You are dismissed."

Archelaus went to the throne room and sat in his throne before nodding to the guards. They opened the door and a young woman entered. On her face was a look of both fear and determination. She stopped at the bottom of the steps and curtsied low.

"Rise," Archelaus said. "What is your name and why do you seek my audience?"

"Great and mighty king," she began. "My name is Leda. I have come to beg Burton's assistance for our village."

"What sort of assistance is needed?"

"The marsh has expanded, taking over our fields and rotting our crops. Some of our houses are beginning to sink. Our people are starving and many will die this winter. I have been sent to offer myself to you as your bride or slave in exchange for Burton's assistance."

Archelaus was shocked by her words. This was a sacrifice that no one should have to make. There had to be a better solution.

"I have a bride already," Archelaus told her gently. "Queen Marriah of Brinley and I are engaged to be married. I have no desire to keep anyone as my slave."

"Oh, then I have failed," Leda cried as she collapsed to the floor, tears running down her cheeks.

Archelaus went down to where she knelt on the floor and gave her his handkerchief.

"How large is your village?"

"Fifty families," she replied after wiping her tears.

"Would they be willing to move to a place south of here?"

"Away from the marsh? I think so."

"I think that we can work out a solution beneficial to both of us, one that doesn't require you to sacrifice your freedom."

She looked up and met his gaze.

"I have been thinking that if Brinley and Burton are to join, that there needs to be a village or town midway between them. I know of a place with a river and fertile ground that would be perfect. We could name it Union."

"My village could move there?" Leda sniffled.

"There should be houses, shops, a school and a large building with many rooms for travelers to stay in," Archelaus said as he sat on the bottom step. "The wedding could be held there."

"Our men could build such a place," she volunteered.

"Even better, there is an abandoned town that is in need of repair. Burton could provide food and supplies in exchange for rebuilding the town. Crops could be planted in the spring and travelers could be charged to stay in a room for the night."

"That way we could support ourselves."

"Burton's army could provide protection for the town, and we'll find a teacher for the school in exchange for a small percentage of each family's annual income."

"Taxes?"

"Yes, but only after each family can afford it without putting them back into poverty," Archelaus replied. "I want all of my subjects to be well housed, well fed, well clothed, and educated."

"I think that my village would agree to those terms."

"Good," he said as he stood up. "You will stay for lunch and I will have the proposal written up to take with you. Do you think that there is someone from your village that could be responsible for directing the workers?"

"No one in my village can read, not even my father." Leda confessed hesitantly. "He is the one that everyone in the village looks to as a leader."

"I will send one of my guards to accompany you and read the proposal to the village. He can write down the response and return to Burton. I will want to take your father with me to inspect the abandoned town as soon as he can come."

"It might be about a week before he could arrive here."

"You look tired. I'll have someone take you to a room where you can rest and freshen up before lunch."

"Thank you, wise king. It is a long walk to our village."

"You will return on horseback then," Archelaus said. "I have some business to attend to now, but I will see you at lunch."

He went up the steps again and pulled the cord hanging near his throne. In a few minutes, Charles appeared and bowed low.

"Take Leda to a room and have a woman attend to any need she has," Archelaus commanded. "Then bring Aurella and Garman to my sitting room."

Charles bowed again and said, "Come with me please."

Archelaus went to his study and wrote a letter to Marriah explaining his plan and the location of the town. He also wrote a letter to Bryant before writing up the proposal to the village. He hoped that they would accept his proposal. It would solve the problem of where to hold the wedding. He was just finishing when Charles returned with Aurella and Garman. He sealed the proposal and set it aside.

"I will need a guard to return with Leda to her village. He will be required to write down their response after he reads this proposal. Make certain he has everything necessary. Leda will need a horse. Probably a very gentle horse," he ordered as he handed the letters and proposal to Charles.

"I will make the arrangements," Charles responded with a bow and left.

"The reason I called for you is so we could arrange a schedule," Archelaus explained.

"We are at your service," Garman replied.

Archelaus smiled. There was much to do before the wedding.

*****

It was a week after Archelaus returned from Brinley before Leda's father, Yves, arrived to explore the deserted city. Sergeant Thaxter along with four palace guards went with them. When they arrived at the collection of buildings that had once been the town of Carleton, Archelaus could see that the stone structures were mostly intact. The sun was setting as Sergeant Thaxter led them to a home with a roof.

"This is where I usually stay while on patrol in this area," he explained. "There's a barn around back that I've made some repairs to. The horses will be safe in there."

They unloaded their saddlebags and bedrolls before Sergeant Thaxter showed the guards where to put the horses. They returned with some firewood and soon a fire was crackling in the fireplace. When Archelaus woke in the morning Sergeant Thaxter was walking in with a bucket of water.

155

"The well water is sweet and cold even in the heat of the summer," he commented as he poured some in a pot.

After eating breakfast they started exploring the town. Many of the buildings were intact, but needed repairs. When they arrived at the central plaza there were weeds growing between cobblestones but no trees. Archelaus was anxious to explore the large building Sergeant Thaxter had told him about with a meeting room and kitchen.

"I want to add an upper floor to this building," Archelaus said. "With guest rooms on the upper floor this would make a great inn. I'd want one large room to spend my wedding night in."

"Does the upper floor have to be stone?" Yves asked scratching his chin. "Wood is easier and lighter to build with."

"Probably faster to build with," Archelaus commented and Yves nodded. "Getting this building rebuilt in time for the wedding is critical. If wood will get it finished in time use wood."

"We can get it finished," Yves assured him.

"Let's walk around the homes," Archelaus said as they left the building. "Then I'd like to see the church."

Some of the homes were damaged by trees growing too close to the walls, but most were in better condition just needing new roofs and floors. When they reached the church Archelaus noticed that there was no cemetery around it. One of the roof beams had collapsed into the chapel blocking the minister's office.

"I would like to see that amphitheater," Archelaus said

"It's a long walk," Sergeant Thaxter replied and Archelaus nodded.

"We'll provide tents and food to get you through until the homes can be rebuilt. There will be a lot of guests for the wedding. I know it's not possible to get everything rebuilt in time, but the buildings along this main plaza should be a priority. I really appreciate your village's willingness to help me accomplish this."

"It is thanks enough to know that that our efforts to prepare this town to host your wedding will give us a safe new home," Yves replied as they headed south.

The amphitheater appeared to be on the edge of where the stone was quarried for the town. The levels were uneven, but Sergeant Thaxter was right about it being usable without much work.

"We'll need a platform here in the center so we can hold the wedding right here," Archelaus said and Yves nodded. "I think I've seen enough if Yves has."

"Our men can definitely get done what you need in time for the wedding," Yves nodded. "Cutting down the trees that have damaged homes and roads will help get the wood we need. Not having to worry about growing food this year will leave us free to repair the town."

Archelaus smiled.

Chapter 16 -Protecting Her Subjects

Marriah yawned as she stepped out onto her balcony for some fresh air. There was so much to be done. She had been meeting with her grandmother, the ministers and district governors all day. She was finding out that Brinley had some serious problems. At least in Dracona she would be able to ask Bryant, Sonje and Auberon for suggestions. She looked out over the city. She had learned that if Brinley's city expanded any further there would not be enough fields for the crops to feed all the people. The outlying villages were nestled in small mountain valleys and could not expand any further. At least that was one problem she had a solution to. Once the people of Glynis left Dracona, over crowding could be solved by moving some of Brinley's people to Dracona and then Merton after they left for Trinan. Tomorrow after breakfast she would be leaving for Dracona. Reluctantly she went back inside. Janina and Katina were waiting for her.

"You look exhausted, My Queen," Janina said gently.

"You should get some sleep," Katina added. "You must have had a long day. Fyodor is hoarse from translating."

"We should all get some sleep," Marriah said. "We have a long journey ahead of us."

Marriah lay awake for a while after going to bed. It seemed she had only slept for a few minutes before Katina was waking her.

"There is someone here to see you, Queen Marriah," she said as Marriah sat up.

"This early?" Marriah asked. "Who is it?"

"Fyodor's parents," Katina answered. "I met them yesterday. I really love them."

Marriah dressed quickly and Katina put her hair in a simple braid.

"Is Fyodor here to translate?" Marriah asked.

"They speak our language," she replied. "In fact they insisted that he not know they were here to see you."

Marriah nodded.

"Go make sure everyone else is packed and ready to go. I will see you after breakfast in the courtyard."

"Yes, My Queen," Katina said as she curtsied.

Marriah went into the sitting room where they were waiting for her. As she entered, they knelt.

"Rise," Marriah told them. "Come and sit down."

They looked a little nervous as they sat down. Marriah could see where Fyodor got his good looks.

"What can I help you with?" she asked as she sat down.

"First, we would like to express our gratitude to you for introducing Fyodor to Katina," the mother began. "She is such a wonderful young woman."

"We are also grateful that you have chosen him to go with you to Dracona," the father added. "It is a great honor for him."

"I am glad to hear that," Marriah replied.

"We were wondering if you could tell her parents," she said, then hesitated. "If they were interested of course."

Marriah smiled and said, "I think you should know that I chose Fyodor to accompany me back to Dracona to give him the chance to ask Katina's parents for her hand in marriage."

"Tell them that we give our blessings for Fyodor and Katina to be married," he said.

"Thank you," Marriah replied with a smile. "I will let her parents know."

There was a tap at the door and Fyodor's parents got up quickly. Marriah motioned for them to exit through the servant's quarters.

"Enter," she said once Fyodor's parents had left.

Fyodor entered with a tray of food. He placed it on a table with several chairs around it. Marriah stood as he turned and knelt before her.

"Rise," she said.

"Are your saddlebags ready to be taken to your horse?" he asked.

"There are a couple of things left to load," she replied. "I'll take care of that now so you can take them while I eat."

Marriah went into the bedroom and put the last of her belongings in. She took them in to where Fyodor was waiting.

"You should not have to carry such heavy things," he said, rushing to meet her.

"I have carried things much heavier than this," she told him. "As queen, I must not forget the burdens of my people. I must not become a burden to my people. Just as you are my servant, I am the servant of the people."

"I'm so grateful we have such a wise and kind queen," Fyodor said as he went to the door.

After the door closed behind him, Marriah smiled. Fyodor returned just as she finished eating. Soon they were mounted up and on their way with a packhorse following behind. The people that they passed waved. As evening approached they picked a spot to camp for the night. Gavynn and Fyodor began to set up the tent. Suddenly Fyodor cried out. Marriah turned to see a snake crawl away from him. She drew her sword and cut off the snake's head.

"Quickly," she said. "Get a cup."

Katina brought a cup. Marriah held the snake over the cup allowing its blood to drip into the cup.

"Katina, get Fyodor laid down with his head up a little and keep him still," Marriah ordered. "Gavynn, start a fire. Janina, get a pot of water ready to boil. Keep this from spilling."

"Will he be alright?" Katina asked with a tremor in her voice.

"You must keep him calm and still while I get the herbs for the medicine," Marriah said firmly.

Katina went to where Fyodor knelt on the ground. She helped him to lay down with his head on her lap. Marriah began to search for the herbs. She found several of the plants she needed. The last one was a special moss that grew only on certain trees. Her search took her farther from camp.

The sound of voices drew her attention. Two men were fighting and next to them was the tree she was looking for. One of the men was wearing the same tunic worn by Brinley's border patrols. The other man was larger and stronger than the patrolman. He cut the patrolman's sword arm, then stomped his left leg. She dropped the herbs next to the tree as she drew her sword and the patrolman collapsed to the ground.

"No!" she shouted as the man raised his sword again then turned to her.

His laugh only made her more determined. She deflected his first blow. His second slashed her right shoulder slightly. She concentrated on his blade until she saw her opportunity and deftly disarmed him. The sword fell at her feet and she stepped forward, putting her foot on it. Just then, two more patrolmen emerged from the trees at a run. They stopped short at the sight of her with her sword at his throat. They shouted something, but she couldn't understand their words. They had their swords drawn and looked confused. She tore open her sleeve with her left hand, exposing her wound and her armband. The man she held at sword point went white as the other two ran over to where she stood. One of them threw the man to the ground. The other looked a lot like the injured man.

Marriah cut several dead sticks into usable lengths. She plucked several leaves from a numbing plant at the base of the tree. She held up the leaves for the wounded man to see motioning to her own lips. He nodded and opened his mouth. She placed the leaves into his mouth. Next she began to rip strips of cloth from her petticoats. She handed one to the patrolman who stood watching her and pointed to the man's arm.

He began to bind the wound while she gathered the sticks she had cut. She knelt at the wounded man's feet. She first handed his companion a short stick then pointing to the wounded man as she put a second short stick between her own teeth. The man nodded and spoke to the wounded man. Once the stick was between the man's teeth, Marriah took the other's hands and put them around the broken leg above the knee. Marriah grabbed the wounded man's ankle and met the patrolman's gaze. When the man nodded, Marriah gave a hard tug. She carefully felt the leg and found that the bones were set. She splinted the leg with the sticks and strips of cloth. She stood and met the wounded man's eyes. He nodded as he removed the stick from his mouth.

Marriah took the sword and pried a piece of moss from the tree then picked up the moss and the herbs. She motioned for the wounded man and the patrolman who helped care for him to stay. She motioned to the other patrolman to bring the prisoner and follow her. As he was pulling the man to his feet, the grey wolf stepped out of the bushes. The men froze.

"We will need two of you to guard the prisoner and another rabbit for supper," she said.

The wolf nodded and disappeared into the forest. She motioned again for the man to follow her with the prisoner. When they entered camp, Fyodor was looking very pale.

"Gavynn, get some rope and tie the prisoner to a tree," she said as she went to the fire.

She dropped the herbs and moss into the cup with the snake's blood. She tore another piece from her petticoats and placed it over a second cup. After pouring some boiling water into the first cup, she carefully poured it into the second cup. She gathered the edges of the cloth up over the herbs and moss then lifted it from the cup to drip for a moment. After squeezing the remaining water from it she carefully stirred the mixture until it was cool enough to drink.

"Drink," she ordered as she pressed the cup to Fyodor's lips. "All of it."

He began to swallow the medicine.

"Will he be alright?" Katina whispered.

"I have done what I can, only time will tell," Marriah replied. "Gavynn, go with this man. One of his companions has a broken leg. Bring them back here."

"What about him?" Gavynn asked as two wolves stepped out of the forest into the tiny clearing.

"They will stand guard," she said as she stood up.

The wolves sat down on either side of the patrolman. They bared their teeth and growled softly. All of the color drained from the prisoner's face. The patrolman turned to her and smiled. She pointed in the direction of his companions and motioned back to the camp. He nodded. He and Gavynn went to get the other men.

A soft moan drew her attention back to Fyodor. His color was returning. He would recover.

She knelt down beside him and said, "Welcome back to the living."

He smiled weakly and whispered, "I'm supposed to be taking care of you."

"You're not the only one who needed my help," Marriah said.

"You're bleeding," Fyodor observed and tried to sit up.

"I've survived much worse," she said as she put her hand on his shoulder pushing him gently, but firmly back down. "Besides, right now I need your translating skills more than your protection."

Fyodor nodded.

"You will be weak for a few days," Marriah said.

"Let me look at that," Janina offered as she knelt next to Marriah. "It's not very deep. Let's get it cleaned and wrapped."

Janina had just finished bandaging Marriah's wound when Gavynn and the other men returned.

"Lean him up against this tree," Marriah said. "Put his leg up on those rocks."

Gavynn helped one of the men with the wounded man while the other tied the horses. Then the patrolmen knelt at Marriah's feet.

"Rise," she said.

They looked up and she motioned for them to follow her to where Fyodor was laying. They stopped as three wolves dropped rabbits near the fire and then left. The one who looked like the wounded man dropped to his knees at Fyodor's side and began to speak rapidly. Fyodor and the man spoke for a few minutes with the other man making an occasional comment.

When they had finished, Fyodor said, "They had heard that Brinley had a new queen, but had not expected her to be a warrior."

Marriah stifled a laugh and asked, "Who is this man who is now our prisoner?"

"He is a thief who has killed several people. He beats them unconscious then robs them. He stabs them several times and lets them bleed to death. Queen Aurita had ordered his capture and execution."

"We will need a grave dug then," Marriah said.

As Fyodor translated, Marriah glanced at the man. At hearing what she had ordered, he hung his head. Gavynn and the two patrolmen took small shovels from their saddlebags and went into the trees. Marriah brought a saddlebag to put under Fyodor's head so Katina could help prepare supper.

"My Queen," Fyodor said.

"Yes?"

"I am still learning the customs of Burton and Langward. I need to ask your advice."

"About?" Marriah asked, guessing at what he was getting at.

"How does one arrange a marriage in Langward?"

"I suggest that you ask Katina's father for her hand in marriage."

Fyodor nodded and said, "Then if he says yes, what do I do?"

"Notify your parents. I'm certain Katina and her parents will doing most of planning for the wedding."

"What if he says no?"

"I'm guessing that if you let her talk to him first, you will get the answer you want from him. You make her very happy. When she looks at you, I see the same look that Regina Sonje gives Regis Bryant."

"Thank you," he smiled.

"Rest now," she told him.

163

He nodded and closed his eyes. Marriah finished staking the tent while the women cooked dinner. She then got out her journal and began to write. She would have a lot to report when she arrived in Dracona. Gavynn and the two patrolmen returned looking dirty and tired. Marriah stood next to Fyodor and motioned for the prisoner to be brought before her. The two men untied him and led him to her. They released his arms and he dropped to his knees before her, face down, palms up.

"For your crimes against the people of Brinley, you must be punished," Marriah said, then waited for Fyodor to translate. "You will pay for the deaths of your victims with your own life."

The man sat up and nodded. Gavynn and the two patrolmen began to draw their swords. Marriah put up her hands and they stopped.

"I cannot ask my subjects to do something I am unwilling to do myself," she said to them.

They looked confused at Fyodor's translation, but sheathed their swords.

"It is by my hand that you will be executed."

The men looked shocked and opened their mouths to protest, but Marriah put up her hands again.

"Take him to his grave," she ordered and they complied.

The man fell to his knees next to the grave. He removed his belt which had a pouch on it and layed it at her feet. He then turned with his side to her and bowed his head. She drew her sword and raised it high before bringing it down on his neck. The man's head fell into the grave as his body collapsed beside it. She stood there for a few minutes, watching the blood run down her blade and drip on the ground. She understood how Bryant had felt about Larkin's execution. She finished ripping the loose piece of cloth from her sleeve and wiped her blade clean before sheathing it. The men dropped the body into the grave. Then they took up their shovels and began to fill the shallow grave.

"Look," Gavynn said as several wolves appeared.

The wolves began to dig at the piles of dirt, filling the grave more quickly than the men could. The grey wolf sat next to Marriah and watched with her hand resting on its head. When the task was complete Marriah turned to return to camp. Gavynn caught up to her.

"Are you alright, My Queen?" he asked.

"Taking another's life should never be an easy thing," she replied.

One of the patrolmen handed her the man's belt and pouch. It was heavy, so she opened it. The pouch was filled with coins. Once back in camp, they ate their meal in silence. It was fully dark when they finally spread out their bedrolls. The wounded man was given more leaves to deaden the pain and made as comfortable as possible.

Marriah was the first to awaken. She stirred the coals and rekindled the fire. As she added more wood, she wondered how Archelaus would react.

'He understands,' Tasia's voice was clear in her head. 'I had Haskell tell him last night. Haskell says both Archelaus and Bryant are proud of you.'

'That makes me feel better,' Marriah replied as she heard voices behind her.

She filled a pot with water and put it on the fire to heat. As she found the dry porridge, one of the patrolmen came over and pointed towards Fyodor. She handed him the porridge and went to see what Fyodor wanted. Fyodor looked much better than he had the night before.

"Feeling better?" she asked as she knelt down next to him.

"Much better, My Queen," Fyodor answered. "I'm still light headed and a bit weak."

"That should pass before we reach Dracona," she replied.

"I have something to ask you," he said. "These are my cousins Davon and Dallon. Davon told me how you set Dallon's leg with his help after disarming the thief."

"I had to set Father's arm once," Marriah explained and shrugged her shoulders.

"They were waiting for their replacements. They're due this morning," he continued. "They want to accompany you to Dracona. They owe you Dallon's life and what one does, the other does as well."

"I cannot claim a debt for that."

"I told them you would feel that way, but they insisted. Dallon insists that he can ride."

Marriah sighed and said, "Well, once in Dracona, I can get Brenndah and Raphello to repair his broken leg."

"They can repair broken legs?"

"Brenndah has before."

"How is that even possible?"

"Each person has different abilities and talents," Marriah said. "It is difficult to explain, but Dracona is a very different place. The people of Glynis live longer than we do. They have abilities that we don't. Remember the things you learned and saw in Langward?"

"I still can't believe that Regis Bryant is over two hundred and seventy," Fyodor said. "He only looks twenty seven."

"Look into his eyes," Marriah responded. "You can see it there. For over a hundred years he lived at Dracona with only his father. There are other things about Dracona that are different from Brinley or even Burton."

"Davon and Dallon want to send a message back with the other man so their parents know why they aren't coming home when expected."

"I want him to take the money back to be returned to the rightful owners," she said as she stood. "I'll get pen and paper."

Marriah got the writing materials for Fyodor. Soon the message was written and they had eaten breakfast. By the time they were packed, the relief patrol had arrived. With difficulty, they got both Dallon and Fyodor on horseback. Davon knew of a pass that would take a whole day and a half off their journey.

By evening they had crossed the summit. By the time they reached Langward, Fyodor was feeling much better. They discovered that Katina's parents had gone to Dracona. The villagers fed them and gave everyone a place to sleep for the night. Early the next morning, they left for Dracona. They stopped for the night early because Dallon's leg was aching. Marriah found more of the pain killing herb for him.

"Tell him that by this time tomorrow, he will be up and walking with hardly any pain," she told Fyodor.

"You're certain about this?"

"Tasia told me yesterday that Brenndah would meet us in the castle courtyard to heal his leg."

Fyodor nodded and spoke to his cousin. Dallon had a look of confusion and disbelief on his face.

"Tell him to have a little faith," Marriah said as she patted Dallon on the shoulder. "And that he will see many things in Dracona that he would not believe unless he saw them for himself. Tell him about what Regis Bryant did with the piece of wood."

As Fyodor spoke to his cousin, Marriah went to her saddlebags and drew out the wooden armband. Dallon's eyes widened as she handed it to him. He turned it over in his hands and examined it closely before speaking.

"He says that he still finds it hard to believe, but he will trust you," Fyodor said.

Chapter 17 - Return to Dracona

The next morning, Marriah gave Dallon more leaves before breakfast. She kept the pace slow. By midmorning they were approaching the outskirts of town. One of the men working on a new house waved and climbed down the ladder as they got to the house. Marriah dismounted and handed her reins to Janina.

"Marriah!" Bryant said. "You made it! We were getting worried."

"Dallon's leg hurt a lot yesterday, so we stopped early for night," she replied. "Can I meet with you tomorrow afternoon?"

"Of course."

"We had best get going for Dallon's sake,"

"Yes," Bryant said. "Haskell is getting impatient to see you."

"Regis!" a man called down from the roof. "We're ready for the last batch of shingles."

"Coming up," Bryant said as a large bundle of shingles began to rise up off the ground.

Marriah stifled a laugh as she saw the look on Dallon's face as he watched the shingles settle on a platform on the peak of the roof. The others had similar looks of shock and disbelief on their faces.

"There's a letter from Archelaus waiting in your room," Bryant said as he began to climb the ladder. "I'll see you for lunch."

Davon said something as she mounted and Fyodor asked, "Why is a king doing common labor?"

"You don't think he got all those muscles sitting on a throne?" she replied. "Later I'll tell you some of Dracona's history, but Regis Bryant rebuilt many of the roofs in the center of town by himself, including the church roof. Also there isn't an actual throne to sit on anywhere in Dracona."

Fyodor looked very puzzled. He translated as Marriah waved to people.

"Everyone seems to know you," Katina commented. "They all seem happy to see you."

Marriah just smiled. Soon they were at the castle. Philip and General Edgard were waiting with Brenndah and Raphello.

"I'm so proud of you, I could burst," General Edgard claimed as he lifted Marriah from her horse.

"Your training saved my life and his," Marriah said indicating Dallon.

Edgard and Davon lifted Dallon from his horse and sat him on the cobblestones. Brenndah carefully untied the splint.

"I'll need the boot off," Brenndah said.

"We'll have to cut it off," Marriah replied. "It's too swollen."

Dallon's eyes went wide as General Edgard produced a knife. Fyodor spoke to him.

Marriah took the knife and said, "I'll get him a new pair of boots."

She very carefully cut down the shank of the boot and along the sole until the boot could be pulled easily off. Then she cut his pant leg open. His leg was several colors of blue, purple and black.

"General Edgard, Raphello," Brenndah said as she put her hands on the swollen limb.

The men put their hands on Brenndah's shoulders. Dallon looked frightened. Fyodor took his hand and spoke to him. When Dallon nodded Brenndah and the men began to glow.

"You did a great job of setting the break," Brenndah complimented as the swelling shrank at her touch. "That makes this much easier."

Brenndah closed her eyes as her hands settled over the break. Her glow intensified for a moment before she opened her eyes and sat back on her heels.

"The rest of the bruising will clear in a day or so," she said. "Raphello, have a look at Marriah's wound while I heal the one on his arm."

"It's alright if there is a scar left," Marriah said. "That one I earned."

General Edgard laughed as the wound closed under Raphello's touch leaving a faint scar. Marriah smiled.

"Katina!" a woman's voice called from the direction of the castle.

"Mother! Father!" Katina cried as she ran to them. "I've missed you!"

"You look happy," her father said. "Agatha sent us to help with your belongings and to show you to your rooms."

Servant Queen

Katina led them over to the group. Fyodor had Dallon on his feet. Dallon smiled from ear to ear as he took a few steps. He then knelt before Marriah and Brenndah. Brenndah glanced at Marriah.

"He's grateful to you for healing his leg."

Brenndah nodded as Dallon got to his feet. Katina's parents bowed to Marriah.

"Welcome back, Queen Marriah," they said.

"Thank you," she replied.

"Mother, Father, you remember Fyodor," Katina said as she put her hand on his arm. "And Janina and Gavynn."

"So good to see you again. Welcome to Dracona," Katina's mother said.

"This is Fyodor's cousin, Dallon, and Fyodor's cousin Davon," Katina said, her hand still on Fyodor's arm. "They don't speak our language, but Fyodor is going to teach us theirs."

"Then we should learn to speak it as well," Katina's father replied with a smile.

"Why don't you start taking things up?" Marriah said. "Fyodor and I need to take Dallon to the tailor and cobbler shops. Davon can help you."

Philip brought out a small carriage while Katina, her parents, General Edgard and Davon picked up the saddlebags and headed for the castle. Dallon said something to Fyodor which made him blush. As he helped her into the carriage, Fyodor was still blushing.

"I suggest you talk to her father directly after lunch," Marriah said as they started out the portcullis. "I think he has guessed what is going on already. He didn't seem upset by her show of affection toward you."

Marriah glanced back to see Fyodor's face get even redder before he hid it in his hands. Dallon began to laugh and elbowed him.

"What will my parents say if I come home engaged or married?" Fyodor moaned through his hands.

"I wouldn't worry about that too much," Marriah said. "Here we are."

She led them into the tailor's shop. Aurora was busy with measuring a child when they entered.

"I'll be right with you, Marriah," she said. "I see you'll need some pants for him."

Soon she was finished with the child and began to measure Dallon.

"I think I have a pair of pants that will fit," Aurora offered. "They were returned because the man's wife didn't like the color."

Aurora disappeared into the back then emerged carrying a pair of grey pants. Dallon spoke to Fyodor.

"He likes the color of the pants," Fyodor said.

Aurora pointed to the fitting room door and handed the pants to Dallon. He soon came out of the fitting room holding three small brass coins. Aurora smiled and took the coins.

"Thank you," Marriah said as she motioned for the men to follow her.

They went down the street to the cobbler's shop. The cobbler promised to have some boots ready by suppertime after measuring Dallon.

Fyodor asked. "I have never heard that language before."

"You'll hear it a lot around here," Marriah responded. "He'll have the boots ready by suppertime."

Once back at the castle, Marriah took them up to their rooms. Davon said something to Fyodor after kneeling before Marriah.

"He says this room is not servant's quarters," Fyodor said.

"There are no servant's quarters in this castle," Marriah explained. "Nor in all of Dracona."

"None?"

"None," Marriah said firmly. "It will be time for lunch soon. Tell Dallon not to worry about having bare feet at lunch. News travels fast around here. The dragons know everything that is going on and soon everyone else does as well. I will come to get you for lunch."

Marriah was grateful to get a bath and put on clean clothes. She sat down and read Archelaus' letter. She liked his idea of building a town named Union between Brinley and Burton. She wrote a reply, sealing it with wax and the imprint of her signet ring. She sighed as she realized that it was time for lunch. She knocked on the door of Janina and Gavynn first. Katina was in her parents' room. Fyodor answered the door and called to his cousins. Dallon had found some boots in the closet, but they looked loose. She got them settled at a table before taking her seat at the head table. Bryant stood and the room fell silent.

"We are glad to welcome our friend, Queen Marriah of Brinley, back to Dracona," he announced. "And we would like to welcome our new friends from Brinley."

Marriah smiled as she saw the men's surprised expressions at the announcements. As they ate, she watched Fyodor glancing at Katina's father.

"Haskell has been laughing over Fyodor and Katina" Bryant commented. "He says they are in love."

"If he can get up the nerve to talk to her father, there will be a wedding soon," Marriah confessed with a smile. "His parents told me they give their blessings for him to marry her. They requested he not be told that they had spoken to me."

"You're joking."

"No," she replied. "And as queen of Brinley, I can marry them."

"No wonder Haskell has been in such a good mood."

"If he doesn't talk to Katina's father before supper, I will," Marriah said. "I think he's a bit nervous around Ethan."

"Haskell says he's terrified of Ethan," Bryant laughed.

"I've got to go talk to Haskell. I'll take them to see the cavern."

"Is your message to Archelaus ready?"

"Yes, it's up on my table."

People were beginning to leave the room as Marriah made her way to where her servants sat. The idea of having her own servants was still strange to her.

"It's time for me to go tell Haskell all about everything since I left Dracona," she said as she reached the table. "He is anxious to meet those of you he hasn't met."

"We'll all go," Katina's father said.

They all followed her out to the great hall and into the cavern where Haskell was waiting at the entrance to his den.

"The sand is cooler near the wall," Marriah told them.

Fyodor and his cousins were talking. Davon and Dallon sounded panicked as she led them up the steps to the ledge. Marriah heard Haskell's laugh in her mind.

'They are visualizing me eating them,' Haskell told her.

Marriah went over to where they stood at the top of the steps.

"Tell them that dragons never eat people, only cattle," Marriah said. "Then tell them that this dragon saved my life."

They calmed down a little, but still seemed unconvinced.

"Tell them that if there was any chance of Haskell eating them that I would not do this," she said and went over to Haskell.

He put his head down and she stroked his cheek. Then she sat on his foreleg and settled back against him. She tried not to laugh as their mouths hung open. At Fyodor's urging, they finally came closer. Fyodor walked up to Haskell and knelt before him before stroking his cheek. Dallon and Davon's eyes grew wide as they watched. They then knelt before Haskell.

"Tell them that I guarantee their safety in Dracona," Marriah said.

They were a bit calmer after hearing the translation. Marriah noticed that Katina's father and mother were watching Katina with pleased looks on their faces. Katina was watching Fyodor.

"Haskell, you know Katina and her parents, Ethan and Kora as well as Janina and Gavynn. You met Fyodor in Langward. These are his cousins Davon, and Dallon."

'Welcome to Dracona,' Haskell replied.

After Fyodor had translated, Marriah said, "You can go do whatever you want to for about three hours. I'll be in the library. It's on the third floor above the dining hall."

While the others began to leave, Katina's parents stayed. Katina noticed they weren't coming, but left when her mother motioned for her to go.

Once the others had left the cavern, Ethan bowed and said, "We would like to speak with you for a moment, Queen Marriah."

"Certainly," Marriah responded, curious as to what they wanted.

"Katina has told us all about Fyodor and that she loves him," he said. "It is obvious that he is fond of her as well."

"She is so happy now," Kora said. "Her eyes light up when she speaks of him or hears his voice."

"I have noticed that he has the same reaction to her," Marriah commented which seemed to please them.

"He appears to be a very suitable husband for Katina," Ethan said.

"You might be interested to know that his parents have met Katina and love her," Marriah said.

Their faces lit up at the news.

"In fact, they give their blessings for Fyodor and Katina to get married," Marriah confessed. "I told Fyodor that it is customary for a man to ask a woman's father for her hand in marriage, but he is very nervous and shy."

"What will we do if he doesn't ask?" Kora fretted.

"We have to give him plenty of opportunity," Marriah suggested.

Katina's parents smiled and nodded.

"Why don't you take Katina down to the tailor's shop to be measured," Marriah said, pointing to Kora. "You take a carriage and show the others around town. That will give him a chance to get a little more comfortable around you."

"Then how do we arrange a more private meeting between Fyodor and me?" Ethan asked.

"I'll think of something," Marriah assured him. "Near suppertime Kora can take Katina and go the cobbler's to see if Dallon's boots are ready."

'They are standing out in the great hall trying to decide what to do,' Haskell informed her.

"Go now while they are still trying to figure out what to do with three hours," Marriah told them.

Once they were gone, Marriah began to laugh. Haskell was shaking with laughter. One way or the other, Fyodor and Katina would be engaged before the day was done.

She visited with Haskell for a while before going up to see Sonje. Marriah found Sonje sitting at the table reading.

"Marriah, you do look like a queen," she said. "I'm so happy for you."

"It's such a relief to finally know about my father's past," Marriah replied. "But, Brinley has a lot of problems that Archelaus and I will have to deal with."

"Bryant and I will be happy to give you any help we can."

"Thank you," Marriah said as she sat down. "I have asked Bryant if we could meet tomorrow afternoon."

"We'll have to meet here or in the library. The stairs are just too much, so unless I walk down to the library, I'm stuck here."

"I'm certain it will be worth it," Marriah said as she gave Sonje a hug.

"Go and see Hoyt now," she replied.

Hoyt was very interested in every detail of Marriah's trip. They talked about it until Fyodor and his cousins came into the library. Their arms were loaded with papers and packages. They were talking about something they seemed excited over as they placed the things on a nearby table then knelt before Marriah. Hoyt looked astonished.

"Rise," she commanded. "Hoyt, I would like you to meet Fyodor and his cousins Davon and Dallon."

They each bowed in turn as they were introduced.

"This is Hoyt, Minister of Education," she introduced. "What are all those papers and packages you brought in?"

"Everywhere we went, people stopped us and insisted we wait for them to write a note to you or bring a package to you," Fyodor replied. "Even some of the children!"

Dallon made a comment.

"They would also ask Dallon how his leg was," Fyordor explained.

Dallon said, "Much better, thank you."

"I see," Marriah laughed as the others walked in.

"We are surprised to find that even the children here can read and write," Fyodor continued. "In Brinley, few besides the nobles, castle servants and some of the military officers are taught to read and write."

"In Glynis and Dracona, we have always started teaching children at a young age," Hoyt explained. "Being able to read and write can help everyone."

"I donated all the property that I held to the village for a school," Marriah added. "If I had been able to write, I would have been able to tell someone what had happened."

"Everyone here is so happy," Fyodor said. "I wish Brinley could be like Dracona."

"I want my grandchildren to be able to read and write," Ethan mentioned. "Whether they learn at school or their father teaches them."

Both Fyodor and Katina blushed at the comment. Marriah could see the hint of a smile play on Hoyt's face.

"I do want to make certain that everyone can read and write," she asserted. "And we can solve the overcrowding problem by moving people to Merton and Dracona once they are vacant."

"Merton?" Fyodor asked.

Marriah found a map and laid it out on the table.

"Here is Dracona, and here is Merton," she pointed out on the map.

Davon said something and Fyodor gave a long response. Both Davon and Dallon gave looks of confusion and disbelief.

"Do you think that Regis Bryant would help explain why Merton and Dracona will soon be vacant?" Fyodor asked.

*****

"I'd be happy to," Bryant acknowledged from the mezzanine where he had been watching for a while.

They all looked very surprised. Peregryn and Haskell had kept him apprized of what was going on. He knew how Fyodor felt about asking a potential father-in-law for his daughter's hand.

"Davon and Dallon don't quite understand why those of Glynis must leave," Fyodor explained. "Perhaps you could show them?"

"I think so," he said as he took off his shirt.

He brought a chair to the railing and stood on it. Once his wings were ready, he stepped on the railing and off the mezzanine. He circled the room before landing near them. Davon and Dallon had rushed toward the doors to catch him. Katina had her face buried in her hands against Fyodor's chest.

Fyodor was patting her back saying, "It's alright, dear. He isn't hurt at all."

Ethan and Kora were smiling at his efforts to calm Katina. Bryant put his hand on her shoulder.

"Katina," Bryant said. "Look at me."

She turned around slowly, peeking out from between her fingers.

"Even without these wings, I would be able to do that without being hurt. I can lift things with my mind."

Katina nodded as she put her hands down.

"Soon more of the people of Glynis will have wings like these. In time all of us will. We have learned that our stay in this place was only meant to be temporary. Before a year from now, we will all leave and move onto the ship that brought our people here. We will leave a few years later to return to our true home."

Fyodor began to translate for his cousins. Davon reached towards a wing and Bryant nodded. His touch was gentle, as he spoke to Fyodor.

"They are amazed that a man could have such wings," he said. "When did you find out that you had them?"

"Quite recently," Bryant replied. "But I learned about Sonje's the night before our wedding."

"What did you do?"

"It didn't matter to me," Bryant admitted. "By then I loved her too much for that to bother me. Besides, I had finally gotten her father to like me. I couldn't give up then."

Fyodor still had his arm around Katina's shoulders but dropped it suddenly after glancing at Ethan.

Fyodor cleared his throat and said, "I need to speak to you, Ethan."

"I'll need some help getting these things up to my room," Marriah chimed in and the others began helping her pick up the papers and packages. "Katina, can you see if Dallon's boots are ready? Gavin and Janina can show you the way."

*****

Marriah led the men up to her room. She was glad that Fyodor had decided to talk to Katina's parents. Bryant had actually been a big help in giving him just the nudge he had needed. They came out of the room just in time for Katina to show up with Dallon's boots. He looked very pleased as he put them on. Kora and Ethan came down the hall behind her.

"Katina," Kora called as she and Ethan saw them. "You are wanted in the library."

"Who?" Katina began to ask.

"Just go," Ethan said.

Marriah nodded and Katina left. Once she was out of earshot, Marriah gestured Kora and Ethan to into her room.

"Well, what happened?" she asked.

"He did it!" Kora exclaimed.

"He's waiting for her in the library," Ethan added.

Bryant said, "Sonje wants to have a welcome home party. She's not been able to go up and down the stairs. She needs something exciting to do."

"That would be great," Marriah smiled. "Let's go down to supper."

Gavynn and Janina came out of their room as Marriah knocked on Dallon and Davon's door. As they reached the third floor, Dallon touched Marriah's arm and pointed across the great hall. Marriah turned to see Fyodor and Katina in front of the library doors.

"Look," she said as they kissed.

"Much better," Dallon said.

"Yes, much better," Kora agreed.

Before supper, Fyodor came up to the head table to speak to Marriah. He looked very happy.

"He called me his son!" he said excitedly. "And Katina said she wanted to be my wife."

"Congratulations," Marriah replied. "We can talk about the wedding after supper."

"Thank you, My Queen," he said. "Thank you."

"He has no idea," Bryant surmised in the language of Glynis. "Does he?"

"That everyone has been plotting to get him engaged to Katina since before we left Brinley?" Marriah replied in the same language. "It seems that she has no idea as well."

Bryant laughed. Marriah watched the happy couple as she ate. At last supper was drawing to a close.

When she saw that everyone was finished eating Marriah went over to the table.

"We've been invited to a party. Follow me," she said.

They all followed her up to the royal apartment. Sonje hugged her as she entered the room. Auberon was there along with Hoyt, Ruth, Edgard, and Agatha. Cherie and Olvan were talking to Ruth and Auberon. Riva arrived with Jonath shortly after Marriah did. It was a while before she had a chance to talk to Riva.

"You look so beautiful and happy," Riva complimented as she hugged Marriah.

"You look happy as well," Marriah replied.

"I still miss Xylia, but my life is not quite so empty any more," Riva said. "For the first time in a very long while, I feel content to stay where I am."

"With people who love you and who will live as long as you will."

"Yes."

"We wanted to thank you for introducing us to each other," Fyodor said as he and Katina came up to her.

"I spoke to your parents and they gave their blessings for you and Katina to get married," Marriah revealed.

"Let's make some plans so your parents can come for the wedding," Kora suggested

"That would mean so much to me," Fyodor replied. "It's hard to believe this is real."

"I feel the same way," Katina agreed.

Fyodor kissed Katina.

Bryant watched Marriah closely as she turned away from Fyodor and Katina. He put his hand on her shoulder. As she turned towards him, he saw a tear roll down her cheek.

"I know that right now it seems that your wedding day is forever away," he told her. "The best advice I can give you is to keep busy. Why don't you go read the notes Fyodor and his cousins collected?"

"Thank you," Marriah said. "I think I will go visit Haskell for a while too before going to bed."

Bryant watched as she walked down the hall. Sonje joined him. They both knew what Marriah was going through. Haskell would let them know if she needed anything. People left in twos and threes until the room was empty.

Chapter 18 - Dealing With the Past

Bryant awoke after being asleep for only a few hours.

'Marriah needs watching over,' Haskell told him. 'I have not been able to keep her dreams from thoughts of Larkin.'

Bryant swiftly pulled on a pair of pants. He went to Fyodor, Dallon and Davon's room and woke them. They were confused, but got dressed. Bryant took them to Marriah's room. She was tossing and struggling.

"Marriah!" Bryant said as he put his hand on her shoulder. "Marriah, wake up!"

She opened her eyes and sat up. She put her face in her hands and began to cry.

"Larkin is dead," Bryant reminded her gently as he sat down on the bed and drew her into his arms.

Fyodor and his cousins were talking quietly before coming over to the bedside. They spoke gently to her and patted her back. Davon began to sing something softly. Marriah began to relax at last and lifted her head.

*****

"Are you going to be alright?" Bryant asked as he wiped her tears from her cheeks.

"I think so," Marriah said softly. "My father used to sing that song when I was very little. Could you bring me my drawing board?"

Bryant brought the board and case. She took out a piece of charcoal and began to draw. She drew her father as she last saw him, battling Larkin so she could escape. She then drew Larkin's execution. Finally, she drew her father holding a baby and singing.

"Messo Langward," Davon said pointing to the drawing.

"Yes," Marriah nodded. "Marriah."

Dallon and Davon nodded as she pointed to the baby. She turned to the drawing of Father and Larkin.

"Langward and Larkin," she said pointing to each in turn.

Davon and Dallon began talking with Fyodore. She didn't understand their words, but she understood the angry tone of voice they were said in. She turned to the drawing of the execution.

"Regis," Dallon said.

"Regis Bryant," Marriah acknowledged. "And Larkin."

She tore the drawing of the fight from the board after putting away the charcoal. Bryant handed her a dress and motioned the men out into the hall. Marriah was soon dressed and led them down to the caverns. Tasia was waiting for them.

'You have those two very confused and concerned,' Tasia's voice came into her mind along with images of Dallon and Davon. 'The third one is also concerned for you.'

Davon and Dallon's eyes grew wide as Bryant bowed low before the queen dragon followed by Fyodor. They cautiously stepped forward and knelt before her.

'I know,' Marriah thought back as she stroked Tasia's neck. 'I didn't think that Fyodor's engagement would affect me so strongly.'

'Even Haskell could not turn your thoughts.'

'It seems like forever until my own wedding. Perhaps when I spend each night in Archelaus' arms, I will truly feel safe.'

'You must keep yourself too busy to worry over such things,' Tasia said. 'Come burn that drawing. Haskell can explain to them why you have nightmares.'

"Have Haskell explain my past to them," Marriah said and Bryant nodded.

He motioned to the men to follow him as Marriah turned towards the tunnel leading to the volcano. Tasia walked beside her to the edge of the crater. She watched the drawing as it fell fluttering like a bird trying to escape.

'Go back to bed now,' Tasia commanded as she nudged Marriah in the direction of the great cavern.

'Thank you, Tasia,' Marriah said as she walked down the tunnel. 'You are a true friend.'

The men were waiting for her. Fyodor and his cousins quickly knelt at her feet. As they rose she saw tears flowing down their faces.

"We understand now," Fyodor admitted. "You are far braver and stronger than any warrior we have ever known."

Once back at Marriah's bedchamber, Bryant said good night, then left. Davon and Fyodor lay down at the foot of her bed while Dallon sat in a chair next to her bed. She slept soundly until morning. When she woke, Davon was in the chair and the other two slept at the foot of the bed.

"Thank you," she said softly to Davon before getting out of bed.

She gathered fresh clothes before going into the bathing chamber. She bathed and dressed before going back into the bedchamber. Dallon and Fyodor were beginning to wake when there was a tap at the door. Davon opened the door and General Edgard entered with a tray of food.

"You missed breakfast," he said. "Bryant said you were tired from the trip."

"Something like that," she confessed. "I think a practice duel or two would do me some good this morning."

"I'll be waiting in the armory for you," he replied as he bowed and left.

Marriah motioned for the men to come and eat. They looked at each other hesitantly.

"You will sit and eat with me," she commanded and Fyodore translated.

This time they quickly complied. They ate in silence, watching her closely.

'They are very nervous about eating at your table,' Haskell told her.

'They must learn that things are different in Dracona,' Marriah replied as she finished eating.

She stood up and they quickly rose to their feet. Dallon picked up the tray.

"Go get cleaned up. I'll be fine," she said and they quickly left.

Marriah sat down and began to write a letter to Fyodor's parents. She knew that they would be glad to learn that Katina's parents were eager to see the couple married as well. She was sealing the envelope when there was a knock at the door.

"Come," she said.

The men entered. They were freshly shaved and wore clean clothes. She led them down to the armory. General Edgard was polishing a shield when they arrived. Marriah got her practice blade and entered the practice ring. They looked alarmed as General Edgard entered the ring with his sword. Marriah held her hand out palm up and ran the edge of the blade across her palm. They relaxed a bit after seeing how dull the blade was.

General Edgard and Marriah circled before exchanging their first blows. General Edgard won the first match, but Marriah disarmed him in the second. They paused for a drink and brief rest before beginning the third match. This time she had found her concentration. The match lasted longer than the first two as General Edgard adjusted to her renewed strength and skill. This time she controlled the anger she was trying to vent. At last she saw her chance, and deftly disarmed General Edgard. She caught his sword in her left hand and brought its tip to join hers at his throat.

"Perfect," he panted.

They were both breathing hard as she returned his sword. He dropped to one knee before her with his blade laid across his palms.

"Rise," she said as she heard cheers from the side of the ring.

Janina, Gavynn and Katina had joined Fyodor and his cousins.

"That was incredible," Fyodor commented. "You could take the instructor at Brinley's Military Training Camp."

"I'll have to remember that when we return to Brinley," she said. "General Edgard is an excellent teacher."

"You are a dedicated student," General Edgard countered. "She is in here almost every day."

"Part of why I practice so often is because I still have a lot of anger for what Larkin did," she explained.

"King Archelaus practices with the castle guard almost daily as well," Gavynn revealed.

"I'm not surprised," Marriah said.

"It's almost lunchtime," Janina announced. "Would you like Katina and me to help you get cleaned up?"

"Yes," Marriah replied.

After lunch Marriah took Fyodor to meet with Regis Bryant and Regina Sonje. Regis Auberon joined them as well. This meeting became a regular event and grew to include Hoyt, General Edgard and Agatha. Marriah received a thank you letter from Fyodor's parents with the second report from Brinley. Fyodor was kept busy teaching Dallon and Davon to speak the local language, along with teaching Marriah and the rest of her servants the language of Brinley. Marriah was pleased to find that she learned more quickly than the others. She was also pleased to find that she caught on quickly to using the paints she bought at the Spring Festival at Burton. She painted several portraits of Archelaus and hung them in her room. After that, she slept better at night.

Chapter 19 - Not a Dream

Archelaus studied the language of Brinley between his regular duties as king of Burton. He also spent a lot of time training with the castle guards to keep his mind off the wedding. He inspected the town he had renamed Union twice and was pleased with the progress.

Two weeks before the wedding, Archelaus received a message from Dracona that Sonje had delivered the twins the day after Bryant's birthday. It was accompanied by a drawing from Marriah. Sonje and Bryant had named their daughter, Tsifira, and their son, Zayle. He laughed as he read that because of Malvin's Heart, it took Bryant three days to get back on his feet after the babies were born.

One week before the wedding, Archelaus went to Union to stay until after the wedding. There were many of the details that he wanted to oversee personally so everything would be perfect. The inn had been completed first, followed by some of the shops and houses. Yves, turned out to be very adept at coordinating the work. Leda and her sister Lyla were skilled wood carvers and provided beautiful pieces to decorate the inn with.

Burton's cook had come with Archelaus to set up the bakery and begin preparing the food for the wedding. Charles and Aunt Althea worked hard at coordinating the details of the wedding and guest accommodations.

"We should have started this a year ago, not two months ago," Charles exclaimed the evening before the wedding as he sank into the chair across from Archelaus.

"I had just gone from being a scullery boy to king of Burton a year ago," Archelaus responded with a yawn. "At that time I wasn't even thinking about getting married, but everything seems ready. Has she arrived yet?"

Before Charles could respond, Leda brought two men in and said, "My King, these men insist on delivering this in person."

At her words, the two men in matching tunics quickly knelt before him with their swords across their palms.

"Rise," Archelaus said in the language of Brinley. "What do you have for me?"

"We bring a message from Queen Marriah's own hand," one man said as he offered the envelope to him.

Archelaus broke the seal and pulled out the letter. It included a drawing of Marriah and him standing together.

'Dearest Archelaus, We have arrived safely. I count the minutes until we can be together. Until then, I have sent you a drawing of us. I send this message in the capable hands of Dallon and Davon. They are yours to command. With all my love, Marriah.'

"She has arrived," Archelaus told Charles with a smile. "These gentlemen can help with anything last minute. They are Dallon and Davon of Brinley."

Each man bowed as he was introduced.

"There isn't anything to do tonight," Charles said. "But, I'm certain that there will be plenty to do tomorrow."

"This carving is beautiful," Dallon commented. "Who carved this, My King?"

"Leda's sister, Lyla, carved it," he said as he stood up. "Leda did this one over here."

*****

Davon moved between Charles and Archelaus. He handed Charles a small folded paper and put his finger to his lips. He opened the paper quietly. It was from Regis Bryant.

'Charles, Queen Marriah is unaware that I have instructed Dallon and Davon on some modifications to the room King Archelaus and Queen Marriah will spend their wedding night in. Help them get King Archelaus to go to bed, so they can accomplish their mission. Regis Bryant'

Charles smiled as he stood up and motioned for Davon to follow him.

"You look tired, My King," Charles said. "Tomorrow is your wedding day."

"I am tired," King Archelaus admitted. "I'll let you get these men settled for night."

"Sleep well, My King," Dallon said.

"Good night," Charles added as King Archelaus left the room.

"He should be sound asleep within five minutes," Charles said quietly. "What did you have in mind?"

"We brought everything we will need," Davon responded. "I'll go get the bags off the horse."

He soon returned with two large bags and saddle bags over his shoulder. Dallon took one of the bags from him. Charles motioned for them to follow him up the stairs. He led them to a set of double doors near the top of the stairs. King Archelaus had personally overseen the finishing of the room and it was beautiful. All the decorations were in purple and blue. Dallon opened one of the sacks as Davon put down the saddlebags. Dallon drew out some cloth.

"We will need something to stand on," he told Charles.

Charles went into a room down the hall and found a step stool.

"Perfect," Dallon said as he took the stool and placed it under a beam.

Before long the two men had hung sheer curtains surrounding the bed by using poles tied to the roof beams.

"That makes it much more intimate," Charles said.

"Intimate?" Davon asked.

Dallon looked confused as well.

"Intimate," Charles repeated, blushing slightly. "Man and woman together alone."

"Yes," Dallon agreed. "Intimate."

Davon laughed and nodded as he drew an ornate gold bowl from the saddlebags. This he placed on the night stand next to the bed. He then placed a gold decanter on the stand next to the bowl.

"What's that for?" Charles asked.

Davon blushed and said, "Sweet oil to help make intimate."

"Oh," Charles nodded, also embarrassed by the explanation.

"We are finished," Dallon announced as he picked up the saddle bags and stuffed the sacks into them.

"We will sleep outside of King Archelaus' room," Davon said as they extinguished the lamps and left the room.

"I will get the bedrolls," Dallon added.

Charles showed Davon the door to the room of King Archelaus. He settled into his own bed with a smile on his face. He was glad Regis Bryant had thought of the improvements to the room.

*****

Marriah woke just after dawn. Janina and Katina were already awake and preparing breakfast. The wedding was scheduled for the afternoon. As she ate breakfast, Marriah realized it would be a long morning.

V.J.O. Gardner

"Don't look so serious," Sonje chided as she entered the tent with Aurella. "Today should be the happiest of your life."

"I just wish that this was lunch instead of breakfast," Marriah replied.

Sonje, Katina, Aurella and Janina all laughed.

"We'll keep you too busy to think about that," Sonje promised. "First you will need a bath and your hair washed."

Marriah was led into another tent where a large metal tub was filled with water. They washed her from head to toe including her hair. When she was dry, they gave her a robe to wear. They trimmed and buffed her fingernails and toenails. Then they showed her the most beautiful white gown she had ever seen. The dress was similar to the one she had worn in Brinley with the right shoulder left bare, except instead of metal plates, there were hundreds of tiny clear gems forming the pattern. The skirt was very full with a long train behind. The entire dress was sprinkled with tiny glittering clear gems. They brushed her hair until it shone before curling it with heated rods. They polished her circlet and armband. By then it was time for lunch. As they ate the delicious food they talked and laughed.

After listening for a while, Marriah asked, "What do I need to know before tonight?"

"Just remember that Archelaus loves you very much," Sonje told her. "You will know what to do if you follow your heart."

"I still feel nervous," Marriah admitted.

"Everyone feels nervous before their wedding," Janina laughed.

"I was nervous when I got married," Katina admitted. "But it was the best thing I ever did."

"I'm glad to hear that," Marriah said.

"King Archelaus has been nervous too," Aurella revealed. "He has been so very concerned about whether or not you would like everything."

"You and Archelaus belong together," Sonje stated. "You have been apart for long enough."

Agatha stepped into the tent and curtsied.

"I'm sorry to disturb you," she said. "But a couple claiming to be Fyodor's parents seek an audience with Queen Marriah."

"Send in just the woman," Marriah responded. "I can meet with both of them tomorrow."

Agatha curtsied and left. She soon returned with Fyodor's mother who placed two boxes at Marriah's feet before kneeling before her.

"Rise," Marriah said in Brinley's language. "It is good to see you again."

"Queen Aurita sends her love. She felt she could not travel so far at her age, but her heart is with you. She sent the royal wedding cloth and something Queen Aurita said she wanted her sons' wives to wear on their wedding days since she had worn it on her's. Your mother never got to wear it, but she said that it is now yours to wear."

She opened the square box to reveal a beautiful necklace and matching earrings. The blue stones of Brinley were complimented by diamonds.

"Thank you so much for bringing this," Marriah said as she put on the necklace. "This means so much to me."

"It was the least I could do after what you have done for our Fyodor and dear Katina," she replied.

"It is time to get you dressed," Sonje announced as she stood up. "I must feed the babies, so I will leave you in their hands now."

"Thank you," Marriah said as she hugged Sonje. "For everything."

Fyodor's mother stayed and helped the others get her dressed. They put a veil on her that fastened to her circlet before placing the bridal wreath on her head. Marriah hardly recognized herself when they held up a polished shield for her to look into. Even the veil had gems in it.

Archelaus' Aunt Althea entered and curtsied to Marriah before saying, "I just wanted to let you know how glad I am that you and Archelaus will soon be married. After his parents died, he became like a son to me."

"I'm happy to call you my aunt," Marriah responded as she hugged Aunt Althea.

"I must go now, but I'll see you later," she said before leaving.

When Sonje returned, she had changed her dress and Bryant came with her. Fyodor's mother went with the others when they went to change.

"You look so beautiful," Bryant told her. "Your father would be so very proud of you. I know that I am."

"Thank you so much for standing in for him," Marriah said. "You rescued me when I had lost all hope for survival. You saved my life in more ways than one. You have been like a father to me."

Bryant smiled and hugged her.

"Sonje thank you for standing in for my mother. You gave me back my dignity and honor. Besides giving me a chance to learn to read and write, you taught me how to be a queen, a ruler of people, and a servant of those people. You have been like a mother to me."

Sonje had tears in her eyes as she hugged Marriah tight.

"I'll never forget what you have taught me," Marriah promised. "And the love you have shown me."

Katina, Janina, and Aurella entered wearing matching blue gowns. Sonje and Bryant put on their crowns. After they arranged the veil over her face, Marriah was led out of the tent to a beautiful white carriage pulled by four white horses. Katina, Janina and Aurella sat in the front seat facing backwards. Bryant sat on Marriah's left and Sonje on her right in the back seat facing forward. Philip drove the carriage slowly through the town to a platform in front of a natural amphitheater.

"Are you ready?" Bryant asked as he helped Marriah from the carriage.

Marriah nodded. Through her veil, she could see that there were so many people that there was no room to sit. Brinley's Ministers and District Governors lined the path between the carriage and the platform. As she passed, they knelt. When they reached the top of the stairs, those on the platform curtsied or knelt including Archelaus.

"Rise," Marriah said, first in the language of Brinley, then in that of Burton.

As Archelaus stood, she felt her heart beat faster. He was also dressed all in white. He wore a tunic with patterns on it worked in clear gems like on her dress. His chest seemed broader, and his arms thicker than she remembered. He had a look of awe on his handsome face. Bryant lifted her veil from her face and kissed her cheek before placing her hand in Archelaus'. Sonje wrapped the royal wedding cloth around their hands.

Bryant waited for a moment before saying, "I, Bryant Donley, Lord Dracona, Regis of Glynis, Merton & Dracona, give this woman, Queen Marriah of Brinley, to this man, King Archelaus of Burton, that they become husband and wife. Before this happy occasion, they have each suffered trials of great magnitude. Trials of pain, sorrow and survival. Through these trials, they have learned lessons about the value of love and kindness. Today these two individuals will join as husband and wife to become one."

Bryant paused for a moment to let Fyodor finish the translation.

"Do you take this woman to be your wife, to love, honor and cherish in faithfulness for all your life?"

"I do," Archelaus said, first in Burton's language, then in Brinley's.

"Do you take this man to be your husband, to love, honor and cherish in faithfulness for all your life?"

"I do," Marriah said, as Archelaus had in both languages.

"Let it be known as they kiss, they seal their commitment and shall hereafter be known to all the world as husband and wife."

As Archelaus kissed her, his kiss grew from tender to passionate. She was almost dazed as their lips parted.

As she removed the cloth, Bryant held up two rings and said, "A ring is a circle that has no end. These rings symbolize that their love and commitment to each other has no end."

He held the rings out for them. Archelaus took the ring he had given her from her finger and slipped the other part in place before returning it to her finger. She took the ring she had designed for Sonje to make and placed it on Archelaus' finger. Then she took the bridal wreath from her head and threw it into the crowd.

"Today we unite more than just a man and a woman, we unite the Kingdom of Burton and the Kingdom of Brinley. Under their leadership they will flourish. There will be adjustments to be made along the way, but with unity comes strength," Bryant announced.

Charles came forward with a crown on a cushion. It matched the one that Archelaus wore, but was smaller and more delicate. Archelaus smiled as he picked up the crown.

"At my coronation as king of Burton, I promised the people of Burton to find a woman who was kind and noble of spirit and pure of heart to become my wife and their queen." Archelaus said. "You have these very characteristics. With this crown, I proclaim you queen of Burton."

He smiled at her as he placed the crown gently on her head. The crowd cheered. Aurella brought Marriah a cushion which held the armband for the king of Brinley.

She waited for the crowd to quiet before picking up the armband and saying in the language of Brinley, "As queen of Brinley, I have a similar responsibility to my people in choosing their king. I have found you to be kind, wise and trustworthy. The changes you have made in Burton have improved the lives of your subjects. I know that you will treat the people of Brinley with the same care and respect that you show the people of Burton. With great pride and joy, I place the royal armband of the king on your arm and proclaim you king of Brinley."

As she slid the armband in place the cheering of the people was almost deafening. Archelaus placed her hand on his arm and led her back to the carriage. She was glad to see the ministers and district governors were cheering as well. The carriage took them to a plaza in the center of the town. There were long tables along the center of the plaza that were laden with gifts. In one corner of the plaza, men were holding the lead ropes of a dozen horses, a large bull and six cows.

"All for us?" she asked Archelaus.

"Yes," he replied and patted her hand. "They have been arriving for a week now."

She could not believe the variety and generosity of the gifts. Scattered among the gifts were even drawings by children. Marriah could tell that some of the gifts came from the wealthy and neighboring royalty, but many came from the poor. She understood all too well the sacrifice made by giving these gifts. It was a sign of great respect. On the end of the last table, Marriah saw Evelina's gift. Sonje had created two dragons, each with a forefoot on the stone.

"This one is from Evelina," Marriah explained as Archelaus ran his hand along one wing. "She told Sonje how to mount it shortly before she died."

"These are a gift from Leda and Lyla," Archelaus said as they arrived at the end of the plaza.

In front of the inn were two carved thrones on a low platform.

"They are beautiful!" Marriah exclaimed as she stepped onto the platform.

She sat down in one of the thrones and Archelaus sat in the other. In small groups, people began to stand in front of them to pay their respects and offer congratulations. Dallon and Davon approached with an older couple. They were still wearing the lavender tunics and purple pants that they had worn for the ceremony. All four of them knelt before the man spoke.

"My name is Karl and this is my wife Sephira. We wanted to express our gratitude to you, Great Queen," the older man said in the language of Brinley. "We are in your debt. You saved Dallon's life and gave him and Davon the opportunity to go beyond being border patrol guards."

"I can claim no debt for doing my duty," Marriah responded. "As queen of Brinley, it is my sworn duty to protect and care for my people. Sometimes more literally than most of the time."

"We are told you were wounded in the fight," Sephira said. "But when you saw the healer in Dracona, you chose to keep the scar rather than let him heal it without any scarring."

"It is an honor to bear a scar earned while protecting another," Marriah explained. "It will remind me that I must strive daily to care for the safety and well-being of my people."

"We also wanted to thank you for allowing Davon and Dallon to accompany you to Dracona," Karl said. "It is a great honor for them to guard our queen."

"They were a great help to me while in Dracona. They did a lot to help me feel safe while I was away from King Archelaus," Marriah smiled.

Both Dallon and Davon blushed at her praise. After them, more people came and left. The ministers and district governors of Brinley came with their families. Most of them expressed surprise at Marriah's grasp of their language.

"How is it that you can speak the language so much better than I can?" Archelaus asked her between visitors.

"Hoyt thinks that because I had learned a second language that the third language was much easier," Marriah replied. "I'm still not fluent, but at least I no longer need a translator for every conversation."

The village council from Langward came and wished them well. Also some of the kings and queens from neighboring kingdoms offered their congratulations. Near suppertime, Bryant and Sonje came out of the crowd.

"Your supper has been delivered to your room," Sonje said. "And they are bringing over the cake for you to cut now."

"After that, you are free to go," Bryant grinned.

Marriah was glad to hear that. It had been a long afternoon with few breaks. It would be the first time in over two months that she and Archelaus would be alone and left undisturbed. The cake was carried over by six men and set in front of the thrones. Marriah had never seen such a large cake in all of her life. They cut the cake and fed each other a few bites before excusing themselves.

Archelaus' hand was trembling as he led her inside and up the stairs. At a pair of double doors, he stopped and turned to face her. As her eyes met his, something in his expression made her heart leap. He unlatched the door before he kissed her tenderly. Her heart began to beat even faster as he lifted her into his arms and carried her through the door.

He gently set her down near a table with a tray of food on it. He held her chair for her before taking his own seat. They ate in silence, just watching each other. He was so very handsome and regal. So much had changed since they had first met, yet it was still sometimes hard for her to believe that he had chosen her to be his wife and queen.

When they had finished eating, Archelaus stood and took her hand in his. She stood up and he led her to a chest of drawers. He took his crown and placed it on the chest of drawers. She placed hers beside his. She then took her circlet and veil off before placing them on the chest of drawers. She then removed the earrings and necklace, placing them next to her crown.

As she turned around, he dropped to one knee before her with his head bowed and said, "I am at your service, My Beloved Queen. Your wish is my command."

Her heart froze for a moment. She had certainly not expected this. He glanced up at her.

"My dearest Archelaus, words cannot begin to describe the longing in my heart for you," she said as she took his hand in hers and pulled gently.

As he stood, his eyes met hers.

"What Larkin sought to take by force, I give to you willingly," she said as she unbuttoned the buttons on the right side of her dress.

She then took his left hand in her right hand.

"Within me is an aching desire for the touch of your hands, your lips," she continued as she placed his hand on her waist where the dress was unbuttoned. "And for the feel of your bare skin against mine."

She closed her eyes as his lips met hers and she felt his hand on her back inside the dress. His kiss grew more passionate as she found the fasteners down the front of his tunic. She began to understand what she wanted of him the most, and he seemed to know exactly what she desired.

Chapter 20 - A Reward and a Duel

Bryant entered the inn with Edgard, Fyodor, Garman and Gavynn. Their wives had come in earlier and not come out yet. Charles met them in the great room.

"King Archelaus is sitting over there," Charles told them. "He sat down a half hour ago without saying a word and hasn't moved since."

Bryant chuckled as Charles led them to Archelaus. He was slouched in the chair, staring at the opposite wall with a half a smile on his face.

"I know that look," Bryant said to the others.

"It reminds me of the way Fyodor looked the day after his wedding," Gavynn affirmed with a laugh as Fyodor blushed slightly.

"Definitely the look of a newlywed," Garman agreed.

"Hi," Archelaus said as his eyes finally turned their way.

"We see that you had a very good time last night," Bryant observed.

"Oh, yes," Archelaus sighed.

"What's that on your neck?" Garman asked.

Archelaus unbuttoned three shirt buttons and held his collar open. Bryant could see that there were several bruises on his neck and shoulders.

"I returned the favor," Archelaus confessed with a sly smile. "But hers will be completely hidden under her dress."

"You must have had some night!" Bryant exclaimed.

"In her arms, I experienced pleasure more intense than any pain I have ever endured," Archelaus boasted with a smile on his face. "She is a very passionate woman."

The men all laughed at the expression on his face.

"Haskell was right," he added. "It was definitely worth waiting for."

"You are a lucky man, my friend," Bryant congratulated him as the women came down the stairs.

Archelaus quickly buttoned his shirt and sat up straight in the chair. Sonje said something as she glanced at Archelaus. All the women laughed. Archelaus blushed slightly, prompting laughter from the men.

"You can't hide much from women," Bryant chuckled. "And what one knows, they all know soon enough."

"You don't think that?!" Fyodor asked as his hand went to his own neck.

"Probably!" Bryant replied, laughing as Fyodor blushed red in spite of his dark skin.

Even Archelaus laughed then.

"Bryant," Archelaus said as the laughter died down. "This morning I realized that there were curtains around the bed that I didn't hang. And there was a bowl of oil on the night stand. You wouldn't know how they got there would you?"

"It was my idea, but Dallon and Davon volunteered to do all the work," Bryant admitted.

"Thank you," Archelaus said. "They helped make everything perfect. I'll have to think of something to do for Davon and Dallon in thanks."

"Do you know who they are?" Bryant asked indicating the two young women who had just walked in.

"Yes," Archelaus replied. "That's Leda and Lyla. Why?"

"Davon and Dallon have been watching them all morning," Bryant revealed as the women approached. "In fact, I bet they will come through the door in a minute or two."

Archelaus smiled and nodded as the women were close enough to hear what they said. They curtsied before Archelaus.

"My King, we have more requests for carvings than we have wood," one said. "Lyla and I need to go search for more wood in the forest."

"There are so many people around, that I worry about your safety," Archelaus noted in a serious tone. "I will send two men to assist and protect you."

"Thank you, My King," the other said.

"Dallon, Davon," Archelaus called. "I have need of you."

Bryant kept a straight face with difficulty knowing that the men had just shut the door behind them. They quickly crossed the room and knelt before Archelaus.

*****

"Rise," Archelaus said.

"What is your command, My King?" Davon asked.

"Leda and Lyla need to gather wood for carving from the forest. You will accompany them to protect them from harm and assist them in collecting the wood."

196

V.J.O. Gardner

"As you wish, My King," Dallon said, as he was obviously trying to not smile.

"Charles, have the cook pack a lunch for the four of them," Archelaus commanded as he struggled to remain serious. "Davon, Dallon, go get a work wagon from the stables. Yves will help you. Bring it back here to pick up Leda and Lyla."

"At once, My King!" Davon replied.

Once the men had gone, Archelaus revealed, "They are from Brinley and still learning our language. They are hard working and experienced swordsmen. You will be safe with them."

"Thank you, My King," Lyla said.

"You are most kind," Leda added.

Once the two women had left, the men began to laugh. Their wives joined them.

"What was that all about?" Marriah asked.

"Dallon and Davon were the ones who hung the curtains and set out the bowl of oil," Archelaus explained. "They volunteered to do it when Bryant explained the idea. I was just, ah, thanking them."

"They have been watching those women all morning," Aurella commented.

"So I heard," Archelaus smirked. "Little do they know that I just sent them to get a wagon from Leda and Lyla's father."

Everyone laughed at that revelation.

"You must come see Tsifira and Zayle," Marriah insisted before kissing his cheek.

"Yes," Bryant agreed. "Come see my children."

Marriah showed Archelaus the twins with Bryant and Sonje looking on. They sat side by side, each with a baby in their arms. He marveled at how tiny and perfect Zayle was. Archelaus laughed as Zayle pulled his finger into his mouth with his tiny fist.

"He's sucking on my finger," he laughed at the sensation. "His hands are so tiny, yet perfect. He's amazing!"

Marriah pulled Tsifira's booties off and said, "Look at her feet."

"What tiny toes!" Archelaus exclaimed. "Babies are so incredible."

"Just wait until you have to feed them and change their diapers in the middle of the night," Sonje laughed. "Every night."

"It would be worth it," Archelaus replied. "To have a son or daughter to hold in my arms and watch them grow. To teach them

197

what I know. To know that after Marriah and I die, a part of us lives on."

"I'm glad to hear you feel that way," Marriah admitted. "I want to bear your children and have our home filled with their laughter. To teach them to read, to write and to love."

"And every one of them, boys and girls, will learn how to fight, negotiate, cooperate and survive in the forest," Archelaus added.

"That would make my father very happy," Marriah said softly.

Archelaus leaned over and kissed her cheek as Zayle began to fuss.

"What's the matter, little one?" Archelaus asked. "Are you hungry?"

"It is time for them to be fed," Sonje acknowledged as she knelt in front of Archelaus.

He kissed Zayle's forehead before handing him to Sonje. He then put his arm around Marriah and played with Tsifira's feet. Bryant followed Sonje into their tent.

*****

After lunch more people came to congradulate them. During a brief break Marriah noticed General Caddaric arguing with a man. The argument became quite heated before the man finally stormed off leaving the general standing in the plaza shaking his head.

"That looks like trouble," Archelaus echoed her thoughts.

"I wonder who that was," Marriah pondered as General Cadderic turned towards them.

Marriah motioned for him to come over to them. He strode over with a troubled look on his face.

"We noticed you arguing with someone," Marriah said before he could kneel. "It appeared if he hadn't left you would had drawn your swords."

"Tarl and I don't agree with each other at all," General Cadderic admitted. "Your uncle appointed him sword instructor as a favor to Tarl's father. He claims he will be taking my position as commander of the army."

"Davon and Dallon have told me a lot about Tarl and I learned a lot from reading Uncle Burkhart's jounal," Marriah confided. "Fyodor echoed their opinions. Although I would prefer to not change anything right away I feel something really needs to be

done immediately about Tarl. Have a guard deliver a message to
him that he is challenged to a duel in an hour behind the stables."

"You want me. . ."

"No," Marriah interrupted him. "I am the one who will face
Tarl, but I don't want him to know that."

"My Queen, you should not endanger yourself by facing
him," General Cadderic pled. "I dare not repeat what he said about
you and your father."

Marriah was touched by his concern, but knew she would
have to be the one to defeat Tarl. She already had an idea of what to
do with him, but hadn't thought she would need to deal with him so
soon.

"I am perfectly capable of defeating Tarl in a duel," Marriah
assured him. "I want Davon and Dallon to witness the duel."

"I'll send them a signal," General Cadderic said and
Marriah shook her head.

"No, I don't want Tarl to know who he will be dueling and
who will be watching until the time is right. I'll get the message to
them."

*****

Dallon was enjoying spending time with Lyla while they
ate. Davon and Leda were getting along well. They spent a couple
of hours cutting and loading wood into the wagon.

"The wagon is full," Dallon said as he wedged one last
piece in place.

He noticed that Lyla almost seemed disappointed. As he led
the horses to turn the wagon around, he heard a squeak. Leda was
pointing in the direction of the road. A grey wolf stood in the
middle of the road.

"It's the queen's wolf," Davon remarked. "It will not hurt
us."

The wolf looked at them, then towards the town several
times.

"Has Queen Marriah sent you?" Davon asked.

The wolf nodded.

"It is a summons from the queen," Dallon explained. "We
must go now."

He tucked the axe in next to the basket as Davon helped
Leda to the seat of the wagon. As he helped Lyla up, he realized that
there was nowhere for Davon and him to ride.

199

"Get up here," Leda said.

The men obeyed, not knowing what she had in mind. When they got halfway up to the seat, Leda stood and moved closer to Lyla.

"Sit down, Davon," she ordered.

He sat hesitantly on the seat where Leda had been. Once he was seated, she sat on his lap with one arm around his neck and Davon blushed. Dallon swallowed hard as Lyla stood up. He sat down and she sat on his lap. He dared not speak, knowing that his brother was also wondering what Yves would have to say when they pulled into the stables with his daughters sitting on their laps. They returned to the stables as quickly as they could without losing any of the wood.

There were some people in the yard behind the stables as they pulled into the passage between the stables and carriage house. Dallon pulled the horses to a stop just behind Fyodor and Garman. Brinley's sword instructor, Tarl, stood alone in the center of the yard.

"Am I to fight one of those two pups?" he sneered pointing to Dallon and Davon.

"No," Queen Marriah countered as she stepped forward. "It is me who challenges you."

"You certainly have more spine than your cowardly father," Tarl jeered. "Maybe I'll put on a blindfold to make it a fair fight."

"You will need both of your eyes open," Queen Marriah stated calmly. "I know the truth of why my father left Brinley. He was no coward."

"He told you lies," Tarl growled.

"Actually he told me nothing about the matter or Brinley," Queen Marriah answered as General Edgard brought the practice blades into the center of the yard. "I found a letter he wrote to his mother, Queen Aurita. And I have read King Burkhart's journal. Both give the same explanation for him leaving Brinley. It had to do with respect, something you know nothing about."

Dallon smiled at that. The sword instructor respected no one. Tarl snarled and raised his blade, preparing to attack. Queen Marriah stood perfectly still. The man charged her, but his blade met only air. He turned quickly to find her ready for the next attack. This time, her sword deflected his blow and she slid her blade along his chest as if to cut it.

That seemed to anger him even more. He attacked again, but again her blade deflected the attempt and slid across his chest. He backed off a bit and circled. His next attack came without warning, but Queen Marriah had no trouble countering the attack. As he came in for another try, she met him solidly and knocked his sword into the air.

His face went white as her sword point rested on his throat. She caught his sword and brought its point alongside hers. Dallon laughed and his brother joined in. They both had been on the receiving end of Queen Marriah's wins. The man had it coming. His personal mission was to humiliate others. It was good to see him suffer a little humiliation himself.

"Davon, Dallon," Queen Marriah called.

Leda and Lyla stood and allowed them to leave the wagon. They hurried to the center of the yard and knelt before her, one on each side of Tarl.

"Rise, faithful ones," she commanded. "Take him to the inn and sit him on a chair on the porch. He is not to move until I command it."

"At once, Great Queen," they replied in unison as they each took an arm.

*****

Marriah lowered the swords and they drug Tarl out of the yard. She smiled as she watched them go.

"They enjoyed that," Archelaus observed as he joined her in the center of the yard.

"I knew they would. That is why I wanted them to see it," she replied. "His swordsmanship is poor and his teaching methods are crude and cruel. Even Burkhart complained about his treatment at that man's hand, and apparently his father was one of Burkhart's friends."

"It sounds like he needs to be replaced," Archelaus said as they walked to the stables. "What will we do with him?"

"I have an idea I think you'll like," Marriah responded. "But first I think we should help get that wagon unloaded. It will give Tarl some time to think."

Yves was asking his daughters what happened while they were gathering wood.

"They were complete gentlemen, Father," Lyla insisted.

"It was my idea that they sit up on the wagon seat with us on their laps. The wagon was too full for them to ride anywhere else," Leda added.

"Is there a problem?" Marriah asked.

"I'm just wondering if Dallon and Davon's intentions toward my daughters are honorable, considering they rode into town with my daughters on their laps," Yves said.

"I trust those two with my life," Marriah assured him. "You have nothing to worry about. They know that they are expected to ask your permission if they want to pursue any relationship with your daughters."

"That makes me feel a little better," Yves said.

After the wagon was unloaded, Marriah and the others went to the inn. Marriah's things had been moved into the Bridal Suite. She put on her sword and picked up Burkhart's journal before returning to the porch. A small crowd of curious onlookers including Brinley's ministers had gathered. Davon and Dallon stood at attention watching the prisoner intently. Marriah paused to keep from laughing before stepping off the porch and into the plaza.

"Bring the prisoner," she ordered as she and Archelaus stepped onto the platform and sat down on the thrones.

Dallon and Davon each had a firm grip on an arm as they led Tarl in front of the platform. The man was very angry.

"In the last two months, I have learned much about your career as sword instructor at Brinley's military training camp," Marriah announced.

"From these two?" Tarl accused with contempt in his voice.

"And from the journal of my uncle, King Burkhart," she replied as she held up the journal. "His comments agree with Dallon and Davon's completely. I have learned that your methods include humiliating your students every chance you get, subjecting them to degrading punishments and encouraging the torture of the weaker students by the stronger ones. This has resulted in several students being permanently disabled or disfigured."

Marriah paused to let her words sink in.

"It is time for great changes in Brinley. The first change is that you will no longer teach swordsmanship," Marriah continued.

Tarl's face contorted as he snarled. Marriah stood up and stepped forward.

"Tarl, you will spend one year imprisoned learning to carve stone. At the end of that year, you may be released if your attitude has improved. At the time of your release, you must live by the following three rules. First, you must earn enough to feed, clothe, and house yourself. Second, you will never be allowed to teach again. Third, and most important, if you ever hold a sword again you will be executed."

The man lunged at Marriah, but stopped short at the sight of her drawn sword. She had anticipated this reaction from him.

"This is no practice blade," she assured him calmly. "I personally executed the man who attacked Dallon with this same blade after confirming that Queen Aurita had ordered it upon his capture."

All of the color drained from Tarl's face and he fell to his knees.

"As for my father," Marriah continued. "Prince Langward left Brinley because King Burkhart had no respect for him. From reading my father's journal, I learned that he had known for years that the only way he could get that respect from anyone would be to leave Brinley and start a new life."

"That is why he did not return to claim Brinley's throne," Tarl surmised quietly.

"No," she replied. "My father was killed just over six months ago protecting me from the man who killed my mother then enslaved Father and me for almost eight years. He gave his life so that I could live. The village where we lived now bears his name."

"I take back everything I ever said about Prince Langward and you, Queen Marriah," Tarl apologized, speaking the names for the first time. "Prince Langward was a greater man than anyone knew, and you are far superior to me with the sword and in wisdom. I can now see that my father and I are in part responsible for Prince Langward leaving Brinley and his death. I will serve my sentence knowing I do not deserve such generosity."

With that, he laid out flat on the ground, face down and palms up. Marriah glanced out of the corner of her eye to see how Brinley's ministers were reacting to this. They were staring at her.

"Rise and return to your chair on the porch until more secure quarters can be found for you to stay in."

The man got to his feet and returned to the chair without needing to be drug by Dallon and Davon. Brinley's ministers came and knelt before Marriah and Archelaus. Marriah sheathed her sword and sat back down.

"Rise," she said.

"Brinley is fortunate indeed to have such wise and compassionate rulers," Prime Minister Adamok said. "We want to know how we can help to make these changes you spoke of."

"We will meet tomorrow morning," Marriah answered. "Come to the great room of the inn after breakfast and we will go over the changes we have planned."

"Notify the district governors of the meeting," Archelaus added. "They are expected to be there also."

"At once, My King!" Adamok responded and they hurried off.

"Dallon and Davon enjoyed that even more than seeing him beaten by you at the stables," Archelaus told her as they left the platform. "I am very proud to have such a wise wife. You handled that as though you had been queen of Brinley all of your life."

"I'm glad you feel that way," she replied. "You at least knew that Burton's throne was rightfully yours. I didn't even know Brinley existed three months ago."

Bryant and Sonje found them as they walked up the plaza.

"The wagon we used to transport Larkin in is on its way here," Bryant advised them.

"Thank you," Marriah said. "Now we just need to find somewhere we can lock him up until the wagon arrives."

Yves came up to them and bowed low before saying, "As we were repairing houses on the west side we discovered one that appeared to actually be a place to keep prisoners."

"Let's have a look at it," Marriah said as Sonje and Bryant went back toward their tent.

Yves led them to the building that was on the edge of the town near the waterfall. The main room had a desk with a chair in the center and a wall at one end. On the other side of the wall there was a single bed and a chamber pot.

"How soon can it be finished enough to house the prisoner?" Archelaus asked.

"We can finish the roof over one cell before the end of the day," Yves answered. "I found the keys in that desk."

Archelaus pulled open the center drawer and picked up the keys. He unlocked both of the barred doors. Each room had a bed, a chair, a small table and a chamber pot.

"Please let me know as soon as this is ready," she requested as Archelaus set the keys back in the drawer.

"Yes, My Queen," Yves replied as they left the building.

When they arrived at the inn Davon and Dallon were still guarding the prisoner. Fyodor and Garman stepped out onto the porch as they arrived.

"Can you two relieve Davon and Dallon long enough for them to eat?" Marriah asked them.

"Our pleasure," Garman responded.

"Has the prisoner been fed?" she asked.

"Not yet, but the cook was going to send out some food for him," Dallon replied.

"Here it comes," Davon noted as a man opened the door holding a plate and a mug.

"Good," she said. "Go eat."

They went inside and were quickly served. As they left the dining room Archelaus commented that he wanted to write in his journal so Marriah took her drawing board out on the porch. She was just finishing a drawing of Dallon and Davon when Leda and Lyla came up and curtsied to her.

"Where are Davon and Dallon?" Leda asked.

"They're inside eating supper," Marriah answered as she put the board down on the table next to her.

"Good," Lyla responded. "We wanted to ask you something."

"What?"

"Are they married?" Leda asked.

"No."

"Do they have girlfriends in Brinley?" Lyla inquired.

"No. Their cousin, Fyodor, told me that they haven't had much luck finding two women that are willing to do everything as two couples instead of one," Marriah explained. "They come as a pair. What one does, the other does as well."

The women looked at each other and smiled.

"We have the same problem," Leda confessed. "Do you think that they might be interested in us?"

"Regis Bryant said that they had been watching you before King Archelaus sent them to help you gather wood," she replied. "And by the looks on their faces when you arrived at the stables, I think they are definitely interested in you."

"Do you think that we will have the chance to do something with them again?" Lyla asked.

"I'll make sure of that," Marriah promised. "Their parents are here. Would you like to meet them?"

Lyla blushed a little as Leda said, "Yes."

"Wait across the plaza. I'll have Fyodor take you to meet them. He will enjoy translating for you. Davon and Dallon teased him mercilessly before he was married to Katina. I think he'll be happy to help you with them," Marriah said and picked up the drawing board.

"That's them," Leda noticed as she pointed to the drawing.

"Would you like to keep this?" Marriah asked.

"Yes, please," Lyla replied.

Marriah laughed to herself as the women left with the drawing. Davon and Dallon came out of the inn to relieve Fyodor and Garman.

"Fyodor, I have need of you," Marriah called.

Fyodor knelt before her.

"Walk with me for a moment," she said as she stood up and stepped off the porch. "I have a task for you that you should enjoy."

"I heard what you were talking to your visitors about," he replied with a smile as they moved away from the inn. "I think I know what you have in mind, and you're right, I will enjoy this assignment."

"Yves has met Davon and Dallon. It's time for their parents to meet Leda and Lyla. They are waiting for you across the plaza."

"I will take care of it at once," Fyodor said as he headed towards where Leda and Lyla were looking over the drawing.

Marriah headed back towards the inn. As she reached the inn, Yves met her and bowed.

"We are ready for the prisoner, My Queen," he informed her.

"Thank you. Bring him."

Tarl walked willingly between Davon and Dallon to where he would be locked up. Marriah glanced into the cell. She drew the keys out of the desk drawer and the prisoner went into the cell without complaint.

"We volunteer to guard the prisoner tonight," Dallon offered as Marriah locked the door.

"Thank you," she replied. "I will have your things sent up to you. Someone will relieve you in the morning."

After they were out of earshot, Yves said, "May I ask you something, My Queen?"

"Yes."

"You seem to know those two pretty well, and my daughters seem interested in them," he began. "I need to know some things about them before I have to make any decisions about my daughters' futures."

"What I can't answer, you can find out from their cousin, Fyodor, or from their parents," Marriah replied, understanding why he was wondering.

"You see, my daughters have not been separated since Lyla was born, except when I sent Leda to King Archelaus to plead for assistance for our village. It nearly killed them to be apart for two days," Yves continued. "I need to know that Davon and Dallon will not keep them apart."

"You don't have to worry about that. Davon and Dallon are the same way. They are inseparable and do everything together."

"The other thing I need to know is if they will make good husbands and fathers. Garman told me about some of the jokes they had pulled in Brinley."

"They are very thoughtful and caring. When they found out that I sometimes have nightmares, they began keeping watch outside my bedchamber door. One would stand watch while the other slept on the floor in the hall. I tried to get them to just sleep in their own room, but they refused," Marriah said, trying not to laugh at the memory. "After Regis Bryant and Regina Sonje's babies were born, they volunteered to tend the babies several times a week so that Hannah and Lizzette could have some time off."

"Volunteered?"

"At first I thought they were still trying to repay me for saving Dallon's life, but they said that someday they would find wives," Marriah explained. "They wanted to know how to take care of babies so they would be good fathers."

Yves began to laugh.

"That makes me feel a lot better about them," he said at last. "Perhaps they are a good choice for my daughters."

"I should warn you that your daughters wanted to meet Davon and Dallon's parents after finding out that the men were unmarried," she revealed.

"Maybe I should too," Yves pondered. "Do Davon and Dallon know?"

"No, but Fyodor is certain to tease them about it tomorrow," Marriah replied. "It should be interesting to see what happens."

"That must be Fyodor there with my daughters."

"Yes, let's wait here for a few moments," Marriah said. "When they're gone, I'll take you to see Karl and Sephira since their sons are guarding the prisoner tonight. I don't want Fyodor or your daughters to know yet."

Yves nodded and they watched as Fyodor went back to the inn while Leda and Lyla walked behind the stables. Marriah led Yves to the tent that the men's parents were staying in.

"This is Yves, the father of Leda and Lyla," Marriah told them. "He asked to speak to you about your sons."

"Tell him that his daughters are wonderful young women," Sephira said. "He should be very proud of them."

Yves smiled at the translation.

"I am impressed with their sons as well," he responded. "I am looking forward to getting to know them better."

"We are happy he feels that way," Karl said. "We can tell that his daughters are just as close to each other as our sons are."

"Yes, they are," Yves replied with a smile. "I'm beginning to understand that Davon and Dallon would be very suitable husbands for my Leda and Lyla."

"We feel the same way," Karl agreed.

"Hopefully they will come to the same conclusion soon," Yves said. "I have been worried about finding husbands for my daughters. I would be pleased to have Davon and Dallon marry my daughters."

"We are staying for a couple more days. We have to get back to our farm," Sephira explained. "Having the wedding before we leave would be wonderful."

"I was thinking the same thing," Yves admitted. "Before meeting Davon and Dallon I thought I'd have to arrange marriages for my daughters."

"I have some plans for Dallon and Davon. Having them married would certainly fit into those plans well. We could have the wedding the last full day you are here. They will return to Brinley a few days afterwards," Marriah told their parents then repeated it in Burton's language for Yves.

All three smiled and nodded. Karl extended his hand towards Yves who shook it.

"What about wedding clothes?" Sephira asked.

"I'll order some from the tailors in Dracona. They have all your sons' measurments already," Marriah offered. "I'll have them delivered by the dragon."

Sephira wiped away a tear as she smiled. They left the tent.

"I'll need to find out your daughter's measurements so I can order wedding dresses for them," Marriah said as they walked back toward the stables.

"They both just gave me dresses that were too worn out to wear. I'll give you those to measure," Yves responded, "I suppose my daughters will have to learn their language."

"King Archelaus and I plan to give everyone the opportunity to learn to speak, read and write both languages," Marriah revealed. "As more people learn both languages, Burton and Brinley will draw even closer together."

When they arrived at the stables Marriah measured the dresses against herself and relayed the order for the wedding clothes through the dragons.

Chapter 21 - Payback and a Chance to Prove Their Skills

Archelaus found Marriah asleep in his arms when he woke up. Marriah opened her eyes and smiled at him.

"Good morning, my beautiful wife," he greeted her.

"Good morning, my handsome husband," she replied. "Today will be a busy day. Yves met Davon and Dallon's parents last night after Leda and Lyla met them."

"Do Davon and Dallon know?"

Marriah shook her head.

"But I'm certain that Fyodor will mention the women's visit to them in the most embarrassing way possible," Marriah laughed. "They teased him mercilessly about Katina before he got married."

Archelaus had to laugh over that.

"Sometime today, I will draw a picture of Leda and Lyla then show it to Davon and Dallon," she said. "I want to see if they can tell them apart."

"Good idea," he agreed. "If they are falling in love, they would know. I know that I would recognize you by even the back of your neck or by your smell."

"As I would you," she replied. "Let's get ready for breakfast."

During their meeting with the ministers and district governors of Brinley, they explained their plans for Burton and Brinley.

"Why do you want everyone to learn to read and write?" Prime Minister Adamok asked. "Certainly a farmer doesn't need to read or write."

"By being able to read and write, a farmer can keep record of what was planted, how much was harvested and what it sold for each year," Marriah explained. "This can show him which crops are in demand and which do better than others. This enables the farmer to use the land more efficiently and increases the production of crops."

"I have begun to set up schools in Burton," Archelaus mentioned. "There has been a very good response from the people."

"People will not be forced to learn to read and write, but it will be available to everyone," Marriah added. "We will strongly encourage people to send their children to school."

"What about these changes at the military training camp?" General Caddaric asked. "We are now without a sword instructor."

"I have a couple of ideas about replacing the sword instructor," Marriah replied. "But it may take a week or two."

"What about the other instructors?" General Caddaric pressed.

"We need to review each one individually. We will replace any that are incompetent," Marriah answered.

"How did you become so experienced with a sword?" General Caddaric asked.

"Eight years of being beaten and verbally assaulted left me with a lot of anger," Marriah admitted. "Regis Bryant suggested that General Edgard train me in self defense and swordsmanship to help control my anger. I practice almost every day. I can now beat General Edgard in a duel and he has centuries of experience."

The men looked surprised. Marriah glanced at Archelaus to find him smiling.

"We also want to review tax income and laws," Marriah said. "We want to avoid forcing our people into poverty by overtaxing. We should also choose some people to go to Merton to learn to sail the ships and harvest food from the ocean."

"Are there no fields in Merton?" Eldwyn, the Minister of the Interior asked.

"Merton is located on a windswept cliff above the ocean," Marriah replied. "There is very little soil. There is an herb garden for the healer and tiny patches of salt grass. They only keep about five horses and ten cows for milking. Regis Bryant has shown me several places between Dracona and Merton that villages could be built, but there would be deep snow in winter and a very short growing season."

"How many people are needed to sail a ship?" Adamok asked.

"Six to ten," Marriah said. "The most important are the ship's captain and navigator. Often they are a married couple according to Regis Bryant."

"I suggest that each district send at least two individuals to Merton," Archelaus said. "It would probably be best to send married couples for now."

The men nodded.

"We will probably have Haskell fly them at least from Dracona," Marriah said. "Otherwise, someone will need to take their horses back to Dracona."

The men seemed alarmed by the idea of flying on dragonback.

"I personally guarantee the safety of our people that Haskell takes to Merton," she assured them. "It is almost lunchtime. We will send additional instructions by messenger."

"We go to Burton after spending about a week here," Archelaus said. "We need to set up a council in Burton before we can return to Brinley."

"As you wish," Adamok acknowledged. "We will follow your every instruction."

Just then, the door opened and the cook entered. He lay on the floor at Marriah and Archelaus' feet.

"Rise," Archelaus commanded.

"Lunch is waiting for everyone, My King," the man announced. "You may eat at your convenience."

"We are ready now," Marriah said as she stood up.

She took the arm that Archelaus offered and they went into the next room where lunch was laid out for them. As they ate, they talked.

Eldwyn asked, "Is the cook the same who . . ."

"Yes," Archelaus replied. "He is responsible for many of the scars on my back."

"Why is he not imprisoned?" Eldwyn asked.

"He is not a bad person, he has scars he received from Gustave," Archelaus explained. "He no longer takes his anger out on anyone else. When he realized who I really was, he punished himself."

"As king, you could have had him executed," Adamok commented.

"I know that and so does he," Archelaus acknowledged. "That is why he always lays down before me instead of bowing as is customary in Burton. That is his choice, not my command."

"I have been thinking about the difference between kneeling as is customary in Brinley and bowing which is customary in Burton," Marriah commented. "I am still getting used to people showing their respect for me in either fashion. I know that kneeling is customary in Brinley, but I feel that bowing is a bit more practical and just as respectful. Kneeling could be reserved for formal occasions."

The men looked surprised.

"It would take some getting used to," Adamok said at last. "But, if that is your wish, we will bow unless the occasion is formal."

"I and my tired knees will be happy to comply with your wishes," Eldwin said as several others nodded.

"There will be many adjustments to be made," Marriah pointed out. "I do not want to abandon all of Brinley's traditional ways, but Brinley is no longer the isolated kingdom it used to be. The people of Brinley need to learn more about the traditions of Burton and the people of Burton need to learn about Brinley's traditions."

"Much of this can be taught in the schools," Archelaus suggested.

Just then, the door opened and Davon entered followed by Dallon. They stopped short when they saw the ministers and district governors, but Marriah motioned for them to enter. They quickly crossed to Marriah's side and knelt.

"Rise," she told them.

"May we please have just a moment of your time," Davon began.

"To ask you something," Dallon added.

They kept glancing at the ministers and district governers. She realized they didn't want to talk in front of the men.

Marriah glanced at Archelaus before replying in Burton's language, "What is it you want to ask?"

They glanced at each other before Davon spoke softly in the same language, "We have wanted to give Leda and Lyla gifts, but couldn't think of anything to give them."

"We spoke to Mother," Dallon added. "And she suggested that young women like new dresses."

"But there are no tailors in town."

"Would you . . .?"

"Could you . . .?"

Marriah glanced at Archelaus. He had his elbow on the table and his hand over his mouth, but she could see the laughter in his eyes.

"Do you have any specific style or color in mind?" Marriah asked.

The two looked at each other and shrugged their shoulders as Marriah struggled to keep a straight face.

"We hadn't thought about that," Dallon admitted.

"I'll take care of it," Marriah said.

"We will pay for the dresses," Davon promised.

Marriah nodded and the two left.

"What was that all about?" General Caddaric asked. "You know those two are trouble makers."

"Actually those two have not given me any trouble at all," Marriah replied. "In fact, I trust them with my life."

The men looked very surprised, especially General Caddaric.

"They were always playing practical jokes on someone and refused to be assigned separately," he cautioned.

"I think you'll find they are settling down," she said. "They make such a good team that separating them would be a mistake. Besides, King Archelaus and I have been setting them up on a practical joke of our own."

"I would love to help," he offered. "I owe them some payback."

Marriah glanced at Archelaus.

"I have an idea," he said. "You heard them mention the names Leda and Lyla."

"Yes," General Caddaric replied as some of the other men began to show interest.

"They are skilled wood carvers and made all of the carvings here at the inn," Archelaus explained. "They are sisters who are just as inseparable as Davon and Dallon."

"I'm beginning to get the idea," General Caddaric chortled. "I believe I need a wood carving of, say, two men wrestling."

"Exactly," Archelaus agreed with a smile. "Fyodor will be happy to help you order the carving."

"They teased Fyodor mercilessly about Katina before they got married," Marriah revealed.

"Thank you," he said. "I'm going to enjoy this. They were always rigging a bucket to dump water or something on me."

"I suggest you go as soon as we finish eating," Marriah said.

After lunch Marriah and Archelaus hurried over to the stables to find Yves.

"What may I do for you?" Yves asked as he bowed low.

"We have some news," Archelaus began.

"Davon and Dallon have asked me to help them get dresses for your daughters as gifts," Marriah revealed.

Yves laughed.

"The other thing we wanted to tell you is that Brinley's Minister of Defense is ordering a carving of two men wrestling," Archelaus informed him.

"Fyodor is translating for him," Marriah added. "I'm certain that he will suggest Davon and Dallon model for it."

"I like it," Yves laughed. "In the past, my daughters have turned down anything that required them to view a man without a shirt because it embarrasses them. I'll go make sure they take this job."

Yves hurried off as Marriah and Archelaus headed back to the inn.

"His attitude towards Davon and Dallon has certainly changed," Archelaus commented.

"Last night their parents and Yves agreed to arrainged marriages," Marriah admitted with a laugh. "We'll have the wedding in a few days. I'll get the dress order added to the order for the wedding clothes. We're keeping it a secret from them hoping they will ask to get married."

*****

Fyodor was surprised that the Minister of Defense was interested in ordering a carving. General Caddaric's office contained only functional items. Nothing decorative was allowed. He led General Caddaric to where Leda and Lyla did their carvings.

"General, this is Leda and Lyla," Fyodor introduced them. "This is General Caddaric, Brinley's Minister of Defense."

"Pleased to meet you," the women responded as they curtsied.

"General Caddaric wants to order a carving," Fyodor said as Yves joined them.

"Tell them I want a carving of two men wrestling," General Caddaric said.

Fyodor nodded, he was beginning to suspect why the general wanted the carving.

"He wants a carving of two men wrestling," Fyodor told them.

"We usually . . ." one began to say, blushing slightly.

"We've never . . ." the other added as she blushed as well.

"You should get Davon and Dallon to model for you," Yves suggested causing both women to blush even more.

"But, Father," they said in unison.

"They would be happy to do the carving," Yves insisted, cutting the women off. "I'll go find Davon and Dallon myself and ask them to model for it."

General Caddaric smiled and nodded at the translation. He bowed before he and Fyodor left.

"It appears that their father is in on this," Fyodor speculated as they walked towards the inn.

"They remind me of how Davon and Dallon act when they are together. I think I will display this carving in my office," the general replied, much to Fyodor's surprise. "Like a trophy."

Fyodor laughed, recalling his cousins bragging about the number of times they had drenched the general with buckets of water over his office door. This carving would be a trophy of sorts, especially if it got Davon and Dallon married. Besides, once they were modeling for the carving, he could mention Leda and Lyla's visit to his aunt and uncle.

*****

"Well?" Marriah asked when General Caddric returned.

"They remind me of Davon and Dallon," the general chuckled. "I'd love to check in on the progress a bit later."

Several hours later they walked down to see how the carving was coming along. They met Yves and Fyodor along the way.

"You should have seen the looks on their faces when I asked them to model for the carving," Yves chortled. "Then when I had them take off their boots and shirts you would think that I had closed the gate on a cage."

Marriah laughed. Fyodor translated for General Caddaric with difficulty because he was laughing so hard. When they reached where Leda and Lyla were carving it was hard to not laugh. The brothers were crouched and leaning into each other as though they were just starting a wrestling match.

"What do you think?" Fyodor asked.

"Perfect," General Caddaric replied. "It will look very good in my office. It is good to see that these two have learned to obey orders."

Marriah heard one of the men groan.

216

"There was one order I could not get them to obey in Dracona," Marriah recalled. "No matter how many times I told them not to, I would find them outside my door every morning, one on guard and one asleep on the floor."

"They have always been persistent," the general agreed.

"These talented sisters requested that I take them to meet my aunt and uncle," Fyodor commented. "I took them last night for a nice long visit."

Davon began to blush followed by Dallon.

"When they get married, they will have to learn to sleep in a bed," Marriah observed, causing both men to blush even more.

"They will learn to obey their wives, or they will be sleeping on the floor," Fyodor jeered.

"That's the last place I want to be sleeping," Archelaus added as they walked away laughing.

*****

"I'm so stiff from posing," Davon complained as they walked toward the tent they were sharing with their parents. "I suppose we deserved the teasing we got today."

"I guess so, but it was so worth it," Dallon sighed. "I want to marry Lyla."

"I definitely want to marry Leda," Davon agreed just before they entered the tent.

"It looks like you had a good day," Mother commented as she dished up their food.

Davon glanced at Dallon before nodding.

"We have guard duty tonight," Dallon said.

Mother nodded as Father called to her from outside. They hurried to relieve the other men after supper, glad to not have to answer any questions.

"We need to talk to Yves," Davon muttered.

"I'm not looking forward to that even if he was in a better mood today," Dallon groaned as they stopped near the side of the prison.

"There's no avoiding it though."

"We will have to ask permission from our king and queen also."

"What about where we will live?" Davon asked, not expecting an answer. "They won't want to travel a lot. They wouldn't be able to carve."

217

"Our queen will know what to do," Dallon assured him as someone approached.

It was General Caddaric escorted by General Edgard and Regis Bryant.

"We thought you two might like a couple of practice duels," General Edgard offered. "Fyodor said they gave you two a pretty hard time today."

"Marriah sent these and said Haskell would deliver your order tomorrow afternoon," Regis Bryant informed them as he handed Dallon some rolled paper. "She also suggested that General Caddaric might like to watch the duels."

"Yes, thank you, Regis," Davon said as he and Dallon dropped to one knee before them. "I'll go first."

General Edgard handed him a practice blade and one to Regis Bryant. They moved away from the building and Davon turned to face Regis Bryant. As he did, he noticed the prisoner was watching out the window. He put that out of his mind knowing he would have to focus or this would be a very short duel. His muscles were sore from posing so long, but he ignored the pain and fought harder. He knew if he didn't he would find Regis Bryant's sword at his throat. At last he found his opening and disarmed Regis Bryant. He was breathing hard as he returned to the side of the building and leaned against it.

"Impressive," General Caddaric praised. "I've never seen some of those moves."

"We learned more than language in Dracona," Davon explained as he watched Dallon and General Edgard square off. "Queen Marriah liked having several dueling partners to choose from."

"You dueled with our queen?" General Caddaric asked in a surprised tone.

"It was almost three weeks before I was able to disarm her," Davon revealed. "She seemed happier about it than I was."

The general shook his head. They watched as General Edgard and Dallon dueled.

"Dallon is doing better than I remember," General Caddaric commented.

"He's tougher than most people realize," Davon pointed out. "He rode three days on horseback with a broken leg to get to Dracona."

"Not many men would do that," the general agreed. "Our queen can be just as determined I've noticed."

"She had to be to survive," Davon explained. "Few people know exactly what she survived. When Haskell comes, I will ask him to show you. You will then understand why she duels so much."

Dallon and General Edgard's duel lasted a bit longer than Davon's had. They finally called it a draw.

"General Edgard has been teaching swordsmanship for around four hundred and seventy five years," Davon said as the two returned to the building and sat down. "We learned a lot from him."

"When you get back to Brinley, can I talk you into teaching me what you learned in Dracona?" General Caddaric asked.

Davon was speechless with surprise.

"We would be happy to," Dallon responded.

"I'm sure that you will have others that will be interested as well," the general said as he began to leave. "I'll see you two tomorrow."

"We had best be on our way as well," Regis Bryant admitted.

"Thank you for the duels, Regis," Davon replied as he unrolled the drawings that Queen Marriah sent. "This one is of Lyla, and here is my Leda."

"Thank you for bringing these, Regis," Dallon said as he looked at the drawing of Lyla. "Please thank Queen Marriah for us."

They went inside and found the two guards were ready to leave.

As they shut the door, Davon said, "I'll take first watch. Get some sleep."

"I want to apologize to you two," the prisoner said.

Davon could see that Dallon was as surprised as he was.

"For?" Davon promted.

"For calling you pups," Tarl said. "I see now why Queen Marriah trusts you. You are better swordsmen than me and I would not have ridden horseback with a broken leg."

"After she saved my life, I would give my life freely to save hers," Dallon declared.

"As would I," Davon agreed.

"If anyone deserves to instruct swordsmanship at the military training camp, it is you," Tarl said. "Both of you. You are better men than I am."

With that, Tarl laid down on his bed. Davon looked at his brother who shrugged his shoulders. Instructing at the military training camp was not an option that he had considered. General Caddaric obviously thought they were qualified to teach swordsmanship.

*****

"They picked out the correct drawings," Bryant said as he entered with General Edgard and General Caddaric.

That pleased Marriah. She nodded.

"What do you think, General?" she asked in Brinley's language.

"They would be perfect if they are ready to settle down," he approved. "I want them to teach me what they have learned."

"I know that they have been looking for women who would be willing to do everything as two couples instead of one. Leda and Lyla are just as inseparable as Davon and Dallon. If they are as serious about Leda and Lyla as I think they are, they will soon ask permission to get married," Marriah said. "Then after they are married we can offer it to them."

Chapter 22 –Granting a Request

The next morning, while Marriah and Archelaus were waiting for breakfast to be ready, Davon and Dallon came into the great room looking nervous. Marriah nudged Archelaus.

"I didn't think it would be this soon," she whispered.

The brothers knelt before them.

"Rise, faithful ones," she said.

"May we speak to both of you?" Davon asked.

Marriah nodded and waited for them to speak.

"Since coming to Union, we have had the opportunity," Davon began.

"The privilege of spending time with Lyla and Leda," Dallon interrupted him. "We wanted to thank you and ask."

"Beg your permission to marry them," Davon finished.

"What do you think, My King?" Marriah asked in a serious tone.

"Only if Yves gives his permission for them to marry his daughters," Archelaus replied solemnly.

The two men looked very relieved as they fell to their knees again.

"Thank you, most generous King and Queen," Dallon beamed.

"We will go find Yves immediately and beg for his permission," Davon added. "But first we need to ask your advice."

"About?" Marriah asked, not expecting the request.

"If we are to marry, we need to work out how our wives can continue to carve and we can continue our duties," Davon explained.

"We do not want to selfishly abandon our obligation to you and the kingdom for our own happiness," Dallon assured them.

"A solution is certain to present itself," Marriah replied, careful not to smile. "Go find Yves before you are due to pose for General Caddaric's carving."

"At once, Wise Queen," Davon and Dallon chorused before leaving.

Once the door shut, Marriah and Archelaus burst out in laughter.

"Now we just need to keep them busy until Haskell gets here," Marriah said.

"This should be fun," Archelaus chuckled. "Fyodor told me what they did to get him ready for his wedding. I think we can do the same for them. In fact, several men have volunteered to help."

"I think that Leda and Lyla will require the same sort of assistance," Marriah laughed. "We can have the ceremony just after supper."

Yves showed up as they were finishing breakfast. He bowed low before speaking.

"I have given Davon and Dallon permission to marry my daughters," he informed them. "The difficult part was not laughing."

"Tell us all about it," Marriah insisted.

"They found me in the stable yard and knelt in front of me like I've seen them kneel before you," Yves revealed, making Marriah laugh. "I didn't know quite what to think and they didn't move until I told them to get up."

Archelaus began to laugh as well.

"I asked them what they wanted and one would begin a sentence, then the other would finish it," Yves related. "They asked my permission to marry Leda and Lyla. They told me that they would find a way to let Lyla and Leda keep carving if they wanted to, but promised that they would support my daughters."

"How would you feel about them moving to Brinley?" Archelaus asked.

"I considered that when I saw them taking a break yesterday," he admitted. "As I watched them, they talked and laughed for a while before they got more serious. As they kissed, I realized that I had made the right decision, especially knowing that Davon and Dallon will not try to separate them."

"We're going to make Davon and Dallon an offer," Marriah confided. "It would mean that they would have to settle down in Brinley."

"It sounds like I will need to learn Brinley's language," Yves nodded.

"I'm glad you feel that way," she replied. "Haskell is bringing the wedding clothes along with the dresses. We will have the ceremony just before supper."

"Leda told me that when the carving was finished, they were going to have lunch with Davon and Dallon," he mentioned. "They were going to have fish."

"Not to worry, they will come very quickly when Haskell arrives," Marriah assured him.

"Once they give the dresses to the women, some men and I will make certain that Davon and Dallon are properly cleaned up and dressed for the wedding," Archelaus confided.

"The women and I will take care of your daughters," Marriah volunteered. "But right now, we'll have someone prepare rooms for them while they are busy."

"I will go back to the stables and keep a watch on them," Yves said with a smile and left.

By noon there were two adjoining rooms decorated and ready for the couples. Yves came and informed them that Davon and Dallon had taken his daughters to the small lake in a carriage. By mid-afternoon, they had not yet returned. Marriah heard Haskell circle the town before landing in the plaza. General Caddaric and the other ministers went with Marriah and Archelaus to meet the dragon.

"My Queen, last night, Davon suggested that I could understand and get to know you better if Haskell would show me what you have survived," General Caddaric said.

"That is a good idea," Marriah agreed. "The other ministers should be shown as well."

While Marriah and Archelaus got two large bags from Haskell's shoulders, General Caddaric spoke to the ministers. Marriah saw Davon, Dallon and the women coming in the carriage as Archelaus checked the bags. The men bowed to Haskell before dropping to their knees at Marriah and Archelaus' feet.

"Rise, faithful ones," Marriah said. "Thank you, Davon, for suggesting Haskell show General Caddaric what I have been through. I want the other ministers to know as well."

"You are welcome, Wise Queen," Davon replied.

"Haskell will not hurt you," Marriah said as she saw Leda and Lyla's frightened looks.

She walked over and stroked Haskell's cheek before sitting on his foreleg. Davon and Dallon went and stood with the women.

"Please show these men what I endured at Larkin's hand," Marriah told Haskell out loud.

She watched the men's faces as Haskell showed them. By the end, even General Caddaric was pale and looked shaken.

"We had no idea it was that bad," the general quavered. "I will have nightmares from that."

"I do have nightmares," Marriah confessed. "That is why I can not fault Davon and Dallon for disobeying my orders and standing watch at my door every night. They have spent some very rough nights with me. I am in their debt."

The two blushed slightly as the ministers turned and looked at them. Prime Minister Adamok stepped before them and bowed low. The brothers blushed even more.

"We are grateful to you for your service to Our Queen," he told them.

The other ministers bowed to them as well. Marriah heard Haskell laughing as Archelaus handed Marriah one of the bags.

"Your order has come from Dracona," Marriah told the brothers as she saw Yves cross the plaza. "I think it is time that you took care of that."

They brought Leda and Lyla with them to Haskell's side. Marriah held out the bag for Davon and Dallon to take out the dresses. They looked at Marriah as they noticed there were two dresses for each woman. Marriah smiled and nodded.

"We wanted to give you a gift," Davon said as they held out the dresses to the women.

Leda and Lyla unfolded the top dresses and held them up.

"We were hoping . . ," Dallon began, but was cut short as Lyla put her arms around his neck and kissed him.

For the first time, Davon couldn't finish his brother's sentence because Leda had done the same to him. Marriah could see Yves smiling from ear to ear. Davon and Dallon's parents were standing next to Yves looking proud. Once the two women were finished showing their appreciation for the gifts Marriah pulled Davon and Dallon aside.

"Have you asked them yet?" Marriah inquired in Brinley's language.

The two shook their heads.

"You had better ask them before you no longer have a say in it," she advised them as she looked at their parents.

The men's eyes were wide as they watched their father shake hands with Yves.

"This is something you will not be able to do as brothers," she said. "You each must do it for yourself."

They both nodded and went back over to Leda and Lyla.

"Do you think they can do that?" General Caddaric asked.

"It doesn't matter at this point," Marriah revealed as they watched the brothers take the sisters around the side of the inn. "Their parents and Yves have agreed that their children should be married."

General Caddaric laughed as she pointed out Fyodor translating for Yves.

"In a little while, Fyodor, Archelaus and some others will take Davon and Dallon to get cleaned up and dressed for their wedding," Marriah said. "Would you like to help?"

"I wouldn't miss it," General Caddaric answered. "Here they come back and it looks like they got the answer they were hoping for."

Davon and Dallon were smiling as they escorted the women back toward Haskell.

"Just follow along," Marriah said. "Fyodor can translate for you."

"We would be honored, Great Queen, if you would perform the wedding ceremony," Davon requested.

"I plan to," Marriah answered. "But first, Davon and Dallon, you will go with King Archelaus and Regis Bryant. You will do exactly what they tell you to do, or Regis Bryant has my express permission to drop you in the middle of the lake."

The women started to laugh as Regis Bryant said, "And you both know I could do that without even touching you."

Davon and Dallon looked at each other with almost frightened looks before nodding.

As the men left, Marriah said, "Leda and Lyla, you will come with us."

*****

Davon noticed that General Caddaric was among the men leading them to a large wagon.

"I'm glad to see you two getting married," the general said as he came up between them. "Your wives will get you to settle down and be serious."

"I don't know," Dallon said. "Lyla and Leda filled their buckets with runny marsh mud."

225

"Oh, no!" the general groaned, eliciting snickers from Fyodor, Garman and King Archelaus.

"Just joking," Dallon claimed. "I think we are past rigging buckets over doors."

Davon smiled to himself realizing that Dallon hadn't promised to quit playing practical jokes. They got into the wagon and rode to the lake. He had no doubt that General Caddaric would be the one dumping rinse water over their heads. Davon was beginning to regret how helpful they had been getting Fyodor ready for his wedding.

Once they were shaved, they were scrubbed from head to toe. Then King Archelaus produced two pairs of white pants and tunics. They were dressed and their hair brushed.

"The brides are not ready yet," Regis Bryant said. "So we have a chance to offer some advice to the grooms."

"Never do something to someone you wouldn't like done to you," Fyodor cautioned.

"I think we've learned our lesson on that," Davon affirmed.

"Always remember that you can do anything you want, as long as your wife approves," Garman added.

Everyone laughed at that.

"Trust me, Sons," Father said. "You can't go wrong following that advice. It's kept me married all these years."

"Mess up and you will be sleeping on the floor," General Caddaric promised with a laugh. "And after tonight that is the last place you'll want to sleep."

All of the men agreed with him. In that case, it had to be even better than kissing Leda. Kissing Leda was something he definitely enjoyed.

"Now you need to find houses," Gavynn reminded them.

"Houses?" Dallon asked as Yves arrived driving a carriage.

"Probably two or three houses each if you have to travel with us," King Archelaus added with a grin as Father helped Mother from the carriage.

"With spare beds so we can visit our grandchildren," Yves insisted.

Davon felt himself begin to blush.

"They're both very good with babies," Regis Bryant asserted causing Davon to blush even more.

"Your brides are almost ready," Yves said. "But, I wanted to tell you something before the wedding."

He walked over and stood in front of them.

"When I first met you, I had heard some things about you from Garman. He mentioned your penchant for practical jokes and some other things. I had already opened enough doors only to be drenched by runny marsh mud. I was worried when you rode into town on the wagon with my daughters on your laps. I wasn't sure that you would be the sort of men I wanted my daughters to know," Yves admitted then paused. "When I confronted Leda and Lyla about it, they defended you. Our Queen Marriah also vouched for your character. I decided I should meet your parents."

Davon glanced at Dallon. That explained Yves' change of attitude.

"I now know that I couldn't ask for better husbands for my daughters," Yves proclaimed before hugging first Davon, then Dallon. "I must go now, but I just wanted you to know that I'm proud to have you as sons."

Yves left on a horse that had been tied to the back of the carriage as Fyodor finished translating for their parents. Mother was in tears as she hugged Davon.

"Don't cry, Mother," he said as he patted her back.

"I can't help it," she admitted. "I'm so happy. My sons have grown into fine men. And you have chosen such wonderful women to be your wives."

She then hugged Dallon.

Father put his hand on Davon's shoulder and said, "I'm so proud of both of you. It's amazing how much you have matured since leaving Brinley. From what Fyodor has told me, gaining Queen Marriah's trust is not an easy thing, yet I see that she trusts both of you."

"We learned a lot in Dracona," Davon said.

"It was worth getting my leg broken," Dallon added. "We learned things we could not have learned in Brinley."

"They are ready," Regis Bryant announced.

"Before we go, I have one last question," Davon said.

"Yes, what do. . ," Dallon began then stopped.

The men laughed.

"My Sons, every man asks that before his wedding," Father said. "Have faith in yourselves. When the time comes, you will know exactly what to do. Just don't be in a hurry. Let your wife set the pace and the rest will be easy."

Servant Queen

"Absolutely the best way to go," King Archelaus agreed with a smile that made the other men laugh.

Chapter 23 – Appointing New Sword Instructors

After breakfast, many of the wedding guests began to pack up to leave. Brinley's ministers and district governors met with Marriah and Archelaus. Bryant, Sonje and Dracona's council also attended. Garman, Aurella and Fyodor translated. The men from Brinley were very interested in learning more about Dracona.

"I find it hard to believe that there is almost no crime in Dracona," the Minister of the Interior observed.

"Education is an important part of that," Bryant replied. "Also, everyone is considered an important part of the whole. The man who sweeps the streets is treated with the same respect that the cobbler is. The cobbler is treated with the same respect that the healer is. And the healer is treated with the same respect that everyone in this room is due."

The room fell silent as the men from Brinley considered what Bryant had said.

"In Dracona, everyone treated me with respect and caring starting the first day I was there," Marriah broke the silence. "Everyone that came to Dracona to serve me was not treated as a servant or a stranger, but an equal and a friend. So many people asked Dallon how his leg was that the first words he learned in Burton's language were 'much better, thank you.' I hope to teach the people of Brinley to have the same respect for each other."

"I want the people of Burton to learn the same thing," Archelaus echoed.

"Would it be possible for me to visit Dracona?" Adamok, the Prime Minister asked. "I want to see this for myself."

"We would be happy to have you," Sonje assured him.

"Aurella and I volunteer translate for you in Dracona, Adamok," Garman offered.

"Be ready to leave just after lunch," Bryant advised them.

"I see that it is time to address the replacement of Tarl as sword instructor," Marriah observed as she saw Davon and Dallon coming down the stairs.

"Yes," Archelaus agreed. "Davon, Dallon, come here please."

The two men hurried over to kneel in front of Archelaus and Marriah.

"Now that you are married men," Archelaus began before the men had risen to their feet. "You will want positions that require less travel so you can start families."

"Yes, My King," Davon replied and Dallon echoed.

"Have you discussed any plans with your wives?" Marriah asked.

"Not yet," Dallon replied.

"But we are going to as soon as they come downstairs," Davon added.

"Go get your wives and bring them here," Archelaus commanded.

"At once, My King," they answered in unison and hurried back up the stairs.

Marriah smiled. This would be interesting.

"Do you think they will accept?" General Caddaric asked.

"They would be foolish not to and they are not fools," Marriah assured him. "Besides, they are the only ones qualified for the position right now. They will not disappoint us."

"Here they come," Archelaus announced.

"We felt that you should have some say in your husbands' careers," Marriah said as the women curtsied. "Have you thought about living in Brinley?"

"We knew that we might have to travel or move," Leda replied.

"We want to learn Brinley's language," Lyla volunteered.

"And how to read and write," Leda added.

"Good," Marriah said. "We have a need of Davon and Dallon for something very important."

"It would require them to live in Brinley and they would be needed for years to come," Archelaus added.

"We would be happy to make our home in Brinley," Leda assured them.

"As long as Father can visit us," Lyla interjected.

"He will want to visit his grandchildren," Leda added and the two men blushed slightly.

"I don't see any problem with that," Archelaus responded. "Do you, General Caddaric?"

Marriah had a hard time not laughing at the looks on Davon and Dallon's faces.

"I see no problem with that, but they would have to learn to sleep in a bed instead of on the floor," General Caddaric replied. "They would be reporting directly to me and they would have a great deal of responsibility."

"Do you think you could handle that?" Archelaus questioned.

"Yes, My King," they replied in unison even though they looked a bit apprehensive.

"In that case," Marriah said. "Davon and Dallon shall be promoted to the rank of Captain and assigned to Brinley's military training camp. There they will assume the duties of sword instructors."

Davon and Dallon's eyes were wide as they dropped to their knees at Marriah's feet.

"Rise, Captain Davon and Captain Dallon," Marriah commanded.

"Thank you," Davon exclaimed.

"We will not disappoint you," Dallon promised.

"You have proven yourselves to be faithful in performance of your duties and skilled swordsmen," Marriah praised. "You have earned it. You will still be expected to serve as my dueling partners upon request."

"Our pleasure, Great Queen!" they replied.

"You escort Tarl back to Brinley," Marriah ordered. "You will make certain that he is reasonably comfortable and adequately fed during the journey."

"As you wish," Dallon acknowledged and Davon nodded.

"The wagon to transport him is on its way and should be here in a day or so," Bryant informed them.

"That will give Leda and Lyla time to finish their carvings," Davon said.

"Bring your swords to me before I leave," General Edgard requested. "I'll sharpen them and give them a permanent edge as I did your King and Queen's."

"We will," Dallon beamed. "Thank you."

"You are dismissed," Archelaus said and two couples left.

"We will return to Brinley in about two and a half weeks," Marriah informed Brinley's council. "We will expect a report in just over a week. Your first order of business is to choose people to send to Merton. Volunteers would be best, but if there are none, select those you wish to send. Just remember that no one should be forced to go."

The governors nodded. After Marriah and Archelaus stood, the others began to leave the room. Bryant and Sonje waited for the rest to leave before saying their goodbyes.

"I will miss you," Sonje admitted as she wiped a tear from her cheek. "You always knew how to make me smile, but I am so proud of you. I am glad that you are happy now."

"I have you and Bryant to thank," Marriah insisted. "Without your help I would not have survived. Also, I would have never met Archelaus."

"We will remember you and the lessons you taught us for generations to come," Bryant vowed as he hugged her. "Both of you will be known by every man, woman and child on Trinan. Your strength and courage will inspire our children. Your suffering will serve as a reminder to the men and women."

Marriah looked at Archelaus. He looked surprised as well.

"We will not let the people of this world forget either," Archelaus promised.

"I know that your father is very proud of you and watches over you," Bryant continued and Marriah felt the tear roll down her cheek. "I will always be grateful for the kindness he showed my father when he was injured."

"He was a great man. He raised his daughter to be a very wonderful woman," Archelaus claimed as he put his arm around Marriah's shoulders.

"Yes, he did," Bryant affirmed. "Riva once told me that I would help someone when they needed it the most and they would preserve the kingdom their parent left. I now know that you are the person she told me about. I know you were born to be queen of Brinley."

"Marriah, you are a great queen," Sonje said. "I know that we could not have taught you everything about ruling a kingdom. The rest you learned from your father."

Sonje hugged Marriah and kissed her cheek.

"I know that you two will have wonderful children who will be well loved and cared for," she said. "We want you to come to see us before we leave for Trinan."

"We will," Archelaus promised and Marriah nodded.

Bryant and Sonje left as Marriah turned to lay her head on his shoulder. He put his arms around her and stroked her hair.

"Let's go up to our room for a while," he suggested softly. "You need to rest."

She nodded and allowed him to lead her up to the room.

"Are you alright?" he asked as she sat down on a chair.

"Yes," she reassured him. "Your parents raised their son to be a very wonderful man."

He knelt in front of her and kissed her hands.

"You were able to see me as an equal, even when I couldn't," she confessed. "You healed my heart and made me feel whole again."

"You have done the same for me," he admitted softly. "When we were apart I did not feel whole, as though a part of me was missing. I trained with the castle guards every day so I wouldn't jump on a horse and ride to Dracona just to be with you."

"I noticed at our wedding that your chest seemed broader and your arms thicker," she recalled, blushing slightly. "That night I was sure of it."

"When I saw you in your wedding dress, I thought I was dreaming. You were more beautiful than ever. That night I knew I had married perfection."

Her blush deepened as he kissed her hands again. He stood and pulled her to her feet. He kissed her tenderly. She laid her head on his shoulder.

"In your arms I feel safe," she sighed. "At last I can sleep without fear. I won't need paintings of you to watch over me."

"Paintings of me?" he asked in shock.

"I'll show you," she said and left his arms.

She untied the cord on a large flat package leaning against the wall. She pulled off the thin blanket to reveal a portrait of him as he was dressed for Xylia's funeral.

"You painted this from memory?"

"Yes," she said as she moved the painting aside.

In the next portrait he wore the purple suit and his crown. It was like looking in a polished shield. She moved the painting, revealing a third.

"This one is my favorite," she confessed.

"From our dream," he whispered.

The painting was of him and his parents. He was wearing a tunic, his armband and his crown.

"It's so life like," he said. "It is my favorite as well. You are a very gifted artist."

233

"I've been working on one of me and my parents, but it's not finished yet."

"We have this whole week to do anything we want," he said with a smile. "Or nothing at all."

"Anything we want?" Marriah repeated with a mischievous grin.

"Anything."

She put her arms around his neck and smiled at him. He drew her close and leaned down to kiss her. As their lips met her fingers slid through his hair and her kiss grew more demanding, which left him no doubt as to what she wanted to do first.

The days that followed were filled with horseback rides, moonlit walks and just relaxing. Marriah finished several paintings including some that would be given to Bryant and Sonje. Fyodor began to teach Archelaus what he had learned about swordsmanship from Marriah and General Edgard.

*****

The day before they were to leave for Burton, Archelaus returned to the inn after dueling with Fyodor. He found Marriah on the porch with her drawing board. She smiled as she looked up at him.

"You look like you had a good duel," she observed as he sat next to her.

"I finally beat him," Archelaus bragged. "What are you drawing?"

"I had a dream last night about building a castle here against the hill near the lake," she said as she turned the board for him to see.

"It's beautiful!"

"I've been wondering about how we will divide our time between the three kingdoms. Will we move between castles every month or so?"

"For a while I suppose we will have to travel a lot until everything is running smoothly," he speculated. "After that we will be able to settle down to live in one place and only have occasional trips."

"I guess we can decide at that time where we will call home," Marriah conceded. "Do you want to go for a ride?"

"Sure," he replied. "Do you want to take that upstairs first?"

"No, I don't think anyone will bother it."

The next morning as Marriah and Archelaus were preparing to leave, the cook came and lay on the floor before them.

"Rise," Archelaus commanded.

"May I speak with you, Great King and Queen?" the cook asked.

"Of course," Archelaus responded noticing that the man was nervous.

"I know that my life is yours to command, My King," he began. "I have come to beg you for release from my duties in Burton that I might remain in Union."

Archelaus was surprised at the request. He glanced at Marriah. She seemed very surprised as well.

"Is there any particular reason why you wish to stay here in Union?" Archelaus asked.

He bowed his head and wrung his hands before answering the question.

"Something has come up that I feel the need to take care of," he replied after a few moments. "Once it is taken care of, I would return to my duties in Burton if that is your pleasure."

Archelaus was curious. What could have come up that the man would need to take care of?

"If you say no, I will understand and obey, My King. I live only to serve you."

"You have served well during the last year," Archelaus admitted.

"You can summon me at any time and I will come at once."

"I will grant your request if you will answer one question," Archelaus proposed. "In all the years I have known you, I have never heard you called anything but Cook. What is your name?"

"M. . .my name is Edwyn," the man stuttered with a surprised and relieved look on his face.

"You may stay in Union, Edwyn," Archelaus declared.

"Thank you, My King. Thank you."

As he left, Marriah asked in Brinley's language. "Any idea what that was about?"

"No," Archelaus replied, "But it seemed very important to him. I have a feeling that we will find out eventually."

Chapter 24 - Haunted by the Past

Once Archelaus and Marriah got to Burton they met with the council that the people of Burton had chosen to represent them. Since Burton had never had a council, the six men were not sure what was expected of them and none of them were literate. Archelaus explained what was expected of them and assigned each of them a scribe that would also teach them to read and write.

The rest of the day was spent taking care of things that had come up while Archelaus had been gone.

The next morning Archelaus went to train with the castle guards while Marriah wrote in her journal. After a while, she left the table and went to the open window. She leaned against the casement and looked towards Dracona thinking about the past. Her thoughts were interrupted by a tap at the door.

"Come," she responded without moving.

"Pardon my intrusion, My Queen," Charles' voice said. "Thinking of Dracona?"

"And the past," Marriah confirmed as she turned to face him.

"King Archelaus would stand in that very spot for hours between meeting you at Xylia's funeral and the Spring Festival," Charles said as Marriah felt herself begin to blush. "I suspect that he loved you since the moment he met you."

"At that time I was afraid to love anyone, yet I could not forget his kindness and sincerity," she said. "When he invited me to the Spring Festival, I could still recall every detail of his face. What was it you wanted?"

"There is a messenger from Brinley and another from Dracona here for you," Charles said. "Also something is wrong with Lady Althea. She will not let anyone in her chambers and refuses to come out."

"I'll see what I can do after meeting with the messengers," Marriah replied as she headed towards the door.

"Thank you, My Queen," he said as he led her to the throne room.

When they entered the throne room, Marriah recognized the messenger from Dracona. It was Absalon. He bowed as the messenger from Brinley knelt.

"Rise," she told them. "Welcome to Burton."

The messenger from Brinley handed her a thick packet before saying, "There are several letters in addition to the reports you requested."

"Thank you," she replied. "Charles, find quarters for these men tonight. They can leave in the morning."

"At once, My Queen," Charles said and led the man from Brinley out of the room.

"I'm afraid that I have more than a few letters," Absalon said holding up the bulging messenger pouch. "Everyone has been very interested in how you are doing."

"It looks like you might have to stay for a few days," she laughed.

"Actually I was planning on spending a week if you don't mind," he replied as Charles returned. "Lady Althea and I have been exchanging letters and she invited me to come visit her. I even brought her a gift."

"Absalon will be staying with us for a week," Marriah said.

"Very good," Charles replied with a bow before taking the pouch and packet from her. "She is always very excited to receive your letters."

"Perhaps you should take him to deliver his gift now," Marriah suggested. "I'll find Archelaus and we'll check on her shortly."

"The king is out practicing with the guards," Charles said. "I'll show you to your room and then to Lady Althea's room, Absalon."

Charles led Absalon away and Marriah headed towards the door. A guard at the door bowed to her before leading her out to the courtyard and to the armory. Archelaus was wrestling with one of the guards. He pinned the guard shortly after they got there. Archelaus stood up and smiled as he saw her standing there.

"What brings you here, My Queen?" he asked as he kissed her hand.

"Messengers arrived from Brinley and Dracona," Marriah replied with a smile. "I have other news, but first I think I would like a duel."

"Fyodor isn't here, but I bet captain of the guards would duel with you," Archelaus said as the man stepped forward and bowed. "Bring two practice blades, Captain Burke."

Soon she stood blade in hand facing her opponent. Marriah raised her sword. The captain seemed hesitant.

"I warn you," Marriah told him. "You will have to work very hard to beat me in a duel."

He raised his sword and began to circle. It was several minutes before he made his first move. Marriah deflected the blow easily. His next blow came quicker, but she was ready for it. She deflected his sword and slid her blade across his chest. This seemed to surprise him. He backed off and circled again. She struck his sword solidly before sliding her blade across his sword arm. He attacked again, but she knocked his sword out of his hand. He tried to reach for it but stopped when he felt her sword point on his throat.

"It looks like we need to change our training methods," Archelaus observed as she lowered her sword.

Captain Burke retrieved his sword and knelt before her with it laid across his upturned palms.

"Rise," she said. "I will be requiring a dueling partner several times a week. In time, you will improve."

"Yes, My Queen," Captain Burke replied. "I am at your service."

Marriah noticed Fyodor had joined the group along with Charles.

"Thank you," Marriah said. "Now I want a duel with a more experienced opponent. Fyodor, if you would please."

"I am at your service, My Queen," he replied as he stepped forward.

The captain handed Fyodor the practice blade and joined the onlookers. Marriah smiled as Fyodor raised his sword and began to circle. She focused on his blade and put everything else out of her mind. She had to work very hard to keep him from breaking through her defenses. She did manage to slide her blade across his arm twice. They fought until they were breathing hard and their blades began to droop.

"Draw?" she said at last.

"Draw," Fyodor acknowledged as he dropped to one knee before her and laid the sword across his open palms.

"Rise, Faithful One," Marriah said. "Thank you. It had been too many days since our last duel."

"Where did you learn to use a sword, My Queen?" Captain Burke asked as he took the practice blades.

"In Dracona," Marriah replied. "That is where Fyodor learned as well."

"Could he teach us?"

"He will be teaching others to speak, read and write in Brinley's language, but Gavynn would be able to teach you," Marriah said. "We will need to put together schedules for the training."

"Thank you, My Queen," Captain Burke said as he bowed low.

As they left the armory, Charles commented, "I had no idea you were so skilled with the sword, My Queen."

"You didn't see her defeat Tarl, did you?" Fyodor asked.

Charles shook his head.

"She disarmed him on his fourth attack and caught his sword in mid-air," Fyodor said. "You should have seen the look of surprise on his face when he found himself unarmed with both sword points at his throat."

"It is too bad you missed it," Archelaus laughed.

"I think it's time to check on Aunt Althea," Marriah suggested.

"She wouldn't let anyone in her chambers this morning, nor would she come out," Charles said. "Absalon came from Dracona and is in with her now."

"Is she alright?" Archelaus asked as they approached Aunt Althea's door.

"She was crying when she answered her door and said one word – wings," Charles replied.

They stopped in front of her door and Marriah tapped softly on it. After a few moments, she opened the door just enough to look in. Absalon sat in a large chair with Aunt Althea cradled in his arms, asleep. Marriah opened the door after Absalon looked up and smiled at her.

"This is a familiar scene," Charles observed.

Marriah glanced at Archelaus who smiled. Charles and Fyodor left as Marriah and Archelaus entered. Marriah could see the tender expression on Absalon's face as he looked at the woman sleeping in his arms. He kissed her forehead softly.

"Wake up, Althea," he whispered as he stroked her cheek.

She opened her eyes and sat up on his lap.

"Are you feeling better?" Marriah asked. "We knew it wouldn't be much longer before your wings grew in."

"A little," she replied. "I've worried about what would happen when I got wings. I don't want to abandon you."

"After everything you have done for me, it is your turn to be taken care of," Archelaus assured her as he took her hand. "You helped me find happiness. Now we want you to find happiness for yourself."

"Are you hungry?" Marriah asked.

"Yes," Aunt Althea replied. "And I want to clean up and change my clothes."

"We all probably need to clean up and change our clothes," Marriah said as Aunt Althea stood up.

"I will meet you at lunch," Absalon said as he kissed Aunt Althea's cheek. "I'd love to see you in the outfit I brought for you."

*****

Archelaus waited with Absalon in the dining hall for the women.

"I will miss her, but I hope that Aunt Althea realizes that she belongs on Trinan with the people of Glynis," Archelaus said. "You seem quite fond of her."

"I hope that she decides to go to Trinan as well. I thought of Althea often after giving you two the tour of Dracona. Through her letters I have fallen in love with her," Absalon replied. "Since you are her only family I wanted to ask you for her hand in marriage."

"I would be very pleased to have you as my uncle," Archelaus answered with a smile. "I know she will live a long happy life as your wife."

Archelaus smiled as Absalon's attention was drawn by the women entering the dining hall.

"She wore the dress I brought for her," Absalon commented as he rose.

Aunt Althea was wearing a dark blue dress trimmed in gold. The colors suited her. The skirt ended just below her knees in front revealing close fitting pants. Absalon met the women halfway, bowing low to them before taking Aunt Althea's hands in his and kissing them.

"I don't need to foresee the future to know that we will be having a wedding soon," Marriah said in Brinley's language as she took her seat.

"He just asked for my permission," Archelaus replied in the same language as the pair joined them at the table.

During the meal, he observed Absalon was very attentive to Aunt Althea and she seemed to enjoy his attention.

When they had finished eating, Aunt Althea asked, "Would you like a tour of Brinley?"

"I would," Absalon replied as he stood up. "I would like to see where you lived while Gustave was in power."

They followed Absalon and Aunt Althea out of the dining hall. Charles met them in the hall.

"One of the maids, Tyrzah, has asked if she could speak to you," Charles said after bowing to them.

"We will be in the sitting room going through the messages," Marriah said.

"You may send her there," Archelaus added.

Charles bowed and left. Once in the sitting room, he saw the packet and messenger bag on the table. Marriah picked up the packet and opened it. They began to read the reports sent by Brinley's ministers. Halfway through the second report, there was a tap on the door.

"Come," Archelaus said.

A woman entered nervously and curtsied.

"What can we do for you?" he asked.

"I just wanted to ask a question, My King," she quavered.

"We will answer if we can," he replied, glancing at Marriah. "Ask your question."

"The cook, Edwyn, is he . . . did you . . ?"

A tear ran down her cheek that she quickly wiped away as she bowed her head. Archelaus looked at Marriah. She shrugged her shoulders.

"Edwyn is alive and well in Union," he replied. "He requested release from his duties here while he takes care of something in Union."

The woman's head snapped up and she finally met his gaze. She grasped the back of the chair she was standing next to.

"Do you need to sit down?" Archelaus asked with concern.

She nodded and collapsed into the chair.

"He is very important to you," Marriah surmised and the woman nodded.

"For several years we have been spending time together during our off-duty hours. Gustave forbid us to see each other. We married in secret shortly before you took the throne. I know that

Edwyn's life belongs to you, My King, and why. When he did not return with you I was worried that you had . . ."

Tyrzah wiped her eyes again.

"That I had ordered him executed?" Archelaus asked.

"It is within your right and power."

"I know that, but I also know what he suffered at Gustave's hand. He has proven himself changed. He is no longer the same man who took out his anger on the kitchen staff. I granted his request because he had earned it and whatever he wanted to do in Union seemed very important to him," he replied. "We will be passing through Union on our way to Brinley in a week. You may accompany us to verify his health for yourself."

"Thank you, My King," she replied. "I will be ready to go at your pleasure."

"Charles will notify you of when we are ready to leave," Marriah said.

Tyrzah curtsied and left.

"Interesting," Archelaus commented. "I wasn't aware that he had a wife."

"He certainly hid it well," Marriah replied. "But she didn't."

They continued reading through the reports from Brinley. The people had responded positively to the announcement that schools were to be set up for them to learn to read and write. Several shopkeepers had offered to allow evening classes to be held in their shops. All of the church ministers had agreed to let their churches be used during the weekdays for classes.

General Caddaric sent a detailed report on the changes at the Military Training Camp. He praised Davon and Dallon's progress with retraining the men in swordsmanship. He was pleased with them in spite of finding his office completely rearranged one morning. Both Archelaus and Marriah laughed over that, but the second report from General Caddaric silenced their laughter. Troops from Mannton to the south had been seen gathering near the border.

Eldwyn, the Minister of the Interior had volunteers from four of the districts willing to go to Merton. Fyodor's parents were teaching them enough of the language that they would be able to communicate once in Merton. They also sent a letter to Fyodor and Katina.

"I'm tired of going through reports," Archelaus said as he stood up and stretched. "I'm glad Absalon isn't returning to Dracona for a week."

"It might take us that long to get through all the messages," Marriah agreed with a laugh. "There's about an hour until supper. We could see if there are any of my paintings you want to hang. I noticed some spots in the halls that looked like a painting was missing. What happened to them?"

"I'll show you," he said knowing he couldn't keep his parent's royal quarters locked forever.

After collecting the key from the desk Archelaus led her to where the door was covered by a tapestry.

"I haven't been in here since my parents were killed. Gustave poisoned them. Aunt Althea figured out what was happening and switched a sleeping draught for the poison. If not for that she and I would have been poisoned too," Archelaus said.

"How did you get out of a busy castle without being seen?" Marriah asked.

"There's a secret passageway next to the fireplace. My father kept a desk in there so he could work on things without being disturbed. It comes out in the servant's quarters in Charles' room. He helped us get out at night," Archelaus explained as the memories of that night began to surface. "Gustave slashed the paintings of the family. Others some of the servants hid, but those have been rehung since I took the throne."

"It looks like he had quite a temper," Marriah commented as she looked at the ripped paintings.

"Only Charles was allowed in the royal quarters. Gustave took the largest guest suite and turned it into his royal quarters. He publicly announced that the original royal quarters would remain untouched as a memorial to my parents and me. Soon after I started working here a new guard started and he told the guard that he was to report immediately if anyone other than Charles set foot in old royal quarters. I realized he knew there was no body in my coffin and he was hoping to catch me trying to retrieve my belongings and kill me," Archelaus recalled as he looked around the room. "Eventually I'll go into my old bedroom and go through my things, but not just yet."

"There are more paintings than I thought there would be," Marriah said as there was a knock near the door.

"I've been looking for you," Charles said from the doorway. "Supper will be served shortly. Lady Althea and Absalon have returned."

"Thank you, Charles," Archelaus replied as they left the room.

"Do you want the rooms cleaned, My King?" Charles asked.

"No," Archelaus said and locked the door behind them. "Not just yet."

When they arrived at the dining room, the messenger from Brinley was waiting for them. Aunt Althea and Absalon arrived shortly afterwards. They both looked very tired. While they ate, Marriah asked the man from Brinley about himself. He was in his second year of training at the Military Training Camp. He elaborated on General Caddaric's office being rearranged. Marriah translated when the messenger struggled with the language, but soon they were all laughing at the details the general had left out.

When the meal was finished, they went to their rooms. Archelaus noticed that Absalon escorted his aunt to her room and kissed her goodnight. He was feeling tired as he prepared for bed. Marriah brushed her hair as she looked out onto the balcony. She smiled at him as she turned to face him. She put down her brush and got into bed. He lay awake for some time just watching her sleep. When he did finally sleep, his dreams were strange, disjointed images of his past where he was desperate to escape Gustave's wrath.

Chapter 25 - Closing the Past and New Beginnings

Marriah was awakened by Archelaus struggling and crying out in his sleep. She had been expecting this.

"Archelaus, wake up!" she said as she sat up and turned towards him. "Gustave is dead. It's just a nightmare."

He sat up suddenly, his eyes wide with confusion in the moonlight.

"Gustave is dead," she repeated as she placed her hand on his cheek. "You are King Archelaus of Burton and my husband."

His eyes finally focused on her as he whispered, "Marriah."

"Yes," she said as she saw the tears begin to roll down his face.

She put her arms around him and held him tight. There was a quiet knock at the door before it opened and Charles' worried face appeared.

"Althea needs. . . ," he said quietly then stopped.

"Wake Absalon and send him in to comfort her," Marriah suggested.

"But . . ," Charles began.

"She wanted Absalon to know what she had been through," Marriah responded firmly. "He should know this as well."

"As you command, My Queen," he replied before shutting the door.

It took a while before Archelaus spoke again.

"Now you know all of it," he said softly.

"The past cannot be changed, but we can learn to not make the same mistakes," she responded. "I understand why you had kept that room locked and hidden for the last year."

"When I became king, Charles kept suggesting that the king should live in the royal suite, but I couldn't bring myself to go in there again. He finally gave up."

"I didn't think I would be able to go inside of Larkin's house until I realized that what Father had carved might be writing," she admitted. "What is done with the royal suite is entirely up to you. I am happy wherever you are."

He drew back and looked at her.

"If you want to lock it up, or turn it into a place to display things, I will abide by your wishes," Marriah promised.

Archelaus finally smiled and brushed her hair from her face.

"Thank you for understanding," he said softly. "I still don't know what to do with it."

"I would not be able to repair the paintings, but if you would like I could paint copies of them."

"I would like that," he acknowledged with a sad smile.

"I wonder how Aunt Althea is doing," Marriah pondered. "Charles looked very worried."

"We should check on her then," he said. "In the past year, she has not given any indication that the past upset her until now."

"She was probably too busy taking care of you to let herself feel anything. Now that we have each other, she has finally started the healing that you started a year ago."

Archelaus pulled on a pair of pants and she put on a robe before they went to Aunt Althea's room. Charles was pacing in front of her door. He bowed low when he saw them.

"It is her turn to begin to heal," Marriah said.

Charles nodded and said, "Absalon is in there with her. It is quiet now, but I hope she will be alright."

Archelaus opened the door slowly. Absalon motioned them in. He sat with her in his lap, cradled in his arms. She was sobbing with her face buried in his shoulder.

"Let it out," Marriah urged softly as she placed her hand on Aunt Althea's shoulder. "We are here to watch over you."

After about an hour, she began to calm down. Marriah was relieved. She knew how hard it could be to let yourself grieve and trust others to take care of you.

"Are you going to be alright?" Archelaus asked softly as she looked at him.

"I think so," Aunt Althea whispered.

"I have been wondering when you would finally let yourself deal with the past," Charles admitted. "You have been too strong for too long. I have been afraid that the burden would break you."

"I had to be sure that Archelaus was safe first," she replied quietly. "I had a dream before the nightmares started. I dreamed that Marriah and Archelaus had eight beautiful children, but I was not here to help care for them. I dreamed I was standing on a balcony over the ocean looking out at a violet sky. Absalon was at my side and I held a baby."

"Bryant and Sonje told me that Trinan has a violet sky over tall red cliffs and an ocean. There are balconies in the cliffs and homes built into the rock," Marriah said.

Absalon glanced from Aunt Althea to Marriah and back.

"If your dream came true, I would be the happiest man alive," he delared. "Please say you'll marry me."

Aunt Althea glanced at Archelaus who smiled and nodded slightly.

"You are certain you want me for your wife?" she asked as she looked into Absalon's eyes.

"Completely certain," he replied without hesitation.

"Before I met you I had not even considered marriage. But you are not like any other man I have ever met. I wanted so much to answer yes when you first asked me, but I needed to know you could accept my past."

"I knew most of it before I wrote the first letter to you. I even brought a ring in hoping you would say yes."

"Then my answer is yes," she confirmed. "I would be happy to be your wife."

Absalon and Aunt Althea kissed.

"You can travel with us to Union before going to Dracona," Marriah offered.

"I can't just abandon," she protested.

"You belong with the people of Glynis," Archelaus intterupted. "I have Marriah to take care of me and I can take care of her. It's time for you to have a life of your own."

"I'm excited to have you meet my family," Absalon said.

"I think we should all get some sleep," Marriah suggested. "It will be morning soon."

"I'll be alright alone now," Aunt Althea said as she stood up.

"I'll see you in the morning then," Absalon replied as he stood and left the room.

Marriah led Archelaus and Charles out into the hall. Charles left but Absalon was waiting for them.

"I am able to carve stone with my hands, but everything I carve that way glows blue. While we were at the cave I carved into the wall, 'In this sanctuary hope for Burton survived.' That hope was both you and Althea," Absalon said as he put his hand on Archelaus' shoulder. "I know I'll be taking her from you, but I promise she'll be happy."

"Thank you," Archelaus responded. "During those long years she was my strength and my hope. Now Marriah is my strength and hope. I know Aunt Althea deserves all the happiness you can give her."

*****

The next morning Marriah was up early. Janina and Katina were drawing the baths when she went into the bathing chamber.

"Aunt Althea and Absalon got engaged last night," Marriah announced.

"That's wonderful," Katina said.

"I'm glad she finally found a husband. She has always seemed a bit sad," Janina added.

After breakfast Archelaus and Marriah wrote responses to send to Brinley. Once completed they sent the messenger on his way before starting on the ones from Dracona. By lunchtime they had only read a quarter of the messages. There was a quiet tap on the door.

"Lunch is ready at your leasure," Charles said when Archelaus opened the door.

When they reached the dining room, Aunt Althea and Absalon were already waiting for them.

"I can't remember the last time I saw her so happy," Archelaus commented to Marriah in Brinley's language.

"He seems very happy as well," she replied.

After lunch, they all went for a ride. Charles insisted that four guards go with them. When they returned to the castle, Marriah worked on her paintings while Archelaus met with the council and took care of other business. The following days were all about the same and by the end of the week they were ready to leave for Brinley. Aunt Althea and Absalon would travel to Union with them before turning east to Dracona. Tyrzah, Kora, Ethan and four guards would go with as well.

"We'll leave just after lunch," Archelaus said as they ate breakfast. "Charles, please notify Tyrzah."

"Immediately, My King," Charles replied. "I will have two wagons readied as well."

The morning was spent packing and taking care of last minute things. After eating lunch, Marriah and Archelaus went out to the courtyard. Tyrzah and the guards were waiting for them. Absalon was with Aunt Althea while she said her goodbyes. Ethan and Kora joined them just before Absalon and Aunt Althea did.

248

They mounted up and were soon on their way. They stopped to make camp for the night. As the meal was being prepared, Marriah noticed Archelaus take Aunt Althea aside. He said something and she nodded.

"What was that about?" Marriah asked as they sat down to eat.

"Just a favor I need her to do when we get to Union," he replied cryptically. "I have an idea I think you'll like."

She wondered what he had in mind. The following day she noticed Tyrzah was very quiet. When they camped for the night Tyrzah still sat staring at the fire when the others were going into their tents for night.

"Are you alright?" Marriah asked her as she sat down next to Tyrzah.

"I'm just so worried about the future," Tyrzah admitted as she wiped away a tear. "After what Edwyn did to King Archelaus."

"Have faith and hope," Marriah said. "I know that it can be hard, but things work out for the best eventually."

"I've wanted children, but we haven't dared," Tyrzah confessed in a whisper.

"We should reach Union by tomorrow evening," Marriah said. "We can get everything worked out then. Try to get some sleep."

Tyrzah stood and offered Marriah a hand up. She then went slowly to her tent with her shoulders sagging as Archelaus joined Marriah.

"I promise by tomorrow this time she will be happy," Archelaus said. "Come to bed."

When they stopped for supper the next evening, Archelaus sent two of the guards ahead. When they reached Union, they went to the inn. Their thrones were in the great room. Archelaus had them pulled out from the wall a few feet. He sent Ethan to get the two guards who had been sent ahead.

"Now, in order for this to work, I will do all the talking," Archelaus insisted. "Tyrzah, what I will say will sound much worse than the situation really is. You are going to have to trust me on this and remain silent. You will remain hidden behind my throne until I signal you with my hand to step into view."

"I trust you, My King," Tyrzah replied.

"Good," he said. "Now quickly take your places. They should be here soon."

Marriah was even more curious as she sat down. There was a tap on the door and Archelaus nodded to the guards. They opened the doors and Ethan entered. Behind him was Edwyn, the cook, flanked by the two guards. He looked very nervous as they stopped in front of the thrones. He quickly dropped to the floor and lay face down at Archelaus' feet.

"Get to your knees, Cook," Archelaus commanded in a stern tone.

The man quickly complied.

"It has come to my attention that some of your recent actions have caused another to suffer," Archelaus continued as the man's face lost all color. "In light of this, I have decided to take action to prevent any further suffering."

The man began to tremble as Archelaus paused.

"I have decided that you need closer supervision," he said sternly. "I will assign an individual to this task. This will put an additional responsibility upon you. You will be required to provide food, housing and clothing for this individual. If this person is satisfied with your behavior, you will be happy, but if you make this person dissatisfied, the consequences will be swift and severe."

Marriah could see the fear in Edwyn's eyes. He nodded, but did not speak.

"There is one thing to do before I formalize this new arrangement," Archelaus announced. "Remove your shirt."

Marriah saw the man swallow as he removed his shirt with trembling hands. Without being asked, he turned his back to Archelaus and knelt with a bowed head. Marriah drew a quick breath as she saw that in addition to the scars from a whip, Gustave had cut his name on the man's back. Aunt Althea stepped from beside the thrones and traced the letters with her fingers. After she had finished, the scars from the whip remained, but the name had been erased.

"Stand and face me," Archelaus commanded.

"You are not going to whip me?" Edwyn asked, speaking for the first time. "I deserve two lashes for each scar that you bear."

"No," Archelaus replied, his voice firm, but gentle. "I know exactly how you suffered at Gustave's hand. The night he carved his name on your back, I saw you return to the kitchen with blood on the back of your shirt. I swore that Gustave would some day pay for such cruelty with his life. I also know the full extent of the power I have over your life. I have had Gustave's name removed from your back by the same hand that hid my true identity from him. The other scars have been left as a reminder. With that, the past is closed. You will not be punished in any way for what happened while Gustave was alive. You will no longer lie on the ground before me. You will bow as is customary in Burton."

"Thank you, My King. I will not disappoint you," Edwyn vowed.

"Good, it is time to formalize your new arrangement," Archelaus reminded Edwyn as he held his hand out and motioned Tyrzah into view.

Marriah allowed herself to smile a little as Edwyn dropped his shirt in surprise.

"Now I formally and officially recognize that Tyrzah is your wife," Archelaus declared.

He stood and led Tyrzah over to Edwyn. He put her hand in Edwyn's.

"I don't want to hear that she is afraid that you have been executed ever again," Archelaus stated.

"Yes, My King," Edwyn replied.

"Now go and I don't expect to see either of you until noon tomorrow."

"Thank you, My King," Tyrzah said. "It is as you promised."

Edwyn picked up his shirt and they left holding hands.

"You even had me worried there for a while," Marriah admitted.

"I wanted him to realize how frightened she had been for his life," Archelaus explained as he put his arm around her. "And I wanted to make him understand that I am not anything like Gustave. I can't erase the past, but at least I could have Gustave's name erased from Edwyn's back."

The next morning they wanted to check on the repairs on the houses, but every time they approached the doors someone would stop them with some matter or another. Finally around lunchtime, they asked Ethan what was going on.

"Edwyn has sworn everyone to secrecy, My King," he said in response. "He wants everything to be complete before turning it over to you."

"Turning it over to me?" Archelaus asked in confusion.

"I can't tell you what it is, but I can tell you that it will be worth waiting for. What he has accomplished so far is amazing."

"Why is he doing this for me?"

"I asked him that and he said he wanted you to understand how grateful he is that you are King of Burton and that you have spared his life. I can't tell you how he got this particular idea, but I can tell you that regardless of his motive, when you consider everything, it does make sense."

"Alright," Archelaus conceded with a sigh. "I'll quit asking questions about it. Can we at least go out and see how they are coming on getting everyone into houses?"

"I'll find Yves for you. He can show you around without spoiling Edwyn's surprise," Ethan offered with a laugh.

"I wonder what he could be doing," Marriah pondered as they waited for Yves.

"Whatever it is, I suppose we will just have to wait and see," Archelaus admitted. "The last time I was told it would be worth waiting for, it definitely was."

"Oh?"

"Haskell told me that our wedding night would be worth waiting for when I left you in Brinley," he admitted as he drew her into his arms.

"Yes, it was," she replied just before he kissed her.

Yves came in and bowed to them before saying, "Ethan said you wanted to check our progress."

"Yes," Archelaus replied. "I want everyone to be out of the tents before the weather turns cold."

"About half of the houses have been repaired," Yves stated as he led them outside. "We have planted some crops, but it won't be enough to see us through the winter."

"I'll make certain that Burton sends enough to get you through," Archelaus replied as they walked down the plaza. "I see more of the shops are open for business."

"Yes, a tailor and a cobbler have decided to make Union their home," Yves smiled. "And we are repairing the church so it can be used as a school until one can be built."

"Good," Marriah said.

As they walked along, a wagon loaded with large square stones passed by, and turned toward the hillside on the west of town. The stones were grayish with shining white flecks on them.

"What are those for?" Marriah asked. "Are you building new homes?"

252

V.J.O. Gardner

"Oh, those are for a special order," Yves explained. "They come from a quarry just south west of here. The stone splits off into square blocks that require little smoothing."

"Sounds like they would make a good sturdy wall or building," Archelaus speculated, hoping for more information.

"I suppose so," Yves replied.

"What about the west side of town?" Marriah asked as they reached the tents at the south end of town.

There were far fewer tents than before.

"It looks just like this side of town," Yves replied as Edwyn came out of a nearby tent.

He hurried over and bowed very low. He looked different than Archelaus had ever seen him. He was happy and relaxed.

"It seems that being married agrees with you," Archelaus teased as Tyrzah came out of the same tent and curtsied.

"Yes, it does, My King," Edwyn beamed. "I'm sorry I didn't tell you that I was married to Tyrzah. We've had to hide our love for each other and marriage for so long. Also I didn't want to anger you."

Archelaus put his hand on Edwyn's shoulder and said, "I had been trying to figure out a way to convince you that I am not angry with you and that you had punished yourself enough."

"Thank you for bringing us back together," Tyrzah said. "Edwyn had refused to reveal our marriage to you."

"We could see it in your eyes when you asked where Edwyn was," Marriah admitted.

"Ethan said your project is going well," Archelaus commented.

"Yes, My King," Edwyn responded. "Many have volunteered to help once they learned about it. There are many who are grateful that Burton has such a wise and compassionate king. It will probably be ready to show you in time for your birthday in a year and a half."

"Alright," Archelaus conceded. "We won't try to find out what you are doing if you will let us see it on my birthday."

"I promise," Edwyn said.

As they walked back toward the inn, Marriah was quiet. Archelaus felt her hand begin to tremble as they walked in the door. He took her up to their room.

"What's the matter?" he asked her as he brushed the hair from her face.

"I don't know when my birthday is," she whispered. "I know when Larkin's birthday is because he demanded to be given gifts on his birthday, but we were not allowed to even mention our own birthdays."

"There must be someone who knows," he said as he drew her into his arms. "We will find out."

She just nodded. He would ask Kora if she knew when Marriah's birthday was. If she didn't, he would send a messenger to Burton to find out if Katina did.

"Are you hungry?" he asked her softly.

"Yes," she said as she looked up at him.

He kissed her before saying, "Let's go down and eat then."

Aunt Althea and Absalon were in the dining room along with another man from Glynis.

"A message from Regis Bryant," the man said as he held out an envelope.

Marriah opened it and read the message.

"What is it?" Archelaus asked as he saw her face.

"Bryant and Sonje want us to go to Dracona to get the keys to the castle in preparation for them leaving," she said. "I didn't think that it would be so soon."

"We should send a messager to Brinley," Archelaus offered.

"I noticed some men from Brinley yesterday," Marriah said. "Perhaps one of them would be willing to carry a message I'll go write the message."

Archelaus nodded and went outside. Two guards followed him. It was a few minutes before one pointed out a man from Brinley. Archelaus hurried over to the man as he prepared to mount his horse.

"I have a question for you," Archelaus said in Brinley's language.

The man looked at him before quickly kneeling.

"Rise," Archelaus said. "I need to get a message to Brinley would you be willing to carry it?"

"No, My King. I do know someone who can help you, but they're at . . . ," the man trailed off. "I'll go get him for you."

"I'll be waiting inside the inn," Archelaus nodded.

The man mounted his horse and galloped off. He wasn't certain if anyone would be coming or not from the man's odd response. He returned to the inn and found that food was being served.

"Did you find someone?" Marriah asked as she came down the stairs holding a small scroll.

"A man said he knew of someone but wouldn't say where they were. He galloped off after promising to get them for me."

"We'll deal with it after we eat."

When they returned to the main room of the inn a man from Brinley was waiting near the dining room. He quickly knelt.

"I was told you need to send a message to Brinley, My King," the man said as he got up. "I can carry it for you. Who do you want it delivered to?"

"Deliver it to General Caddaric," Marriah replied as she handed him the scroll.

"I will," the man responded. "I was going to leave this morning to return to the military camp anyway."

They went inside where Ethan and Kora were packing the trunks.

"We're leaving for Dracona immediately," Marriah said. "How soon can we be ready?"

"Within a half hour," Kora replied.

"I'll get the wagon," Ethan said. "Yves asked about traveling with us to Brinley."

"He is welcome to come with us," Marriah said.

When they stopped for the night Marriah was quiet. Archelaus knew she would miss Bryant and Sonje as much as he would miss Aunt Althea.

Chapter 26 - Saying Goodbye

When Marriah and Archelaus arrived in Dracona the town was bustling with activity. Wagons were being repaired and loaded with belongings as they passed on their way to the castle. There were wagons in the courtyard showing signs of repair as well. Absalon and Aunt Althea went to his parent's home while Marriah and Archelaus continued to the castle. Bryant and Sonje came out of the castle as they were dismounting.

"Thank you for coming so quickly," Bryant said. "We've opened the Temple of Origin and it is now at Merton so our people can begin to learn how to live on the ship and how to operate it."

"How soon will you need to leave?" Marriah asked as she tried to control her conflicting emotions.

"It might take years before everything is ready," Sonje assured her. "The ship needs a lot of cleaning on the inside and people need to get used to living in such a strange place."

"The outside of the ship is encrusted from being in the ocean for so long. It will take some time to clear all of that off," Bryant added.

"Your rooms are ready so you can get cleaned up and rest before supper," Sonje said.

Marriah was glad to get a warm bath and put on a clean dress. She was relieved that the Temple of Origin would not be leaving immediately, but knew it would happen all too soon.

"What's the matter, My Queen?" Kora asked as she put the last clip in Marriah's hair.

"Just sad to know that some of the people that have come to be like family to me will soon be gone forever," Marriah confided. "I'm grateful that I now have Archelaus and that we can build our own family."

They knocked on Adamok's door and took him down to the dining hall.

"This is a beautiful palace, but very different from Brinley's," Adamok commented as they sat down at the head table. "It seems so strange to have such a large dining hall that everyone including the servants eat with the rulers."

Marriah explained some of Dracona's traditions to Adamok during the meal. After the supper Bryant invited them to the sitting room outside his office along with Aunt Althea and Absalon.

"I'll miss you but I know Absalon will take good care of you," Archelaus admitted as he hugged Aunt Althea.

"I'll miss you as well," Aunt Althea replied. "I know Marriah will take care of you. Together you can heal from the past."

She hugged Marriah tightly and kissed her cheek.

"You have given me such peace of mind knowing that Archelaus will be happy now," Aunt Althea confided.

"I'll miss all of you," Marriah replied.

"We had best go finish packing Althea's things," Absalon said. "We're leaving for Merton tomorrow morning. I've already got an apartment on the ship. She'll stay in my parent's quarters until we get married. We'll send you an invitation."

"We wouldn't miss it," Marriah promised.

There were more hugs before Aunt Althea and Absalon left. Bryant took Archelaus and Marriah into his office.

"I didn't know if you would be able to come again before we left for Merton," Bryant said as he shut the door behind them. "There are a few things you should know about."

"Will you be taking the chairs?" Archelaus asked as he pointed to the chairs behind the desk.

"Yes," Bryant replied as he put his hand on one of the chairs. "This one was my wedding gift to Sonje. I made it when I discovered I could work wood without tools. We will be taking mostly records and things of sentimental value. We want you to have our horses, the black stallion, Llewellyn, and the white mare, Gwen. They will be in the cattle pasture with the other horses."

Bryant opened the desk drawer and drew out two sets of keys.

"These are the keys to the castle," he explained as he handed one set of keys to Archelaus. "As people move out, the keys to each room will be locked into the room. These three keys will open the doors of the living quarters. There is one key for each floor. The rest fit the other doors. I'll leave this set in the stables above the door when we leave."

He looked around at the room and stroked the surface of the desk before whispering, "I'll miss this place."

"You will always be remembered here," Marriah reassured him. "I have been painting portraits to hang here of you, Sonje and the children."

Bryant smiled.

"That means a lot to both of us," he said. "There is one last thing. Come around here, Archelaus."

Archelaus went around the desk.

"Put your hand down the dragon's throat," Bryant said. "There's a lever."

Archelaus put his hand into the dragon's mouth. Suddenly he looked up at Bryant.

"There are two levers," he said. "Which one?"

"Two?" Bryant asked in a surprised tone.

"See for yourself," Archelaus insisted, withdrawing his hand. "One on the right and one on the left."

Bryant reached in.

"You're right," he agreed after a moment. "Father showed me the one on the right, but I had never noticed the other. The one on the right opens this bookcase."

The bookcase he pointed to swung silently forward. Bryant opened it wider. Marriah and Archelaus both gasped at the sight. There was a room behind the bookcase. Bryant's light was reflected back by hundreds of gems.

"Sonje and I have taken what we wanted and the things Mother requested already," Bryant informed them. "The rest are yours. We will have no need of them. The guardians say that Trinan has gems of its own. There is a peephole to check the office."

Marriah could see the small disk that he pointed to on the back of the bookcase. They went back into the office and the bookcase swung shut behind them.

"We certainly didn't expect you to leave anything this valuable," Marriah protested and Archelaus nodded.

"You are like family to us," Bryant insisted. "We want you to have it."

"I have always thought of you as family," Marriah admitted.

"As have I," Archelaus agreed. "I want to ask you about something. You have a first name and a family name passed down from Lord Fanchon. As there gets to be more people, I can see that a family name would help identify people even if they have the same first name as someone else. I wanted to ask your permission to use Donley as our family name."

"I would be honored by that," Bryant smiled as he put his hand on Archelaus' shoulder.

Bryant reached into the dragon's mouth again. The bookcase opposite the first one swung open. Bryant opened it wide so they could see.

"Another bookcase," Archelaus commented.

"A few of these look like," Bryant began, then stopped as he picked up and opened the last one on the bottom shelf. "It's my father's journal. Thank you for finding these. They are worth more to me than all the gold and jewels in the whole mountain."

"I'm glad I found them," Archelaus said.

"Reading my father's journal brought me closer to him than I had ever been. I hope these will do the same for you," Marriah added as he closed the journal.

*****

The following morning Archelaus woke to see Marriah standing at the window. He silently joined her. She leaned against him and he put his arm around her. They stood in silence until there was a quiet tap on their door.

"Come," Marriah responded, but her voice was strained.

Kora and Ethan entered and bowed. Soon Marriah and Archelaus were bathed and dressed. They went down to breakfast.

'Take good care of her,' Haskell's voice said as Archelaus began to eat.

'She is my life now,' Archelaus replied.

'Help her to heal. She needs to know when her birthday is,' Haskell said. 'She is worried about you healing from your past.'

'With her I am whole. I promise I will find out when her birthday is.'

After breakfast, a soldier from Brinley was brought to them.

He quickly knelt with sword across his upturned palms and said, "I have an urgent message from General Caddaric."

"Rise and give us the message," Marriah prompted.

"Queen Aurita died four days ago. Mannton attacked two days later. There have been small skirmishes and no deaths so far, but he fears they are preparing for a full battle," the man replied as he sheathed his sword.

"We should leave for Brinley immediately," Marriah insisted as Adamok joined them.

They said their goodbyes as the horses were packed before mounting up. Yves and Adamok rode with them along with Garman

259

and Aurella. Once they were out of Dracona, Archelaus could see the wolves keeping pace with them. It was almost nightfall when they found a place to camp for night. It was south of the village of Langward and nearly to a mountain pass Marriah knew of.

"My King!" one of the guards said with alarm as they were setting up the tents.

Archelaus turned to see the grey wolf followed by two others enter the clearing.

"They will not harm us," he assured them as the wolves dropped three rabbits at Marriah's feet.

"Thank you," Marriah said. "Will you be keeping watch tonight?"

Archelaus heard Adamok gasp as the grey wolf nodded. As the other two entered the forest, the grey wolf followed Marriah. He could see the fear on Adamok's face as the man watched the wolf lay beside Marriah when she sat near the fire.

"That wolf is of the pack that traveled with Riva and Xylia when they saved Regis Bryant's life," Archelaus explained. "When Marriah traveled to Xylia's funeral, that wolf became her friend and protector. The rest of the pack will protect our camp while we sleep."

Archelaus watched Marriah rub the wolf's neck with one hand as she sat watching the fire.

"Our Queen seems a bit sad tonight, My King," Adamok commented. "I suppose she is mourning the death of her grandmother. Queen Aurita will be missed."

"It's more than that, she will miss the people of Dracona. Also Larkin took a lot from her and her father including their birthdays," Archelaus said. "She has no memory of when her birthday is."

Adamok shook his head.

"I know who to ask to find out the date," he continued. "When I have the date, I will declare that day a holiday."

"Let me know as soon as you find out," Adamok said. "We will organize a celebration or festival in her honor."

Archelaus smiled and nodded. Marriah had enjoyed Burton's Spring Festival, so he was certain she would like attending one in her honor. He went over to her and knelt beside her.

"You look like you've got a lot on your mind," he said softly before kissing her hand.

She just nodded without looking at him. He put his hand under her chin and gently turned her face towards him.

"What ever troubles you, we can face it together. We will find out your birth date, I promise," he vowed. "And if ever I do anything you dislike or don't agree with, tell me at once. I would never do anything like that intentionally."

"I know that," she said softly.

He leaned closer and kissed her lips tenderly. As he brushed a wisp of hair from her face, she smiled.

Kora brought them their dinner. As he ate, he noticed Adamok watching them. He was glad the man was concerned about his queen's mood. Once they had eaten, he led Marriah into their tent. After they had prepared for bed, he kissed her again, this time with more passion than before. She stroked his face with her hand before returning his kiss.

Chapter 27 - Defending Brinley

The next morning, they were on the road early. They stopped briefly for lunch and were within a half day's ride of the city by the time they stopped for the night. Archelaus noticed that Marriah joined in the conversation as they ate, but went inside the tent soon afterward.

They reached Brinley by early-afternoon the following day. Marriah smiled at the people's warm welcome. Some even gave her small gifts. By the time they reached the palace, the whole palace staff was waiting for them. They were led to the royal suite to bathe and rest.

"I want to visit my grandmother's grave," Marriah said as Kora braided her hair.

"Anything you want," Archelaus replied noting the sad tone of her voice.

One of the guards at the door led them to the tiny graveyard where the fresh grave had not been covered by flagstones yet. There were fresh flowers on the grave and the marker stone sat in line with the others.

"Queen Aurita, beloved wife of King Brook," Marriah read aloud.

"She was loved by all of Brinley, My Queen," the guard said softly. "She died surrounded by the palace staff. I was present at her death. At the end she began speaking to King Brook as though he was there. She told him that Prince Langward's daughter was strong and beautiful. She told him you are King Brook's true heir who would lead and defend Brinley with King Archelaus at your side. Her last word was your name."

Marriah began to cry and Archelaus gently drew her into his arms.

"I'm sorry. I just," the guard stammered.

"No, I'm glad you told me," Marriah insisted as she lifted her head and turned to look at him. "I wish I had been able to be here when she died."

"I'm sure she understood," the guard assured her. "She had a soft smile on her face as she died."

"I think we should find Yves and go to the Military Training Camp," Archelaus suggested.

"That's a good idea," Marriah agreed. "I'm in the mood for a duel."

"I could use some practice myself," he said knowing a dual would cheer her up.

The guard led them back into the palace. They were walking toward the stairs when they met Yves and a guard coming down from the guest quarters.

"We were just coming to find you," Marriah said as the men bowed low.

"I am at your service, My Queen," Yves responded.

"We are on our way to the Military Training Camp," Archelaus said. "Would you like to come with?"

"I would, My King. Thank you."

The two guards led them down to the courtyard. Soon they were mounted on fresh horses and on their way. The camp was just southeast of the city. It was nearly deserted when they arrived and no one seemed to notice them. The guards led them to a large building. As they tied their horses there were shouts and sounds of swordplay coming from behind the building. As they got to the rear of the building they found Davon and Dallon at the center of the small group of young men. They watched until the two brothers disarmed their opponents.

"Captain Davon, Captain Dallon, your services are needed," Marriah called loudly in Brinley's language.

The brothers rushed to kneel before her with their swords across their open palms.

"Your wish is our command, Great Queen," they said in unison.

Archelaus heard many gasps as all the men quickly knelt. He could see the hint of a smile play across her face, betraying her serious expression.

"Rise," she commanded. "Bring me a practice blade."

"My blade is yours," Davon replied as he offered it to her hilt first.

"Captain Dallon," she said. "You will serve as my opponent."

"With pleasure, My Queen," he grinned as the crowd shifted, providing space for them to duel.

Archelaus watched as Marriah and Dallon dueled. He knew that this would improve her mood greatly. It was silent except for the swords. Dallon was certainly not allowing her to win easily, but suddenly she knocked his sword into the air. Archelaus smiled as she caught the sword and brought its point beside her own,

"I am pleased," she praised. "You almost had me a couple of times."

"Next time perhaps, My Queen," Dallon replied.

The men broke into a cheer as she lowered the swords.

"Your turn," she said as she handed him a sword.

"Captain Davon," he said.

"My pleasure, My King," Davon replied.

He concentrated on Davon's blade as they dueled. Davon was definitely more skilled than Fyodor. He was able to slide his blade across Davon's chest once, but couldn't disarm him. Soon after he slid his blade across Davon's chest a second time, he managed to knock Davon's sword from his hand.

"You show great improvement, My King," Davon congratulated as he knelt with his blade across his palms.

Archelaus smiled remembering that their duel in Union was brief and ended with Davon's sword at his throat. The men cheered as he returned to Marriah's side.

"You are dismissed," Davon announced loudly.

The men left the yard quickly.

"I see my daughters have husbands who are well respected," Yves said as he put a hand on each of their shoulders.

"Would you like to see our office?" Dallon asked.

"It's next to General Caddaric's," Davon added as they walked toward the building.

"Probably so he can keep a watch on you," Marriah jested.

Archelaus laughed as did Yves.

"We heard about his office getting rearranged," Archelaus said.

Davon and Dallon laughed as they entered the building. The brothers led them upstairs and down the hall.

"Last week he turned all the furniture in our office upside down," Dallon admitted as Davon opened the door.

"Come in and sit down," Davon said.

Just as they sat down, there was a tap at the door. Dallon opened the door and General Caddaric stepped into the room, bowing to Marriah and Archelaus.

"I hear you are giving these two the same treatment they have been giving you," Marriah said.

"Yes," he replied with a smile. "In Union, I found I enjoyed playing practical jokes on these two."

"We never did get to see that carving," Archelaus said.

"It's in my office. You are welcome to come see it," General Caddaric offered.

"Let's have a look at that carving," Marriah said as she stood up

Yves stayed with Davon and Dallon while Archelaus and Marriah followed the general to his office. The carving was on the top of a chest for storing maps. It had been stained and rubbed with oil. It was very detailed and almost seemed to move.

"I see that Leda and Lyla are very talented," Marriah commented.

"Yes. I have commissioned a couple more for my home, but I think this one will remain my favorite. Because of it, I no longer worry about getting drenched when I leave my office."

Archelaus and Marriah both laughed.

"Once we get this battle with Mannton won we need to observe the other instructors," Marriah said.

"I can set up a schedule for you," General Caddaric replied.

"Actually, I would prefer to observe them unannounced before meeting them in person," she informed him. "That will give me a more realistic assessment of their skills."

"As you wish."

"After I have observed all of them, then we will schedule appointments. How is the battle going? What do we know of this King Yitzhak?" Marriah asked. "What language does he speak?"

"He speaks our language," the general replied. "His father tried to invade once while your great grandfather King Langward was in power and three times during your grandfather's reign. King Yitzhak has tried twice during your uncle's reign. We have driven them back each time."

"What do we know about his kingdom?" she asked.

He drew out a map and laid it on a table.

"It is a little smaller than Brinley and bordered on the south by the ocean. They have no shortage of land, but it doesn't contain very much metal," General Caddaric explained as he traced the border with his finger.

"He has probably learned of Queen Aurita's death," Marriah speculated. "He may think that Brinley is vulnerable at this time."

"He may not know that an heir was found," General Caddaric nodded. "He would never acknowledge your grandmother as ruler of Brinley. He has a wife, but she holds no title."

"Is there anything else we should be aware of?" Archelaus asked

"So far there have been some injuries during small skirmishes, but no deaths. I'm certain that it will soon become a full scale battle. The last time they attacked King Burkhart seriously wounded King Yitzhak and sent him back to Mannton. It seems he's trying to capture Weston again, but it might be an attempt to distract us while he slips around the main battle to attack the palace," General Caddaric replied. "I have increased the patrols along the entire southern border and sent a message to Okiah. They have joined us in battle against Mannton before. I will notify you immediately if it becomes a full-scale battle."

"Good. I expect reports on the situation at least twice a day," Marriah replied as there was a tap on the door.

"Come," General Caddaric responded after Marriah nodded.

A man entered with a sack and knelt at Marriah's feet.

"Rise," she ordered.

"I have a gift for you, My Queen and for you as well, My King," the man said after standing up.

"You were the third member of Davon and Dallon's patrol," Marriah remembered.

"Yes," the man responded. "I know that the life you saved could have been mine instead of Dallon's so I wanted to show my appreciation to you."

He knelt and opened the sack. Archelaus heard Marriah gasp as he withdrew a chain mail shirt and leather undershirt. The collar on the chain mail shirt was worked with inlaid brass in the patterns customary in Brinley. The leather undershirt had the patterns dyed along the hem and sleeves.

"My wife is a seamstress in the palace," he said. "She was one of the two who made the coronation dress for you."

"It's beautiful," Marriah remarked as she took them from him. "And most thoughtful."

"I have one here for you as well, My King," the man said. "I felt that if our queen is a warrior, that she should have the proper protection."

"Thank you," Archelaus responded as he took his shirts from the man. "I am grateful that you are concerned for our safety."

The man bowed and left.

"He's not an easy man to impress," General Caddaric admitted. "That's why I assigned Davon and Dallon to his patrol."

Archelaus smiled to himself. He knew how important the respect of others was to Marriah.

"I wanted to tell you something," General Caddaric said as he turned to Marriah with a serious expression on his face.

"What is it?" Marriah asked.

"Right before he died, my grandfather found your father in the village," General Caddaric confided. "He delivered your great-grandfather Burkhart's carving tools to him and told him that his brother would never know where he was. He was under direct orders from King Brook. I was the only person he ever told. He swore me to secrecy and told me that when you arrived in Brinley that you would need my help. I have observed that like King Brook and his father, King Langward, you were born to be a ruler over people."

"Father never mentioned his past to me," Marriah divulged. "Even when I asked he would not tell me anything, but I knew he was sad about it. He even submitted himself to slavery in exchange for Larkin's promise to never reveal his past to anyone."

"I know that King Burkhart was completely wrong about his brother," General Caddaric asserted. "I wish King Burkhart had removed Tarl as sword instructor long ago. Although King Burkhart was a good king for the most part, there were times I saw conflict in his eyes."

"I read a letter that Grandfather wrote to me about the prophecy he was given," she said. "I know that he was well aware of what was going on. In the letter he said that he did not intervene on Father's behalf even though he knew what he suffered at his brother's hand. He knew that we both would suffer pain and sorrow. I cannot fault him for his actions. I feel he did what he knew was right."

"I was with King Brook when he spoke to the fortune teller," the general admitted. "He said that her words gave him hope. It nearly killed me when King Brook died. I would have given my life to preserve his and I would do the same for both of you."

General Caddaric drew his sword and knelt with it laid across his open palms.

267

"Rise, General," Marriah commanded. "I have wondered how you and the other members of the council felt about me taking Brinley's throne and joining with Burton."

"We were all astonished at first," General Caddaric conceeded as he sheathed his sword. "I was expecting Prince Langward's son, not his daughter. We all soon realized that you were rightfully queen by more than just blood. Our first meeting was enough to prove that once we were told who you were."

"We should get back to the palace," Marriah smiled. "We'll expect another report in the morning."

General Caddaric bowed and smiled. The two guards were waiting for them in the hall. When they reached the palace they went to their quarters. Ethan and Kora were there along with Karl and Sephira. Garman and Aurella came in from the servant's quarters.

"I think I would like to change my dress before dinner," Marriah stated

"Kora," Archelaus said. "I need you to attend to something out on the balcony for a minute."

"Yes, My King," Kora responded and followed him out to the balcony.

He shut the door behind them and said, "I need some information that only you and Katina might know."

"What information is that?"

"Marriah doesn't remember when her birthday is. Larkin never let her and her father even mention any birthday except his."

"That is terrible," Kora shook her head. "I was the midwife at her birth. Katina was just three months old at the time. She was born on the fifth day of the month of First Snow, the same day that Larkin was executed."

"Somehow I can't think of a better gift than the certainty that Larkin could never harm her again," Archelaus commented.

"Yes," Kora acknowledged. "It's not what one normally gets on their birthday, but it is certainly a good gift."

"From now on, that day will be a holiday," Archelaus nodded.

"She should like that," Kora said as he opened the door.

Ethan was waiting for them just inside the door.

"We have fresh clothes for you to wear to dinner, My King," he offered.

V.J.O. Gardner

"Thank you," Archelaus replied as he followed him into the bedroom.

Marriah was sitting at the polished shield while the women put up her hair. Archelaus followed Ethan into the walk-in closet where Garman and Karl were waiting. As he removed his shirt, Karl gasped.

"I had heard about your scars, My King," he said. "But I did not realize how many you had. I can't begin to imagine how you survived those eight years."

"I still have nightmares sometimes," Archelaus replied as they began to dress him. "But my happiness now far out weighs the pain I suffered."

Once he was dressed, he went back to the bedroom to find Marriah waiting for him. Just as his clothes were new and featured the designs popular in Brinley, so was her dress.

"You are more beautiful than ever, My Queen," he complimented her as he bowed and kissed her hand. "I have a surprise for you, but you'll have to wait until we get down to the dining hall."

"I guess I can wait that long," she smiled and stepped closer.

He drew her into his arms and kissed her before they left the bedroom.

Once they were seated in the dining room, Archelaus said, "I have a very important announcement to make."

All of the ministers and governors fell silent.

"Although I would normally let Queen Marriah make the final decision on this sort of thing in Brinley, I wanted this to be a surprise for her. I will also announce this in Langward and Burton."

As Archelaus paused, he saw Adamok smile and nod.

"I officially declare the fifth day of the month of First Snow to be a holiday to honor Queen Marriah's birthday."

All the men were excited about the idea, but Marriah just stared at him.

"I realized that if anyone knew your birth date, Kora or Katina would. Kora told me that she was your mother's midwife for your birth," he told her in Burton's language.

"That's the same day," she stammered.

"I know. It's the same day that Larkin was executed," he acknowledged. "I know that nothing can replace the birthdays he took from you, but I wanted you to know how much I love you."

269

Marriah smiled at last.

"When is your birthday, My King?" Adamok asked.

"The third day of the month of Planting," he replied. "It's during Burton's Spring Festival."

"If it pleases you, Queen Marriah, Perhaps Brinley could have a fall festival similar to Burton's Spring Festival," Adamok proposed.

"Yes, that does please me," she replied. "It was on King Archealus' birthday that he asked me to be his wife and queen."

"I could never want for anything better on my birthday than your acceptance of my proposal," Archelaus confessed. "I shall always treasure that day in my heart."

"As will I," she smiled.

For the rest of the meal, they discussed the new festival. Archelaus was pleased with the men's enthusiasm. When the meal was over, he and Marriah returned to the royal suite.

*****

They were awakened at dawn by Garman and Aurella.

"What's the matter?" Marriah asked when she saw the look on Aurella's face.

"General Caddaric sent a man to tell you that King Yitzhak was seen near Brinley's southern border," Garman answered and Aurella nodded.

"Then it's time to settle this," Marriah stated as she went to the closet.

Aurella helped her into her riding habit. While Archelaus got dressed, Marriah put on the leather undershirt and then the chain-mail. Archelaus put his on as Aurella braided Marriah's hair. They buckled on their swords before going down to the stables. The soldier was waiting with their horses and four guards. They galloped through the streets and past fields before reaching the border. General Caddaric was waiting with Davon and Dallon.

"It's as I suspected," General Caddaric confirmed. "There's a battle going on to the west over that ridge. He's trying to slip around to attack the palace directly."

They approached the border where Marriah could see Brinley's soldiers watching King Yitzhak's soldiers. A man wearing a crown rode out of the forest with eight soldiers.

"General Caddaric," the man shouted. "Haven't you died yet? Both of the kings you served have died."

"I'm sorry to disappoint you, King Yitzhak," General Caddaric yelled back. "But I've got a few years left in me."

"Why don't you just give up? Brinley needs a king," King Yitzhak countered as he raised his arm and signalled the attack.

General Caddaric glanced at Marriah who nodded. Brinley's soldiers surged forward to meet the attack. The battle raged around them and soon both Marriah and Archelaus had drawn their swords to defend themselves. Marriah soon found herself separated from both Archelaus and General Caddaric. As she spotted King Yitzhak nearby there was a commotion in the forest to the east of King Yitzhak. Three men were dragging something out of the trees.

"My King!" one of the men shouted. "There is a monster among us!"

As they approached their king, Marriah could see that they were dragging a man who was bruised and bleeding. As they turned to face their king, she could see the man had wings on his back. King Yitzhak dismounted and walked towards the man.

"You've hid among us for ten years, only to turn on us now. I even trusted you to guard my wife."

General Caddaric approached from Marriah's left but was blocked by several soldiers as King Yitzhak raised his hand then struck the man across the face. Marriah could watch no longer. Her mount leapt forward at her urging. She dismounted as the horse came to a stop.

"Wings do not make a man a monster!" she exclaimed as she stepped between King Yitzhak and the man.

"Who is this girl, Caddaric?" King Yitzhak roared.

"You will address me directly," Marriah demanded. "I am Queen Marriah of Brinley and Burton."

"Impudent wench!" he exclaimed as he raised his hand.

Marriah sidestepped the blow, grabbed his arm and threw him to the ground. He lay on the ground for a moment with a shocked expression on his face before several soldiers helped him to his feet. He raised his sword with a snarl. Marriah held her sword already. She saw out of the corner of her eye that Davon and Dallon had followed her and were ready to attack. She shook her head slightly and they obeyed.

"I'll put you in your place," King Yitzhak growled.

His first attack was almost careless and she easily deflected it. His second attack was more forceful, but again she deflected it, this time sliding the flat of her blade across his chest. He was obviously enraged by her action. She met his next blow solidly and knocked his sword into the air. His face went white as she caught his sword and he felt both points at his throat.

"Now that I have your complete attention, I suggest you listen closely," she commanded. "I am Queen Marriah of Brinley and Burton. You will address me directly with the same respect you expect for yourself."

He swallowed before saying, "I did not think King Burkhart produced an heir."

"He did not," she replied. "I am the daughter of Prince Langward."

"He disappeared years ago and was thought to be dead."

"He died almost a year ago protecting me from a man who was a real monster, a man whose pleasure was to beat and torture others. Call off your attack and I'll order my soldiers to stand down."

"I suppose I have little choice," King Yitzhak grumbled.

"It's time to end this conflict once and for all," Marriah declared. "We both have more to gain from peace than from battle."

A man on horseback charged towards them from the west.

"Call off the attack!" King Yitzhak shouted at the man. "Now!"

The man pulled his horse to a stop and looked confused.

"Call off the attack!" King Yitzhak repeated. "Send someone to call off the main battle as well."

"Yes, My King," the man replied.

"Davon signal General Caddaric," Marriah ordered.

"At once My Queen!" Davon responded raising his sword and twisting it rhythmicly.

Soon the battle subsided around them.

"You do not seem alarmed that this man has wings," King Yitzhak commented. "Why?"

"I lived among his people following Father's death," she replied. "If you will behave yourself, I will return your sword. However, I must warn you that my sword is razor sharp and will slice easily through a man's neck in a single stroke. Also, both these men will obey my command without hesitation or question. They would both give their lives to defend mine."

King Yitzhak nodded and she lowered the swords.

As he sheathed his sword he asked, "How do you know that blade would cut through a man's neck?"

"I have executed a man with this blade," she revealed. "This man needs a healer's attention, but he needs his broken bones set immediately."

"I'll send for my healer."

"No," she replied. "I will summon a healer from his people. Davon, Dallon, you know what I will need to set his bones."

"Use my tunic, Great Queen," Dallon offered as he removed it. "We will return in a moment."

"He is loyal to you," King Yitzhak observed.

"They are brothers," Marriah explained as she began to rip the tunic into strips. "I saved his life. He rode three days with a broken leg when they insisted on returning to Dracona with me."

The king shook his head in disbelief. While he thought about that, Marriah silently called out to Tasia.

'It is good to hear from you, Sister Queen,' Tasia responded.

'We need Brenndah and Raphello to come to Brinley right away,' Marriah told her. 'We have found another from Glynis, and he is injured.'

'Bryant and Aurora will be coming as well,' Tasia replied after a brief pause. 'Where should they meet you?'

'Where Haskell landed last time he came.'

"Is something wrong?" King Yitzhak's voice broke into her thoughts.

"No," she said as Davon and Dallon returned. "The healer has been summoned. We will need a way to get him to the palace."

"I know what will work," Davon proclaimed and hurried off.

Dallon handed Marriah several leaves of the pain killing herb.

"I have something to ease your pain," Marriah told the injured man in Glynis' language.

"What language is that?" King Yitzhak asked as the man's eyes opened.

"It's his native language," Archelaus explained as he and General Caddaric knelt next to Dallon.

"Chew this and swallow it," Marriah told the man. "Then I will set the broken bones."

The man nodded and opened his mouth.

"There have been many changes since you left Glynis," Marriah told him as he chewed. "The people of Glynis have found the man of the riddle. They have moved from Glynis to a kingdom east of here named Dracona."

The man swallowed and asked, "Are you of Glynis?"

"No, but I lived among your people while I healed," she replied as she picked up a short piece of stick. "Later I will explain more. Bite on this while I set your bones."

With Dallon's help, his arm and wing were soon set and splinted. The man passed out before she finished setting the bones.

"What did you tell him?" King Yitzhak asked as the man was placed on a litter.

"Only that his people had moved and there have been many changes. After he has been seen by the healer, I will explain to him about the wings."

"You mean he didn't know he had wings?"

"No, his people learned about the wings just six months ago," Marriah answered as they followed the litter back toward Brinley. "I'm certain he was just as surprised and frightened as the men who witnessed the change. He is still the same man he has always been, only his appearance has changed."

King Yitzhak was silent for a minute before he admitted, "I can see that I was too hasty in my judgements of both you and him. My people have never allowed women to be treated as equals to men, yet I have seen the respect these men regard you with. You said you are Queen Marriah of Brinley and Burton. What did you mean by that?"

"Let me introduce my husband, King Archelaus of Burton and Brinley," Marriah replied.

Archelaus gave a shallow bow to King Yitzhak.

"Why didn't you come to defend her?" King Yitzhak asked as he looked from Archelaus to General Caddaric. "Why would her guards stand ready without using their swords?"

"As you have noticed, my queen is quite capable of defending herself. Besides, Brinley is hers to rule. She will tell us if our assistance is wanted," Archelaus pointed out

King Yitzhak shook his head as Archelaus helped Marriah mount.

"Perhaps it is time that my kingdom and yours sign a peace agreement," Marriah proposed as a man brought King Yitzhak's horse. "Come to the palace with us. Bring eight guards, two advisors, and your wife."

"Li has not been outside the palace since I took her as my wife," he admitted after he was mounted.

"Perhaps it is time she gets a change of scenery," Marriah suggested. "She will have everything she requires for her comfort."

"You four with me," King Yitzhak said to his men. "You four bring Joris, Yuri and my wife to Brinley's palace."

Three patrolmen knelt beside Marriah's horse.

"Rise," she told them.

"We volunteer to guide the party from Mannton to the palace," one man said after they had stood back up.

"Thank you," Marriah replied before urging her mount forward.

Chapter 28 – Transformation of a Queen

They rode in silence until they reached the outskirts of the city. Suddenly, Davon turned his horse and rode back to Marriah's side.

"He is awake again, My Queen," Davon said. "He is speaking the language of Glynis and seems panicked."

Marriah urged her mount into a trot until she rode beside the litter.

"Where are you taking me?" the man was asking.

"You are safe," Marriah replied. "We are going to Brinley's palace. Two healers from Dracona will meet us there to heal your bones."

"King Yitzhak," he started.

"Has realized he should not have thought you to be a monster or a traitor," she interrupted. "I told him there was no way for you to have known about the wings."

"He actually listened to a woman?"

"I think he is realizing that he has much to learn," Marriah replied. "Besides, after I threw him to the ground, then disarmed him in a brief duel, I had his attention. I suppose it is hard to ignore someone who is pointing their sword and yours at your throat."

The man let out one laugh and then groaned.

"You can laugh about it later," she said. "Save your strength. We will be there soon."

The man nodded and she returned to ride beside Archelaus.

"Why is he only speaking that language?" King Yitzhak asked. "He has spoken only ours for ten years."

"Yes, but he spoke his own for probably three hundred years before learning ours," Marriah replied.

"Three hundred!?"

"His people can live for up to a thousand years," Archelaus revealed as they entered the gate in the wall surrounding the palace.

"As you will soon see, there are other things that set them apart, but do not be frightened," Marriah added as she heard the familiar flapping of Haskell's wings.

"What is that beast?!" King Yitzhak asked as he looked up at Haskell approaching.

V.J.O. Gardner

"That is a dragon named Haskell. I guarantee your safety. I had better explain this to the man before he panics again."

The man's eyes were wide as Marriah reached his side.

"That is Haskell," she told him. "He is a dragon and my dear friend. He brings the healers."

The man nodded as Haskell landed near the palace.

"Welcome to Brinley," Marriah greeted them as she dismounted. "Thank you for coming so quickly."

"You are welcome," Bryant replied as he bowed to her.

"We should do this inside," Brenndah suggested as she hugged Marriah.

"Yes," she agreed as the men from Mannton stared at Haskell.

She patted Haskell's cheek before leading the group inside. They went to the throne room to find that a lounge had been placed in the center of the room. Raphello set the saddle bags he was carrying on the floor and pulled a thin strap out of each pouch. He put one on his own wrist as Brenndah put the other on her wrist.

"I am going to lift you over to the lounge," Bryant told the man. "Do not be frightened."

Marriah heard King Yitzhak gasp as the man rose into the air. Brenndah and Raphello gently removed the splints. King Yitzhak moved to the foot of the lounge to watch.

"The bones are cleanly set," Raphello commented and Brenndah nodded as their glows increased.

Archelaus put his arm around Marriah's shoulders as she watched King Yitzhak. Aurella entered and knelt before Marriah.

"Lunch has been set for everyone," she announced after she stood.

"Thank you," Marriah replied.

"Amazing!" King Yitzhak exclaimed. "The gash on his forehead closed under her hand. I can't even see a scar."

"Perhaps later I can explain more," Marriah offered. "But they will need to eat and rest soon after they have finished."

"We are finished," Brenndah confirmed as she and Raphello removed the straps from their wrists.

"How are you feeling?" Marriah asked the man as she approached the lounge.

"Better, thank you," he replied. "I feel a bit weak though."

"What is your name?" she asked.

"Lucjen."

Marriah glanced at Bryant. Could he be?

"Do you know a man named Edgard?" she queried knowing that Bryant was wondering the same thing. "He's five hundred and fifty years old and teaches swordsmanship."

"I have an older brother named Edgard." Lucjen replied. "I don't even know if he is still alive, but that could be my brother."

"If it is, then he is now General Edgard and Minister of Defense for Dracona," Marriah told him. "You should eat and rest now, but when you wake I will have a drawing of General Edgard for you to look at."

Lucjen nodded as he slowly sat up.

"Brenndah and Raphello are Dracona's healers," Marriah introduced. "And this is Bryant Donley, Lord Dracona, Regis of Glynis."

"I'm glad Marriah found you in time," Bryant said. "You will need to stay in Brinley for a few days to recover, but Marriah and Aurora can help you catch up with the changes that have happened in the last hundred years."

"I knew a man named Absalon whose little sister was named Aurora," Lucjen commented as Bryant and Archelaus helped him to his feet.

Aurora blushed as Marriah said, "I think you'll find she's not so little any more."

Once they reached the dining hall the ministers and district governors joined them. As they ate, Marriah noticed that Aurora was seated next to Lucjen and had let her own wings grow out for him to see.

"All of them have wings?" King Yitzhak asked her.

"Yes," Marriah confirmed. "It is a very long story, but soon they will return to their original home. It is a place of tall cliffs above an ocean with homes built into the cliff sides."

"That is why they have wings?" he asked.

"Yes, but we can discuss that later," Marriah responded.

"I almost forgot," Bryant interrupted. "This is for you."

He handed Archelaus an envelope.

"It's from Aunt Althea and Absalon," he said after he opened it up. "Aunt Althea is enjoying living with Absalon's parents, but is very busy with cleaning Absalon's home and wedding plans. Absalon is excited to be learning a lot of new things but comes home exhausted at the end of the day."

Marriah laughed and said, "I'm so glad they're happy."

"You're not talking about her brother are you?" King Yitzhak asked, pointing to Aurora.

"After lunch we can tell you some of our history," Archelaus replied. "But, yes, Aurora's brother Absalon will soon be my uncle. Aunt Althea is descended from both Burton and Glynis."

The man shook his head with a confused look on his face.

"We can explain further later," Marriah assured him as they stood up. "Garman will take you to your suite. We will see you in about an hour."

Before they reached the door, Garman entered with a guard. They both knelt at Marriah's feet.

"Rise," she ordered.

"This man just came off duty from guarding the prisoners," Garman explained. "He said he has a message for you."

Marriah nodded.

"Tarl asked me to tell you that he has prepared a gift for you, Great and Compassionate Queen," the man stated. "He says that although he is unworthy of your presence, he begs your indulgence that he might present the gift to you personally at your leisure."

"I will grant his request sometime today before supper," Marriah replied.

The man knelt again before leaving.

"Isn't Tarl Brinley's sword instructor?" King Yitzhak asked.

"Not anymore," Marriah replied. "Davon and Dallon are now filling that position. I am going to go visit with Haskell for a while."

"I'll make sure everyone gets settled," Archelaus offered as he drew her into his arms. "I'll come join you later."

She nodded before he kissed her. As she left, she noticed King Yitzhak's surprised expression.

*****

"Your wife is unlike any woman I have ever met," King Yitzhak confessed as Marriah left.

"Yes, she is," Archelaus replied with a smile and began to tell King Yitzshak about Marriah's past and their first meeting.

King Yitzhak seemed both amazed and confused by the story.

"When she arrived in Burton, she saw a boy being beaten. I saw her leap out of a moving carriage to defend the boy. In that moment, my heart was hers."

They walked in silence to where King Yitzhak would be staying.

"You knew then that she would have Brinley's throne?" King Yitzhak asked.

"No," Archelaus replied. "And I would have given up everything to marry her. She has a nobility about her that none of the princesses sent to meet me had."

"I still don't quite understand."

"In time you will. I'll see you in an hour."

*****

Marriah and Haskell were laughing over things when Archelaus and King Yitzhak approached, deep in conversation. Just as they reached Haskell and Marriah, the gates opened and six men rode in followed by a wagon. They stopped when they saw Haskell.

'They think I am going to eat them,' Haskell laughed to Marriah.

"We had better go greet them," Marriah told King Yitzhak.

He nodded and followed her to where the group from Mannton had stopped.

"Welcome to Brinley," Marriah greeted them. "Haskell will not eat you, nor harm you in any way."

The guards nodded, but the other two men and the woman riding in the wagon looked at King Yitzhak with confused expressions.

"This is Queen Marriah of Brinley and Burton," King Yitzhak explained, turning their expressions from confused to surprised.

"Perhaps this would be a good time to see what Tarl has for you," Archelaus commented quietly in Burton's language, making Marriah want to laugh.

"And this is King Archelaus of Burton and Brinley," King Yitzhak added as Garman rode up leading three horses.

Garman dismounted and knelt before Marriah. She could hear Haskell laughing.

"Rise," she told Garman. "Have Tarl and his gift waiting for us when we arrive in the courtyard."

"It shall be done, My Queen," he said before mounting and riding back to the palace at a gallop.

As King Yitzhak mounted, Marriah said in Burton's language, "If they're surprised now, they will be shocked after watching Tarl present his gift."

Archelaus nodded as he offered her his clasped hands so she could mount. As she settled into the saddle, she heard a gasp. She glanced over to see the two counselor's mouths hanging open and Li's expression of amazement.

"I see that women in Mannton do not ride horses," Marriah commented as Archelaus mounted.

"No, they don't," King Yitzhak confirmed as they headed toward the palace.

'The woman seems interested and excited,' Haskell commented. 'Yet I still sense a lot of apprehension, fear and grief from her.'

'She hasn't been outside Mannton's castle since becoming his wife,' Marriah replied. 'Nor has she seen any woman treated with respect by her husband or any other man. Perhaps that can change in time.'

Soon they were entering the palace courtyard. As they dismounted, four guards escorted Tarl into the courtyard. He was dragging a small wagon containing something covered by a blanket. When Marriah stepped towards him, he stopped the wagon and hurried to lay flat on the cobblestones, palms upturned at her feet.

"Rise," she told him after a moment.

He rose to his knees with bowed head before her and said, "Wise and Compassionate Queen, I know that I am unworthy of your presence. I will live and die at your command. I humbly present you with this gift to demonstrate my faithful compliance with the terms of my sentence."

"Present your gift," she responded.

He got to his feet and removed the blanket revealing a stone statue of a wolf. As she approached the wagon, he dropped to his knees again. She circled the wagon as she examined the statue.

"Your gift pleases me," she said as she stopped before him. "When you are skilled enough, I will have a project for you, one which you will be paid for upon completion."

He looked up at her in surprise, meeting her eyes for the first time.

"I will work hard to gain the required skills, Great Queen," he said. "I will not disappoint you."

He then lay out before her again.

"I will find a place suitable to display this," Marriah said. "You are dismissed."

He rose to his feet and returned to his guards.

As Marriah turned around, King Yitzhak stuttered, "How? What?"

After Marriah explained how she had defeated Tarl in a duel and about his sentence she said, "Garman will show you to your rooms. I will see you at supper."

Once she and Archelaus entered the royal suite, they began to laugh.

"I'll never forget the looks on their faces!" Archelaus exclaimed.

"They wouldn't have been surprised if Tarl had presented his gift to you," she agreed. "But none of them has ever seen a woman receive such respect. They will just have to get used to the fact that Brinley is different than Mannton. Let's get bathed and changed."

Soon after they were dressed, there was a knock at the door.

"Come," Marriah said as she sat down with her drawing board.

King Yitzhak entered escorted by two guards. The guards knelt before leaving.

"There is only one bedroom in the quarters assigned to me and my wife," he said.

"You sleep in separate rooms?" Marriah asked in surprise.

"That is the custom in Mannton," he nodded. "In fact, most women apparently sleep on a mat on the floor in the kitchen of the home."

"I would not tolerate sleeping on the floor or being separated from Archelaus each night now that we are married and neither would any married woman in Brinley and Burton."

"The men and I wouldn't stand for it either," Archelaus asserted as he entered the room. "In fact, if a man is not sleeping in the same bed as his wife, it usually means that he has angered her and he is the one sleeping on the floor."

King Yitzhak seemed stunned as he sat down.

Marriah finished her drawing of Edgard and turned to one of Bryant carrying Sonje to their tent on the way to Xylia's funeral.

"Look at this," Marriah demanded as she turned it for King Yitzhak to see.

"That's Regis Bryant," he said.

"I will always remember this," Marriah said before explaining how seeing Bryant's love for his wife helped her begin to trust people again.

"I have seen this expression on King Archelaus' face as he speaks of you," King Yitzhak commented.

"Do you love Li?" Marriah asked.

"I care for her," he admitted after a few moments. "But now I see that I really don't know what love is at all."

"I think that the people of Mannton would be much happier if the men learned to love and respect their wives," Marriah suggested.

Archelaus sat down next to her and kissed her hand before saying, "I have discovered that the love of my wife holds pleasures far greater than anything I had imagined."

"May I speak with your wife?" Marriah asked. "Perhaps we can help you understand love better. You might learn that your wife is capable of so much more than just bearing children."

"I don't know if she will agree to anything, but you can try," he conceded.

"You two take this drawing to Lucjen while I talk to Li," Marriah said as she tore the drawing of Edgard from the board. "We will join you there."

*****

She took her board with her while Archelaus led King Yitzhak down the hall.

"I do hope that Queen Marriah can get Li to listen to her," King Yitzhak confided. "There is something special about Li. She has the intelligence of a man at times."

"I can imagine she might be terrified if she hasn't been outside your palace since becoming your wife," Archelaus commented. "That's something Marriah will be able to understand."

"Li is very brave for a woman," King Yitzhak replied as they reached the small suite where Lucjen was resting.

Bryant and Aurora were there along with Garman.

"I brought a drawing," Archelaus said as they entered.

"I'm almost afraid to look," Lucjen admitted softly. "I actually ran away from home and family after. . ."

As Garman translated Bryant put his hand gently on Lucjen's shoulder and Aurora took his hand in hers.

"Edgard often spoke of the brother that he missed with all of his heart. He never would quite tell me what happened, only that he was sick with grief for quite a while," Bryant said and Garman translated.

Lucjen held out his hand. He closed his eyes for a moment then drew in a quick breath as he looked at the drawing.

"It is my brother," he confirmed in Brinley's language before turning to Bryant.

Regis Bryant and Aurora began talking with Lucjen. King Yitzhak motioned to Archelaus to follow him to the other side of the room.

"I had once asked him where he came from but he told me it didn't matter since he could never go back," King Yitzhak revealed. "I was worried that he was a criminal and pressed him for answers. He assured me that he had not committed any crimes before swearing complete loyalty to me. He said he would do anything I asked. I had him do some jobs that no one else wanted to do. He did them without any question or complaint. When the man assigned to care for my wife tried to poison her I decided he would be the one person I would be able to trust. Li told me that he treated her kindly and made certain she got food that she liked. That was very important to me."

"It seems that you do care very much for your wife," Archelaus commented.

"I chose her as my wife because I could see that she was different from other women. She cared for others," King Yitzhak replied.

They rejoined the others and King Yitzhak began asking questions about Bryant and the people of Glynis. After a while there was a knock on the door. Archelaus opened the door and smiled as his eyes met Marriah's. Li's appearance had gone from being that of a peasant to a queen. King Yitzhak's back was towards the door. He and Bryant were talking to Lucjen with Garman helping with translating. Bryant stopped mid-sentence when he saw them enter. King Yitzhak turned to see what had caught Bryant's attention.

"Li?" he asked in a surprised tone as he stood.

"Yes, My King," Li replied.

He quickly crossed to where she stood. He stood with a shocked expression before reaching out and gently stroking her face.

"I told her he would notice," Marriah said softly in Burton's language as Archelaus put his arm around her waist.

They watched as Li stepped closer to King Yitzhak.

"Are you pleased?" she asked as she stepped even closer.

"Yes," he whispered as he leaned down to kiss her lips as he had seen Archelaus kiss Marriah.

"The next few days should prove to be very interesting," Archelaus surmised softly as Bryant joined them.

"You certainly helped her get his attention," Bryant commented as King Yitzhak drew Li into his arms and kissed her again.

"I think she understands what she needs to do to keep his attention," Marriah affirmed as Li put her arms around King Yitzhak's neck.

"Obviously," Archelaus grinned.

"I think the women of Mannton will be seeing some changes soon," Marriah speculated as King Yitzhak led Li over to where they stood.

"Regis Bryant," King Yitzhak said. "Queen Li."

Bryant bowed and Li smiled. They then walked back to where Lucjen sat.

*****

Marriah was pleased with King Yitzhak's response to Li's appearance. Li obviously was as well.

"You have done something I didn't think possible," Lucjen said in Glynis' language. "She is the first woman of Mannton to hold any title, let alone that of queen."

"It is the least I could do after all I have been given," Marriah replied.

"You were right," Lucjen admitted. "Edgard is my brother."

"His training saved you," Marriah said. "He will be happy to see you again. He spoke of you often."

"I heard the guards talking about you having wings," Li said.

"Yes, I have wings, Queen Li," Lucjen responded. "I am feeling too weak to show you mine, but perhaps Regis Bryant will show you his."

"I would like that," Li replied. "Could you ask him if he would?"

Bryant smiled and nodded at the translation. He removed his shirt and turned his back. King Yitzhak put his arm around Li as Bryant's wings began to grow.

"Amazing," Li exclaimed as Bryant turned around. "May I touch them?"

Bryant nodded at the translation. During the next hour, they discussed the similarities and differences between their peoples. While they talked King Yitzhak was holding Li's hand or had his arm around her. Li was smiling. At supper, King Yitzhak was watching how the other men treated their wives. After supper Bryant, Brenndah and Raphello returned to Dracona. King Yitzhak and Li retired soon afterward.

"You will never cease to amaze me," Archelaus told her as they watched the sunset from the balcony. "You made me very proud today."

"Did you see King Yitzhak's face when he saw her?" Marriah asked with a laugh.

"I bet a gentle breeze would have knocked him over," Archelaus commented.

"She loves him. She wants so much for him to love her. She was worried that he wouldn't notice the change in her appearance."

"Trust me, every man in that room noticed. Even Bryant forgot what he was saying," Archelaus assured her as he laughed.

"The guards outside their suite noticed."

Archelaus drew her closer and kissed her.

"We should get to bed," he suggested. "Tomorrow should be very interesting."

Chapter 29 - Negotiations and a Reunion

The next morning at breakfast, the advisors from Mannton questioned Archelaus about the whereabouts of King Yitzhak.

"I doubt he'll come out of the bedroom before noon," Archelaus told them, causing them to look confused.

"We suggested that perhaps he should try one of Brinley's customs," Marriah explained.

"Sleeping until noon?" one of them sneered.

"Sharing a bed with his wife," Archelaus replied with a grin.

"All night?" the other asked.

"He was quite distracted by her last night," the first one commented. "I had no idea she could be . . . was so . . .so."

"Beautiful," Archelaus finished for him. "Apparently he had no idea either."

Archelaus and Karl gave the men a tour of Brinley while Marriah met with Brinley's ministers and district governors. Just before lunch, Archelaus and the advisors from Mannton knocked on the door of King Yitzhak's suite. Garman opened the doors and bowed low.

"Where is our king?" Yuri asked.

"Out on the balcony," Garman replied indicating the door to the balcony.

Archelaus led the men out onto the balcony. King Yitzhak was leaning on the railing with both hands, looking out over the city.

"Did you have a good night?" Archelaus asked.

"Very," he responded with a smile as he turned around.

The two advisors dropped to their knees.

"Joris, Yuri, last night I realized that we have been making a big mistake for many years."

"Mistake?" they asked in unison as they stood up.

"When we return to Mannton, I will start to correct our mistake by decreeing that the wife of the king will hold the title of Queen of Mannton and will be treated with the same respect the king is due."

The two men stood with their mouths hanging open.

287

"Also, women will be allowed to attend public meetings," he added. "From now on, Queen Li will share my bed every night."

"The palace staff will talk, My King," Joris argued. "What will the men think?"

"I'm expecting them to talk," he asserted as he opened the door to go inside. "You are beautiful this morning, My Queen."

"What have you done to him?" Joris demanded as King Yitzhak crossed the room to take her hands.

"Why is he acting so strangely?" Yuri fretted as he kissed his wife on the lips.

"He's acting like a man who has discovered he is in love," Archelaus smiled. "He is learning that a woman can do more than bear children."

"She has been his wife for two years and there are no children."

"Give them six months," he replied. "She will be with child by then."

King Yitzhak led Queen Li over to where they were standing.

"We want to thank Queen Marriah," he said.

"And I would like to learn to ride a horse if it is not too much trouble," Queen Li added.

"Garman?" Archelaus asked.

"I will see to it personally, My King," Garman replied.

"When we return to Mannton, Queen Li wants to learn to read and write," King Yitzhak announced.

"But, My King," Joris protested. "Women are not capable of such things."

"If Queen Marriah can speak, read, and write in three languages, I can certainly learn to read and write in one language," Queen Li replied.

"Three?" one of the men asked.

Both Archelaus and Garman nodded.

"It is nearly lunchtime," Garman reminded them.

"Take us to Queen Marriah," Archelaus responded.

When they reached the room, the district governors were beginning to leave. The ministers excused themselves and Garman went with them.

"We wanted to thank you personally," King Yitzhak said as he bowed to Marriah. "In the two years she has been my wife, we had barely spoken to each other before last night. I learned many new things about the women of Mannton and their importance."

"I will be learning to ride horses and when we return to Mannton, I will learn to read and write," Queen Li said. "Thank you for giving me the encouragement I needed and for letting me use the dresses."

"Aurella said they have been in storage," Marriah responded. "You are welcome to keep any that you want. I'll have a trunk found for you to put them in while returning to Mannton."

"Thank you," she replied. "I would like that."

"So would I," King Yitzhak added before kissing her hand.

Aurella entered and announced that lunch was ready.

*****

As they followed her to the dining hall, Marriah said in Burton's language, "I thought his advisors were going to fall over at his last comment."

"I've had the hardest time not laughing at them this morning," Archelaus admitted. "Especially when he told them that he would officially title her, and would continue to share a bed with her when they got home."

"I have some idea of what I will be asking of Mannton on the peace treaty," Marriah said as the food was brought out. "I'll make certain that Burton, Union, Langward, Dracona and Merton are included."

"Good," Archelaus replied. "If you don't need me then, I'll observe some of the instructors at the Military Training Camp."

After lunch, Marriah took Adamok and General Caddaric to the meeting with King Yitzhak and his advisors. By suppertime they had most of the details worked out. King Yitzhak would nod slightly as Marriah outlined each point, but his advisors argued everything. She realized that he was satisfied with her proposal, but was letting the advisors learn that she was just as capable of being a ruler as King Yitzhak was. The treaty would include provisions for trade between the kingdoms. Mannton would trade food and wood for metals, gems and other things. Both agreed to come to each other's aid in time of crisis, both military and otherwise.

"You are one of the toughest negotiators I have ever seen," Joris admitted to Marriah as they walked toward the dining hall. "I never realized a woman could be capable of much of what you do."

"Thank you," Marriah responded. "When I arrived in Dracona, I was nearly dead. Before escaping Larkin, I believed that

I was nothing, much like Queen Li believed before yesterday. In Dracona I learned the truth about the importance of every individual person, including me. They healed my body and my mind, but it was Archelaus who healed my heart and made me whole again."

"King Archelaus mentioned that he had served as a scullery boy and was beaten before gaining Burton's throne," Yuri said.

"Yes," she replied. "He still bears the scars."

"Why keep them if Dracona's healers could remove them?" Yuri asked. "And why have you kept the one on your arm?"

"Archelaus chose to keep his scars as a reminder of what our people could suffer," she explained as they entered the dining hall. "And this scar I got while saving the life of one of Brinley's new sword instructors."

"It's about time," Archelaus said before taking her hands and kissing them both. "I invited Yves to join us along with Davon, Leda, Dallon and Lyla."

"Excellent," she said. "Come meet Brinley's sword instructors. They are my favorite dueling partners."

"Then the guards were not exaggerating when they told us the sword you carry is not just for looks," Yuri surmised as they crossed the room.

Davon and Dallon quickly knelt before Marriah.

"Rise, faithful ones," Marriah said. "I see your wives have made friends with Queen Li."

"Yes, Great Queen," Davon acknowledged. "She was telling us of your efforts on her behalf."

"And of how much she admires you," Dallon added.

"I would like you to meet King Yitzhak's advisors, Yuri and Joris," Marriah introduced them with a smile.

"Our pleasure," they responded in unison.

"This is Captain Davon and Captain Dallon, Brinley's sword instructors."

She and Archelaus left them to talk and joined King Yitzhak where he was talking to General Caddaric and Adamok.

"Your wife is a tough negotiator," King Yitzhak said.

"She had to be tough to survive Larkin's cruelty," Archelaus revealed as he put his arm around her waist. "It's one of the things I love the most about her."

During supper, Marriah noticed those from Mannton watching Davon, Leda, Dallon and Lyla. She was pleased that Archelaus had thought to invite them.

"My Queen tells me that the wives of your sword instructors sell wood carvings," King Yitzhak said.

"Yes," Marriah replied. "They are very skilled. General Caddaric has one of their carvings in his office and has ordered several for his home."

"The one in my office is of Davon and Dallon wrestling," General Caddaric explained. "I consider it a trophy of sorts. After all, it was posing for that carving that helped them decide to get married and then they promised not to rig any more buckets of water over my office door."

Everyone laughed over that. The next morning they wrote the peace treaty out and signed it. Marriah was pleased when King Yitzhak even insisted that Archelaus and Queen Li sign it. He had taught to sign her name the night before. She was obviously very happy and Mannton's advisors were very surprised.

After lunch, Marriah showed her paintings to King Yitzhak, Queen Li, Joris and Yuri. They were very amazed that she could paint so well, especially from memory. King Yitzhak asked if she could paint one of him and his wife.

"I would be happy to," Marriah replied noting the surprised looks on Joris and Yuri's faces.

"Queen Marriah told us that you have scars on your back," Yuri said. "Would you mind showing us your scars?"

"Of course not," Archelaus responded as he began to remove the tunic he was wearing.

Queen Li gasped as he turned his back towards them.

"Were your scars this bad, Queen Marriah?" she asked.

"I had scars, bruises and fresh wounds all over when I arrived in Dracona." Marriah replied watching the men's faces go pale. "That is why in our kingdoms, abuse is not tolerated."

"We are setting up schools to educate our people in the hope that there will be less abuse and other crime," Archelaus added. "Every man, woman and child will have the opportunity to learn to read, write and speak both Brinley's and Burton's languages."

"And once the people of Glynis have left for their true home, all of Dracona and Merton will be given to us," Marriah continued. "Since Brinley has a serious problem with overcrowding, the people of Brinley will have the first opportunity to move there."

"To tell the truth, I have known about Brinley's problem of overcrowding and have been worried that Brinley would invade

Mannton," King Yitzhak confessed. "That is why I thought I would seize control of Brinley before Brinley took over Mannton."

"That makes sense," Marriah commented. "But I'm glad I was able to change your mind."

"So am I," he replied with a smile before kissing his wife's hand.

The next morning, as the people from Mannton were preparing to leave, Marriah presented them with a side saddle for Queen Li, a trunk for the dresses she had decided to keep, and samples of sweet oil. Joris and Yuri asked what it was for and King Yitzhak promised to explain it to them later. They were in the courtyard packing the wagon and saying goodbye when their attention was drawn by the sound of dragon wings.

"Tasia!" Marriah exclaimed in surprise as she looked out to where the sounds had stopped.

'I'm glad I had the opportunity to see your kingdom before we left,' Tasia told Marriah as a man climbed down from Haskell's back. 'I want to meet our sister. I have a prediction for her.'

By then the others had joined Marriah on the draw bridge.

"There is more than one dragon?" Joris asked.

"Fifty two more," Marriah confirmed as they crossed the draw bridge. "This is Tasia, queen of the dragons."

As they approached the dragons, Marriah recognized the man.

"General Edgard, welcome to Brinley" Marriah said in Glynis' language.

"Regina Sonje insisted I come and deliver this package to you personally instead of just sending Haskell," he said as he dropped to one knee before her. "But she didn't explain why."

"I think I understand the reason," Lucjen said as he stepped forward.

General Edgard looked up in surprise.

"Lucjen!" General Edgard exclaimed as he leapt to his feet. "Is this where you've been hiding for the last hundred years?"

"I've been here and there," Lucjen replied as General Edgard hugged him and pounded his back. "I hear you're a general and Minister of Defense."

"Yes," Edgard confirmed as he released him.

"He is the man who taught you to use a sword?" King Yitzhak asked.

"And that maneuver that I used to put you on the ground," she revealed.

"I've seen her win a duel with him several times," Archelaus commented.

"You can beat him?" King Yitzhak asked in amazement. "I'm glad you only wanted my attention."

"Queen Li, Tasia wants to meet you," Marriah said. "She has a prediction for you."

They walked over to where the dragons were waiting. Archelaus knelt on one knee before Tasia while Aurora curtsied.

Marriah led Queen Li forward and said, "Tasia doesn't know the language of Brinley and Mannton, but you will be able to hear her voice in your mind and see some images. I will translate for you."

'I am glad to meet you in person, My Sister,' Tasia began. 'You and Marriah will lead your people into a great era.'

Queen Li looked from Tasia to Marriah.

'You will end the suffering of your women, Li. Your works will serve as an inspiration for generations to come,' Tasia continued as King Yitzhak walked up to them. 'This one will provide you five beautiful children.'

Queen Li looked at her husband and smiled.

"How do you know that?" he asked, looking at Marriah.

"Not me," she replied. "Tasia can foresee the future."

'He loves her,' Tasia told Marriah. 'You have done well.'

'It is a small repayment for the kindness of the people of Dracona,' Marriah replied silently as she stroked Tasia's cheek.

'The one who came with Haskell has something for Li.'

"General Edgard, where is that package?" Marriah asked Glynis' language.

"Oh yeah, I almost forgot," Edgard admitted. "Regina Sonje said you would know what it was for."

He drew a rectangular package wrapped in cloth from the pouch he had been carrying and handed it to Marriah.

"What did he say that was for?" King Yitzhak asked.

"He was told only that I would know what it was for," she replied as she removed the cloth revealing a piece of gold. "I believe it is meant for you to present to Queen Li when you return to Mannton, but not in this form."

"A crown?" he asked. "That would take several days at least."

"Lucjen, come here a moment," Marriah said. "I'm guessing that you are able to shape stone and metal."

"How did you know?" he asked.

"Otherwise, Regina Sonje would have made the crown herself," she replied in Glynis' language as she handed him the gold. "You might want your brother to give you some of his energy."

Lucjen sat down on the ground. General Edgard knelt behind him and placed his hands on Lucjen's shoulders. Those from Mannton gathered around to watch. Soon he held in his hands a delicate crown matching the one King Yitzhak wore. A row of pink gems were set just above the bottom of the crown.

"Perfect," King Yitzhak approved.

"The first time it is placed on her head, it will adjust to a perfect fit," Lucjen told King Yitzhak as he handed the crown to him.

"Tomorrow morning, I will proclaim you Queen Li of Mannton," King Yitzhak declaired as he faced his wife. "Then I will place this crown on your head."

Queen Li began to cry.

Marriah and Archelaus stepped back to give them some privacy.

"We should stay in Brinley for a week," Archelaus suggested.

"Perhaps we should travel though some of the villages on our way back to Burton," Marriah suggested and Archelaus nodded.

Goodbyes were said and those from Mannton left just before the dragons left for Dracona with General Edgard, Lucjen and Aurora.

Chapter 30 – A Place to Call Home

It was almost the month of First Snow when Marriah and Archelaus left Burton so they would be in Brinley for Marriah's birthday. It had been a busy year with constant travel and only staying in one place for two or three weeks at a time. Archelaus was very worried about Marriah travelling so much now that she was so close to delivering their first child. He had a coach built with wide seats that were thickly padded in case she wanted to lie down.

Ethan and Kora were staying in Burton until Katina delivered her baby. Fyodor's parents had come from Brinley to be there as well. It was nearly nightfall when they reached Union. It was raining hard when Edwyn greeted them at the inn.

"The inn is full tonight, My King," Edwyn said as he bowed.

"We could sleep in the great room," Archelaus said. "Queen Marriah is exhausted."

"I know somewhere that will be more suitable," Edwyn said. "It is on the edge of town."

"Take my horse and lead the way," Archelaus said. "I will ride in the coach so I can explain to Queen Marriah."

"Yes, My King," Edwyn said in a surprisingly pleased tone.

Archelaus took off his wet cape after shutting the coach door behind him. Marriah opened her eyes briefly.

"Are we there?" she asked sleepily as she sat up.

"Soon, My Love," Archelaus replied as the coach began to move. "The inn is full, but Edwyn has somewhere for us to stay the night."

"I've thought about staying in Dracona until our baby is born, but then it's so empty with Bryant and Sonje gone."

"I miss them and Aunt Althea too," Archelaus replied. "They're on their way to where they belong. I'm glad that Aunt Althea married Absalon."

"We still need to decide which city we will live in most of the time," she said softly as Archelaus felt the coach start up a hill. "A place to call home."

"I feel the same way," he said as he took her hand in his.

The coach turned three times before coming to a stop. Soon Edwyn opened the door.

"We are here, My King," he said. "I sent someone ahead to prepare your chambers."

"Thank you," Archelaus said as he stood up.

She slowly stood up as Archelaus left the coach. Once out of the coach, he could see that they were under a roof of some sort. He helped Marriah from the coach and they followed Edwyn through a set of double doors guarded by soldiers from Burton. As they went down a hall, two guards from Brinley opened another set of doors. Tyrzah was waiting inside. Archelaus could see the bed in the firelight. Janina had followed them in. Tyrzah and Janina began to prepare Marriah for bed.

"Where are we?" Archelaus asked as he turned to Edwyn.

"That will be easier to answer in the morning, My King," Edwyn replied cryptically. "It's not completed yet, but when news came that there would soon be an heir to the throne we worked specifically on making this ready for you to stay in. We're working on getting the rest finished as quickly as possible."

"I don't understand, but I'm too tired to ask any more questions," Archelaus said. "I'll see you in the morning."

"Just pull this cord if you need anything," Edwyn said. "Tyrzah or I will be here in a minute."

Edwyn, Tyrzah and Janina bowed and left. Archelaus got undressed, laid down beside Marriah and was soon asleep.

*****

Archelaus was still asleep when Marriah woke up. She stood up slowly and looked around. There was an open door on the wall closest to her side of the bed. She looked in and was grateful to find it to be a bathing chamber similar to those in Dracona's castle. She was looking forward to soaking in a tub of nice warm water, but first she was hungry. When she returned to the bedchamber, she saw a cord hanging near the bed. She pulled on it once and soon Tyrzah entered the room.

Marriah led her into the bathing chamber and said, "I want a bath, but first I need to eat."

"At once, My Queen," Tyrzah said with a curtsey and left.

Marriah went back into the bedchamber and sat down in one of the two chairs at the small table. Archelaus began to stir.

"Marriah?" he said as he sat up.

"Tyrzah went to get us some breakfast," she said. "Where are we?"

"I'm not certain, but I think we are on the hilltop west of Union," he replied as he stood up. "I suspect it has to do with Edwyn's mysterious project. He promised to explain this morning."

Archelaus slipped on his pants before looking around.

"I found the bathing chamber in there," Marriah said, pointing toward the door.

"I'm glad you found it," Archelaus said. "You don't go very long in between trips lately."

"It will be worth it," Marriah said with a laugh.

Tyrzah brought her a robe. After helping Marriah put on the robe, Tyrzah opened the door. Edwyn came in with a large tray of food.

"Did you sleep well, My Queen?" Edwyn said as he set the tray on the table.

"Very," Marriah responded as he bowed. "The bed is very comfortable."

"I'm glad to hear that," he said as Archelaus came out of the bathing chamber. "I hope the food meets with your approval as well."

"I'm certain it will," she said as he put a plate of food in front of her.

"If it pleases you My King, after you have eaten and gotten dressed, I will give you a tour and an explanation."

"Yes," Archelaus said as he sat down. "I am most interested in your explanation."

Tyrzah and Edwyn bowed and left the room. Marriah was so hungry that she ate most of what Archelaus didn't. When she was finished, she settled against the back of the chair with a sigh.

"Better?" he asked her.

"Much," she replied as there was a quiet tap on the door. "Come."

Janina entered along with Tyrzah. Soon Marriah was bathed and dressed. Archelaus took some clothes into the bathing chamber. By the time he was dressed Janina had Marriah's hair done.

"Tell Edwyn I am ready for that tour and his explanation," he said.

"So am I," Marriah said as she stood up.

Tyrzah left quickly, but soon returned with Edwyn. He bowed low before speaking.

"I want you to know that many people have donated their time, materials and money to building this," he said. "Through this door is a sitting room."

He led them into the next room. It was large and open. There were two fireplaces to warm the room. It was beautifully furnished.

"I like it," Archelaus said.

This seemed to please Edwyn as he led them through another door into a hall. There were narrow windows lighting the hall and a wide staircase leading down. Marriah was glad to see a metal handrail attached to the wall going down the stairs. The lower level was lit by torchlight.

"We were concerned for your safety, My Queen, as well as your comfort," Edwyn said as he placed his hand on the rail.

"Thank you," Marriah replied.

He led them down the stairs to a large, open crescent shaped room with seven fireplaces. There were men building walls to divide the room.

"What is this room?" Archelaus asked before Marriah could.

"It will be for the children," he replied cryptically as he led them to another staircase.

Archelaus glanced at Marriah and shrugged his shoulders. On the next level down, there was another hallway. Edwyn led them past a staircase and turned at a pair of double doors.

"Where does that lead?" Marriah asked as they passed the doors.

"Out to a courtyard and stables," Edwyn said as he opened a set of double doors at the end of the hall. "I think you will understand what we are building when you see this."

They found themselves in a very large throne room. The thrones carved by Leda and Lyla sat at the other end of the room on a dais. There were purple and blue drapes along the walls. In the center of the room there was a table containing a model of the waterfall and cliff face along with an exact replica of the castle Marriah had dreamed about after their wedding.

"I beg your forgiveness, My Queen," Edward pled without looking up. "I heard you talking about your dream and waited for you to leave before carefully memorizing every detail of the drawing."

"There's nothing to forgive, Edwyn," Marriah assured him. "I left the drawing on the porch of the inn knowing someone might see it."

"A castle? A whole castle? How? Why?" Archelaus stammered as he collapsed into a chair near the table.

"You spared my life and in gratitude for your service as our rulers," Edwyn replied.

Archelaus just stared at him. Edwyn knelt at his feet.

"After everything I did to you I expected to be executed, but instead you freed me," Edwyn confessed. "You brought my wife to me and gave me hope. Even this castle is nothing compared to what you have given me and all of Burton."

Archelaus put his hand on Edwyn's shoulder and smiled. Edwyn stood and removed the top two layers of the model revealing a dining hall and several other rooms on the same level with the throne room.

The next floor down is guest quarters for ten and the final floor is kitchens and servant's quarters," Edwyn explained.

"This is the business you had to take care of?" Archelaus asked and Edwyn nodded. "How did you build it so quickly? It takes far more than two years to build this much."

"There have been many people contributing money and materials to the project including donations from neighboring kingdoms," Edwyn replied. "Many of the workers are from Okiah, the kingdom to the west. They were excited to learn the new building techniques to use in their own kingdom. I had heard about Dracona's castle and asked Regis Bryant about it before he left after the wedding. A week later a messenger arrived with a copy of the building diagrams of Dracona's castle. I studied them and learned more efficient building techniques from them. With many hands to help, the building is going very quickly."

Tyrzah entered and curtsied.

"There are people here asking if you will be granting audiences, My King," she said.

"Of course," Archelaus said after Marriah nodded to him. "Get someone to help Edwyn move this model into another room before letting them in."

Tyrzah curtsied again and left. Soon two men arrived and helped Edwyn move the table. Archelaus offered Marriah his arm and they climbed the dais steps. Once they were seated Archelaus nodded to the guards who opened the doors. People began coming in and bowing to them. Most of the matters were minor and easily cleared up. One dispute that was brought before them resulted in one person being sentenced to a year in prison.

Once everyone had left Marriah and Archelaus went back upstairs to the sitting room. Marriah went out onto the balcony and looked out over the forest and city.

"I've been thinking about the choices we have as to where to call our home," Archelaus commented as he joined her on the balcony. "Burton's castle just doesn't seem like home to me. It's a memory of the past, but nothing more."

"I feel the same way about Dracona's castle and even the village," Marriah said as she looked toward the dark mountain in the distance. "Brinley's castle is a piece of my father's past, but not home either."

"Here we can build new memories together," Archelaus suggested. "Our children can grow up in a place that isn't haunted by our pasts."

"It does feel more like home than anywhere else," Marriah agreed. "Most couples get married and build a house or at least change a house to suit their needs."

"Here we can make this castle suit our needs without disturbing memories of the past."

"And we can serve all of our people," Marriah smiled. "We have found a place to call home."

"Home at last," Archelaus said before he kissed her.

*****

A new life forged by a sacrifice of blood, reveals a throne waiting for the prophesied heir. In choosing a life of service leading a new nation, the servant queen brings peace and prosperity to all.

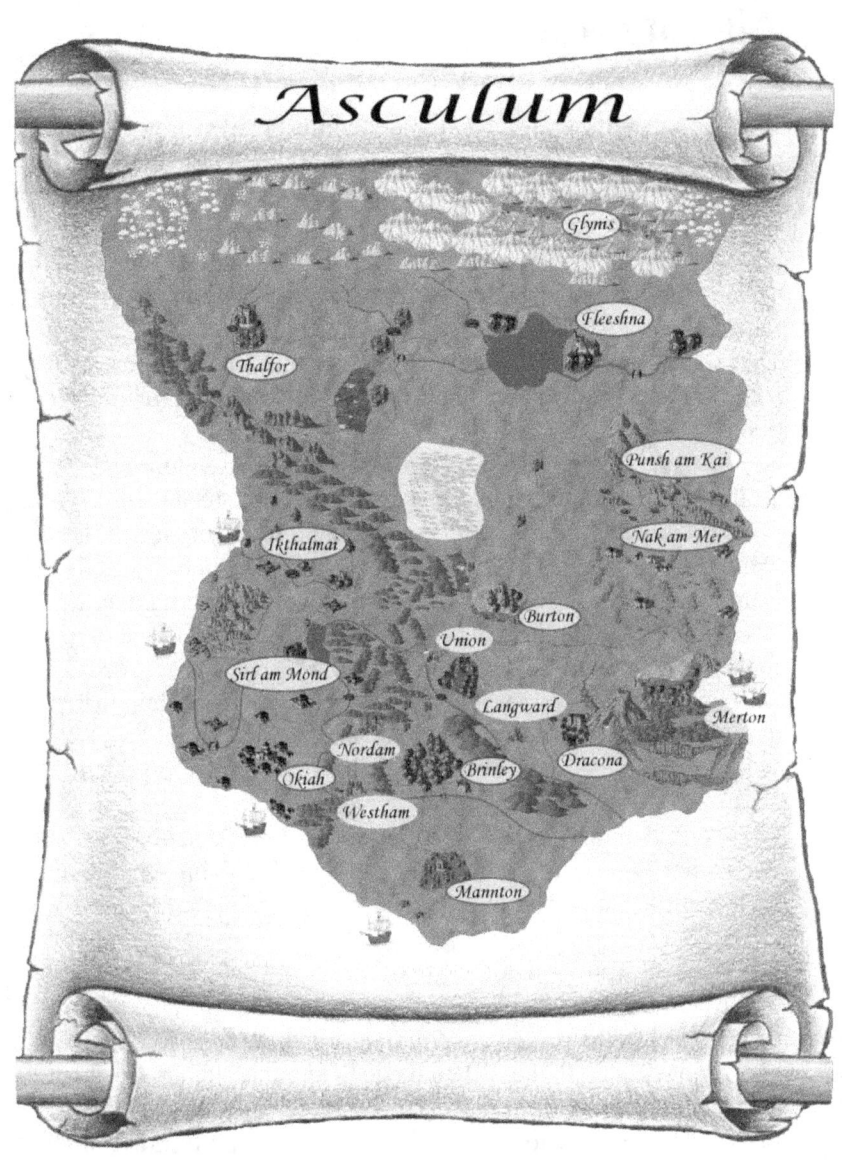

Asculum

Tales of Asculum

A group of refugees stranded in the hostile snow covered north divide up hoping to find shelter on this world they call Asculum. All of the dragons and some of the people fly south in search of warmer climates while the rest of the people face a journey they are ill prepared for. They are lost and freezing as their leader urges them forward through the blizzard into the mountains for as a seer she knows that they will find temporary shelter there. They manage to stumble out of the snows into a paradise created by a ring of active volcanoes. Their magical talents become vital in building a city they name Glynis.

As they begin to settle into their new home their leader sends out small scouting parties to discover who inhabits this world. They find that while the people of Asculum look very much like them, they are a short lived primitive people. The people of Glynis learn what they can from these people without revealing that their past and magical abilities. They begin to make wagons and carriages for cargo and people. They even learn to make and use swords along with bows and arrows they've seen the people of Asculum using. As the people of Glynis search for a new home away from the volcanoes that could destroy their valley their past is forgotten.

It is in this environment that the **Tales of Asculum** are set. Each book is meant to be a standalone book involving a particular region of the planet and the characters that inhabit that region.

You would think the life of a prince would be great, but for the crown prince of Brinley that's far from the truth. The only others near his age in the palace are children of the servants who all tease him for having no name. When he goes into the military he must conceal his identity but finally gains some friends. When he is sent to deliver a message to the overthrown tyrant King Burkhart he falls in love with the one woman he knows he can't have.

Aurita knows everyone hates her and her father but everyone is forbidden to tell her why. What she does know is that for her and her father the village is their prison and to leave seals their deaths. King Langward controls their lives including who she will marry when she is of age but he is kind to her. When King Langward's son sends her a gift her father teaches her to read and write so she can send him a note to thank him. They begin to exchange letters. As the years pass she looks forward to the letters she gets from the prince but doesn't dare admit she has fallen in love with him. When she meets the handsome corporal sent to deliver a message to her father her heart is torn between him and the prince.

The last Lord of Dracona is a lonely man with a dark past who is thrust into unexpected responsibilities. He lives alone in an empty castle in the center of the deserted town of Dracona. He faces tasks that he has no hope of accomplishing on his own and no one to turn to for help. Lord Dracona's story includes a nation in search of the answer to an ancient riddle and another nation in the grip of a tyrant king. When he falls in love with a mysterious woman he goes from desperate for companionship and purpose to overwhelmed by new responsibilities as new citizens begin to arrive.

The new King of Burton is in search of a wife but is dissatisfied with the spoiled princesses sent by neighboring kingdoms to court him. At a dear friend's funeral he falls in love with a beautiful servant girl that had a life of slavery and abuse. Through their love and perseverance they are able to unite several kingdoms in peace.

In the dying kingdom of Mannton women are not treated as people. They work for scraps of food and sleep on woven mats that will become their burial wrappings. This all changes after Li is purchased by the king to provide him an heir. He soon finds that she is no ordinary woman.

For more information and social links see www.vjogardner.com

Aurita and her father are imprisoned in a village and hated by everyone. The only friend she has is the crown prince of Brinley who has no name. When she falls in love with a kind and handsome soldier her heart is torn between him and the prince knowing she is betrothed to a stranger.

As a young adult novel 'Blood of Ancient Kings' has romance, action and a touch of fantasy. It has gotten rave reviews from readers of all ages.

As the last Lord of Dracona Bryant faces a life of loneliness
and insurmountable tasks. When he saves a stranger in the forest he
demands the man's daughter live with him at the castle. Sonje
accepts knowing she has a responsibility as crown princess to find
her people a new home. Both have no idea what they've agreed to.

As the second book in the Tales of Asculum series
Dracona's Rebirth has a dragon with an unusual sense of humor,
romance, mystery, adventure and a touch of magic.

About the Author

Valerie J.O. Gardner is an award wining author of full length fractured fairy tale fantasy novels. She has found success with both self published and traditionally published works.

Always fastinated by both medieval times and sci-fi she was an avid reader and enjoyed a wide variety of literature and authors. She began writing in in the late 1980's after graduating from Dixie State University in St. George, Utah, where she studied Fantasy Lit and Writing. Valerie is a member of the United Authors Association and LDS Publishing Professionals Association.

Valerie is a co-founder of V&E Enterprises a service to support and educate authors. She also does freelancer formatting and final edits for both publishers and for self published authors.

Valerie has been an invited panelist at Tree City Comic Con (Boise, ID.) and at Salt Lake Comic Con (Salt Lake City, UT.) She also has been a panelist at several writers conferences including LTUE (Provo, UT.) The topics she specializes in are World Building, Maps, Indie Publishing and Female Protagonists.

You can visit her at www.vjogardner.com.